THE STORM DRAIN MURDER

THE
STORM
DRAIN
MURDER

JACK CAMERON

Visit Jack Cameron's website,
JackCameronWriter.com

Follow Jack Cameron on
Instagram and Facebook
@jackcameron_writer

CONTENTS

PART 1

THE BODY

CHAPTER 1

The village of Sea Cliff slept beneath a blanket of fog.

On Bluffside Drive, just above the Pacific Ocean, the windows of the houses were black at two in the morning. Dense gray air clung to the roofs and trees like a shroud. The night was quiet as death, save for dripping drizzle and lapping wavelets.

An idling engine and scraping wipers joined the sounds of nature. A silver minivan inched along the narrow road. The van's headlights were off, and the driver leaned out the open side window, as though searching for a landmark in the fog. The passenger slumped against the door and half-open window.

A wraithlike man in ragged clothes snuck through the mist behind the van, hiding behind each hedge or bush that offered cover.

The van drove a few feet, stopped, crawled forward, and stopped again. The man, crouching behind a garbage can, coughed in the damp air. He cringed. He raised his head just enough to peek over the lid.

The van's passenger window slid down. "Who's there?" the driver demanded in a gruff whisper. "Someone there?" The man dropped to his knees and froze, holding his breath. A minute later, the van inched forward again.

Bluffside Drive meandered along the bluff tops, 30 feet above the rocky shore. The van crept the length of the road and turned into the Vista Point parking lot. It stopped near a sawhorse blocking a dirt path that led to the Point. A sign with handwritten STEEP DROP—KEEP OUT was taped to the sawhorse. Just beyond it, in the center of the path, a gaping storm drain was open to the beach below.

The van's engine died. Murmuring waves and dripping dew filled the silence. A few yards away, the ghostly man crawled behind a large boulder.

The driver climbed out of the minivan, closing the door with a *thunk*. A light behind a curtain went dark in the house next to the parking lot. A second later, the curtains parted.

The driver wore all black—oversized sweatshirt and sweatpants, and a baseball cap pulled down low. The shapeless clothes concealed any hint of identity as male or female, stocky or slight. The driver moved through the mist like a billowy shadow.

Circling the van, the driver opened the door and hefted the passenger out of the seat. "You screwed too many people, and got wasted once too often," the driver whispered hoarsely, propping the limp form face-first against the van's door. "So here you are, as dead as you can be."

"Amen to that, you son-of-a-bitch," the ghostly man whispered behind his rock.

The driver lifted the body under the armpits and dragged it backward by its heels to the dirt path, stopping at the sawhorse. Gasping and struggling to hold the body upright, the driver reached down and shoved the sawhorse aside. The body lost its balance. It swayed to the left. The driver swore and yanked the body sharply to gain control.

Fighting for breath, the driver heaved the body backward up the path and around the storm drain before stopping. The drain's rusted cover lay several feet behind them, invisible in the gloom. "OK," the driver rasped, "to the Point and down you go."

One step backward. Two steps. On the third step, the driver tripped over the rusted cover. Falling while holding the body's dead weight, the driver shoved it away, as chance would have it, toward the storm drain. The body's boot toe caught on the lip of the drain. For five heartbeats, the body teetered over the gaping opening.

Arms flailing for balance, the driver thrust out clumsy hands to grab the body, but pushed it instead. It tumbled headfirst into the open storm drain, crashing into the bottom grate 30 feet below.

"Shit!" the driver cried, hitting the ground on a hip, then a shoulder. "Damn! Damn! Damn!" The driver crawled to the drain and stared into it before limping back to the minivan, muttering and swearing.

The ghostly man watched, peeking over the boulder where he hid. He held up his fingers in a sign that wards off evil. "You can ride that drainpipe straight down to hell," he spat.

CHAPTER 2

A week after the events of the foggy night, Jason Brinkman jogged along the bluff trail above the Pacific Ocean where Sea Cliff meets the sea. His thighs burned, pain shot up his shins, and his lungs were ready to burst. And, he wanted a cigarette. God, how he needed a cigarette. Gasping, he paused at a bench atop a rise. He twisted to feel his left shoulder and found the nicotine patch, still there despite being soaked with sweat. He reached around to his right shoulder and felt the second patch.

The sun was bright and the sky was blue at eight o'clock this morning, which was unusual for foggy, gloomy June. A light breeze from the ocean cooled his sweaty body as he began to get his breathing under control. He'd jogged the mile from the trail's south gate at Vista Point to its north gate, and halfway back. His goal was the full two miles, but he decided a mile and a half wasn't too bad. Feeling a little lightheaded, he sat on the back of the bench and let the breeze wash over him.

The trail twisted and turned along the bluff tops. A few yards to the west, at the foot of the cliffs, the Pacific Ocean surged against boulders and craggy rocks. To the east were 100 acres of green meadow, and behind it, golden hills with swaths of dark-green pine and eucalyptus trees. The trail and meadow were favorites of local runners, as well as tourists who were awed by the rugged coastline.

Despite its familiarity, the beauty still pulled at Jason's heart. Whitecaps riding blue-gray waves marched to the rocky shore. They crashed against sandstone bluffs, whose gnarled fingers clawed into the seabed. The sun dazzled on the water while a white fogbank lurked on the horizon. The crashing waves spewed ocean mist as high as Jason's bench.

He closed his eyes and breathed in the salty air and the sweet scents of wildflowers and grasses. Meadowlarks sang and blue jays scolded, and for a moment, he experienced total contentment.

"Things will get better soon," he promised himself. "On a day like this, I know I can make it here."

* * *

When Jason was ten, he found a map of California. He traced the coastline with his finger from Los Angeles, where he lived with his mother, to San Francisco, where his father lived. He saw that Highway 1 ran along the coast through his grandmother's hometown of Sea Cliff, and he discovered that it was exactly halfway between the two cities.

In those days, Jason shuttled back and forth between his parents on alternate weekends, holidays, and summer months. He began to believe that if he could live in the middle between his mother and father, they'd stop arguing and fighting over him.

Jason's parents had enjoyed too much success early in life and not enough later. With success came drugs and alcohol, and as success dwindled, more drugs and more alcohol. Each blamed the other as money and possessions disappeared, until the night, forever branded on Jason's mind, when they squared off with kitchen knives.

"What are we doing?" Jason's mother cried, dropping her knife on the counter. "For God's sake, Barry, what are we doing?" She snuck out of their San Francisco tenement early the next morning and fled with her child to Los Angeles, where she entered rehab.

Jason's father and mother then began their battle for control of his body and soul. Each argued, "I only want what's best for my son," by which each meant, "He's mine and no one else can have him, especially you, and damn the consequences to the boy." Their lawyers dutifully filed stacks of motions and evaluations with the court to prove their client's entitlement.

When Jason was twelve, he decided he wanted to know who was making him fly to San Francisco every two weeks to live with his drunken, disciplinarian father. He asked his mother to take him to one of the court hearings, and after months of pestering, she finally agreed.

Jason sat at the counsel's table with his mother and watched the tired judge on the dais and bored lawyers at their podiums. When the lawyers paused, Jason climbed out of his chair and walked solemnly around the table to stand midway between them. The bailiff bolted toward Jason, but the judge motioned him to stop. The courtroom silenced.

"Your Honor, sir," Jason said in a little voice, "I want to live with my GG in Sea Cliff."

The judge glared at Jason over his half-glasses before turning to the surprised lawyers. "What did the child say?" the judge asked them.

"The child wants to live with its grandmother in Sea Cliff, Your Honor," one of them said.

The judge studied Jason, and he stared back without flinching.

Finally, the judge said, "OK, Counsel. Get the evaluations, and we'll see. Clerk, call the next case."

* * *

The rhythmic stride and controlled breathing of another runner brought Jason back to the present. He heard the *crunch-crunch* of gravel and felt a rush of air as the runner passed his bench. Opening his eyes, he saw a bouncing blonde ponytail and long, tan legs sprint north up the trail. He admired the woman's figure and effortless speed, but her strong pace brought home his own failure. "I still haven't made my two miles," he berated himself. "Two miles used to be my warm-up. What the hell is the matter with me?"

Recognizing this failure opened the door to others that had been festering. Two years ago, Jason had been a well-paid associate at a big law firm in downtown Los Angeles. When his marriage soured, he'd quit the firm. Moving back to Sea Cliff, he'd opened his own one-man law office. "Local Track and Baseball Star Opens Law Office in Village," the headline in the *Sea Cliff Crier* shouted, and Jason waited for the clients to line up at the door. A trickle did at first, but the trickle slowed, and now his practice was about to go belly up.

His difficulties suddenly filled his head. His office rent and the lease payment on his Porsche were due. He was behind on his credit cards and other monthly bills. Medical, malpractice, and car insurance premiums were coming up at the end of the month.

It was chump change in his old life. In those days, Jason and his wife spent lavishly, chasing the good life after 80- and 90-hour workweeks. The downtown penthouse loft, matching Porsche convertibles, custom Armani wardrobes, and $1,500 midnight dinners had taken their financial toll.

He'd managed to bring a $60,000 nest egg with him to Sea Cliff, but it was nearly depleted. Half had gone to setting up and running his office. The other half was invested in a luxurious ocean-view house being built on speculation, which seemed like a guaranteed money-maker when he'd committed the funds.

A meadowlark landed on a scrubby bush next to his bench. The bird cocked its head, eyeing him cautiously. Jason sat completely still. Its sweet, lilting song lifted his spirits. *I can't lose hope when there's so much beauty! I'll get my nest egg back, and some profit, when the spec house sells. I know I can find some clients with money in Sea Cliff.*

Jason lifted his black baseball cap and smoothed his hair. He stood reluctantly and stretched, preparing his muscles and mind for the half mile back to the south parking lot. Out of habit, he looked up the trail to the cliffside boulder where he'd scattered his grandmother's ashes and admired the purple lupine and golden California poppies growing beside it. They were her favorite wildflowers, and he knew she'd love to have them so close.

With the blonde runner on his mind, Jason set a good pace and high-kicked the last half mile to the Vista Point parking lot and his car. He made it with his breathing barely under control. As he fumbled for his key fob, he heard his father's slurred voice in his head: "Failure is never an option, boy, and you failed to achieve your goal." For an instant, Jason relived one of his father's drunken lectures about setting goals and achieving them, and about how failure meant you were roadkill. He beeped open his Porsche 911 Carrera S and slipped behind the wheel. "Fucking hypocrite," he muttered. "Advice for a successful life from the biggest loser ever."

His cell phone chimed in his gym bag on the passenger's seat. Hoping it might be a new client, he pulled out his black sweat suit and found the phone at the bottom of the bag next to an unopened Marlboro pack. The chiming stopped and the screen announced a text message from Courtney, his soon-to-be-ex-wife in LA.

Call me. Must tlk.

And that was the other black cloud hanging over him. His ex-wife, who now was a partner at his former law firm, earning hundreds of thousands of dollars a year, was demanding child support from him. He punched *Delete* and threw the phone back in the gym bag.

Jason motored slowly down Bluffside Drive toward Del Mar Road, which would take him through the hills to his grandmother's house, where he lived. The Porsche's 440 Teutonic horses growled in his ear. As he rolled past the house directly across from the Vista Point parking lot, he recognized the dark-silver Range Rover parked in front, with its sky-high suspension, blacked-out windows, and the license plate MOVEOVR.

He snapped his car around the next left corner and stopped. *That guy owes me money!*

CHAPTER 3

Jason sat in his car and tried to remember the man's name and how much he owed him. He recalled the guy was a paving contractor from Fresno who rarely used his Sea Cliff house. He'd hired Jason two years ago to sue the prominent local builder-developer who'd constructed the house. Water leaks, a cracking foundation, and a faulty furnace were some of the issues. The builder was Geraldo O'Brien. Jason had filed suit against O'Brien, and quickly negotiated a good settlement for his client. O'Brien was so impressed that he retained Jason for his own legal work.

A minute later, Jason remembered that the man's name was James Paige and that he owed him $2,500. He got out of his car and pulled his black sweat suit over his running gear. Grabbing some business cards out of the glove box, he stuffed them in his pocket. Then he drove around the block and parked behind Paige's Range Rover.

Jason took several deep breaths to center himself, like he did before entering a courtroom. He checked the visor's vanity mirror to make sure he was presentable after his jog. "Look at me," he said to his reflection. "I'm about to dun a client for $2,500. I used to make $25,000 a month for shuffling papers." He shrugged. "That life had no connection with reality. This guy had a real problem, and I fixed it for him. I actually earned this money." The dark-brown eyes in the mirror stared back at him without wavering. "I earned this fee, and now I'm going to collect it—in person. It doesn't get more real." He climbed out of his car and walked to the front door.

A brass plaque on the jamb read *The Paige's*. Jason was about to ring the bell when the door opened. A little boy and girl, both towheads, stood just inside with towels and plastic buckets and shovels. The buckets were stenciled with *Slade* and *Hayley*. The boy might've been seven and the girl five. They looked up at him in surprise. Paige stood behind them in a wrinkled golf shirt and cargo shorts, looking annoyed. "Whaddya want?" he demanded.

"Mr. Paige, I'm Jason Brinkman. I did some legal work for you a couple of years ago? The builder? Geraldo O'Brien? The leaky roof?"

Paige grunted recognition and looked more annoyed.

"My secretary was reviewing my receivables," Jason continued, "and it appears your account was never closed." He paused. "May I ask that you settle your account while you're in town?"

Paige squatted down. "OK, you two. You go down to the beach and play while I talk to Mr. Brinkman. Dude, you're in charge of your sister. Be careful crossing the street, and watch the steps. Don't get close to the water. And play nice!" He patted Hayley on the head and fist-bumped Slade.

The kids looked up at their father, then at Jason, and dashed across Bluffside Drive to the Vista Point parking lot. Paige stood and punched a thick finger in Jason's chest. "You don't never call me a deadbeat in front of my kids," he snarled. His breath stank of stale cigar. "Send me a bill." He slammed the door before Jason could speak.

Jason held his finger on the bell. It bonged repeatedly before Paige finally opened the door, eyes afire and fists clenched. Jason leaned forward just enough to violate Paige's space. At six feet and 185 pounds, Jason could be intimidating when he chose to be. His athletic build had thickened, but he looked fit in his early thirties. He said, "Mr. Paige, you owe me $2,500 and it's at least a year past due. Drop the check at my office today and my secretary will give you a zero-balance statement." His eyes bored into Paige's. "I wouldn't want to embarrass you further by filing a collection action." He held out his business card.

Paige said, "Fuck you." He slammed the door.

Jason stuck the card in the jamb and walked slowly back to his car, fuming. "Next time," he vowed, "the fee gets paid out of the settlement proceeds. How could I be so stupid?" He kicked himself for having been naïve, and cursed Paige for being an asshole.

He punched the *Start* button, jabbed the accelerator, and peeled away from the curb, heading home for a long, hot shower before going to his office.

* * *

A mile to the south, at the opposite end of Bluffside Drive, Sheriff's Deputy Duane U. Hardesty parked his patrol car in a pullout. Deputy Hardesty loved being a cop. He loved his utility belt and its holster and cartridge clips. He loved his gun. He loved how his handcuffs jingled when he walked, and how his nightstick bumped his thigh. He loved his patrol car, with its lights and siren and shotgun, and all the new computer equipment that helped him identify perpetrators.

He liked being stationed in Sea Cliff well enough, although he sensed the villagers didn't appreciate the majesty of the law as much as he did. Deputy Hardesty tolerated no breaches of the law on his beat. He'd sit in his patrol car, patiently waiting for the final minutes to expire on a meter so he could ticket the offending owner. He'd cite litterers instead of giving them warnings, and ticket cars parked too far from the curb or over the lines. And he enjoyed using his lights and siren to bring jaywalkers to heel.

"The Law is a strict mistress," he repeated to himself when he cruised the village looking for offenders, "and it's my job to make the citizens understand this simple truth." The locals had quickly sized up Deputy Hardesty and nicknamed him "Deputy Hardass," which he secretly considered a badge of honor. They avoided him, leaving the tourists to feel the sting of his strict mistress' lash.

The deputy rolled down his window and listened to the murmur of the waves in the distance. He rested his coffee mug in the cup holder and propped his *Peace Officer's Legal Field Guide* between the top of his belly and the steering wheel.

The sheriff's department had just announced a promotional exam for the rank of sergeant. Deputy Hardesty was eligible, with three years' seniority, and he'd decided to go for it. He intended to ace the test. He thought the best way to do that was to memorize the section numbers and titles of the important criminal laws. He knew the big ones, of course. *Section 23152, Driving Under the Influence. Section 211, Robbery. Section 187, Murder.* He also planned to memorize other important, but less commonly violated laws. Like *Section 236, False Imprisonment. Section 451, Arson. Section 490a, Larceny. Section 487, Grand Theft.* That way, he could impress his colleagues and the test administrator, and understand the dispatcher more easily.

While Deputy Hardesty fully intended to memorize all the important sections and titles, his passion was to memorize the ones having to do with sex crimes. It was his secret mission to rid Sea Cliff of every one of its *preverts.* Once Sea Cliff was cleansed, he planned to turn his attention to the rest of the county. As a sergeant, he could assign this task to the deputies under his command, thereby multiplying his effectiveness many times over.

He sipped his coffee and opened the field guide to the *Sex Crimes* tab. "*Section 314, Indecent Exposure.*" He repeated it until it stuck, then moved on. "*Section 646.9, Stalking. Section 647, Peeping. Section 318.5, Topless Waitresses,*" and so on, until he reached the next tab.

CHAPTER 4

Slade and Hayley Paige ran full speed across the Vista Point parking lot to the north corner, where rickety stairs went down to the beach. They paused on the top landing to catch their breath. Hayley whined, "I wanna go over there." She waved her hand in the direction of the Point, across the parking lot. "I wanna see the bunnies."

Slade remembered they'd seen one rabbit a long time ago when they'd walked on the dirt path all the way to the Point. Now his sister wanted to see "the bunnies" every time they were allowed to play outside. He didn't like the path because it was close to the edge of the bluff and it scared him. There was also that big hole in the middle of the path that his father said was a storm drain. One time last year, Slade looked through the rusted grate and down the drain all the way to the beach below. He got dizzy and nearly threw up.

"Uh-uh," Slade said. "I wanna make a sandcastle on the beach. Besides, the path is way on the other side, and it stinks over there." He sniffed the air. "Must be red tide."

"What's a reb tibe?" Haley asked.

"It's when the beach smells like dead fish and rotten seaweed. Stuff girls don't like."

"Ick! I don't wanna go down there. I wanna see—"

Slade interrupted, "Father said I'm in charge, so you havta do what I want, and I'm gonna build the best sandcastle you ever saw." He ran down the steps, yelling, "C'mon!" over his shoulder. "We'll go see the bunnies later."

Hayley cried, "Wait for me!" Taking one step at a time, she shouted at his back, "Father said you havta be nice!"

On the beach, Slade set to work smoothing the sand.

"I wanna help," Hayley demanded.

"Nuh-uh," Slade said. "You'll just mess it up."

Tears welled in Hayley's eyes and she started to wail. Slade went rigid, looking up at the Vista Point 30 feet above them. "Shh, Hayley, don't cry. He'll hear you." Thinking out loud, he said, "I'll tell you what. You can find stuff I'll need for my castle."

The wailing stopped. "OK," Hayley said, wiping her eyes and nose with the back of her hand. "Like what?"

"I don't know," Slade said, exasperated. "Stuff you need for a sandcastle. Like those branches over there." He pointed to the base of the bluff near the bottom of the storm drain.

The drain ran from the edge of the bluff at the top, straight down the rock face, and ended about four feet above the sand. Slade's father had explained it to him last summer. He'd said, "That there drain is a old-time corrugated sewer pipe. It's oversized and you can see it's rusted to hell. See how it's bolted to the cliff by those heavy steel brackets? I never seen anything like it. They must've had a bad drainage problem a long time back and fixed it with what they had on hand. Down at the bottom, there's a metal grate up inside the pipe that's welded in place. I never seen that done either. There's supposed to be a grate just like it at the top, but it ain't welded, and someone keeps taking it off."

Slade glowed with pride because his father spoke to him like an adult for once. "How do you know so much, Father?"

Paige said, "A paving contractor's gotta know everything about drainage."

Slade began shoveling the sand and shaping it with his hands and pail. Hayley brought him twigs and branches from the base of the cliff. "It stinks over there," she said.

"Uh-huh," Slade said. "Red tide." He added some towers and stuck black twigs in the battlements. They were cool, like witches' fingers. He said, "Get more twigs, and some stones."

Hayley scurried to the base of the cliff, but turned around and ran back to Slade empty-handed.

"It's real stinky over there," she said, squeezing her nose closed. "I think I'm gonna frow up." She dropped to her butt, glassy-eyed.

"Jeez, Hayley, don't be such a girl. Just bring me one more handful."

"OK," Hayley sulked, "but you havta say 'xactly what you want."

Slade looked at the base of the cliff, thinking he needed something to finish off his castle. He had enough twigs and stones. The rocks were too big and the seaweed was full of flies. He scanned all the debris that had collected where the beach met the cliff. "There's gotta be something," he told himself. Something that would make his castle perfect and make his sister feel useful so she wouldn't tell their father he'd been mean.

The sunlight caught some shiny, silvery, stringy stuff hanging from the storm drain's bottom grate. He looked again and saw there was lots of it. Some of it was so fine it almost looked like hair. "It's perfect!" he exclaimed. "I can lay it in the moat to look like water." He said, "Hey, Hayley, see that silvery string over there?" He pointed at the grate. "It's hanging out of that thing, that storm drain."

Hayley squinted. "Uh-huh."

"Get me as much as you can. Get it all, even if you have to reach up inside." Hayley started to object, but Slade said, "Jeez, Hayley. You said you wanted to help. That's what I need, so go get it."

Hayley trudged slowly toward the storm drain, holding her nose. When she reached it, she tugged on the silvery strings. They didn't come out. She pulled again. They didn't budge. "I can't get it," she whined loud enough for Slade to hear. "It's 'tached to something an' won't pull out."

Slade sighed. *Girls!* He yelled, "Look up there and see what's holding them."

Hayley got on her hands and knees at the edge of the drain and craned her neck to look inside. "I can't see," she yelled. She backed away for a moment before crawling under the grate and peering up into it. "Now I can see," she called to her brother. "It's a … it looks like a …." She shrieked a bloodcurdling cry. "EEEKKK! EEEKKK!"

CHAPTER 5

Jason lived in his grandmother's house at 135 Crescent Lane, a sleepy street on Conifer Hill on the west side of Highway 1. GG's house was a modest stucco bungalow with a wide front porch, a brick walkway from the curb, and a rundown detached garage at the end of the driveway. Stands of tall pine trees lined the side and back yards. Roses and geraniums bloomed beside the house and drive, despite being neglected since she died.

Crescent Lane meandered through the neighborhood in a rough semicircle. It joined Del Mar Road at its east and west ends, both of which were marked by crumbling stone gateposts. The street was so narrow that everyone treated it as being one way, always entering through the east gate and exiting through the west.

After showering and shaving, Jason strode down the walkway to his Porsche parked at the curb. He drove slowly around Crescent Lane's long curve to the west gatepost and turned right on Del Mar, the main road between the Pacific Ocean and Highway 1. Enjoying the sunshine and warm temperature, he motored lazily over Del Mar's hills and around its curves, through pine forests and residential neighborhoods, to the highway. The light turned green just as he reached the intersection. He crossed through it and continued down Main Street to his law office.

Jason's office was the end unit on the ground floor of a ramshackle building on Charles Street, a block up from Main Street, in Sea Cliff's business district. Next to his office was the Ocean Wave Hair Salon, and next to it, the Real Estate Office of Mags Turlock. A creaky deck connected the three first-floor units. The Tats by Inky Dink tattoo parlor occupied the entire second floor.

About ten o'clock, Jason headed up the brick walkway to the steps and his front door. Unlocking the deadbolt, he kneeled and scooped up the mail from the floor. All bills.

"Good morning, Christina," he said, dropping the bills in the pile on the empty secretary's desk. It was a stupid ritual, he knew, but he still missed her cheery smile a year after he'd had to let her go.

The Law Office of Jason Brinkman was a 20-foot square-room painted industrial beige. The reception and public areas were separated from his desk and office by a 15-foot-long, six-foot-tall bookcase. It was crammed full of used law books on both sides, and created both a visual and physical barrier between the two spaces.

Jason did all his legal research online, but clients expected to see law books, so he dressed his set accordingly. He obtained out-of-date books from a friendly clerk at the county law library and bought others at Goodwill and estate sales.

He flipped on the fluorescent ceiling lights. They flashed and buzzed as he walked the length of the bookcase, dragging his finger along the spines of the books. Rounding the end, he walked slowly to his desk and dropped into his chair. He hit the spacebar on his desktop computer to wake it up. No emails or instant messages from clients or any court where he had cases pending. No "friends" needed his services. Nothing new on LinkedIn. He checked his cell phone. No messages, no tweets.

He settled into his chair and listened to the quiet, thinking it was just another day at the Law Office of Jason Brinkman.

* * *

Jason missed the frenetic energy of a real law office at moments like this. After graduating from Loyola Law School in Los Angeles, he'd been lucky to land a position in the LA office of Whatley, Thelen & Füchs. The multi-national law firm was expanding in LA, and was willing to hire young attorneys like Jason—highly qualified but not quite up to the firm's usual exacting standards—to double its roster immediately. He seized the opportunity to become one of the firm's 600 lawyers.

He was assigned to the team of senior partner Gretchen Fautz, which he also considered to be great luck. Gretchen was legendary. She was a ferocious litigator who, in 40 years with the Whatley firm, had never lost a trial and had recovered billions for her clients. Unknown to Jason at the time, Gretchen also was legendary for consuming her junior associates. Male or female, it didn't seem to matter, as long as the associate fit her whim at the time.

Jason refused Gretchen's advances. Twice. The second time, he was banished to what he called "the basement." The firm occupied the top 30 floors of the Whatley Tower in downtown Los Angeles, and his new workstation was on the first of the floors, far from the marble and walnut of the firm's public spaces. He sat at a desk in a little cubicle and received his assignments by email. When he finished an assignment, he sent the hard copy to Gretchen or one of her lieutenants by an inter-floor runner.

Jason's work was solid and insightful, and eventually he was promoted to leading a team of associates whose sole duty was to review and analyze discovery for the firm's litigation teams. He spent his days, and many nights, in a smoke-filled basement conference room, scouring thousands of documents grudgingly provided by the corporate opponent of the moment.

Jason was suicidally bored, but was mollified somewhat by his $300,000 salary. To earn it, he was required to work at least 4,000 hours each year, and bill at least 3,000. He was constantly on the verge of leaving the firm to do something more meaningful than helping the firm's corporate clients win piles of money from their corporate opponents.

Everything changed the day he met Courtney.

All of the firm's upper-floor conference rooms were in use, so Gretchen's litigation team had descended to the basement to confer with Jason's discovery team in one of its dingy meeting rooms. He was captivated by Courtney the moment he saw her. He also recognized her as one of Gretchen's lieutenants. Their eyes met and the spark was combustible. When she placed a pack of Marlboros on the table above her note pad, he knew he had his opening.

He walked up to her during a break. "Can I bum a 'Boro?" he asked. She shook the pack to slide a cigarette out for him. "I didn't know girls smoked Marlboros," he said, lighting the cigarette.

"I didn't know you liked girls," Courtney replied. They both looked at Gretchen.

"She's saying I'm gay?" he asked. Courtney nodded, her green eyes twinkling and quizzical.

The meeting lasted another hour, but Jason could only focus on saying something to Courtney that would make him unforgettable. He decided the situation required boldness, and came up with a plan.

Out of the reams of documents he'd reviewed in the lawsuit, his brief-case held a handful of emails between the opponent corporation's board of directors. Jason knew the contents would bring them to their knees. Like any ambitious associate striving to get ahead, Jason's usual practice was to reveal this kind of evidence to the litigation team only when it was to his best advantage. At that moment, however, the only advantage he sought was with Courtney.

"Stay a moment," he whispered as she rose to leave when the meeting ended. He removed the emails from his briefcase. "Look at these." She scanned them. He said, "We know that the bond prospectus and registration statement were full of lies, and that our clients bought the bonds and lost millions because they believed those lies. These emails show that—"

She interrupted him. "That none of the directors read the documents and didn't exercise any due diligence at all—"

He interrupted. "Which means the directors can be personally liable to our clients for the millions they lost—"

"And will want to settle—"

"Generously, to save their own behinds." He paused.

She looked at him as if to say, "And?"

"You take it to Gretchen."

She smiled.

Courtney soon became Gretchen's most trusted lieutenant. She arranged assignments that would make Jason look good in Gretchen's eyes, and worked with him on every case possible. Their romance flourished in the heat of their passion, their shared addiction to Marlboros, the unrelenting pressure and stress of big-firm litigation, and 16-hour days.

In the glow of a $40 million verdict won by Gretchen with Courtney's assistance, and Jason's less obvious assistance, they decided they were in love. The case was *Lancaster v. Estate of Granquist*. It would prove to be both the pinnacle and rock bottom of their relationship. Jason was mesmerized by Courtney's courtroom performance, and she thought his trial strategy and theory of liability were brilliant. They got married over a long weekend between trials, and seemed destined to spend their lives together at the Whatley firm.

Gretchen Fautz had other plans for Courtney and Jason, however.

CHAPTER 6

Footsteps on the creaky deck outside snapped his mind back to the here and now. His office door opened and closed, then high heels clacked on the other side of the bookcase.

The footsteps stopped. A cloud of platinum curls peeked around the end of the bookcase, followed by a waft of jasmine hairspray. The curls framed a teenage girl's face—a fresh, angelic face, disguised by painted eyebrows, long mascara lashes, glitter eyelids, and bright-red lips.

"Hiii, Jaaaason," the girl said.

She curled the rest of her body around the bookcase and leaned against it.

"Nikki Beach!" Jason said. "You're a blonde this week!"

She beamed. "Just a perk of being the Ocean Wave's shampoo girl."

They looked at each other for fifteen seconds. When the silence became awkward, they spoke simultaneously.

"So, Nikki, what's … ?"

"How do you like my new tattoo?" She peeled her sweater slowly down her left arm to reveal a black rose tattoo on her milk-white shoulder. The stem crept down her arm. She pulled up her sleeve to show the stem becoming roots digging into her knuckles. Drops of red blood dripped from the thorns.

It was stunning, Jason had to admit. And ghastly. "Wow, Nikki. Inky really outdid himself this time."

She beamed again and shrugged the sweater off her right shoulder, revealing a screaming skull with flowing black tresses. The sweater, now free of both shoulders, fell to her elbows, exposing her hot-pink tube top. A bare midriff, chartreuse tights, and four-inch teal-blue stiletto heels completed her ensemble of the day.

"You don't match," Jason said, nodding toward her shoulder with the skull.

"I know," she said, a little sadly. "The skull was for my old boyfriend. The rose is for me." She added excitedly, "Jason! I heard a rumor about one of your clients."

"Oh? Which one?"

She didn't answer.

Jason knew that Nikki visited when she wanted to show off something new. Today was a grand slam: her hair, rose tattoo, and outfit. Her real purpose, however, usually was to convince him to drive her up the coast in his Porsche. She had two tactics. She'd flirt and posture, or she'd promise to reveal a tidbit of gossip she'd overheard in the salon. Sometimes she combined approaches.

Jason enjoyed Nikki's quirky energy, but soon grew tired of her flirting and come-ons. He put up with them, at least for a while, because she did often have useful information about goings-on in the village. This apparently was one of those days.

Nikki walked slowly in front of Jason's desk, dragging her fingers along the shelves of law books. She turned her back to him and smoothed her tights. Pulling a book halfway out, she considered the title, pushed it back, and pulled out another, and then a third. She picked up the unopened pack of Marlboros on one of the shelves and put it back in its place. Still facing the bookcase, she said, "Gerrraaaldooo."

"Really? Tell me what you heard."

Nikki turned from the bookcase and took two steps toward the desk. "Do you really want to know?" She ran her finger along the top of a picture frame on his desk.

"Yes, Nikki, I really want to know."

Picking up the frame, she looked at the picture of Jason and his grandmother. She replaced it carefully on the desk. "When are you going to take me for a ride in your Porsche?"

"How 'bout when you're an adult."

"I am an adult! I'm eighteen. Almost."

"Sure you are. When?"

"Eleven months and fifteen days." She looked at him as if she'd scored match point.

"You know, Nikki, you can't always believe rumors about Geraldo. He starts most of them himself."

"Like the one about his scar?"

Geraldo O'Brien had built dozens of houses in Sea Cliff, and was a major local employer. He bragged that one out of every fifteen jobs in the village was supported by the money his construction business generated. He also was Jason's most important client, leaving lawsuits in his wake after every project.

O'Brien had a crescent-shaped scar from the corner of his left eye around the outer edge of his cheekbone. Everyone in Sea Cliff knew he'd acquired the scar under mysterious circumstances.

"Yeah," Jason said. "He always tells people a Mexican drug lord cut his cheek with a machete."

"But it's true."

"No, it isn't. Geraldo and I had some beers down at Mostly's Saloon, and he told me the real story." Jason shook his head. "He was in his garage workshop, cutting some wood on his table saw and watching a football game. He got distracted 'cause he was pissed about a penalty, and the saw kicked back a chunk of wood into his face."

"Whatever. I like the drug lord better." She walked slowly to the wall behind him and began examining his diplomas and certificates.

He decided to change tack. "So, Nikki, if you're not going to tell me what you heard, will you tell me who you heard it from?"

Nikki moved from the diplomas to the credenza behind his desk. She examined the pictures of Jason with his high school track and field medals. Picking up the All-Star baseball bat signed by Jason's team the year he was captain, she read each name aloud. Finally, she said, "Mags Turlock."

"Sea Cliff's 'Real Estate Agent of the Year'? What's she doing at the Ocean Wave Salon?"

"Getting rid of her gray. Everyone wants to get rid of their gray. Except you, with your gorgeous chestnut-brown hair." She reached to stroke his hair, stopping just short of touching it.

Jason was surprised at Mags. She was the most unfeminine woman he'd ever met, and she seemed completely oblivious to her appearance. Yet this ungainly woman, who always wore sweat suits and work boots, was having her dishwater curls dyed.

"You're kidding. Are you going to tell me what you heard?"

"I just love the smell of leather," Nikki sighed, rounding the desk. "And I love the way it feels on my skin, especially when I'm wearing a silk skirt."

"For God's sake, Nikki, can't you get some boy your own age to take you for a ride?"

"That's the problem, Jason." Her expression was cross. "They're boys. And they all drive pickups." Red crept into her white cheeks and she glared at him through mascara lashes. "Are you saying you're never going to take me in your Porsche?"

Jason's desk phone rang, startling them both. He glanced at the screen. "No," he said distractedly, "I'm not saying never."

The call was from Pedro Rodriguez, Geraldo's framing foreman. He let it go to voicemail.

"Mister Brinkman?" Pedro's voice and heavy Mexican accent came from the phone's speaker. "I calling you because I not know where is Geraldo. I no see him two weeks. I need find him. I think maybe you know where he is? You call?" The machine clicked off.

Nikki retreated to the bookcase and sank against it. Jason watched little frown lines appear between her painted eyebrows. She studied the wall behind him. He guessed Pedro had spoiled her surprise, and she was considering her next move.

A minute later, her expression brightened and she plunged ahead. "Mags said Geraldo cashed in everything and moved to Australia. Mags said he'd finally done it. Just like that." She snapped her fingers. "Took his surfboard and his girlfriend and moved to Australia to be a surf bum."

"Huh. Which girlfriend?"

"Danni, I think."

"I thought I saw her the other day. Has she gone gray?"

"Kind of. More silvery, actually. Her hair's long and looks like Geraldo's, but hers is *Silver Highlights Number 3* by Redken."

"Could have been silvery. Anyway, that's it? Geraldo's been saying he's gonna do that as long as I've known him. That's all Mags said? No other details?"

"She didn't…I don't…I mean, I just thought you'd be interested, him being your number-one client and all."

"Yeah, well, it's just a rumor at this point."

Nikki deflated like a pricked balloon, and Jason glimpsed the teenage girl beneath the glam-and-glitter makeup. But only for an instant. "Wait a minute," she demanded, regaining her composure. "What about what Pedro just said?"

Rumor or not, Jason was interested. He did a lot of legal work for Geraldo, and he guessed Geraldo hadn't paid him for two months. But he didn't believe the rumor, or Pedro. Geraldo had been threatening to move to Australia or Fiji to be a surf bum since they first met. Usually, it was when he'd completed a major project, like the big spec house at One Bluffside Drive he'd just finished building. Geraldo always paid Jason eventually, and Jason knew he never missed paying his workers and suppliers. He also knew that Geraldo had some new projects in the pipeline.

Jason could only take so much of Nikki in one dose. He decided it was time to get her to leave, so he asked, "Hey, do you know a blonde who's a runner? Kinda tall, with a ponytail and a nice tan? Maybe you've seen her in the salon?"

For a moment, Nikki's expression reminded him of a kitten whose prey has just been stolen by a bigger cat. She pulled her sweater over her shoulders and wrapped it around herself. "You're so mean, Jason."

She walked to the end of the bookcase and turned to face him. "I'll find out who your blonde is, but I won't tell you until you take me for a ride. A long ride." She turned on her heel, and her stilettos marched the length of the bookcase toward the door.

"Hey, Nikki," he called, "how would Mags know about Geraldo?"

The footsteps stopped. She spoke with exaggerated patience.

"They used to screw each other, stupid."

Jason was dumbstruck. *How could I have missed that one?* He recoiled at the thought of 50something Mags and 60something Geraldo locked in a love embrace.

"You know, Jason," Nikki continued in a voice heavy with sarcasm, "it's a good thing I like you, or you wouldn't know a thing going on in this stupid town."

Her clacking heels continued to his front door. He heard it open, but not close.

"Jason?"

"Yes?"

"Mr. Hoogasian came by today to pick up the salon's rent check. He said to tell you not to be late again this month."

She slammed the door.

CHAPTER 7

Jason returned Pedro's call as soon as Nikki left.

"That you, Mister Brinkman?"

"Please, call me Jason, Pedro."

"OK, Mister Jason."

"What's going on, Pedro?"

"Geraldo no pay me this month. I got rent due three days. I think Geraldo split for Australia like he say. Take surfboard and Danni. I got no money. You know where is he, Mister Jason?"

"No, Pedro, I don't. I haven't heard from him for a couple of weeks. Since he finished the spec house at One Bluffside."

"Aayyeee, the spec house. I give him money for that. All my money in bank. $10,000. All I got. He say he make me rich when he sell house, but he take all the money and split, and my wife kill me."

Jason's gut clenched. *My $30,000—the last of my nest egg!* He'd given the money to Geraldo to invest in the spec house project a year ago. In his mind, he'd divorced the project from the money, and forced himself to forget about it. His law practice had been doing well enough at the time, and he felt comfortable taking the risk. He'd told himself it was like putting the money in a CD where he couldn't nickel-and-dime it, but with a much better return.

Geraldo's pitch had been simple: Build a luxurious ocean-view house on Bluffside Drive for $2.5 million and sell it to some rich geezers for $4.75 million. Everybody gets their money back, plus a proportionate part of the profits. The deal was sealed with a handshake and a couple of beers at Mostly's Saloon. Jason didn't know that Pedro had invested, but knew Mags Turlock was in for $150,000. He thought Walter Crips, Geraldo's accountant, had invested at least $100,000. Mags bragged she made more than half a million a year, and Walter had a trust fund, so they could afford to lose that kind of money, but Jason certainly couldn't.

The blood began to pound in Jason's ears. If Geraldo hadn't paid his right-hand man and hadn't been seen for two weeks, something was seriously wrong. He took a deep breath to slow his pulse. "I'll see what I can find out. Call me if you learn anything."

"OK, Mister Jason."

Jason clicked off and speed-dialed Geraldo's cell phone. *Ring. Ring-ring.* "C'mon, Geraldo," he muttered impatiently. On the third ring, the phone connected. "Geraldo!" Jason said with relief, but the call had gone to voicemail. Geraldo's too-loud voice said, "Leave a message. I'm busy."

"Damn," Jason swore, but said into the phone, "Geraldo, this is Jason. I need to talk to you right away. It's important. Call my cell." He punched *End.*

The next obvious person to call was Walter Cripps. Jason was scrolling through his directory looking for Walter's number when he heard his office door open. "Hello? Nikki?"

There was no answer, but jingling and the squish of crepe-soled shoes approached on the other side of the bookcase, then stopped. He glanced up and recognized Deputy Hardesty's round bulk standing at the end.

Jason couldn't help thinking if a cop was supposed to inspire respect for the law, Hardesty definitely did not. Deputy Hardass was barely five foot nine from his see-through buzz cut to his crepe-soled shoes. His 220 pounds stretched his polyester shirt over his stomach so tightly that the buttons gapped. Coffee dribbles dotted the northern hemisphere of his round belly.

"Duane," Jason said, surprised. "What can I do for you?"

Hardesty tapped his badge and said, "That's Deputy Hardesty."

"OK, Deputy Hardesty. What can I do for you?"

"Your Porsche," Hardesty spat the word, "is parked on an incline."

"So?"

"So, Vehicle Code Sections 22509 and 22502."

Jason drew a blank, but he knew Deputy Hardass well enough to be wary when he started citing Vehicle Code or Penal Code section numbers. "I'm sorry, Deputy. I'm not familiar with those provisions. Can you…enlighten me?"

"Section 22509," Hardesty said contemptuously. "Failure to curb the wheels when parking a vehicle on a hill. Section 22502. Failure to park a vehicle parallel with the curb and within eighteen inches of it."

"Oh, for Chrissake!" Jason swore silently. He said, "I'm kind of in the middle of something right now. Can I move it in a few minutes?"

"I'll give you five minutes before I write a citation."

Jason knew that Hardesty would sit in his patrol car counting down the five minutes. "OK, Deputy. Thanks for being understanding."

Hardesty maneuvered his bulk around the end of the bookcase and squished down the opposite side. The door closed, and Jason said, "What an idiot!" He finally found Walter's number in his contacts and placed the call.

"Hello, Jason," Walter said pleasantly, "what's up?"

"Have you seen Geraldo recently?"

"Yeah, he dropped off the month's bills last week, or maybe it was ten days ago. Why?"

"Pedro just called me because he hasn't been paid this month."

"That's because Geraldo hasn't put the money in the bank yet. That happens sometimes, but usually there's enough left from the previous month to pay the workers."

"So you think he's around?"

"You know Geraldo. He's probably on a binge with some little bimbo celebrating the spec house. He'll surface in a few days."

"Speaking of the spec house, do you know how much the investors put in?"

"I don't know the exact numbers. I'd have to check. But I think there were about twenty investors and about one million dollars."

One million dollars! The number exploded in Jason's mind. He forced his voice to be calm and chatted with Walter about surf conditions, but he was thinking Geraldo could live simply in Fiji for years on $1 million. He ended the call. *That settles it. I've gotta find out what's going on.*

CHAPTER 8

Jason knew exactly where to go for all of Sea Cliff's latest rumors. The Bites 'n Bytes Wi-Fi Café was gossip central before noon, and was always more up-to-date than the GossipGoddessBlog by the village's queen of gossip, Mandi Jo Turowski. But first, he wanted to see how much Geraldo owed him. He opened his billing program and clicked on Geraldo's file.

In the last two months, he'd prepared a bankruptcy petition for Geraldo's Custom Builders No. 8 Inc. Bankruptcy was the final step in the scheme concocted by Geraldo for avoiding liability for construction defects. Jason would create a corporation. Geraldo would build several buildings and houses under the corporation's umbrella. Then he'd have the corporation declare bankruptcy. That way, there wouldn't be any assets for unhappy purchasers to go after.

It made Jason a little uncomfortable that some purchasers wouldn't be able to recover damages for faulty construction—potential damages for possible problems, he constantly told himself. He rationalized that his role in Geraldo's scheme was far less repugnant than aiding the Whatley firm's mega-corporate clients to avoid liability for defrauding their shareholders or injuring thousands of victims.

Jason also had started work on incorporation documents for Custom Builders No. 9 Inc. He'd defended Geraldo's latest DUI and prepared pleadings and interrogatories in the parade of petty lawsuits against Geraldo. It added up to 25 hours. "That's $8,750 he owes me!" Jason exclaimed. "That's enough to pay my rent and bills and keep going for a couple of months."

He closed out the billing program and opened his tickler file. No pleadings, motions, discovery responses, briefs, or appearances for ten days. His calendar reminded him that he was the guest speaker at the Chamber of Commerce luncheon a week from Friday, and that he planned to attend the Rotary Club meeting the following Monday. Both events were opportunities to attract new clients.

Having nothing scheduled for a week was good news, for once.

Before leaving, Jason stepped into the little quarter-bath tucked into the rear corner of his office. He leaned over the sink to rinse his face and looked at himself in the mirror. "Not bad for thirty-three," he judged. His chestnut-brown hair was free of gray, except for an occasional stray at the temple. These he plucked out immediately. Prominent cheekbones and a strong jaw meant his face would hold up well. At least that's what his mother used to say. His skin was taut and a little tan, and his brown eyes were clear. Most importantly, he could look himself in the eye, which he'd found hard to do when he worked for Whatley and lived with Courtney. He ran his fingers through his hair to smooth it, but not too much, and returned to his desk to gather up his cell phone and keys.

Jason walked around the bookcase to his front door and stuck a *Back in 5 minutes* sticky on the window. He flipped off the lights, but changed his mind and turned them back on so it would look like he'd only be gone a short while. On the way out the door, he grabbed his *Jason Brinkman, Attorney/Abogado/Notario* sandwich board sign to set up on the corner.

He locked the door behind him and walked down the steps. Glancing at his Porsche, he was surprised there wasn't a bright green ticket envelope tucked under the windshield wiper. "Deputy Hardass is off his game today," he chuckled.

* * *

Deputy Hardesty sat in his patrol car around the corner from Jason's office, concealed by a tall hedge but with a clear view of the offending Porsche. The timer on his cell phone ticked off the last seconds of the five minutes he'd generously granted Brinkman to comply with the requirements of the law—time the scofflaw had used instead to walk down the hill. Mindful that being efficient was a crucial attribute for an officer of the law, Hardesty had already prepared two citations for violations of the Vehicle Code. His timer chimed when it reached 00:00. Hardesty exited his vehicle and walked ramrod-straight to deliver the notices of violations. He jammed the two fluorescent-green envelopes under the driver's wiper.

That mission accomplished, Hardesty made a beeline back to Bluffside Drive. He liked to be erratic when he patrolled his beat, popping up in the business district, then in a residential area, so he could catch lawbreakers unaware. But he always cruised Bluffside Drive several times a day. It was part of his strategy for getting his sergeant's stripes. He knew that important people lived by the ocean on Bluffside, and his goal was to help them, even if only to carry in their groceries, so they'd support him when he went for his promotion.

Hardesty had an even more important reason for patrolling Bluffside, however. He wanted to bust a prevert. Beaches dotted the shoreline below Bluffside Drive, and Hardesty knew that preverts hung out at beaches. "After all," he reasoned, "didn't the old man in the trench coat choose Venice Beach to flash me?"

The old man had smiled at eight-year-old Duane. When Duane smiled back, the man waved him to come closer.

"Hi there, sonny, wanna little treat?" the old man had asked.

"Yes, sir," little Duane had mumbled shyly.

"How 'bout an all-day sucker, little fella?"

Then, *bam*, the old man pulled open his coat and exposed himself.

As Duane grew older, he researched everything he could about Venice Beach and the preverts who hung out there, so he wouldn't get caught again.

Deputy Hardesty was lost in that memory as he cruised Bluffside. Out of nowhere, a little boy and girl ran from the Vista Point parking lot, across the pavement, right in front of his patrol car. Startled, he screeched to a halt, just missing them.

"Daddy, Daddy," they screamed. "We saw a…. We saw a…." They ran into the closest house and slammed the door before Duane could hear what they saw. But he knew. He could tell from their terrified expressions what they'd seen. They looked just like he did when he told his parents about the man in the trench coat.

Them kids've just been flashed by a prevert.

Deputy Hardass felt the stars align and heard the angels sing. "I'm about to apprehend a flasher and earn points with an important person on Bluffside Drive," he whispered to himself. Judging by the house and the Range Rover in the driveway, a very important person. It would be a personal triumph and a career maker. Looking at his sleeve, he pictured his sergeant's stripes.

He hit the switch for his flashing lights, grabbed his nightstick and digital camera, and ran across the parking lot. He peered up and down the little beach below, looking for the flasher. Nothing. He considered reconnoitering the beach, but decided the stairs were too rickety to bear his 220 pounds. "Besides," he rationalized, "the beach really reeks today. Must be red tide or a dead seal. So, there's only one thing to do. I gotta take incident reports from them kids."

Duane experienced a queasy *déjà vu* feeling as he walked back across the street. This time, he'd be the policeman taking the statement from the frightened children, coaxing them to relive the terrifying incident instant by instant, the way he did every day. He'd be the one forcing them to remember details that would help identify the flasher and lock him behind bars forever.

He retrieved his hat and clipboard from the patrol car, and walked to the door of the house with the Range Rover.

CHAPTER 9

With feelings of anticipation and trepidation, Deputy Hardesty pushed the doorbell of the house the children ran into. The bell bonged inside. No answer. He rang again. Still no answer. He held his thumb against the button.

A man finally opened the door. He looked angry, surprised, and then pleased, probably because a cop appeared immediately after his kids ran into his house screaming in horror.

"Deputy," he said. "Thank God you're here. My kids just saw—"

Deputy Hardesty held up his hand to stop him. "I know what they saw, sir. Please don't say anything else to me or them."

Hardesty saw that the man didn't understand the delicacy required when questioning children about a sex crime. "It's important that you don't influence the children's statements or my report," he explained.

The man nodded, accepting but uncomfortable. "OK. But they're very scared, and I don't want to make it worse, so you'll have to question them together." He started to lead Hardesty into the house, but stopped abruptly. "I'm going to be in the room when you question them."

"Of course, sir," Hardesty said. From his own experience, he knew that a parent must be present while the cop interviewed the victim.

The man led the way to the great room, where the little boy and girl sat on the sofa, huddled in a blanket. He stood in the doorway. Deputy Hardesty strode across the tile floor to the sofa. His handcuffs jingled and his utility belt creaked, and when he stopped, he towered over the children. They seemed oblivious, their eyes unfocused and faces expressionless.

"Tell me what you saw," Deputy Hardesty said sternly, trying to break through their daze.

"Silver hair and big eyes," the girl mumbled.

Hardesty asked, "What was the person doing?"

The boy said, "Staring."

Hardesty decided that meant the perp was sizing up his victims. He asked, "Did the person say anything to you?"

The children answered at the same time. "No."

"Did you notice anything noticeable about the person's person?"

The boy looked across the room at the man, who said, "What the hell does that mean?"

"Sir, I'm attempting to ascertain whether there was anything particularly noticeable about the person," Hardesty explained. "Like did the person have—"

"Stinky," the girl interrupted.

Deputy Hardesty restated his questions several times to be sure the children's answers didn't vary, but they repeated the same words over and over robotically. Frustrated by their rote answers and lack of detail, he asked more questions, taking care not to lead them or suggest the answer.

"How close were you?"

"As close as you."

"How did you see this … person?"

"Looked up," the girl mumbled. "Waiting there."

Hardesty leaned back on his heels, pleased with himself for having elicited this new fact. It meant the prevert was lying in wait to expose himself indecently, which meant the arrest would virtually guarantee Hardesty his sergeant's stripes. He continued, "Where did you see the person?"

"The beach. The drain."

"What was the person wearing?"

The boy seemed confused and looked toward the man. "Don't know," he answered meekly.

Hardesty glanced over his shoulder at the man. He looked perplexed. His body tensed, as if he were about to spring across the room. He stood rigid in the doorway, clenching and unclenching his fists.

"What color was the person's coat?" The deputy pressed ahead, ignoring the man.

"Umm…don't know."

"Did you see any scars or tattoos?"

"No."

The man bolted toward the sofa. "What kind of questions are these? What are you doing?"

Deputy Hardesty raised his hand as if stopping traffic. "Please don't interrupt, sir. I know what I'm doing. I have experience."

The man returned to the doorway. He stood just inside the room, breathing rapidly.

Hardesty continued questioning the children. "Have you ever seen this person before?"

"No."

"Did you see part of the person's body?"

"Silver hair and big eyes," the boy repeated his original answer.

That was good enough for Deputy Hardesty. He wrote the children's statements carefully on his report form and announced his conclusion, which was both obvious and the only one that fit the facts. He cleared his throat. "Sir, an elderly prevert, who was lying in wait, exposed himself to your children. They say he was stinky, so he's probably homeless."

"No, you goddamn idiot!" The man charged into the great room. "They found a dead body in the storm drain." He grabbed Hardesty by the arm. "You're dumber than shit," he roared, dragging the deputy to the front door while the children wailed. "You get the fuck outta my house. You got no right to come in here an' scare my kids even more after they seen a corpse."

The man opened the door and shoved him out. "I'm calling the sheriff. I'm going to have your ass." He slammed the door so hard the house's front wall shook.

Deputy Hardesty retreated to his patrol car, baffled. "So they're saying it's a Section 187, Murder, and not a Section 314, Indecent Exposure?" he asked himself. He was disappointed at first, but heard the angels sing again a moment later. "No!" he decided. "Finding a dead body's way better for my promotion than collaring a flasher!"

He knew he should alert dispatch, but decided he ought to ascertain that there was actually a corpse before he called in. This caused him some apprehension, as he'd never seen a dead person.

Steeling himself, he retrieved his flashlight from his cruiser and walked slowly across Bluffside Drive to the gravel edge of the Vista Point parking lot. He decided a short delay was justified to observe the crime scene. On the left side of the lot, about 20 feet from him, he saw a tipped-over sawhorse at the foot of a dirt path that traced the edge of the cliff all the way to the Point. A few feet up the path there was a large hole in the middle of the dirt. He assumed that was the storm drain. Beyond the hole lay a dark, round object that looked like a manhole cover with wide slits.

Deputy Hardesty sniffed the air. His stomach heaved alarmingly. "What's that smell?" he wondered aloud. He raised his nose like a dog tracking a scent and scowled at the house next to the parking lot. "Oh," he said, "must be their septic leaking."

He walked across the gravel. Now the odor seemed to be coming from near the dirt path. Taking baby steps, he approached the path and the hole in the ground. "Whew!" he said. "It's coming from that hole."

Deputy Hardesty summoned all his courage and leaned over the hole. He shined his light into the blackness. There, perhaps 25 five feet below, were the soles of work boots. *So that's a dead body. What's the big deal?* A gust of wind blew the stench of decomposing flesh and organs up the drainpipe, in his face. Overwhelmed, he almost vomited into the opening. He jerked back, gagging. *THAT'S what that smell is!*

Squeezing his nose, Deputy Hardesty staggered across the parking lot, steadying himself against a large boulder for a moment. He looked around and saw the stairs to the beach. He stumbled to the top landing and sat, gulping fresh air.

He debated whether to check the other end of the body at the bottom of the pipe, but decided not to. "Them stairs look too rotten for my weight," he rationalized. Besides, now he knew what the kids meant. "The body's head is jammed 'gainst the bottom grate," he figured. "Its eyes must be open an' the kids must've seen 'em through the slits. That's what they meant by big eyes starin' at them."

Deputy Hardesty sat a few moments, catching his breath. When his head and body felt right, he fetched a roll of yellow crime-scene tape from his cruiser and cordoned off the Vista Point parking lot. That done, he called dispatch.

* * *

The village of Sea Cliff, population 3,551, was blessed by natural beauty, but lacked any exploitable resources. As a result, the main industries were tourism and real estate, with gossip close behind. Jason had vowed not to get sucked into the small-town rumor and gossip machine when he moved back to Sea Cliff. Still, he knew that certain information could be helpful in his law practice—like what business was about to fail, who was about to default on their mortgage, which contractor was about to go belly up, who'd been in an accident or gotten into a fight over the weekend, who was sleeping with whom, and so on.

"Always have several good sources of information," his father lectured him when he started at the Whatley firm, "and never tell anyone anything you learn."

Jason smiled wryly because that was the only good advice his father ever gave him.

For once, he'd heeded his father's counsel and had developed good sources of information. There was Nikki, who listened to everything that was said at the Ocean Wave Salon. There was his girlfriend, Erin Jones, who waited tables at Sea Cliff's *chi-chi* restaurant and paid attention to diners' conversations. Christina, his former secretary, fed him tidbits now and then from her new position in the village's largest law office. He gave generous tips to his hair cutter and the newsstand owner for solid information. There were his coffee buddies at Bites 'n Bytes and his drinking buddies at Mostly's Saloon, who provided intelligence sometimes. And there was the network of homeless laborers and gardeners, presided over by a homeless Vietnam veteran known as Admiral Bill. They knew virtually every secret in the village. Jason also checked the GossipGoddessBlog every day, although it rarely had anything useful to him.

He walked with his sandwich board down Charles Street's gentle hill toward Main Street. As he passed Mags Turlock's real estate office, he noticed Mags at her desk in the window, talking animatedly on her cell phone. Pictures of her listings lined the window's bottom sill, and in the corner, a poster advertised Geraldo O'Brien Custom Homes. *The finest in contemporary design and old-world craftsmanship*, the poster read. *Unparalleled quality for more than 25 years.*

Jason scoffed, but stopped briefly to inspect Geraldo's picture. It was one he hadn't seen. Geraldo was in his early forties, and his shoulder-length hair was still dark. Where his eyes normally were calculating, the camera caught them with a twinkling, sincere look. He smiled his most engaging smile.

The man in the picture surprised Jason. The dark hair now was the color of sun-bleached driftwood, and the face as craggy as the sandstone cliffs below Bluffside Drive. He continued downhill toward Main Street, thinking that 20 years of hard living, drugs, and working outdoors had really taken their toll.

He set his sandwich board on the corner of Charles and Main, with the arrow pointing up Charles toward his office. The sign was faded by sun and salt air, but it still clearly read *Jason Brinkman, Attorney/ Abogado/Notario. Your problem is my problem. Specializing in DUI, divorce, custody, personal injury, criminal defense, evictions, living trusts, immigration, mediation.*

"And anything else that walks in the door," he muttered, turning left on Main Street toward Bites 'n Bytes.

CHAPTER 10

"I don't care what the buyer's inspection report says," Mags Turlock bellowed into her cell phone. Mags was a little hard of hearing and didn't trust modern technology, so she overcompensated by yelling into the little device. Her voice was deep for a woman's; or maybe not, considering she favored sweat suits, down vests, and work boots.

"The water heater makes hot water and doesn't leak. End of discussion." Mags pushed back from her desk and stood up, holding the phone to her ear with her shoulder. Half-listening to the buyer's real estate agent, she shuffled through the papers in her inbox. The newbie agent argued that Mags's sellers should replace the water heater because the inspection report said it was ready to fail.

"Listen, Cupcake," Mags thundered at the young woman. "Your clients are buying a used home. A used home comes with a used water heater. If they want a new water heater, they should buy a new home. I've got some of those, if they'd like me to sell 'em one."

Mags found the elusive slip of paper with her list of ideas for a new slogan. It was time for a new ad campaign for Mags Turlock Real Estate Inc., and she needed something fresh and catchy. Cupcake argued earnestly while Mags scanned her list of possibilities:

Top producer on Central Coast since 2006.

True, but way too bland. She wanted something memorable. Maybe...

Real Estate is a blood sport.

Or...

Write with me, Right with God.

Although she believed both statements with every fiber of her being, they might be too much for the average client. How about…

Every deal's a done deal.

It was a fact, almost. Since 2006, Mags hardly ever lost a deal once it was accepted. But the slogan was boring.

Something Cupcake said caught Mags's attention. "Missy," Mags boomed, "why don't you just go back to Bakersfield? My clients aren't paying for a new water heater, and there's no way I am. You want to protect your clients? Buy 'em a home warranty, or better yet, pay for the water heater yourself."

Mags returned her attention to the list of slogans. The last one was her favorite:

Mags Turlock—Queen of Central Coast Real Estate.

She'd tried this one on some people in the village, and they all said they liked it. True, it was corny, but Mags's ego swelled every time she read it. In the last five years, she'd made more in commissions than any other local agent, and had closed more transactions. The other agents feared her, and she usually could bend them to her will with a phone call. Except for this little mosquito, who was still buzzing in her ear.

"Hold it, you little bitch," Mags yelled into her phone. "There's no way you're canceling this contract. We're five weeks in, you've lifted the contingencies, and the water heater isn't a material condition." Mags took a breath before moving in for the kill. "If you even try to back out, you'll be dead in this town. I personally guarantee that you'll never close another deal. You won't even write another offer. And I'll have a word with your broker and he will send you back to Fresno or Clovis, or wherever you're from."

Yes, "Queen of Central Coast Real Estate" was perfect. Mags circled it in red marking pen and placed the list on top of the other papers stacked in her inbox. Cupcake was still blathering. Mags held the phone away from her ear and glanced at the street. She saw Jason Brinkman looking at her window display. A minute later, he walked down Charles with his sandwich board sign.

All at once, she'd had enough of this maggot. Mags still missed her old-fashioned desk phone with its receiver she could slam down to end a call. It was hard to get the same effect with a cell phone, but she'd come up with several unpleasant alternatives. "So sue me," she bellowed and punched off her phone. "Damn, I love this job," she said to herself.

After the adrenaline rush, Mags realized her hands were shaking and her head was beginning to ache. She reached under her desk for her cooler and pulled out a half-pint of orange juice. Her cell phone rang as she opened the container.

Mags glanced at the screen between swallows. Walter Cripps, her accountant. She frowned. Walter only called when there was a problem, and she wasn't in the mood for any more problems this morning. "What do you want?" she barked into the phone.

"Good morning to you, too, Mags."

"What is it? If it's a problem, it can wait."

"Actually, Mags, it can't. You've got a big problem, and you need to start dealing with it right now. You need to hear this."

"Yeah, yeah. So call me back tomorrow."

"No, Mags. Now."

"OK, this afternoon."

"Now, Mags. You can't put this off."

"Alright, Walter, tell me all the bad news," Mags sighed into the phone. "I know you're dying to."

Walter cleared his throat. "Your tenants haven't been paying their rent, your commercial buildings are still empty, and you haven't had any income for two months. And you're supposed to be paying for the staging at One Bluffside, but you're not, because you don't have any money coming in. You're so leveraged your whole house of cards is about to crash."

Mags snorted. "You say that every time I have a cash flow problem."

"This time is different. On top of all that, you went and cosigned that $2.5 million note for Geraldo—his construction loan for One Bluffside. Against my advice, I might add. And he hasn't made any payments on it."

"I'll make a sale soon. Can't you stonewall 'til some cash comes in?"

"I can put off most of the creditors, but I can't put off Jamie, the manager of the bank. His ass is on the line."

"He's a pissant." Mags gestured like she was brushing away a fly. "Just shine him on."

"Can't do it. The loan doesn't show any payments, and you and Geraldo got him to release all the funds at once, which violates more rules than I can imagine. He's been notified that federal regulators are coming to inspect the bank's books. He thinks he's gonna get fired, and if he is, all his transactions will be scrutinized. That wouldn't be good for you."

"I just got off the phone about a sale, and I got a call today about One Bluffside from some folks from Beverly Hills. I'll sell it soon. I'll get my 150K back, and some commission, and Jamie will get his money. You'll get your money. Everyone will be happy."

"Sure, Mags. And I'll be the next American Idol. Let me put it to you bluntly. Geraldo is dragging you down. He's gonna destroy you and all you've worked for. Get some money from him. At least 50K. And bring it to me by the end of the week, or watch the wrecking ball come through your window." He ended the call.

Mags stared at her cell phone. "He's gonna destroy all you've worked for." Walter's words rang in her head. She placed the phone on her desk blotter, carefully squaring it with the corner. Sipping her juice, she grew melancholy and nostalgic. "Geraldo, you miserable fuck," she whispered, "we made a good team once. You, for building cheap houses, and me, for doubling our money when I sold 'em."

After making a killing on their first deal together, she and Geraldo invested their profits in more houses and made more money. Both excelled at sweet-talking others into covering most of their risks. They became lovers after celebrating a million-dollar sale with too much cocaine and ouzo. She remembered their affair wistfully. "I still miss your big strong arms, my hairy man, and I know you liked my big hooters. You were like a baby, playing with 'em."

Her need for him kept growing, but he began to lose interest. She wanted their liaison and partnership to continue, so she convinced him to do another major deal together—the spec house at One Bluffside—and then reevaluate. She was certain the financial ties would keep Geraldo close, or at least close enough. Fate intended otherwise, however, when he met Danni and her young daughter, Tiffany.

The sweet memory turned to ashes. "Goddamn you, Geraldo!" Mags swore, draining the orange juice. "You dump me for Danni and her little tramp, and now you steal my money." She smashed the container flat on her desk. "You absolutely deserve to rot in hell."

* * *

Even though it was eleven o'clock, Jason figured most of the regulars would still be at Bites 'n Bytes. He crossed the café's patio, passing a dozen empty tables. He pulled open the heavy door and surveyed the room, hoping to find Geraldo holding court in his usual booth, bullshitting anyone who'd listen. At the least, he expected the normal hum of caffeinated conversation. But there was no Geraldo, no conversation, and no friendly greetings when he walked in. Instead, everyone was glued to the blaring flat-screen televisions suspended from the ceiling.

Jason walked to the counter and waved to get the barista's attention.

"Hi, Jason," Arlene said. Normally she was flirty, but she spoke without taking her eyes off the TV. "What'll you have?"

"Hey, Arlene. Let me have a cappuccino and a warm nut bread. What's going on?"

"Whale-watching boat out of Rock Bay exploded. Forty people dead, maybe twenty injured."

"Jeez. How'd it happen?"

"They think fumes in the engine room."

"You seen Geraldo?"

"Huh?" she said, still focused on the TV. "No, he hasn't been in for a week or so. Here's your scone."

"Don't forget the cappuccino, and I wanted a nut bread."

"Sure," she said, heading for the bean grinder. "Just a minute."

Jason watched the TV and listened to the young woman reporter while Arlene ground the beans for his cappuccino. The scene was a distant shot of a capsized boat in heavy gray seas beneath black clouds. The reporter and the crawl repeated what Arlene had just said.

"Hey, Counselor." Jason was so focused on the television that the voice startled him. "Why ain't you down at the dock in Rock Bay handin' out your business cards?"

Jason recognized the smoke-and-whiskey voice of Admiral Bill. He turned and found the man standing at his elbow, wearing his trademark yellow sunglasses and ragged camouflage fatigues.

"Nah," Jason said, "I let the sharks do their dirty work. They wind up paying me for bailing 'em out 'cause they're overextended."

"You all sharks," the Admiral said amiably. He smiled his odd inverted smile, turning the corners of his mouth down to form an upside-down 'U.' "Some's just smarter 'n others."

Jason let the conversation die. They both watched the TVs.

"Here's your cap, Jason," Arlene said from behind them.

Jason started to ask her for a slice of nut bread instead of the scone, but Admiral Bill interrupted him. "I got some news for ya, Counselor."

Admiral Bill had a knack for showing up unexpectedly, like this morning. Jason hadn't seen him for weeks, but here he was, no doubt wanting to sell his information. Of all Jason's informants, Admiral Bill was the best. He and his gang of homeless veterans were invisible to most villagers, and they picked up all kinds of information as they did odd jobs around town.

Jason once asked Admiral Bill why his men called him the Admiral. "I was in the Navy during 'Nam," Bill explained, "and the guys elected me leader." Jason learned later that Admiral Bill dropped out of college in the 1960s to join the Navy. He'd been a cook's helper, but spent most of his military career in the brig. Whatever the whole story was, the Admiral was loyal because Jason always sprung him from jail when Deputy Hardass busted him for being drunk, peeing in public, peeping, or just being homeless.

"What've you got for me?" Jason asked, forcing himself to ignore the televisions' noise and images.

Admiral Bill looked pointedly at Jason's cappuccino.

Jason said, "Arlene, how about a cap for my friend?"

"Make it a double Americano with double whip cream," the Admiral countered. Jason nodded, and Arlene returned to the bean grinder.

"So, Bill, what've you got?"

"You're close to Geraldo."

"Not really. I just do some work for him."

"Modesty don't sit well on a lawyer," Bill snorted. "Everyone knows you're his right hand. And his friend. Anyway, I got some news he needs to know about."

"What is it?" Jason asked patiently.

"Thing is, I ain't had breakfast this week."

"Arlene," Jason said, "the Admiral here needs a blueberry scone."

Bill shook his head. "How 'bout a egg melt on a English muffin?"

"Fine. Arlene, an egg melt on an English muffin and a double Americano whip, please." He paid for both orders and told Bill to come up to the café's balcony when he got his food.

Jason took his scone and coffee upstairs to the balcony and sat next to the railing. Main Street was directly below and Highway 1 was in the distance. From this vantage point, he saw the blue Pacific beyond the hills and trees west of the highway. The sun sparkled on the water at the moment, but a thick bank of gray fog lurked on the horizon. The sight of the fog made him shiver. *The fog's coming in soon, and it'll be dark and cold.* He suppressed a shudder. *I'll just have to deal with it. It'll be OK.*

Admiral Bill joined him a few minutes later with his coffee and egg melt. Jason sipped his cappuccino and picked at his scone, watching the cars on the highway. Finally he said, "So, what's on your mind, Bill?"

"Well, you know I think Geraldo's 'bout the meanest son-of-a-bitch there ever was, 'cause he treats me and my men bad, never payin' us what he promised an' makin' fun of us 'cause we don't got no square roof."

The Admiral's face grew red and his voice louder as he spoke. "And he's always struttin' 'round town drivin' that big Cadillac with his arm hangin' out the window and all that chrome, and throwin' his money 'round so he can fuck all them young college girls he picks up down at Mostly's."

Someone on the balcony scraped a chair. Bill stopped and looked over his shoulder. When he saw people staring at him, he continued in a normal voice. "But he does pay us now and then, and we do need the money, so even though I hate him, I need him 'round."

"Where're you going with this, Bill?"

Bill leaned closer. "I heard there's a major bad dude in town looking for him. Big Mexican guy. Calls himself El Carnicero."

"The butcher? That sounds serious."

Admiral Bill nodded. "Very serious. They say you gotta see this guy to believe it. Huge and mean. Likes to kill. Muscles everywhere. Got 'El Carnicero' branded into his forehead." He took a big bite of his egg melt and slurped his coffee. "This El Carnicero, he put out the word that Geraldo owes him big-time money, and he'll pay to find him. Says he gonna cut him into little pieces when he does."

"You going to turn Geraldo in for the money?"

"No way. I don't want nothin' to do with that Mexican. He's one scary fucker, so's I hear."

"So, why are you telling me this?"

"Like I say, you're close to Geraldo. If you talk to him. The Mexican rides a big Harley, in case you wanna avoid him."

"Thanks for the heads-up, Bill. I'll be sure to tell Geraldo when I see him."

The two men sat watching the cars and RVs stream past on the highway. Jason finished eating while Bill sipped his coffee and fidgeted. When the silence became uncomfortable, Bill pulled out a folded handkerchief and opened it, revealing three half-smoked cigarettes and a fresh Marlboro. He offered the Marlboro to Jason, who shook his head. "No, thanks," he said, pointing to his shoulder. "Patches."

Bill lit one of the stubs. "Counselor, I hate to ask, but I got no money and my disability check's run out. You got anything I could do to earn a few dollars?"

Jason considered for a moment. He felt guilty because GG's garden looked terrible, and decided he could solve his problem and Bill's by having him do some trimming and weeding. "Sure. Come over later this afternoon." He wrote his address on the back of his business card.

"Thanks, man." Admiral Bill took the card and stuck it in his pocket without reading the address. He smiled his upside-down smile, revealing stubby brown lower teeth. "You won't regret it."

"I know you'll return the favor," Jason said, watching the traffic. "Look at that."

A line of emergency vehicles headed south on Highway 1. A sheriff's patrol car led, followed by an ambulance and a fire truck. They all had their flashing lights on, but no sirens, and were driving the speed limit. At the end of the line, a semi pulled a crane on a trailer.

"Must be heading to Rock Bay," Admiral Bill said.

"I don't think so. No sirens, and they're not speeding. Must be something local."

Jason left the Admiral munching on his egg melt. He descended the stairs into the din of the TVs and was about to leave, but stopped when the young reporter yelled excitedly into her microphone: "Breaking news! This morning forty people died in a boat explosion in Rock Bay. Now a body's been found in a storm drain in Sea Cliff, just twelve miles north of here. I'm Ally Booker, and I'm taking my crew up there right now. Stay with me on KHYP, your news station. Ally Booker gets the story every time."

CHAPTER 11

The tidbits Jason learned at Bites 'n Bytes didn't help much. He walked toward his office, adding up what he knew.

Geraldo hadn't been to Bites 'n Bytes for a week and never gave Walter money to pay his bills. Nikki said that Mags said he'd gone to Australia. Bottom line: He may well have left for good and taken the $1 million with him, including Jason's $30,000.

It was possible Geraldo had been kidnapped by the cartel enforcer, El Carnicero, but Jason considered it unlikely. There were always rumors that Geraldo was selling drugs, but Jason doubted he'd be stupid enough to cross a Mexican drug lord. But there was the story about the scar on Geraldo's cheek ….

Geraldo may or may not have taken Danni with him—Jason was pretty sure he'd seen Danni last week. Geraldo's affair with Danni puzzled him. Geraldo liked girly-girls, like the coeds from Santa Luisa and the young townies he picked up at Mostly's Saloon and boinked in the back of his Escalade. Yet he lived with Danni and her teenage daughter in one of his houses.

Danni Tedeski couldn't have been less girly. She was a big woman—big-shouldered, burly-bodied, five-foot-ten to Geraldo's five-eleven—with a caved-in nose and hollow eyes caused by years of cocaine abuse. A contractor in her own right, she often swung a hammer when Geraldo needed help on one of his building projects. She usually won the arm wrestling and tequila shots contests at Mostly's. A persistent rumor said she'd been a nurse once, but lost her license because she got caught stealing narcotics from her hospital and using them.

Jason figured Danni would know if Geraldo was gone, and her daughter would know if they were both gone. "The thing to do," he decided, "is to go to their house and find out what's going on."

He stopped on the sidewalk at the foot of the walkway to his office. Glancing at his door, he saw the back of a man built like a pro wrestler. He wore an oversized black windbreaker, and was hunched against the window with his hands cupped around his eyes.

"Can I help you?" Jason called.

The man turned around and walked down the steps, scowling and clenching his fists. "Brinkman, am I glad to see you." Jason recognized him, having met him a couple of times—Mack Hammersley, the owner of Sea Cliff's building supply and lumberyard.

"Mack, what's going on?" Jason stuck out his hand and Hammersley shook it, crushing it in his grip.

"I hear O'Brien split town."

"I heard the same thing, and I'm looking for him, too. What can I do for you?"

"That fucker owes me fifty grand for materials. You know, that piece of shit house he built down on Bluffside. He ain't paid me, and I can't make payroll this week."

"You know Geraldo always pays his bills. Well…eventually."

"I ain't got 'eventually.' I need that money now. He knows I'm always close to the edge, and I was thinkin' maybe he left a check with you, you bein' his lawyer an' all."

"Nope. Have you asked Walter?"

"He said to talk to you. Look. If I don't make payroll, I lose my men, and I can't fill my orders. If I can't make money, my suppliers come after me, and I go under. I need that money today."

"Honestly, Mack, I don't know where he is. I'm looking for him, too. I'll let you know—"

"This is personal, Brinkman. My business is my life. I put everything I got into it, and I ain't gonna lose it 'cause O'Brien skipped town to be a surf bum in the South Pacific." His face turned crimson as he spoke. "That sack of shit is dead meat," he dragged his finger across his throat, "and there's a lotta folks gonna be comin' to you to make things right with him." Hammersley shoved past him, slamming his shoulder and knocking him off balance.

"Hey!" Jason yelled at his back. "Don't be looking to me! I'm not his bank!"

The big man stomped across Charles Street and climbed into his pickup. He peeled down the hill.

Jason stood watching the truck slam on its brakes at the intersection with Main. He added Hammersley to his mental list of angry people Geraldo had left behind, along with Pedro, the other investors, El Carnicero, and himself.

He beeped open his Porsche. That was when he saw the two fluorescent-green ticket envelopes jammed under the wiper. Disgusted, he ripped them free and threw them in the passenger's footwell.

Punching the *Start* button, he resolved, "If Geraldo's at home, I'll tell him I want a check for $8,750 right now."

His phone chimed as he shifted into first. The message was from Erin:

Gd news 4 u. C me @ wrk.

* * *

Jason jogged up Posh's back steps and entered the kitchen through the open door. "Hey, Pierre," he said to the cook, who was humming and sweating over his eight-burner range. Pierre looked up and wiped his forehead with his sleeve.

"*Bonjour*, Jason. She's in the dining room bussing." He stirred a pot of bouillabaisse. "The busboy's sick today."

As if on cue, Erin burst through the door, balancing a tray loaded with dirty plates and glasses over her head. She spiraled the tray down to the bussing counter so smoothly that not a single dish clinked.

Jason watched her from across the kitchen, mesmerized by her grace and strength. Her auburn hair was clasped at the nape of her neck and her cheeks were pink with exertion. The overhead lights played off the curves of her body as she lowered the tray. He saw the outline of her bra beneath her white silk shirt for an instant, and when she bent her leg, the cut of her thong.

He rarely saw Erin at work anymore. When they first got together six months ago, he dropped by Posh whenever he could. After a while, she asked him gently, but firmly, to stop.

"Until I can support myself selling my photographs, or win the lottery and leave here forever," she explained, "I'm going to be the best server in town, and you distract me."

She was, indeed, an excellent server. She never wrote down an order, knew how every dish was prepared, delivered each selection flawlessly, and was always cheerful. Her skill and beauty earned her generous tips and loyal customers.

Erin also was a gifted photographer. She produced dreamy, surreal images of Big Sur, capturing the dance of sun and fog along the rugged coastline and among the towering redwoods. Her photographs hung in the village's best-known tourist gallery, and once in a while, she'd call Jason excitedly to say one of her pictures had sold. Jason liked her ambitiousness, but thought she lacked the fire that consumed Courtney. His impression was that, like many other lifelong villagers, Erin's ambitions were trumped by the unknowns of the world outside. That suited him, since he had no desire to leave Sea Cliff after so many years in Los Angeles.

She saw him as she settled the tray and smiled with mischief in her deep-blue eyes. She said, "I need something from the pantry. Will you help me?"

He followed her into the dim pantry, guessing what she had in mind. "Something from the pantry," he said as he closed the door. "I'd love to help. Whatever can it be?"

Erin walked to the bank of storage shelves atop the long counter. She looked up, facing the shelves. "Let me see. I think I need…that big jar of artichoke hearts." She stretched on her toes for a jar that was just out of her reach.

Jason pressed himself against her back as she stretched, feeling her warmth and firm curves. "I've missed you," she said, pushing her body into him with surprising intensity.

They'd been intimate almost from the beginning, and couldn't seem to get enough of each other. She was a hungry lover, and he responded in kind, although they were always gentle. Even so, they'd never promised each other to be exclusive. He knew she saw her boyfriend from junior college sometimes, and Jason dated other women now and then. By unspoken agreement, the "L" word was not part of their relationship.

Jason kissed her earlobe and nuzzled her neck, teasing the silky stray hairs that escaped their clasp. Her perfume and hairspray, and the faint scent of her hard-working body, filled his head. He pulled her hips into him and she murmured approval, swaying gently.

"So, you have some news for me?" he whispered in her ear.

She giggled and said, "It feels like you have something for me, too." She turned to face him and they shared a long kiss. He ran his hand up her flat stomach, savoring her warm flesh beneath the silk, and started to cup her breast. She arched against him, moaning softly, but stiffened and pushed his hand away after a moment.

"No, Jason, don't. It's too much. You understand."

Jason didn't, but he'd learned to accept that her passion could take unexpected turns, sometimes exploding, sometimes shutting down. She sighed. "Anyway, I have to get back, and I can't be all wrinkled."

They looked into each other's eyes, her arms around his waist, his around her neck. He pressed himself against her pelvis and traced the curve of her eyebrow, then her cheek, with his finger. Finally, he turned away to lean against the counter next to her.

They stood quietly, hips and shoulders touching. When their pulses slowed, Erin said excitedly, "I wanted to tell you. I served an elderly couple from Beverly Hills this morning, and they were talking about One Bluffside. They had Mags Turlock's full-page ad. They were saying, 'We could put this piece of furniture here' and 'hang this piece of art there.' And they loved that it has an elevator. Mags is going to show it to them later this afternoon."

Jason frowned.

"Is something wrong?" Erin asked.

"Yeah, it's probably too late. All morning, I've been hearing rumors that Geraldo split for Australia with our investment money. Or it could be that a Mexican drug lord kidnapped him. Either way, it's not good for us investors."

"Your $30,000?"

"Probably gone," he said gloomily. "I was on my way to Geraldo's and Danni's to find out where he is when I got your message."

"But isn't that the last of your money?"

Jason's stomach clenched, but he didn't answer.

"Geraldo wouldn't do that to you, would he?" she insisted. "Just run away with your money and everyone else's?"

"Yeah, he could've," Jason grumbled. "Everything Geraldo does, he does for himself." He stabbed his toe at a sugar packet next to his foot and kicked it across the room. "It's funny, though ... I don't think you've ever met him—"

"Uh-uh."

"But he's got this salesman's personality. You're just drawn to him, like a magnet. He's charming and sincere, and you have to like him. He's your best buddy at the same time he's cutting you off at the knees."

She shuddered. "Sounds like a nut case. Are you friends? I thought he was just a client."

"A lot more client than friend. He's a sleaze, and a macho prick, but his personality's so strong, there's still some kind of bond. Even if it turns out he did steal all our money, I'd hate him, but there's a part of me that would miss him. Crazy, I know, but that's the hold he has on people."

Erin slipped her arms around his waist and kissed him on the cheek. "I'm sorry, baby. I hope it's just a false alarm."

He smiled wanly. "Things will work out, I'm sure."

They stood leaning against the counter in the dim light for another minute. "There's more bad news, I'm afraid," he said. "Two things, actually. I should probably tell you because your customers will be talking about it."

He felt her tense. "What happened?"

"A tour boat exploded down in Rock Bay and forty people are dead. Maybe twenty injured. And, they found a body in Sea Cliff."

"Oh no!" She clasped her hands to her face. "How horrible!" Tears welled in her eyes, and for a split second, Jason was moved to say the "L" word. He settled for wiping her cheeks and kissing each one gently.

Trying to lighten the mood, he reached up and fetched the artichoke jar from the shelf. "Here's your artichoke hearts, lady."

She wiped her eyelashes and forced a smile. "Let me know what you find out at Geraldo's."

"I will. See you tonight?"

"No, I'm working a double. Maybe tomorrow night?"

"Definitely," he said, kissing her goodbye.

Jason walked into the bright kitchen with the jar of artichokes hearts, leaving Erin smoothing her hair and straightening her shirt. Pierre glanced up, his expression both knowing and wistful. Jason selected an apple from the fruit bin and placed the jar on Pierre's worktable. "Here you go, Pierre. We thought you might need this."

* * *

Sergeant Duane Updegraf Hardesty. The sound was so pleasing in Duane's head that he repeated it out loud. "Sergeant Duane Updegraf Hardesty. It's in the bag," he told himself. "After my superior performance this morning, only the award ceremony stands between me and my sergeant's stripes."

It was he who'd discovered the dead body, after all. He was certain no other competitor for the sergeant's position had found a corpse. After finding it, he'd called dispatch and reported his find using his best cop jargon. The emergency vehicles were on their way. He'd even thought to tell dispatch to send a crane to lift the victim out of the storm drain. "My problem solving ability's gotta impress the test administrators," he gloated.

Then, the most extraordinary thing happened. An elderly neighbor in curlers and a cloth coat approached him and told him a tale that made him giddy. The neighbor, Mrs. Dorothy Richardson, explained she lived in the house next to the Vista Point parking lot. She told him she'd been emailing her grandson stationed in Germany at two in the morning a week ago, when she heard a car door slam shut. She looked out her window and saw a silver minivan in the lot. She saw a drunk dragging another drunk across the lot toward the Point, but only one of them returned to the van and drove away.

"I didn't know if it was important," Mrs. Richardson said. "I checked the lot next morning to see if one of them was passed out or dead, but I didn't see anything, and there was nothing on the news. Anyway, I didn't want to get involved. You know how it is."

Deputy Hardesty nodded to show that he did, indeed, know how it was.

"I didn't want to be an old busybody, but my conscience bothered me all week, and seeing you here is like a sign from the Lord that I should report what I saw. So, here I am."

"You're doing the right thing, ma'am." He held his breath and asked, "Did you happen to see the van's license plate?"

"No, Officer. I'm sorry. It was so foggy. But I did see one of those international stickers that people put on their cars. You know, white and black? An oval?"

He said, "Uh-huh," as if he understood.

"It was on the back window on the right, and it said 'IE' or 'IT.' Or maybe it was 'IL,'" she said proudly.

Deputy Hardesty nodded again and made notes on his report form. He thanked Mrs. Richardson and gave her his card in case she remembered anything else.

Although he maintained his professional demeanor, his head was bursting. *I'M the one who discovered the body, AND I've got a good lead to find the perpetrator. How many silver minivans can there be in Sea Cliff? Finding the perp'll be a piece of cake.* A thought blossomed that took his breath away. *Maybe I'm more qualified to be a captain.* Did he dare say it out loud? "Captain Duane Updegraf Hardesty," he whispered to himself. "I like the sound of that!"

He completed his report as he waited for the emergency vehicles, giving himself full credit for finding the body and locating the witness. He didn't mention the little kids, or their unpleasant father. As far as the deputy could tell, the father was the only speed bump on his road to becoming Sergeant Hardesty. *Or Captain Hardesty.* The thought gave him goose bumps.

The scene with the man and his kids was still fresh in his mind, but he pushed it aside. "Best to leave all that stuff out of my report," he rationalized. "It's cleaner if I just take the credit. Anyway, who'll ever know?"

Gloating, he reviewed his report one last time. He looked up when the clatter of diesel engines and the rumble of heavy vehicles approached on Bluffside Drive. A moment later, a semi loaded with a crane came into view, followed by emergency vehicles and a TV news van.

CHAPTER 12

Jason turned right out of Posh's parking lot and drove south on Main Street toward the intersection with Highway 1. The sun was bright at the moment, but streamers of fog reached across the pavement, casting shadowy black fingers. He knew from experience that Geraldo's house and everything else west of the highway would be buried in fog.

Motoring along Main Street, he watched the shadows creep up the hills behind the business district, and realized the entire village soon would be dark and cold. He shuddered, dreading the prospect. "What is it with me?" he asked himself, although he knew the answer. "Why does fog still creep me out after all these years?" He turned up the Porsche's heater to 80, and for good measure, flipped on the seat warmer.

Seeing Erin for even a few minutes normally brightened his day. As he drove past the shops and offices, he tried to focus on the sensations of her firm body, her sexy energy, and that mischievous smile. But despite himself, his mind kept returning to his money problems, looming like the dark cloud he was about to drive into. "Bottom line, I'm broke." Saying it out loud made it more real.

Main Street became two lanes at the end of the business district and snaked up the hill to intersect Highway 1. He accelerated up a short straightaway. Approaching a blind right curve, he stabbed the brakes and downshifted into second. "Stupid, stupid, stupid," he rebuked himself, "to bet the entire $30,000 on the spec house. It's gone. I'll lose everything if I don't get some money from Geraldo." Turning deeper into the curve, he barked a laugh. "I'll be a total loser, just like my old man."

He crossed the highway and turned right on Miller Street, stopping front of 317, the two-story stucco box where Geraldo lived with Danni and Tiffany. The house was one of dozens Geraldo had built in Sea Cliff over the decades. Locals called them "Geraldo boxes" because they were so common.

Drizzle began to fall from the gray cloud overhead. Jason ran to the stairs and took them two at a time. He rang the bell, huddling under the front eaves. When no one answered, he walked back to the street and looked up at the second floor. There was a light in one of the bedrooms. He returned to the front door and rang the bell three more times. Minutes later, footsteps clomped down the stairs inside. A teenage girl wearing just a faded football jersey and UGG boots opened the door.

"Hey, Tiffany."

"What do you want?"

Jason was surprised at her tone and appearance. She usually was well-groomed and as polite as any teenager is to an adult. Today, her hair was dirty and pulled back in a scrunchie. Her face was pale beneath her freckles, and dominated by black bags under pink eyes. He smelled marijuana smoke on her clothes and in the house.

"Are you OK?"

"What do you want?" She might as well have slammed the door in his face.

"I'm looking for Geraldo."

Tiffany glared at him. Her eyes were fierce and sad. Finally, she said, "He's not here."

"How 'bout your mom? Is she home?"

"NO!"

"Do you know where they are?"

"No. Leave me alone."

"C'mon, Tiff. You must know where one of them is. Where's Geraldo?"

"The creep?" she snapped. "He ran away to Fiji."

"And your mom?"

"Probably with him. In Fiji."

"They just left you?"

"Yeah. They left me. They left me with no money and a jar of peanut butter." Her face softened and her eyes filled with tears.

"Can I help you, Tiffany?"

"So now you're the one who's gonna fix everything and take me away from all this?" She began to sob.

"I just meant, can I take you to the Super Mercado or give you some money for food?" he said, trying to console her.

"No," she said, wiping her eyes with her sleeves. "Thanks. I'm sorry." She pushed her sleeves above her elbows.

"Jesus, Tiff, are those needle marks on your arm? Let me see."

"Get away from me!" She pulled her sleeves down and backed from the door. "I … I … gave blood … at the blood drive. At school."

Jason stared at her.

"I'm OK. I'm going to be OK. Now leave me alone." She stood half hidden by the door, studying him.

For a second, he thought she was going to ask him for help. "Call me if I can—" but she slammed the door. He heard her clomping up the stairs, sobbing.

Jason walked to his car in the drizzle. Sitting in the driver's seat, he remembered his despair when he was a kid every time his mother disappeared on a binge. *God, how I wanted some adult to come and rescue me. I have to do something to help her. Yeah, but what?*

Peering through the misty windshield, he tried to make out shapes while he debated solutions. He could give her money for food and drive her to the store, but that wasn't a long-term solution. If Geraldo and Danni really were gone for good, someone would have to take care of her until she turned eighteen … in two years? Did she have friends whose parents would take her in? He dismissed the idea. Tiffany was a good kid, but that would be asking a lot of someone who wasn't related.

The lawyer side of his brain snapped to attention. "Legally, I'm an officer of the court," he reminded himself. "If she's abandoned and refusing help, I have to notify Children's Protective Services."

Jason knew protective custody wasn't a good solution, having been in foster care many times before the judge let him live with GG in Sea Cliff. His mother's and father's stints in rehab often overlapped, and CPS parked him in foster homes for the duration. His stomach twisted at the memory. Tiffany didn't deserve that. But if she really was living on dope and peanut butter, and God forbid, shooting up, CPS needed to get involved.

He imagined a CPS matron dragging freckle-faced Tiffany off to Juvenile Hall. "That can't happen," he vowed. "Danni's screwed up, but she wouldn't just abandon her daughter. Geraldo would, but not Danni." Still, the consensus of the day's gossip was that Geraldo and Danni were gone for good. He realized he was the only one who wasn't convinced.

The drizzle turned to rain. "I will not call CPS until I've exhausted every possibility," he decided, "and there's still one place left to check for clues." He punched *Start* and flicked on the wipers. "The spec house."

* * *

Tiffany fell into her crumpled bed and cried herself to sleep. The *bink-bink* of her laptop woke her an hour later. Wiping her eyes on her sleeve, she turned the computer to see who wanted to chat with her. She wasn't in the mood for any of her stupid classmates, but it was Victoria, her dearest friend in the whole world, so she clicked on.

"hey, T. have you decided what your gonna do?"

"no. i mean yes, but i'm not sure."

"maybe you should talk to someone." The words flowed across Tiffany's screen. "someone who's been through it."

"like?"

"Charlotte."

"Charlotte the Harlot? really?"

"that's what i heard," Victoria typed.

"no surprise. she's to stupid to remember to put on her underwear after she does it."

"lights on, nobody home."

"if i talk to her, everyone will know, just like when i told you about Geraldo."

"i know. my guilt forever."

"no, i have to figure this out by myself. my mom's always yelling at me to grow up. and now i have to."

"you were acting pretty adult there for a while with Geraldo."

"yeah. i thought i was being grown up, but i was just stupid. LOL."

"anyway," Victoria typed, "listen, do you remember what Mr. Pearson told us in Human Development class?"

"no."

"he said teenagers should learn to make decisions based on facts, not emotions or what we think the right answer is supposed to be."

"yeah? so?"

"so you need to get some advice. that's what adults do, at least the smart ones. this is a big decision, T."

"i know, but i'm so confused. you don't understand. i don't want anyone to know about this. it's my secret. mine."

"i know sweetie, but listen to me. there's a place in Santa Luisa near the Greyhound station i heard about called God's Love or God's Hands or God's something. let's go talk to them. they'll help you decide."

"can't."

"why?"

"don't want to."

"your not listening. c'mon."

"no car."

"this is the biggest decision you ever made, T."

"yeah, but no car."

"i'll take you. we'll go in together. let me be your big sister and take care of you. we can take my mom's car. she's passed out from last night. it'll be our secret."

"NO!" Tiffany yelled as she punched the keys. She cried, "Stop pushing me! I'll figure it out. It's no one's business!"

Her screen was blank. She stared at the word in big black capital letters. Victoria didn't respond.

"No one can know!" Tiffany screamed at the screen. Tears dripped on her keyboard. "No one!" she sobbed. "NO ONE!"

She wiped her eyes and waited forever for Vic to respond, but the screen stayed blank. Finally, Tiffany typed, "are you still there, V? i know your just being my BFF and big sister and trying to help."

"c'mon, T. we'll get stoned and sing Beatles songs. it'll be fun."

Tiffany's fingers refused to move. She thought about what Mr. Pearson said and decided he might be right. Maybe she did need to know more. Whatever she decided, it would still be her decision and her most secret of all secrets. Forcing her fingers to type, she barely touched the keys. "ok. but just the happy ones. ok?"

"awesome. pick you up in ten."

"it's near the Greyhound station?"

"yeah."

"ok."

Tiffany clicked off and rummaged in her closet. She pulled on her jeans and threw some essentials in her backpack—a baggie of dope, rolling papers, iPhone, earbuds, laptop, a stale Snickers bar, and a tee-shirt. Reaching under her mattress, she found the birthday card with the hundred-dollar bill in it.

Happy Sweet 16, Princess, the card said. *Buy yourself something sexy for me.*

Tiffany gagged and ran to the wastebasket, but only dry-heaved. She tore the card into a million pieces and pocketed the money. The gray fog out her window reminded her it was cold outside. She grabbed her jacket and backpack and ran down the stairs to meet Victoria.

Sitting on the front steps, she listened for the putter and pop of Victoria's mom's VW Beetle. She dug out her iPhone and stuck the buds in her ears. As she scrolled through her playlist, she had the creepy feeling she was being watched. She held the phone in front of her so she could look across the street while pretending to read the screen.

Behind the neighbor's hedge, she saw a man peering at her through the leaves. She stared, trying not to be obvious, hoping it was the neighbor's gardener, but caught a glimpse of yellow sunglasses. That meant it was Admiral Bill. She shuddered, remembering the times she caught him staring at her through the bathroom window.

Tiffany turned away and leaned against the newel post. "C'mon, Vic," she silently willed her friend, "before that dirty creep gets any ideas." She selected a Beatles song to distract her and hummed along as Paul and John harmonized in her ears:

♩ Silently turning the back door key
Stepping outside, she is free ♩

As Tiffany waited, she remembered Mr. Pearson's class and his earnest lecture about thinking like an adult. She remembered he'd also said revenge is a waste of time and energy for teenagers. *He's wrong on that, totally. Getting revenge is everything. Revenge is all we've got.*

CHAPTER 13

Nikki had a problem. She really, really wanted Jason to like her. He was so handsome and cool, with his expensive LA clothes and cute little butt and strong arms. And that luscious chestnut hair. She wanted to dig her fingers into his hair and smoosh his face into her boobs. And his Porsche. She really, really liked his Porsche a lot.

She wanted him to drive her up the coast to Falling Cliffs on a sunny day with the top down, or maybe all the way to Big Sur, where the car might break down and they'd have to spend the night at Ventana or one of those super-expensive resorts. A dreamy fantasy filled her mind. *I'll wash his hair and scrub his hands 'cause they'll be all greasy after he fixes the car, and he'll be all sweaty so we'll take a long shower—no—a cold plunge and a sauna. Yeah, that's even better, and then*…. She sighed. All of that would have to wait.

Right now, she had to make him like her and not treat her like a kid. She had an idea. After listening to the chatter in the beauty salon all day, she knew who Jason's runner with the blonde ponytail was. Instead of trying to bribe him with information, which didn't work this morning, she decided she'd tell him everything she'd learned. "That way," she figured, "he'll see that I'm nice. And mature, because I kept my promise. And he'll start to like me the way I like him."

There was a danger, of course. Telling Jason about the runner might set her up as a rival. Nikki thought about this carefully while washing her tenth head of the day. With all she'd learned, however, she was pretty sure she could tell Jason things about the woman that would turn him off.

Nikki had another, smaller problem, and that was Erin. She knew that Jason wouldn't be ready to like her until Erin got out of the way, or was pushed. It would be simple to push Erin if she needed to. Nikki's older sister, Brenda, was Erin's best friend, and Nikki knew things about Erin. Yucky things that would make Jason break up with her.

But right now, Nikki thought her best bet was to do something nice for Jason. She was feeling sorry for him because she knew he didn't have any money to spare right now, and she'd seen that horrid Deputy Hardass give him TWO tickets. She knew he couldn't afford them and he was always late paying his rent. That made her wonder if he was always going to be poor. Would she feel the same if he didn't have money, nice clothes, and his sexy, sexy car? *No way. He's a lawyer, and Mother says all lawyers are rich.*

Nikki decided she could make Jason's day better, and score some points, by telling him all she'd learned about the blonde ponytail. She finished rinsing number ten's hair and dried her hands. There was just enough time before her eleventh head. Spinning the salon's greeting card rack, she picked one with a kitten and a puppy and a pink envelope. She grabbed a lavender pen from beside the cash register and began to write.

Five minutes later, she slipped the envelope through Jason's office door's mail slot and hurried back to head number eleven.

* * *

The drive from Tiffany's to One Bluffside Drive should've taken about five minutes, but took more than ten in the heavy mist. Jason drove slowly down Del Mar Road, carefully negotiating its turns and grades, using his wipers and headlights to find his way. The fog grew thicker as the road descended, and the early afternoon was dark as dusk when he reached Bluffside.

One Bluffside, an imposing two-story McMansion, loomed large in the gloom when he pulled into the driveway. The house was painted a foreboding gray with a darker gray tile roof, and combined Spanish, Tuscan, and Craftsman design elements. It sprawled across the corner of Bluffside and Driftwood Lane, and was the only house on Bluffside before it dead-ended. Just across the street, the Pacific Ocean lapped against the sandstone cliffs, and on a clear day, the house would command a spectacular view of the water. While the neighborhood conveyed a sense of solidity and refinement, the spec house conveyed a sense of "lots of house for the money."

Jason hadn't visited the site since groundbreaking, so he sat in his car and appraised the house objectively. He decided it wasn't bad-looking. It had all the design cues—oversized windows, deep eaves, and scalloped rafter tails. Patinaed copper gutters, downspouts, and custom chimney caps gave it an expensive look.

The entry and garage doors appeared to be heavy wood, and the driveway and walkway were stone pavers. A formal entry portico with decorative columns completed the façade facing the street. Did it look like $4.75 million? Time would tell.

He put on his black baseball cap and warm-up jacket and climbed out of the car. Looking at the clouds where the sun should be, his whole body shivered. *What is my problem? Most of my life, I've lived near the ocean.* He fought for breath in the heavy, wet air. *Why does fog still freak me out?* Something scuffled behind him in the gray haze, just out of sight. His flesh crawled. "Get a grip, Jason," he told himself. "Don't think about it. Just do what you came here to do."

Jason knew full well why fog filled him with dread, but he squashed the memory whenever it threatened to surface. "A real man never admits his fear to anyone," his father lectured him repeatedly when he was young, "even to himself."

The words stuck, despite Jason's vow to reject everything his father ever told him. It took GG to coax the memory out of him shortly after he came to live with her.

"Jason," his grandmother asked one dark and cold evening, "what is it about the fog? Why does it scare you so much?"

"I don't know, GG," he'd mumbled, embarrassed that a man of thirteen suffered from such a little-boy fear. Later, after thinking about it, he decided he could confide in her. "Maybe it was when I was six, in my first foster home. You know, the first time Mom and Dad were in rehab at the same time? That was a long time before the judge said I could be with you."

The night before Halloween, he explained, the housefather assembled all the boys, ages six to fifteen, and made them listen to a tape of Stephen King's *The Mist*.

"It's 'bout a small town that gets covered by a thick mist from out of nowhere," Jason told her. "Monsters live in the fog, an' they kill anybody that goes outside, but the worst thing is, you can't see 'em. They just reach out of the fog and eat you."

"My goodness," GG said. "What a story to read to a six-year-old." She sat next to him on the sofa and held his hand. "Tell me about the monsters, so I'll understand."

"Some had tentacles with sharp teeth, and they wrapped around one guy and ate him, and some were like giant bugs. There was one like a scorpion, but it's got claws from a lobster, and there was another one kinda like a dragonfly, only all messed up. The scariest ones were spiders. They're big as dogs. They're called 'Grey Widows' and they can smell you, and they kill you with acid spider webs."

"Why, that would give anyone nightmares," his grandmother said. "I don't understand why people write such stories."

"It gets worse, GG. The next night was Halloween, and all of West Los Angeles was socked in. You couldn't see a thing." He moved closer to her on the sofa. "The big kids didn't like me 'cause I was new, and I guess I was kinda little, so they blindfolded me and tied me up, and carried me to another neighborhood and left me in a alley. I was so scared, GG. I didn't know how to get back. Some of 'em hid in the fog and they jumped out. They were grabbing me and punching. I thought they were Grey Widows, come to kill me. One kid snuck up behind me and put a plastic bag over my head. I couldn't breathe. I thought I was gonna die."

The memory brought tears to his eyes. GG held him in her arms and rocked him gently.

"How did you get home?" she asked after a while.

Jason explained that, hours later, the housefather found him huddled in a doorway, crying. "He dragged me back and locked me in the basement time-out room for a whole day. He was a mean man. He said, 'You ever try to run away again, I'll send you straight to Juvie Hall.'"

Standing outside One Bluffside, Jason zipped up his jacket and pulled his hat tighter on his head. He concentrated on relaxing his tense muscles and taking deep breaths. "There was no noise," he told himself. "There aren't any Grey Widows. No giant scorpions. I'll be OK. I just havta do what I came here to do, and then I can go home."

He knew the house would be locked, but also knew Geraldo always hid a spare key in the electrical panel during construction. Walking toward the side of the building and the panel, he noticed Mags Turlock's FOR SALE sign lying on the bark chips in the front yard. He detoured to hook the sign back on its post before following the dirt path around the corner to retrieve the key. The path was wet from the dripping condensation, and he cursed the mud that clung to his Gucci loafers.

Key in hand, Jason walked on the bark chips to get back to the front door. A piece of paper was taped to the door and hung limply in the moisture. His heart skipped a beat. *That can't be* ....

But it was. The paper was a *Notice of Default.* It stated the house was in foreclosure and a payment of $180,941.94 was required within ten days to reinstate the $2.5 million mortgage.

"That son of a bitch!" Jason roared. "He got a million from us investors and then got a bank loan behind our backs."

All the pieces fell into place. Between the investors and the loan, Geraldo had $3.5 million to work with. The house might've cost $1 million to build and the land $500,00. He kept the rest. He was probably in Australia right now with all the remaining money.

Jason's temples pounded and blood rushed in his ears. He forced himself to take deep breaths. He counted slowly to 50. "It will be what it will be," he told himself. "There's nothing I can do at this point." By the time he counted another 50, his temples stopped pounding. He shoved the key into the lock and let himself in.

The foyer surprised him. Looking around, it actually was quite impressive, even tasteful. Handsome travertine covered the floor. The walls looked like Venetian plaster. He ran his hand across the surface. It was just a faux finish, but well done.

The stairway, trimmed with wrought-iron balusters, curved gracefully to the second floor. Next to the stairs, the elevator door was made of dark wood. The door to the garage, also dark wood, was tucked behind the stairway. "It all looks good!" he exclaimed, feeling a flicker of hope. "Maybe Mags can sell this turkey before it gets foreclosed, and we can get our money back."

Although the entry looked impressive, Jason knew that Geraldo always cut corners and used cheap materials in his houses. He was certain Geraldo hadn't changed his ways when he built this one. A quick inspection confirmed he was right. He opened the elevator door and saw its wood finish was actually veneer about a millimeter thick. The wood paneling inside also was veneer, and the brushed-nickel trim was plastic. The nameplate on the elevator's threshold said *Otes* instead of *Otis*. He decided to take the stairs.

He climbed several steps, stopping to view the foyer from this angle. A trail of muddy shoe prints followed him. With a sigh, he descended and leaned against the wall to slip off his loafers. "Friggin' $300 Guccis," he swore, "and they look like I work in a field." In his LA days, he'd have given them to someone to clean, or ordered new ones. "That was then," he told himself. "Now I've gotta make them last." He kicked the shoes against the baseboard.

The travertine stairs were cold beneath his stocking feet. Reaching the top, he found himself in the great room. Heavy curtains made it pitch black. He barely made out the shape of furniture, and an island or peninsula to his right. The house was cool despite his jacket, and his feet were freezing.

Jason stood stock still in the cold and dark room. The creepiness he felt outside washed over him again, only now it was like living the nightmare where he was trapped in somebody else's house. No, it was worse than that. It was like when he was eleven, when he was snooping in his foster parents' bedroom, and footsteps approached the door.

Like that moment years ago, Jason's arms and legs were leaden, and when he forced them to move, it was in slow motion. He shuddered. Goose bumps rose on his arms. He felt his way to the wall and ran his hand along it, searching for a light switch. No luck. With arms out-stretched, he groped, hoping to find some kind of light. He knocked against a floor lamp, but caught it before it fell. Righting the lamp, he turned it on. It gave off a faint glow.

"Holy shit!" he gasped. The peninsula and kitchen counter were stacked with kilo blocks of hash, pound bags of marijuana, kilos of cocaine, baggies of heroin, and shopping bags bulging with boxes and vials. A gilt mirror lay on the island countertop with two lines of cocaine and the remnants of six others. An empty hash pipe lay beside the mirror. Flattened packing boxes leaned against the refrigerator, and rolls of tape were piled nearby.

For a moment, his curiosity overcame his fear and common sense. He wedged himself between two bar stools to open one of the bags. His stocking foot stepped on something hard. Looking down, he saw the blue plastic top from a disposable syringe. *Someone was shooting up? All that's missing is a rubber tube.* Reaching for the closest bag, he hesitated, worried about leaving fingerprints. He flicked the edge of the bag with his nail to push it back. The bag tipped over, spilling its contents. Oxycontin. Vicodin. Valium. Ecstasy.

All at once, he understood. "Oh my God!" he exclaimed. "There's gonna be a major drug deal here any minute!" A crazy thought followed. *Why didn't Geraldo finish the deal and take the money to Australia?*

The front door slammed closed downstairs. Footsteps crossed the foyer. The elevator whirred as it descended. His heart began to pound. "Jesus," his voice screamed in his head, "they're coming to finish the deal!"

Now it was no nightmare. He really was in a stranger's house and a real person was coming to get him. A real person, who'd be very pissed to find him there. *Should I hide? It's obvious I'm in the house. My shoes are downstairs. The floor's muddy. My car's in the driveway.*

The elevator whirred again, coming back up. He pictured El Carnicero hunched in it, clutching a bloody cleaver. Or a ski-masked gang *capo* ramming a fresh magazine into his Glock.

Time stood still.

Cold panic froze his body. His mind went numb. He had to do something! Shut the light? Hide in the bedroom? Run downstairs while the elevator's coming up? *Can't move. Too late to run. Better hide in the bedroom.*

He turned.

"Hold it," a voice boomed from inside the elevator. "Stop right there. Do that and you're dead."

Jason stood still, paralyzed. *Oh God, they know I'm here. They're coming to get me.* The whirring slowed, finally grinding to a stop with a metallic *SCRREECHHH.*

CHAPTER 14

A mile north of the spec house, at the opposite end of foggy Bluffside Drive, Commander Ramon "Ray" Sepulveda of the sheriff's coastal division was having a bad day. Already on his watch, 40 people were dead in an exploding boat. Now there was a body in a storm drain. "And it's only three o'clock," he grumbled. "I won't get outta here for at least two hours, and my reports'll take all night."

Commander Sepulveda was a veteran cop who'd seen his share of gruesome corpses. He wasn't worried about what the crane would pull out of the drainpipe, although God knew how his budget was going to pay for renting the crane, especially such a big one, but it was the only one available, and how the hell did the body get in there headfirst anyway?

He knew he could deal with those issues. What really irritated him, however, was that the idiot Hardesty found the deceased and filed the report.

Sepulveda had a visceral dislike for the man, who also was the most incompetent deputy he'd ever supervised. Shocked that such a bungler could even be hired, he'd run a deep background check and discovered Hardesty was the cousin of the sheriff's wife. Sepulveda had assigned Hardesty to sleepy Sea Cliff, where nothing ever happened, except that now angry citizens filed countless complaints against "Deputy Hardass." The idea of supervising the man while the death was being investigated made Sepulveda's stomach acid begin to flow. *He'll bring back my ulcer, and if he parlays this into making sergeant, I'll have to shoot him. Or me.*

He glared across the Vista Point parking lot at his bumbling deputy. Like a schoolboy, Hardesty was mesmerized by the crane as it stabilized itself, extending its outriggers and belching compressed air with each movement. Sepulveda scowled at the TV news crew as they set up their equipment and started filming background shots. He glowered at the young reporter with bleached-blonde hair and chipmunk cheeks. She stopped dead in her tracks when their eyes met. She took a step toward him, but hesitated when he raised his fist and pointed two fingers at her, imitating the barrel of a .45 pistol. When he raised his thumb to cock the pistol, she retreated to the camera crew.

"Don't piss off the press too much," the commander reminded himself.

He jammed the wannabe sergeant's incident report into his clipboard and began to scour it, determined to find some flaw. "Deputy!" he yelled. "Get over here!" Hardesty jingled across the parking lot. "Clarify for me how you discovered the body," Sepulveda demanded. "Your report doesn't explain."

"Yes, sir. Of course, sir." Hardesty cleared his throat. "I was patrolling Bluffside Drive with my windows open and smelled something unusual. I exited my vehicle and traced the odor to the storm drain. I shined a light down it and saw the body. Once I confirmed the body, I called dispatch."

The commander swore a silent oath. "You're lying, you sack of meat. You're not that perceptive. How'd you find the witness?"

"That wasn't hard, sir. I canvassed the neighbors, door-to-door, and found Mrs. Richardson. She observed the incident from her bedroom window. She was very cooperative. Her statement is on page—"

"I can read her statement, dammit. She says she saw the vehicle."

"Yes, sir. A silver minivan."

"What about a license plate?"

"No, sir. She didn't get a number."

"Anything distinguishing about the vehicle?" He watched the deputy's eyes dart away for a second. "Body damage? Decals? Stickers?" Sepulveda prompted, certain Hardesty knew more than he was telling.

"No, sir, she didn't mention anything. But it can't be hard to find. How many silver minivans can there be in Sea Cliff?"

Commander Sepulveda reached his limit. "Listen, shit-for-brains," he growled. "Every mother on the Central Coast has a silver minivan, and so does every real estate agent. Don't you use your fucking eyes when you're patrolling?" At the same time, he was certain Hardesty was withholding information so he could find the van himself.

"Yo! Dudes! Officers!" the TV cameraman interrupted. "How 'bout a little quiet over there. We 'bout to go live."

The commander spun around to face this new irritant, a lanky 20-something Black man wearing a backward baseball cap emblazoned with *Spike*. Sepulveda took a half-step toward him but stopped, thinking that getting filmed punching out the cameraman would be bad PR.

* * *

Spike signaled the reporter with his fingers held high over his head: III, II, I. On I, he lowered his arm and pointed dramatically at her.

"Good afternoon," she said to the camera. "This is Ally Booker live in Sea Cliff with breaking news. A short while ago, a corpse was found in the storm drain behind me. As my viewers know, a tragic accident aboard a whale-watching boat out of Rock Bay claimed the lives of forty people earlier today. I've been covering that story all day. Now I'm about to bring you exclusive live footage as the body is hoisted out of the drain by that crane." She smirked at the unplanned rhyme and turned away to hide her expression.

Regaining her composure quickly, she continued, "While the crane's getting ready, I've been asked to read this announcement from the county coroner's office." She read:

"The coroner's office extends its sincere condolences to the families of those so tragically killed in today's explosion, and joins them in their sadness and grief. The coroner's office pledges to work as quickly and diligently as possible to identify each victim and notify family members. Unfortunately, at this point in time, the coroner's office is facing severe budgetary and staffing challenges. Therefore, we are informing the victims' families and the public at large that the identification process may be lengthy. Please do not call the coroner's office. We will contact each victim's family as soon as we have made positive identification. We appreciate your patience and understanding."

Ally raised her eyes and looked at Spike. He made a motion with his hands like he was stretching pizza dough. "So there you have it," she said.

"The coroner is facing staffing challenges and identification of the victims is going to take a long time. That's going to be hard on the survivors." The cameraman made more stretching motions. "Forty bodies," she ad-libbed. "That's a whole lotta dead people to identify. It is gonna take quite a while. Really hard on the families. I wonder how they know where to order the dental records from if they don't know who the bodies are."

Spike motioned emphatically with his hand, making a cutting motion across his throat. He pointed past Ally to the two cops. Picking up the cue, she continued, "Now, about the corpse here. I wonder if the sheriff's department knows who the deceased is." She turned toward the two officers standing next to the patrol car. "Officers, can one of you join me on camera and tell us what you know about the victim?"

Sepulveda was the first to react. He clapped his commander's hat on his head, squared his shoulders, and started toward the reporter.

At that moment, the crane's diesel engine roared to life.

* * *

The ominous voice from the spec house elevator was silent now. The great room was quiet as a tomb, and nearly as dark.

Jason couldn't move. The air caught in his throat. He struggled for breath, reliving the moment his foster father found him snooping in his bedroom. A severe beating followed. "That was a lifetime ago," he told himself. "It's ridiculous to be afraid." Still, like when he was eleven, he wished he was invisible.

In the weak light, Jason barely saw the elevator door fifteen feet away. The door slid open in slow motion, as in a dream. It inched along its track, then made a *clunk* and jammed halfway. An arm in a black sweatshirt reached through the opening. The arm was followed by a shoulder. With a grunt, the shoulder pushed the door.

A muffled voice came from the elevator. "Cheap fucking piece of shit."

Jason stood transfixed. *If I was dreaming, this is where I'd wake up.* But it was real, and there was no escape. His adrenaline kicked in, jolting him out of his daze.

He watched the passenger stiff-arm the elevator door. It opened reluctantly, creaking in protest. A shadowy figure stepped sideways through the opening. Its head and neck were bent down, obscuring its face. Jason watched, confused, until it dawned on him: The passenger was pressing a cell phone to their ear and was straining to listen.

"I wasn't talking to you," the passenger bellowed.

"I know that voice," Jason realized. "Can't place it. Damn. Who is it?"

"OK," the passenger continued, "you're a cheap fucking piece of shit, too."

Mags Turlock strode into the dim light of the great room, cell phone glued to her ear, head bent in concentration. "Hold it right there, little man," she yelled into her phone. "You will not change our contract, and you sure as hell won't cancel it." She stopped, staring down. "Do you want to die? I'll tie you to my trailer hitch and drag you through town. Ask your broker what happened when he tried to mess with me." Head still bent, she turned and paced back toward the elevator. Jason heard the other agent's voice, but not the words.

"No," Mags boomed after a pause, "I'll tell *you* how it's gonna be. This is a sweet deal for both of us, and you're not gonna blow it. So the pest report says there's termites in the rafters. Big deal. The home is in the forest. There's always termites. You just need to understand that no one needs to know about it." The other agent's voice grew louder.

"It's not fraud. It's business as usual. Here's what's going to happen, junior. Get the pest inspector to change his report. Send me an estimate for repairs. My clients and I will pay twenty-five percent. After escrow closes. Your side splits the remainder. End of story. Period."

Mags listened briefly before interrupting. "It's as fair as you're gonna get. Don't fuck up this deal, little man. If you do, I'll personally crucify you." She clicked off and turned back toward the great room. Raising her eyes, she looked in Jason's direction for the first time.

"What are you doing here?" she demanded.

"Looking for Geraldo."

"He's in Australia," she snapped.

"How about Danni?"

"What am I, their keeper? She's with him, I guess."

Jason and Mags tolerated each other, but just barely. Geraldo was their only common link, and they both made a good share of their living from the business he created for them.

"Why are *you* here?" Jason countered.

"I'm showing the home this afternoon. I need to make sure it's clean and the elevator works. Which it never does. Did you hear that noise when it stopped? At least it didn't get stuck between floors this time. I told Geraldo not to use a cheapy, but *noooo*, he had to get one made in China just to save a few dollars."

With that, she flipped on the ceiling lights. "Jesus Christ!" she exclaimed, staring at the bundles and bags of drugs. "Look at this mess. It's a good thing I came over. I can't show the house like this. We've got to clean this up before my clients get here."

The attorney in Jason woke up. "We?" he sputtered. "Clean this up? This is a crime scene! You can't touch anything. It's bad enough our fingerprints are in the house."

Mags ignored him. She hurried into the kitchen and began assembling packing boxes. "You're such a straight-shooter. Who's gonna know? My clients'll be here in thirty minutes, and I've got to sell this home." She tossed bundles of hash and cocaine into one of the boxes. "I need my 150K out of it, and I know you need your 30K, and we've got to get our money before the bank forecloses. So get over here and help me!"

Jason stared in disbelief as Mags taped the first box closed and started loading a second. He knew half-a-dozen criminal statutes Mags was violating, and there were probably at least a half-dozen more. "No way," he said. "You're crazy. I'm outta here."

Mags closed the second box and began on a third. "I can't do all this by myself. If you're going to be a pussy, at least open the drapes and turn on the lights." Jason's greed for his $30,000 overcame his good sense, so he did what she asked. He pulled his jacket sleeves down to his fingertips and opened the drapes. Using just his palms, he straightened out the magazines on the coffee table. Mags was taping up her fourth box, and the bundles and bags in the kitchen were diminishing.

"OK, that's it. I'm gone," Jason said as Mags lifted three full boxes and carried them down the hall toward the master bedroom.

"Shit!" she cried. "Help me!" The boxes swayed and toppled, crashing to the floor. Mags slumped against the wall and slid down it.

Jason ran to the hall. Mags was trembling and ashen, and covered with cold sweat.

"I forgot to eat my snack," she rasped. "You've got to help me." She gripped his wrist fiercely with a clammy hand. "Go down to my car and get my cooler." Jason stared at her, trying to understand. "Please! I think I'm gonna pass out." He didn't move. "Yes, I'm diabetic," she growled. "You tell anyone, I'll kill you. Now get my cooler!"

Jason dashed down the stairs and put on his muddy shoes. He sprinted to Mags's silver Lexus. It was locked. He ran back upstairs. Mags was sitting on the floor, back against the wall, amid the tumbled boxes of drugs.

"Mags, the key!" She searched the pockets of her down vest and sweatpants. She patted her sleeve, found a slinky band with the fob, and handed it to him.

He ran down to the car and opened the door. The cooler was in back. He grabbed it and charged back up the stairs. Mags hadn't moved. Her face was even more ashen.

"Open it," she commanded. "Give me a Snickers bar." Her voice trembled. She held out a shaky hand.

Jason opened the cooler. He pulled out an ice pack, bread slices in baggies, half-pint containers of orange juice, Snickers, several vials of insulin, and a box of disposable syringes with blue plastic tops. He stopped when he saw the syringes. *That's weird. Those caps are the same as the one I stepped on by the breakfast bar.* Shoving the thought aside, he handed her a candy bar.

She ate it in little bites, chewing each thoroughly. Minutes passed. Her color began to come back and her hands stopped shaking.

Jason said softly, "You need to reschedule your showing. We need time to figure out what to do about all of this." He gestured toward the boxes and the remaining bags and bundles.

"No way," she snapped. "My clients are going back to Beverly Hills tonight. I've got to sell this home, and they're perfect for it. They're old enough to need the elevator, and they've got the cash to buy it."

"I know. I need my money, too. But the police—"

"Fuck the police. I'll never be able to sell it once they get involved. And the bank wants to foreclose. It's a goddamn mess. What was I thinking, giving Geraldo my last $150,000?" She leaned back against the wall and stared at the box in front of her. "He's bleeding me dry. My whole house of cards is collapsing. I had this sweet million-dollar deal ready to close, but the buyers found out somebody died in the home a few months ago. They cancelled just before escrow closed. Even I couldn't hold that deal together. Nobody wants to buy a home where someone's just died. That deal would've bought me the time I need."

Mags picked up a container of orange juice and sipped it slowly. Jason saw the fire return to her eyes and the strength to her body. "Goddammit!" she swore as she climbed unsteadily to her feet. "If I lose even one property because Geraldo's got my money, I'll kill him twice!"

CHAPTER 15

The Sky Hi Crane & Hoist Company's Unit No. 3 stood ready to extract the corpse from the storm drain on Vista Point.

Since the death was tentatively considered a homicide, Commander Sepulveda had been assigned to oversee the process. "Rank hath its burdens," Sepulveda reminded himself. He showed his badge to the crane's team members and wrote their names on his report form: Marty, the operator and team leader; Joe, the semi driver; Buddy, the flagger; and Oliver, the trainee.

Marty dug in his pockets, found three toothpicks, and held them in his fist. He said, "Listen up, you three. You gonna draw straws for the honor of attachin' the rope to the body."

Oliver drew the short one. Joe spat a stream of tobacco juice and opened a *National Enquirer*. Buddy high-fived Oliver and smirked, "You go, dude."

Sepulveda dug deep for his nice-cop personality and walked over to Oliver and Marty. "Gentlemen, I need a moment."

Marty said, "Sure, boss." Oliver nodded.

"This is a delicate situation," Sepulveda said, "because the media and public are present. Sheriff's personnel normally would conduct this recovery. A technician should enclose the corpse in a body bag and secure it to a harness, but the exploding boat tragedy has exhausted our resources and supply of body bags. The corpse has been decomposing for a week, so I need you to be mindful of two things." He pointed at Oliver. "It will be important to secure both legs to minimize the potential for dismemberment."

Oliver's eyes grew wide. "You mean, like, if I hook one leg, it might pull off?"

"Exactly." Sepulveda pointed at Marty. "And you will need to operate the cable smoothly, without any jerking. For the same reason."

Marty said, "Unnerstood, boss." He swung into his cab.

The crane's diesel engine clattered at idle, shattering the stillness of the foggy afternoon. The 40-foot boom rested horizontally, dangling several lengths of braided wire cable from its tip. Oliver put on his headlight helmet, elbow-length rubber gloves, and a respirator. He walked the 40 feet from the cab to the tip of the boom, waved at Marty, and pointed down. Marty lowered the tip of the boom and the cable to the ground.

Oliver hoisted the heavy line over his shoulder and trudged it to the edge of the drainpipe. He turned and gave Marty a thumbs-up. Marty set to work, gently pulling and pushing his levers and pedals. The engine thundered, and the immense boom arced into the sky, a black lattice of girders and trusses silhouetted against pewter clouds. It rotated slowly and stopped, positioning the end of the cable precisely over the center of the opening.

Commander Sepulveda studied Marty's every move as he commanded the huge structure to do his bidding. When the movement stopped, the commander noticed Deputy Hardesty standing transfixed in the middle of the lot, next to a large blue tarp spread on the ground.

The plan, grudgingly agreed to by the coroner because there were no body bags, was for the crane to deposit the deceased on the tarp until someone from his office could get there to take possession of the remains. Only then could Sepulveda leave for his office and the mountain of paperwork that awaited him. He popped a Zantac and looked past Deputy Dumbass to Oliver, who was fashioning a heavy orange nylon rope into a noose.

The TV crew was already set up, to Sepulveda's considerable irritation. Spike's camera was aimed at Oliver balanced on the pipe's rim. Ally Booker walked up to Hardesty and tapped him on the shoulder. "Hey, Officer! Move over! You're blocking our shot." He grunted and moved two small steps to the right.

Oliver yanked on the noose to be sure it would hold. He motioned to Marty for more slack on the cable and attached the rope to the loop on the end. Standing on the edge of the drainpipe, he shined his helmet light into the void. He turned back to Marty, waving for still more slack. With great concentration, Oliver bent at the waist and lowered the noose into the opening.

* * *

A small group of spectators gathered near the TV camera—Commander Sepulveda, Deputy Hardesty, two of the crane's team, and an elderly woman neighbor.

Ally and Spike were perfectly positioned for the Emmy-winning shot when the crane hoisted out the body. They went live as Oliver gently moved the rope up and down. "What's he trying to do?" Ally whispered into her microphone. She watched silently, ignoring the dead air. "Oh, he must be trying to hook the noose over the victim's feet. That's smart."

Oliver straightened up and yelled at Buddy. "Get me the *polo*... the pole, and a *paleta*... a paddle head." Buddy jogged to the semi and unstrapped three 8-foot sections of fiberglass pole from the back of the cab. He screwed the sections together and attached the head as he ran back to Oliver, who stood astride the tube. Oliver motioned for slack. He shoved the pole down the inside edge of the pipe and pushed the paddle end toward the center. He quickly lowered the noose.

"I see," Ally explained to her audience. "He must've hooked one of the feet." Oliver circled the pole around to the opposite side and repeated the procedure. "There," Ally said, "now he's hooked both feet."

Oliver motioned for Marty to increase the tension slowly. He shined his helmet light into the opening and signaled Marty to stop. He pulled gently on the rope until it was taut. Apparently satisfied that the noose would hold its burden, he motioned for Marty to haul in the line. The crane's diesel engine roared and the cable began to rise.

Ally had to yell to be heard now. "This is Ally Booker in Sea Cliff with exclusive live coverage of the recovery of the dead body from the storm drain behind me." She looked behind her as the orange rope emerged from the black hole. "And it looks like we're gonna get our first glimpse of the corpse."

The great machine rattled, clattered, and squeaked as the rope inched upward. The little crowd stood still as statues. Everyone held their breath. Even Ally Booker was silent. Only Deputy Hardesty moved, walking toward Oliver.

Orange rope rose from the void. Work boots followed. Then legs. Deputy Hardesty moved closer. The butt and waist appeared. Next came the back. Finally, the body was fully exposed: a bloated carcass blackened by decay and moisture, and dripping with slimy green runoff. The engine silenced and the cable slowed to a stop. The lifeless hulk swung slowly over the mouth of the drain, hanging from the noose by its ankles, its arms and long silvery hair dangling down, its face toward the foggy shore, away from the spectators and the camera.

"OH MY GOD!" Ally shrieked. "There it is, at last! Oh my God! Will you look at that! Exclusive live pictures from Ally Booker. And KHYP, of course. Your local news channel. Does it stink something fierce! Whew!" She walked closer to the camera. "Don't forget, there's more news to come. We don't know who the victim is yet, and probably won't for some time because the coroner's office is short-staffed and has all those dead people from this morning's explosion to deal with first. But stick with me for updates—" She paused. Spike waved like he wanted her to move to the side. *But that'll block the shot of the ....*

Ally glanced behind her. The fat cop stood next to the swaying corpse, smiling proudly, left fist on hip, right arm pointing to the body, like a sport fisherman posing with his trophy marlin at the dock.

And that was the lead picture on KHYP's evening and morning news and on the front pages of newspapers all over California the next day. It went viral minutes after it was posted on the station's Facebook and Instagram pages and website, and became the most popular meme of the week. Millions of people all over the world saw the slimy, decomposed carcass, swinging by its ankles, with Deputy Hardass standing beside it, grinning like the man who won the Powerball jackpot.

* * *

Jason left Mags at the spec house packing the last of the drugs. His Porsche crawled through the fog up Del Mar Road to Highway 1, where the sun was shining brightly.

Now within range of his cell carrier's only tower in Sea Cliff, his phone chimed with three new messages: Erin, Christina, and Walter Cripps.

"Why are these three people calling me at the same time?" he wondered aloud. He parked on the shoulder before crossing the highway, and punched the button to retrieve his voicemail.

"Jason!" Erin's voice cried. "Check the News Channel's Facebook page. They've found the dead body you told me about! It's at Vista Point."

Christina's message was similar.

Walter's message was matter-of-fact. "Jason, in reference to your call this morning, I think I know where Danni is, or maybe Geraldo. Look up the top stories on KHYP. Call me."

"Jesus!" Jason exclaimed. "Danni or Geraldo dead?" He tried to open the station's Facebook page on his phone, but it wouldn't load. He tore across the highway and through town to his office, parked nose to curb, and ran up the steps. With shaking hands, he unlocked the door and stepped on something—a pink envelope that smelled of jasmine hairspray. "For God's sake, Nikki," he swore, stepping over it.

He pulled up KHYP's website and searched through the day's stories. "Corpse found in storm drain in Sea Cliff. Foul play suspected. Exclusive coverage." He clicked on the link.

The picture loaded slowly. A silhouette of a body hanging upside down from a cable. He couldn't see the corpse's face, but recognized Deputy Hardesty standing next to it with a ghoulish grin. *What the hell…?*

He zoomed in on the bottom of the picture, trying to focus on the head, but the face was turned away. All he saw clearly was long, silvery hair. "Oh my God!" he said to the screen. "It's gotta be either Danni or Geraldo. Can't tell…. She's a big woman. Could be either."

Dragging the picture up, down, left, right, he tried to get a clear shot of the head and clothing, searching for anything identifiable. Nothing. But the bloated, rotting flesh and clothes green with slimy runoff made his stomach heave. He took a deep breath and tried to push down the nausea.

"Check the hands," he told himself. Geraldo had "Love" tattooed on the fingers of one hand, and "Hate" on the other. Jason scrolled down and zoomed in. Scrubby grass hid the fingers. "Damn it to hell!" he swore. He punched the "+" symbol—once, twice, three times, four times.

The image that filled his screen was unrecognizable. He leaned closer, studying it. "It's the back of a hand!" he exclaimed. The flesh was black and so swollen it looked ready to burst, like a mottled black balloon. Horrified, he clicked back to the hanging body. His stomach wretched violently. He dashed to the bathroom, barely reaching the sink before he threw up.

When dry heaves took over, he rinsed the basin. He splashed himself with cold water and sipped from the tap. His face in the mirror was sallow and drawn, his eyes dull. "This is what death does," he whispered to his reflection.

Stumbling to his desk, he fell into his chair. He struggled to make sense of what he'd seen, but his thoughts were a jumble. *Is it Danni? What'll happen to Tiffany? Was it murder? What if it's Geraldo? It's a horrible way to die. Oh my God, what if it is Geraldo? My number-one client? My $38,000? Will I ever see it? How will I replace him?*

He felt a pang of loss, which surprised him. "God help me, I did like the man," he admitted, "sleazy as he was. There was a bond, and I'll miss him. If it's him. I'm so confused. No one I know has died, except GG. This is too real."

Jason pushed back from his desk and stood unsteadily. He pressed his hands against his stomach to calm it, thinking he should go to Vista Point before they took the body away. A wave of nausea buckled his knees. "No," he decided. "I've had enough. I'm going home. I'll get the rest of the story tomorrow."

Forcing his limbs to move, he walked out the door and down the steps into the brilliant afternoon sun. Someone called his name as he beeped open his car. "Jason! Jason!"

Looking over his shoulder, he saw Nikki running toward him, platinum curls and pink tube top rising and falling with each step. "Jason," she cried as she ran. "The body…they found a wallet." She stopped in front of him, breathing hard. "Mrs. Richardson…the phone tree…my mother…I know who it is!"

Jason stood rooted to the ground. Time stopped. *I don't want to know!* His every sense tingled, hyper-aware. The scent of Nikki's hairspray. The sun on his neck. The cawing of the crows. The gorge in his throat. He remembered his grandmother's wry comment: "Bad news has wings in a small town." GG's face filled his mind's eye—at her table with a cup of coffee, in her garden tending her roses, in her coffin. *But I've gotta know.*

Nikki gained control of her breathing. Her eyes searched his face. "Jason!" she said solemnly, like she was about to share a deep secret. She arched her back and shoulders. "It's so awful! I never knew anyone dead before." She placed her hand on his forearm. "What does it mean?"

He didn't answer. The image of the grotesque, dangling corpse was seared into his mind. A queasy chill washed over him. "What it means?" he mumbled. "That depends on what you tell me."

Nikki took his other hand and turned so the sun was behind her, making a halo of her curls. He was forced to look at her face or be blinded. He stared at her, but his mind was filled with the hanging corpse. *Jesus! Is it Danni or Geraldo? No one deserves to die rotting in a drainpipe. There'll be consequences for Tiffany, or for me. Her or me. But what…?*

"Jason." Nikki spoke solemnly, bringing him back to the moment. She drew a deep breath, locked her eyes on his, paused.

His heart beat once. Twice. Three times.

"The body…it's Geraldo."

PART 2

TANGLED WEBS

CHAPTER 16

Jason awoke the next morning with the dawn. The sun warmed the little bedroom, releasing the scents of GG's hairspray and talcum powder. The smell always reminded him of the day he finally came to live with her full-time, following months of evaluations, counseling, court hearings, and arguments. He pictured himself as a boy, dropping his backpack and running up the walkway into her arms.

"It'll be OK now," she'd promised him with a hug and a kiss. "Everything will be OK."

He smelled her powder and felt the warmth of her embrace, but pushed the memory away, telling himself, "I've got real problems to deal with today."

During the night, his mind began to sort through the confusion caused by Geraldo's death and Danni's disappearance. He'd come up with preliminary plans of action by dawn. First he'd order copies of the death certificate. Then he'd go through Geraldo's estate planning files and file a Petition for Probate with the court and get himself appointed administrator of the estate. He'd begin to identify Geraldo's assets. Eventually he'd recover a fee, which would be some reimbursement for what Geraldo owed him.

The whole process probably would be delayed because a criminal investigation into the cause of Geraldo's death was inevitable, and the coroner's office had the 40 victims from the exploding boat to identify first. So, realistically, it could be six or twelve months before he saw any of the money.

As for Tiffany, he'd resolved to make inquiries all over town to try to locate Danni. If that failed, he accepted he'd have to call Children's Protective Services.

Jason lay on his back quietly, trying not to disturb Erin. She'd come over at midnight, after her second shift. He'd sipped tea, and she'd finished his bottle of wine, while he tried to explain the emotional roller coaster of the day. He told her about discovering abandoned, doped-out Tiffany, and his worries about her. He described his bizarre encounter with Mags at the spec house. He recounted the excruciating, slow-motion revelation that it was Geraldo who was dead.

"I know he was a gross human being," Jason told her as they cuddled on the sofa, "but he was a big part of my life here. Financially, and personally, I have to admit now that he's gone."

He tipped the bottle to dribble the last drops into her glass. "It's like the hand of death reaches out from behind a curtain that you don't even know is there and snatches someone, and everyone who's left is frozen. And when you come to, you don't know what to do."

"I'm sorry, baby," Erin mumbled sleepily. "I'm sorry you lost your client and all that money."

She nodded off on his shoulder, and he guided her to the bedroom a few minutes later.

Jason lay in bed watching dust motes swirl in a shaft of morning sunlight. He was relieved to have plans for dealing with Geraldo and Tiffany, but was overwhelmed by his financial situation. The numbers crowded into his mind as he listened to Erin's deep breathing. Seventeen hundred dollars for the lease payment on his Porsche. Twelve hundred for office rent. Another fifteen hundred for car and health insurance. *That's more than $4,000 before I turn on the lights, eat, or put gas in the car! This is not the way it was supposed to work out.*

A noise came from the back door, down the short hall from the bedroom. The knob turned. Once. Twice. The door rattled in its frame, as if someone was testing its strength. The knob turned again.

Jason slipped out of bed and found his shorts. He tiptoed to the kitchen and opened the knife drawer, grabbing the cleaver. Holding his breath, he pressed himself against the hall wall and inched toward the door, cleaver ready to strike.

The steps outside creaked. The silhouette of a big man loped across the back yard and ducked behind the garage. Jason saw only a black leather vest, beefy bare arms, and a purple scarf tied around the man's head.

A motorcycle roared to life and *brrrraapppped* into the distance.

Jason's heart beat double time. He realized he was reacting like this was LA, like this guy was an ax murderer instead of a prowler. He leaned against the wall a moment to catch his breath, reminding himself there was virtually no crime in Sea Cliff. "Still, I need to be careful," he told himself. "People may decide to come after me to get what Geraldo owes them." He checked the locks.

After replacing the cleaver in the kitchen, he walked quietly to the bedroom and put on his tee shirt. He went around the bed to pull the sheet over Erin's bare shoulder and watched her sleep.

Erin's auburn hair sparkled with red and brown highlights in the morning sun, and her pale complexion glowed. He couldn't help staring at the profile of her face—the curve of her eyebrow, the slope of her nose, the determined, yet very feminine, set of her chin. For a moment, he watched the gentle rise and fall of her breasts beneath the sheet. "I could love this woman," he admitted to himself.

Slipping on his UGG scuffs, he padded to the kitchen and poured the morning's ration of Peet's beans into the grinder. Coffee was another little worry on his list that kept growing longer. The bag was almost empty, and he doubted he could afford $19 a pound when this was gone. The unopened pack of Marlboros on the table caught his eye. At least his ongoing battle to quit smoking was saving $10 a pack.

He added the grounds and water to GG's coffee maker. His cell phone chimed as punched the *Brew* button. The clock on the coffee maker said 5:45 a.m. The mere idea that anyone would text him at 5:45 a.m. annoyed him, until he remembered it was normal when he worked at Whatley.

His phone's screen said the message was from Courtney at work. He opened it:

Jason: Attached are the final divorce papers for your signature. I get the penthouse loft and custody of Jason Jr. You pay $2,500/month child support. No alimony. It's the best deal you're going to get. Sign and return ASAP.

Jason threw the phone against the wall behind the kitchen table. It crashed to the surface, tipping over the napkin holder and salt and pepper shakers, and knocking the Marlboro pack to the floor. "God damn her!" he swore. He pressed his palms against his temples to soothe the sudden pounding in his head. "She's steamrolling me. She knows I can't fight her. I don't have that kind of resources."

He asked himself the question he'd never been able to answer. "Why's she so vindictive? What did I ever do to her?" His chest tightened and his temples threatened to burst. "Goddamn fucking bitch," he swore, not realizing he spoke out loud.

"Who's a fucking bitch?" Erin asked from the doorway.

Jason started with surprise. "What? Oh. It's nothing."

"It must be something. Your face is all red and you look upset."

"Umm...it's Courtney again, bugging me about the divorce. It's my old life, Erin. I don't want to talk about it."

Erin walked to him and kissed his cheek. "What does she want this time?"

"The same. My son and more money than I have. I don't want to talk about it."

The coffee maker beeped, and Jason poured two cups. They sat silently at GG's kitchen table in their shorts and tee shirts. Jason rested his elbows on the table and his forehead in his palms, studying the white squiggle designs in the red Formica.

Erin reached across the table and took one of his hands. "Sweetheart," she said softly, "you never told me what happened in LA. Why you left Courtney and your firm. I'd really like to know, and it might help to talk about it. I'm sorry I startled you, but maybe now that you've settled down?"

He raised his head and took her other hand. They were soft and warm, and her touch calmed him. He felt a glow of affection for her that he never remembered feeling for Courtney. *Maybe she's right. It might help to tell her a little, I've been holding it in so long.*

He hesitated for a moment, then said, "Leaving was the hardest thing I've ever done." His voice was barely a whisper. "I didn't want to hurt

Jason Jr. He was only three, and so sweet and unspoiled. I didn't want to do to him what my parents did to me—a weekend with one, and the next with the other, and no real home. Plus, it was my relation with Courtney, and my career. I thought if I could stick it out, I could be a father to my son and put up with the rest, but things got worse and worse, and I had to leave. It was so bad …." He trailed off.

"Let me understand, be a part of you." She smiled encouragingly.

"I've never told anyone but my family, and they were no help. Except for my grandmother." He shook his head. "No, it's still too raw. Too close."

"I care for you so much," Erin insisted. "Don't shut me out. Won't you let me help? Let me in, just a little?"

He saw the concern in her blue eyes. Without pulling her hand away, she got up and moved to the chair next to him. She looked into his eyes. "Just tell me a little bit."

"That world is so different from the one you know," he said dully. "I don't think I could make it real to you."

"I do know something about the world outside Sea Cliff, you know. And I certainly know about people who treat you badly. Just give it a try." She smiled encouragingly again. "I'm pretty sure I'll be able to understand."

Jason pulled his hands away and warmed them on his coffee cup. He crossed his arms over his chest. "OK," he sighed, "but it's not a pretty story."

* * *

Dawn's early light set off lightning bolts behind Danni Tedeski's closed eyes. The sound of snoring split her head like a chain saw at full throttle. She pulled the pillow over her head to escape both, but the bed began to spin, so she opened one eye and stared at the wall.

Pictures of Barney, the purple dinosaur, gradually came into focus. They covered the wall. Through half-closed eyes, she watched Barney ride his skateboard. Barney bounce a rubber ball. Barney read to a class of children. Barney in water wings swim in circles, 'round and 'round and 'round.

"Hi," Barney said with his big toothy smile. "I'm Barney. What are you doing here?"

"I don' know," Danni said. "Where am I?"

Barney looked at her sternly. "Every boy and girl should know their address and phone number. You're in the Windy Gulch Trailer Park, space 169. Can you remember that?" He smiled at her again. "So now that you know where you are, what are you doing here?"

Danni had to think, which caused waves of sharp pain to radiate from the center of her brain. Sensations began to filter through the fog. The sheets stank of dried sweat and stale marijuana smoke. Her teeth were dry and furry, and she tasted cocaine when she licked them. She formed a fuzzy image of a man and empty quart bottles of tequila. The man chased her through the trailer's living and dining rooms into the room with the Barney wallpaper. He was naked. And hairy. She was naked.

"C'mon, big boy," she cried as she ran, "come an' get it." She belly-flopped on the bed, shrieking with excitement. He jumped on her. They laughed and laughed, and now her head was about to burst.

"I'm with him," Danni replied, meaning the man who was snoring. She tried to roll her eyes in his direction, but the movement caused stabbing pain. "Wha' you doin' here?"

"This used to be Billy's room," Barney said sadly, "'til him 'n his mom moved away." He was quiet while the man snored, and Danni's stomach sent a wave of nausea through her. "Are you going to stay?" Barney asked after a while. "We can be friends."

Danni wanted to say yes, but knew she couldn't because she had something important to do. *Can't remember wha'. Wonder how long've I been here with hairy man?* "Hey, Barney, do ya know how long I been here?"

Barney scrunched up his face. "'Bout a week, I think, but this is the first time we've talked to each other. You're always busy with him when you're in here."

Memories began to stir. She remembered pounding down shots at Mostly's during the weekly tequila shots contest. "That musta been a week ago," she figured. That really turned her on, because no man could match her when it came to tequila shots. The guy turned out to be a surfer dude called…? She tried to concentrate. *Wha's his name? I been fucking this guy a week, so I oughta know his damn name, but I got no clue.* "Barney, do ya know this guy's name? Snoring surfer dude over here?"

"His name's Byron, but people call him Bunion. 'Cause of his feet."

Knowing she'd been here for a week with Bunion helped Danni organize her thoughts. Despite her splitting head and stomach that wanted to puke, she was happy she'd spent a week drinking, snorting, and screwing with a guy she'd picked up at a bar. "That'll show Geraldo he can't never take me fer granted," she gloated. "Bunion thinks I'm hot an' wants ta make it wit' me, even if Geraldo don't.

"Hey, Barney," she whispered so Bunion wouldn't hear, "do ya know Geraldo? My old man?" Chills surged the length of her body and she thought she was going to blow. She clung to the mattress to stop the spinning. It took minutes for the feeling to pass. "Least he used ta be. He was fucking some other broad. I found out an' I…I…."

An image floated behind her eyes. Geraldo lay face down on the floor in a pool of blood. People stood in a circle staring at him. They walked quickly out of the room. She shook her head, ignoring the gorge that rose from her gut. "No," she protested under her breath. "Uh-uh. Tha's a dream. I couldn't of. Din't. He's my old man. He's all I got."

Tears dripped from Danni's eyes, causing more pain in her pounding head. "Fool," she said to herself crossly. "Lookit me, Barney, cryin' over a no-good son-of-a bitch man. A man who was screwing someone else 'stead a me."

She sobbed great tears that tasted of alcohol. "But I need him, Barney. I need him ta take care a me an' my li'l girl." Her sobs wracked her body. "I were majorly pissed at him. I wanned ta hurt him bad. I run out an' got wasted an' wound up fuckin' with Bunion here. But I left my baby girl alone an' now I don' know where she's at or how ta find her." She moaned so loudly that Bunion sputtered and stopped snoring.

Danni opened both eyes and raised her head. "Tha's wha' I gotta do, Barney. I 'member now. I gotta find my baby. I gotta go find my Tiffany."

* * *

Danni's battered Jeep Wrangler careened out of the Windy Gulch Trailer Park with Bunion's garbage can wedged beneath it. Flooring the accelerator, Danni nudged the hulk up to 80, its top speed. The garbage can broke free, only to be snagged by the front bumper of the pickup ten feet behind her. The Jeep's canvas top flapped and snapped, and the wind whipped Danni's hair. "Gotta find my Tiffany," she whimpered, pulling strands of silvery hair out of her eyes and mouth. "Gotta find my little girl."

She raced north on Highway 1, repeating her daughter's name like a mantra. Despite her spinning head and heaving stomach, she managed to slow down when she saw the flashing lights of a sheriff's car on the shoulder, behind a silver minivan. Once around the next bend, she floored the Jeep again, and it gradually gathered speed.

"Where'll I look if she ain't home?" Danni asked herself. "She gotta be at home. I'll call tha' girl—her friend. Wha's her name? V-something. Veronica? Valerie? Victoria? Or Geraldo. He might know." The image of Geraldo lying on the floor returned, and panic gripped her stomach. "Oh no!" she cried. "Wha's wrong with Geraldo?" Cold air blasted her eyes, causing them to tear. "Ain't my fault," she moaned. "He needs help. Gotta help him. Wha's the nummer for 911? No, Tiffany's most 'portant. Gotta find her first."

Danni blew the light at Highway 1 and Main, swerved onto Miller Street, and caught the curb in front of her house. The Jeep stopped so abruptly she hit her head on the windshield. "No matter. I'm home, baby. Mama's home."

CHAPTER 17

Jason picked up Erin's and his empty cups and shuffled across the kitchen to the coffee maker. He filled both and returned to the table, sitting in the chair next to her.

She took his hand and squeezed. "Tell me your 'not pretty' story."

Jason had bottled up the memory so long, he'd begun to fear he'd never be able to talk about it. In this intimate moment, however, feeling Erin's warmth and concern, he decided that letting some of it go might make his other pressures easier to live with. "Yeah, well," he began, "remember I told you about Gretchen Fautz?"

"The lesbian, switch-hitting senior partner you worked for who wanted to have sex with you on her desk? How could I forget?"

"Well, after I refused Gretchen the second time, I gave Courtney some smoking-gun evidence in a big case. We won a $40 million judgment, and pretty soon, Gretchen made Courtney her chief lieutenant. Things were going along OK, even though I was just a grunt in the basement. Then the time came for our five-year reviews."

He explained that the last weekend of every June, the firm's senior partners deliberated in a secret location to decide the fate of the fifth-year associate attorneys. The ironclad policy was to promote or discharge associates at the end of their fifth year.

On the first day of July, each associate found a sealed envelope on their desk. The letter inside said either, "Congratulations. You have been named a junior partner of the firm …" or "The management of the firm regrets to inform you that your services no longer are required …."

As the firm's top producer for four decades, Gretchen wielded enormous power in these deliberations, and had built a cadre of partners who were loyal to her and her team.

"Courtney was Gretchen's most trusted assistant, and obviously would be named a partner," Jason said. "I was another matter. The office pool gave even odds I'd be discharged, and sixty-to-one odds I'd be made a partner. I gave myself ten-to-one odds because Courtney always told me how she talked me up to Gretchen. But Gretchen had different plans for me."

He explained that although Gretchen never missed an opportunity for revenge, she recognized the value of his contributions to her success over the last five years. She convinced her partners to promote him to the position of senior associate.

Under the firm's rules, that meant he would supervise her team of associates but never become a partner. Gretchen would continue to benefit from his skill and knowledge, and could manipulate him to keep Courtney in line. At the same time, any misstep he made would be held against Courtney.

As a senior associate, he'd be paid handsomely but would have no power in the firm. He could neither choose the cases he worked on, nor decide litigation strategy. He could not select subordinates or team members, or even communicate with any partner but Gretchen. He'd be subject to dismissal without notice for any reason, or no reason. He'd be expected to work 16- to 18-hour days, do what he was told, and produce excellent results. In time, he'd become like the handful of other senior associates—well-to-do, but mere shadows in the firm's corridors, reviled by the associates as failures, and ignored by the partners as nonentities.

"I was willing to accept the position with all its downsides," Jason said, "for the sake of my marriage and my son. You have to understand Courtney's and my relation was all about our careers and our knowledge of the firm's personalities and internal politics. All we talked about was the power shifts among the partners as they won and lost cases, and as their personal lives fell apart. She got really good at positioning herself to take advantage of the fallout. I thought we could make it work. Courtney would get all the glory and I'd toil in the basement. I convinced myself I could maintain my integrity and not become a timid suck-up, like the other senior associates."

He paused and picked up his phone. Courtney's text was still on the screen. His thumb hovered as he debated whether to get rid of the message or print out the divorce papers. He decided to be responsible and sent the document to the printer in the living room. As soon as the printer began churning out pages, he punched *Delete.*

"But it turned out Courtney wasn't on board," he continued with a sigh. In mid-August, he began to realize Courtney was distancing herself from him. She no longer offered him half her lunch wagon sandwich. She avoided meetings he attended, and criticized him when she did attend. She stopped dropping by his cubicle and inviting him upstairs to her office. When he tried to borrow a Marlboro from her purse, she slapped his hand. She refused to share office news and gossip, and information about her cases.

"What's going on, Courtney?" he finally asked late one night in the great room of their penthouse loft. Streamers of ocean mist blotted out the cheery sparkles of downtown Los Angeles, turning the room's 20-foot windows black and foreboding.

"You're a smart guy. You figure it out."

Jason felt like she'd sucker-punched him in the solar plexus.

"I'm in this position because I refused to sleep with Gretchen," he exploded. "It was, and still is, a matter of principle. You used to like that I have principles."

Silence.

"Did you sleep with her, Courtney?" It was the question he'd wanted to ask for five years. "Are you sleeping with her now?"

She glared at him. The green eyes that once beguiled him were hard and hateful. She selected a Marlboro from her pack, lit it, and blew a cloud of smoke at him.

"You're holding me back, Jason. I can be Whatley's national managing partner in the New York office in eight years. I can be Gretchen's boss."

Her words hit him like another punch to the stomach, followed by an uppercut to the jaw. He lurched back, hitting the corner of the suede sofa and falling onto it clumsily.

Courtney stood, arms crossed, in front of the cold, black marble fireplace. It was the exact spot where they made love in the early days, warmed by roaring flames. She cocked her head, examining him. Jason recognized the look on her face. It was her expression when she evaluated last season's business suits: Keep this one, toss that. Save another, discard the rest.

She dropped her cigarette on the Persian carpet.

"It's time for you to go, Jason."

She scrunched out the cigarette with her Prada pump, and walked out of the room.

* * *

At 6:30 a.m., Ally Booker walked briskly into the lobby of the KHYP studio in Santa Luisa, 30 miles south of Sea Cliff. The receptionist looked up from her computer and smiled. "You go, girl!"

Ally wended her way through the newsroom's cubicles to her desk and sat down. She switched on her computer and powered up her work cell phone; 233 new messages popped up, all from viewers praising her story about recovering the body from the storm drain.

"Fantastic reporting."

"Good job."

"You'll be up for an Emmy."

"I felt like I was there."

She opened her email program. More new messages, with subjects like:

"Loved the drainpipe story."

"Keep following this one."

"Zombie apocalypse right here!"

"Excellent local news coverage."

"Tell us who the dead guy is."

All the messages were favorable as she scrolled through the screens. One with the subject "Disgusted" caught her eye, however, and she paused to open it. "I was disgusted. Blatant sensationalism. You are sick. How can you show a rotting corpse on television? How can you make the death of a human being into entertainment? I'm switching to KRP."

Deleting the message, she checked her Facebook, Instagram, and Twitter accounts. Ninety-nine percent favorable and complimentary. *This is my ticket! I can ride this baby all the way to the network in New York. All I have to do is find out who did it, and package the story.*

She pictured herself standing with Lester Holt in the NBC newsroom, reporting her latest scoop. "Great story, Ally. Thank you very much," Lester would say before turning back to the camera.

A knock on her cubicle divider made her jump. Phil Kowalski, the station's news director, leaned over the half-wall and smiled down at her. "Fantastic job, Ally! Keep following this story. We'll use it during sweeps, and I'm sure it'll be in the Top 10 at the end of the year."

"Thanks, Phil." She looked up at him and gave him her brightest smile. *Wish I'd worn a low-cut top.* "This story's got great legs, and you were brilliant to let me run with it yesterday. Letting me broadcast the body being pulled out of the drainpipe, and posting it. More than a million hits just yesterday! That was genius!"

Phil blushed from his rubbery neck to the scalp beneath his jet-black comb-over. "Well, I…you know…when you have good people—"

"Let me identify the body at five o'clock. It'll keep up the interest."

"Geesh, Ally, I don't know. The sheriff hasn't identified the victim positively."

"They found the guy's wallet at the scene. What more do you want?"

"Yeah, but there's no driver's license, and no fingerprint match yet. It's really bad when you broadcast that someone's dead when they're not. I had a friend who was news director in Dubuque—"

"Phil! This is the story of the year! It makes us both look good. Let me do it tonight at five and six." She sensed he was wavering. "I'll go back up to Sea Cliff and do the story from the scene. Picture it. The craggy cliffs. The fog. Viewers will love it! You can run the tape at eleven."

Phil looked across the newsroom at the blank monitors hanging from the ceiling. He tugged the gold medallion at his neck. He pulled his moustache over his upper lip and chewed the ends. "No, Ally," he said decisively. "Not tonight. Give the sheriff a few more days to ID the dead guy. If they don't, and you can identify him independently, then I'll give you the green light. But you have to wait." He paused. "*Capisce?*"

It was just what she'd expected from a guy whose nickname was "Phil Noballsski."

Ally bit her tongue and said demurely, "You're right, Phil. It's better to be cautious."

"Good. Glad you agree. You'll get your chance." He knocked twice on the top of her cubicle wall and walked away.

"Fuckin' wuss," Ally fumed silently. "I'll get a positive ID today, and find the perp by the end of the week." She reached for her personal cell phone.

CHAPTER 18

"It's time for you to go, Jason."

The coldness of Courtney's words still stung him. The woman he'd loved for five years—his wife, the mother of his son, his intimate companion—and that was all she could say to him?

"My sweet baby," Erin said softly, her eyes moist. "She was so cruel. I could never be that mean to you. Or anyone."

Jason pushed back his chair and walked to the sink. He dumped his coffee and poured a fresh cup. He held the pot out to Erin. She shook her head. "So what did you do?"

He stuck his cup in the microwave and pushed the reheat button. "Well, the first thing I did was move to a hotel a block from the office. That way, I could still see Jason Jr., and I'd have more time to work because I wouldn't have to commute." The microwave dinged. He retrieved his cup and returned to the table. "I didn't decide to leave the firm right away."

"Really? After they treated you so bad?"

"It was a lot of money, Erin. A lot. And it was what I was familiar with. It was the only law job I'd ever had. I didn't know what else to do, or where to go." He sipped the coffee, made a face, and stirred a spoonful of sugar into the dark-brown liquid. "I tried to convince myself that I'd never be like the other senior associates. That I wouldn't lose my self-respect and wind up with my *cojones* in Gretchen's file cabinet."

Erin made an "eeuuww" expression.

"But I was fooling myself, and I was miserable. I was completely lost. I've never been so low."

"Didn't you have anyone you could talk to?"

"There was a guy at work I was friends with—Howie Simon. Did I ever tell you about him?"

"I don't think so."

"We worked on a lot of cases together, and he was number two on my discovery team. We used to talk about opening an office together in Santa Monica, by the beach, and taking any case that walked in the door. Kinda like I'm doing here. It was a pipe dream, but when I didn't make partner, he said, 'This is your big chance, man.' I asked whether he was with me, but he said, 'Sorry, man, my kid's about to go to college. Can't give up my salary at the firm.'"

"Some friend."

"No, he's a good guy, and I understand he didn't have the flexibility. Still, I was disappointed."

"What about your family?"

Jason waved his hand dismissively. "My mother called."

"I thought she was in rehab."

"She's always in rehab, but she has this sixth sense that tells her when I'm totally depressed. That's the only time she calls. She said my problem was that I hadn't accepted Jesus in my heart, and that when I did, He would tell me what to do." Jason shook his head. "She said He wouldn't send His answer right away, and it might take a while for me to understand His message when He did."

Erin's eyes lit up for a second, like she'd just solved a problem she'd been trying to work out. He waited for her to share her revelation, but she said, "What about your dad? What did he say?"

"It was classic Barry Brinkman," Jason sighed. He remembered the conversation exactly, but was embarrassed to repeat it.

He'd called his father to ask his advice, and acceded to his demand to meet in person. That meant carving 30 precious minutes out of his jammed 16-hour workday. They'd met in the snack shop in the Whatley Tower's lobby, and Jason had paid for their lattes and scones.

As Jason took his first bite, Barry got straight to the point. "You didn't fuck the old broad. There's your problem."

Jason nearly spit out his mouthful of scone. "So I should be a whore for the money?"

"Your problem, boy, is you're too moral. Where'd you get this overdeveloped sense of morality anyway?"

Jason wanted to say, "Certainly not from you." He said instead, "I wouldn't respect myself. I'd be like a eunuch."

Barry laughed. "Any man who can't blackmail his boss is a eunuch, boy. Take it from me, six figures buys a lot of respect and eases a lot of pain. You'd be set for life."

"I could be fired any minute."

"Then you live on your money, or get another job. You're just pissed 'cause they didn't make you a partner. Give the old broad what she wants and take the money. So what if she's twice your age? A bit of straight pipe from a young stud like you goes a long way."

"Dad! For God's sake!"

Barry made a show of sweeping crumbs off the table. "Or, she might die. One way or another, you'll get your promotion and be a rich guy. It'll work out. You'll see."

"You never prostituted yourself for a deal. Physically."

"What the hell is the matter with you, boy? Do what I say, not what I do."

"Thanks for the advice, Dad," Jason said, standing. He picked up his dishes, dumped them in the bussing tray, and took the elevator back up to his cubicle and piles of documents.

Jason shut his father's voice out of his head. "Basically, my dad said I should swallow my pride, ignore my morals, keep the job, and take the money."

Erin reached under the table and placed her hand on his thigh. She squeezed affectionately. "I'm glad you didn't listen to him. I'm glad you came here and found me."

Jason smiled wistfully. "You can thank my grandmother."

"She must've been a wonderful person. I'm so sorry I never met her. What did she tell you?"

"She was my rock for so long." Jason's voice broke, and he wiped the corner of his eye. "She was my mother, my family, my everything." He paused, looking down at the table. "We talked about it a lot—she actually listened more than anything. She told me this was a crossroad, and the decision I made would shape the rest of my life."

He remembered the decisive conversation with GG. He was in his cubicle at work late one night, surrounded by stacks of depositions he had to analyze before morning. "Jason," she'd said, "that law firm of yours… they'll just work you until you're all used up and throw you out. No amount of money is worth that." She was quiet for a moment before adding, "Let me tell you something. Your Grandpa Larry and I, we pushed your father much too hard to make a lot of money and be successful. I see now it was a terrible mistake, he's so miserable. You need to follow your heart, dear boy, and make the decision that's best for you."

Jason took a last sip of coffee and pushed away his cup. "She challenged me to think about the kind of life I wanted." As he spoke, he arranged the salt and pepper shakers and straightened the paper napkins in their holder. "She asked me things like, 'Do you want to be a slave for partners in New York you've never met? Wouldn't you rather see your clients' smiles when you've won their case? Wouldn't you rather deal with real people than paper?'"

His foot grazed the Marlboro pack under the table. He picked it up and spun it in his fingers. "She told me time and again there are real people in Sea Cliff with real problems, and that I could help them and make their lives better. That was exactly what Howie and I talked about doing, and it sounded so right. She even said I could live here with her until I got established. 'You can bring Jason Jr. with you,' she said. 'You can live together and be a real father to him.' She took me in for the second time when I had nowhere else to go." His voice grew thick and a tear rolled down his cheek. "And, as soon as I got here, she died."

Jason stood and carried his cup to the sink. He slumped over it and grasped the edges. His back heaved as he fought his emotions. "The only problem," he said hoarsely, "which neither of us realized, is the people in Sea Cliff with real problems can't afford to pay to fix them. And now I'm going broke." A muffled sob escaped him, followed by sniffling and throat-clearing.

Erin walked across the room and pressed her body against his back. She reached around his waist and pulled herself to him, kissing him between his shoulder blades. She laid her cheek against his spine, tightening her arms and squeezing him possessively. "I'm so glad we've talked like this," she whispered. "I've never felt so close to you."

She hugged him until his sniffling stopped. When his breathing slowed, she placed her hands on his hips and turned him to face her. She linked her arms around his neck and pressed her hips against him. His arms fell to her waist. Looking up at his eyes, she smiled shyly and said, "There's something I want to say to you."

He nodded.

She looked down for a moment before raising her eyes. "I've never said this out loud to anyone before. My birthday's next month. I'm going to be twenty-five—"

He brightened a little. "I know. We're going to celebrate all weekend. I've got something very special planned—"

"That sounds really nice," she interrupted, "and you're so sweet, but that's not the secret part."

He dredged up a smile and said, "So, tell me the secret part."

"Don't make fun. This is very important to me."

"Sorry. I didn't mean—"

"No, no, it's OK." She paused, looked away again. "Here goes. When I was in high school, I promised myself I'd get out of Sea Cliff by the time I was twenty-five, because that's when my mother had me, and she never got out, but here I am just like her, still stuck here, and now I have you…." She trailed off.

"There's no leeway? A couple of years…?"

"NO! It's already been eight years!" She stiffened in his arms, then relaxed slowly. "I told you about my promise to myself so you'll understand what I really want to say."

Her eyes darted out the window and slowly came back to his. "I don't think Jesus is the answer, like your mother does. But I do believe in Fate. I believe my fate *is* to get out of Sea Cliff, and I think Fate sent you to me to take me away. I think everything you've said this morning and Courtney's text are telling us we should leave here and go to Los Angeles."

Jason struggled to ignore the warmth of her body, the soft swell of her breasts under her tee shirt, the firm pressure of her pelvis. Her eyes were shy and assertive at the same time, and her face a mask of innocence. With great effort, he pushed her away and stood her at arm's length. "I'm not going back to Los Angeles, Erin. I've lived the LA life, and there's nothing there for me."

"I know you have, but I haven't. You'd have me, and we'd be together. Anyway, I'm not going to be stuck in Sea Cliff, like my mother. I'm not going to get knocked up and be trapped here forever, like she's been with me. That's her life. I won't let it be mine!"

"You don't understand. I can't make a living in Los Angeles. I'm damaged goods. I didn't make partner, and I quit the firm on short notice. No one's going to hire me."

They stood a foot apart, taking measure of each other as adversaries for the first time.

"I can wait tables 'til you find a job," she argued, "and I'll find a gallery to sell my Big Sur photographs. It may be hard at first, but we can do it. And ...." She paused, as if deciding whether to complete the thought out loud. "And," she plunged ahead, "if we were in LA, you'd be closer to Jason Jr., and could see him more."

Jason stepped back so quickly he bumped the kitchen counter. "Don't use my son as a bargaining chip!" he said coldly. "Leave him out of this. He's none of your business. I'll be established here soon enough. I know I can do it! I'll be able to bring him here without any problem, and be a father. I just need time."

Erin turned her back to him and started toward the hall. She whirled around. "Don't you see? You're doing to your son what your father did to you, making you travel halfway across the state to see him."

"Dammit, Erin! I feel guilty enough about him!" Every muscle in Jason's body tensed and his eyes smoldered. "Don't you ever try to manipulate me by using my son!" He pronounced every syllable and his voice was unnaturally quiet.

Jason knew he'd never forget the expression on her face. Crimson filled her milk-white cheeks. Her blue eyes were hurt and defiant, and the firm set of her jaw, which he'd loved when she slept, now was obstinate and petulant.

"I think you'd better go," he said more mildly. "We both need some time to think this through."

Erin left him alone in the kitchen and returned several minutes later in her clothes from last night. She stood in the doorway with her fists planted on her hips. "There's another reason I have to go to LA that I've never told anyone."

"What's that?"

"You'll laugh at me."

"You started this, now you won't tell me?"

She crossed her arms over her chest and straightened her back. "My photographs," she said defiantly.

"What are you talking about? I love your pictures. Why would I laugh—"

"Don't patronize me! I'll be thirty in no time. I need to create a market for my photographs in LA now, while I'm young. I have to be there to meet people and network. Gallery owners and critics. Movie people."

"What about the Internet?"

"It's all about personal connections, Jason. That's how artists get established. I can't do that if I'm stuck here. Now you're holding *me* back!"

He jerked like she'd slapped him in the face. "I'm not.... You're way out of.... You'd better leave 'til we both calm down."

"I'm not waiting. You obviously don't care how important this is to me. I'm not getting trapped like my mother, and I'm not gonna let my photographs rot here in obscurity. I'm getting out of Sea Cliff, one way or another. I'd like it to be with you, and I thought that's what Fate intended, but if not...." She shrugged. "I'll find another way."

She stalked to the living room, and he heard her rummaging in her purse. Returning to the kitchen, she tossed his key on the table. "Here. I don't need it anymore."

CHAPTER 19

"The Storm Drain Murder!" Ally said to herself. "The perfect title for my package."

She sipped yesterday's cold coffee and let her imagination run. It was an icky and unforgettable title that would grab the network's attention when she sent it to New York. Her excitement grew. *I'm gonna be famous! I'll go out to lunch with Norah O'Donnell, and Savannah Guthrie and the girls from* The Today *show. I'm gonna be friends with Jenna Bush!*

All she had to do was identify the dead guy and find the perp before the cops did, and she knew exactly where to start. She scrolled through her contacts on her personal cell phone and punched the number for sheriff's dispatch. A man's voice answered on the second ring. "Sheriff's Dispatch. Deputy Peters."

"Hi, Bobby. This is Ally."

"Ally! Hello! How's my favorite ex-girlfriend?"

"Just thinking 'bout you."

"I know you too well, Ally. You mean thinking 'bout how you could get me to do you another favor."

"Bobby. Is that all you think I care about?"

"You can prove me wrong by having dinner with me tonight."

"Tonight? Let me see," Ally said, tapping her keyboard to sound like she was looking through her calendar. "I'm sorry, baby. I'm busy tonight. Is this the only night your wife's away?"

"Damn, Ally. I miss you." Someone spoke in the background and Peters answered at length. Returning to Ally, he said, "Guess I'll just have to take a rain check."

"It's a promise. One surf-and-turf dinner and mudpie dessert with my best used-to-be."

Peters sighed. "So, what do you want, Ally?"

"Have you seen the incident report for The Storm Drain Murder?"

"Yes, I have, and it's just a 'probable' homicide at this point."

"Any witnesses mentioned in the report?"

"A neighbor. Why?"

"Oh, I'm just curious. Poking around, thinking maybe I could speed things up a bit. Who's the investigating officer?"

Peters was silent for a moment. "Deputy Hardesty, I think. He filed the report, anyway."

"The fat guy who posed with the corpse? No way! That guy's dumber than dog shit. He couldn't find his way out of a paper bag."

"Well, that's what we're dealing with. And our forensics team's totally tied up with the victims of the exploding boat. Coroner's investigators, too."

Ally heard the frustration in his voice. "Bobby," she said sweetly, "is there any way I could get a copy of the incident report? You know, just between you and me? I bet I can track down more leads in a week than that guy can in a month. I'll tell you everything I find out, and you can take credit." *But I'll probably broadcast it first.*

"Oh, babe, I don't know. I could get my ass in a serious sling. I've already broken twenty-three rules just talking to a civilian about it."

"Hey," Ally said in her sultry voice. "Remember that place at the beach where we used to sit and watch the moon? The place where I lost my top in the surf? Maybe we could do dinner and watch the moon after, just like the old days."

Ally was pretty sure she had him, but a chorus of male voices boomed in the background. She heard Peters cover the receiver. *Shit! He was ready to roll over for me.*

"OK. OK, you guys, just a minute," Peters said to the people in the room with him. He came back to her and whispered, "I gotta go. I'll do it, but I can't send it from here. I'll have to fax it when I take my break. Where do you want me to send it?"

"Kinko's. Same as last time."

"All right, babe. Look for it in about an hour. And, Ally…"

"Yes, Bobby?"

"You owe me for this one. Big time."

* * *

When Jason was eight, the divorce court assigned Dr. Felicity Patchit to be his family counselor and evaluator. Her advice to Jason was always the same: Compartmentalize.

"Imagine yourself standing in front of a row of lockers," she'd instruct. "Pick an empty one, stuff your troubles in it, and close the door. Lock it with a padlock. Then concentrate on what's good, and focus on the things you need to accomplish today."

Jason tried mightily to stuff away the hurt from his argument with Erin. By the time he'd showered and shaved, he was able to force the door closed on most of it. The hateful words, the hard glances, the feel of her firm body, her dramatic departure—all of it was jammed into the locker in an untidy mess. The piece that wouldn't fit, however, was her using his son as a pawn. That was hitting below the belt. But her angry accusation hit a nerve. *Is she right? Am I hurting Jason Jr. the way my dad hurt me?*

He crammed those thoughts into the locker with the others, and forced himself to focus on going to his office and working through Geraldo's estate files. Concentrating on the day ahead helped a great deal, but another nagging question kept scratching on the locker door: *Was I just the means to an end for Erin? Her ticket out of Sea Cliff?*

Jason gathered his keys, wallet, and cell phone. He locked GG's front door, cursing the sticky deadbolt. Stopping on the front porch, he looked at the morning for the first time. The sky was cloudless and crystal blue, and the sun warm. A light breeze ruffled the top boughs of the pine trees that lined the side and back yards. The breeze carried the roar of the ocean surf, far in the distance. Squirrels jabbered and crows cawed. Doves cooed to each other. Vultures circled high in the sky.

He trudged the walkway to his Porsche, parked as usual at the curb in front of the house. The car fired to life, and he motored slowly around

Crescent Lane's long curve to the west gate, where he turned right on Del Mar Road and headed toward Highway 1.

At his office, the pile of bills remained on Christina's desk, unopened. He bent down and picked up a pink envelope that smelled of jasmine hairspray. *Jason* was written in lavender calligraphy on the front. "Oh, Nikki," he sighed.

Ripping open the envelope, he walked the length of the bookcase and flopped into his desk chair. The scent of jasmine hairspray overwhelmed him. "For God's sake, Nikki," he groaned, "what do you want, today of all days?"

He opened the card and read:

Jason, I found out who your runner with the blonde ponytail is. Her name is Rory. She's from Rodeo Drive in Beverly Hills. She does some kind of beauty treatments with Botox and collagen injections. She rented a house on Bluffside for a month. You owe me a long drive in your Porsche with the top down. I think you should take me to dinner at Falling Cliffs resort. I want the lobster.

xoxo
Nikki

PS. She's not really blonde, and she's gaye.

* * *

Ally and Spike sat in the KHYP news truck outside Kinko's in Santa Luisa. Ally finished reading the first page of the faxed incident report and handed it to Spike. She scanned the second page and dropped it in his lap. The only useful information was that a neighbor, Mrs. Dorothy Richardson, saw someone who seemed drunk drag another drunk across the Vista Point parking lot toward the path to the Point, return alone, and drive away in a silver minivan. The person was dressed in black and limped a little when he or she walked back to the vehicle. The witness did not see the van's license plate.

Ally fished her cell phone out of her purse and dialed Mrs. Richardson's number from the report. The phone rang five times before a recording clicked on: "Village Pizza, number one on the Central Coast. We're closed right now, but you can leave your order after the tone." Ally punched the *End* button in disgust. "Stupid cop didn't even get the phone number right."

She opened her Reverse Directory app and typed in Mrs. Richardson's address. A different number appeared on her screen. She dialed the new number. The phone rang several times before it was answered. She heard women's voices in the background. An elderly woman said, "Hello?"

"Hello, Mrs. Richardson? This is Ally Booker from KHYP, your News Channel. How are you today?"

"My word," Mrs. Richardson said. Covering the receiver, she called, "Girls! It's Ally Booker, the reporter. From the television." The women were quiet for a moment. "Just call me Dottie, hon," Mrs. Richardson said. "I feel like I know you. I watch your stories every night. You got a new hairdo last week."

"I did, Dottie," Ally said, touching her hair. "You're right. It's always nice to meet a fan."

Spike tapped Ally's shoulder and pointed at the phone. She nodded and pushed the *Speaker* button.

"What can I do for you, dear?" Mrs. Richardson said. "I'm hosting my Mah-Jongg club this morning and the girls are waiting for me."

"I won't keep you, Dottie. I understand you saw the corpse being dumped last week, and I was hoping we can do an interview so you can tell everyone what you saw."

"Me? On television? Why, I never dreamed...." The woman was silent while the voices warbled in the background.

"Come on, Dottie," one of them called. "You're holding up the game and our tea and scones."

"Go ahead, girls. Don't wait for me. This is important."

The women's conversation began again, but Mrs. Richardson was silent. Finally she said, "Oh dear, I suppose I could do that. The Lord told me I did a good thing when I reported what I saw to that young policeman. And of course I'd do it for you, hon. Yes, by gum, I'll do it! There's just one thing...."

"What's that, Dottie?" Ally said, forcing herself to be patient.

"Well, hon, I just can't go on television until I've had my hair done. Could you interview me tomorrow afternoon?"

"Of course, Dottie," Ally said, rolling her eyes at Spike. "I understand. You want to look nice. Perfectly natural. What time would be good for you?"

"Well, I'll get an appointment for three o'clock, and then I have to go to the pharmacy before I drive back home. Would four-thirty be OK?"

"Gee, Dottie, I don't think so. That's really crowding my deadline for the five-o'clock news. How about four o'clock at the beauty parlor?"

"OK," Mrs. Richardson said hesitantly, "if that's OK with you."

"It'll be fine. We do interviews in all kinds of strange places."

Ally used her free hand to find a pen and her reporter's notebook. "Dottie, so I can be fully prepared for our interview, why don't you tell me everything you saw. That way, I can remind you if you get nervous and forget something on camera."

"Why, that's a wonderful idea, dear. I suppose I will be nervous."

"OK, Dottie. I'm ready to take notes." Ally balanced the phone on her thigh.

Spike reached over and covered the mouthpiece with his palm. "Why you takin' her statement if you gonna interview her tomorrow?" he asked innocently, but there was an edge in his voice.

"Hey, camera jockey," she snapped, digging her nails into the back of his hand. "I know what I'm doing. You just worry about taking pictures when I tell you to." She pushed his hand away. "Go ahead, Dottie. Just tell me everything from beginning to end."

Mrs. Richardson repeated what she'd told Deputy Hardesty. Ally listened intently, transcribing her every word.

"That's great, Dottie," Ally said when the woman's voice trailed off. "Very thorough and helpful. I'll see you tomorrow afternoon at four."

"Hon? I was just thinking...do you know where the beauty parlor is?"

"In Sea Cliff? I'll Google it, and I'll see you tomorrow at four."

"Oh, of course you can Google it. OK, dearie. Goodbye, then."

Ally ended the call and turned to Spike. "Alright. So she said the silver van had an international sticker on the back window." His face went blank. "You know," Ally explained, irritated, "one of those white ovals with a black border and the initials of a country. She thinks it was IE, IT, or IL. I want you to call—"

"Shiiit, girl. You gonna break that ol' lady's heart when we no-show tomorrow, her being all pretty with nice hair and all. An' she yo' biggest fan. What she gonna tell her old-lady friends?"

"It's a hard business we're in, Spike. Besides, it could turn out we need her anyway. Depends on what else we find out, or if we have time to fill. So this is what I want you to do. Call all the other camera crews and tell them to be on the lookout for a silver minivan with one of those international stickers in the right corner of the rear window. Tell 'em I'll give $50 to the person who finds it first and gives me the license number."

"Fifty dollars?" Spike squeaked. "Shit, Ally, I ain't no fool. I got my cred to keep. I ain't callin' no one for no $50 reward."

"OK. Seventy-five dollars."

Spike plucked Ally's phone from her thigh and turned it off. He took his own phone out of his pocket, pressed the *Off* button, and slipped both into the driver door's map pocket. Turning away, he stared out the windshield, ignoring her.

"OK," Ally fumed. "One hundred dollars. And tell 'em all to call everybody they know who drives for a living—cabbies, Uber and Lyft drivers, tow truck drivers, delivery truck guys, garbage men. We've gotta find that van and the owner. We've gotta scoop the cops." She added silently, "And everyone else, so I can get outta cow town and get my ticket punched for the network and New York City."

CHAPTER 20

Until their fight this morning, Erin had always been sweet, never nasty or manipulative. "Guess I don't know her as well as I thought," Jason muttered to himself as he searched his file cabinets for Geraldo's estate plan folder. "But I do know she always has a backup plan. She sells her Big Sur pictures in case she gets laid off from Posh. Well, that's one reason, it turns out. She's always looking for a new roommate because one might leave." On a personal level, she never trusted just one method of contraception.

Folder in hand, he walked to his desk. *So she must have a Plan B for moving to LA. She must be seeing someone else. Someone with enough money to take her there. Dammit!*

Jason always listened to the rumors about who was seeing whom in the village because it made good business sense, but he hadn't heard anything about Erin. "Who can it be?" he asked himself. "I must've not been paying enough attention."

He selected the file labeled *Next of Kin* and opened it, but his mind was elsewhere. If Erin always made sure she had options, he thought, Geraldo had dozens of irons in the fire all the time. It was impossible to guess which way he'd jump next. Jason figured he'd made so many people angry over the years that he had to keep everyone guessing.

Six months ago, Geraldo instructed Jason to draw up a basic estate plan with a will or a trust, and Jason gave him the necessary worksheets. Geraldo returned them months later, more or less completed, but never told Jason what he wanted done. Jason was examining the documents this morning for the first time. The most important ones were "Next of Kin" because those people had to be notified Geraldo had died, and "Assets." Creditors and other possible claimants would be notified later.

Forcing himself to focus on the pages in front of him, he was surprised Geraldo hadn't named many relatives. Eighteen in all, with addresses scattered through the West and Southwest. Geraldo hadn't bothered to fill in the column that asked for the relationship of each person to him.

Jason grinned at one name, despite his sour mood: Goldie O'Brien. "Sounds like a Jewish-Irish mobster babe," he mused. The name was so absurd, he said it out loud. He wondered, "Where would a person named Goldie O'Brien live?" The worksheet just said LA.

His fingers typed names and addresses into a new estate correspondence spreadsheet, but his mind wandered back to Erin. Should he have pushed her to be exclusive? Probably not. So what if she saw her junior college guy, or if he dated someone now and then? Should make them stronger when they did commit. *But for her to have a backup boyfriend?*

He thought about his next steps with her. He could break it off, but he liked her too much for that. He wasn't going to call and apologize. No way. She picked the fight, after all, and he didn't do anything wrong. After a few minutes, he settled on a strategy: jealousy. He needed to go out with someone new. But that solution was also a problem. Who could he take out that she'd hear about, and that would make her worry?

Picking up the Assets file, he turned to the Real Property pages. There were only five properties listed. The first two were the house where Geraldo lived with Danni and Tiffany, and One Bluffside Drive. Another house on Bluffside, and unimproved lots in Santa Cruz and Mendocino rounded out the list. Jason was surprised, because Geraldo always bragged about all his properties, and all the money he'd make when he sold them.

As he entered the addresses and Assessor Parcel Numbers into his computer, he thought about who he could go out with but drew a blank. He double-checked the street numbers and the APNs on the computer screen. "So," he decided, "I'll have to start hanging out at Mostly's."

The idea didn't excite him. Mostly's Saloon was the late-night place to be seen, but the meat-market atmosphere didn't appeal to him anymore. He imagined the stench of smoke and stale beer, the drunken din, the overheated bodies crushed together. "Doesn't matter," he said to himself. "I'll go there tonight. I *will* do it."

Next, he started to review the Bank Accounts pages. "Holy shit!" he exclaimed. "Look at all the bank accounts this guy has!" There were two dozen accounts, scattered all over the country. If the number of accounts surprised him, it was just like Geraldo not to include balances for any of them. *What the hell was Geraldo doing?*

An explanation dawned slowly. Geraldo was cashing out and hiding the proceeds, and that was why he had so few properties and so many bank accounts. If he'd lived, he'd have emptied all the accounts. He'd have taken that money, the spec house investors' money, and the money from the drug deal, and disappeared.

"Son of a bitch!" he swore. "That wily old bastard!" He dropped the worksheets on his desk and gazed into space, thinking there could be a fortune in the accounts, or a few dollars in each. The Geraldo that he knew could've played it either way. But why would Geraldo bother with an estate plan if he was going to disappear with his money?

He turned his chair to face the wall behind his desk and thought out loud. "OK. Assume he was planning to disappear. If he just vanished, there would be lots of questions. People he owed money to would try to find him. Relatives, too." Jason's eyes roamed over the pictures on his credenza. "So, what would a devious scumbag do to throw people off his trail?"

As Jason pondered this, a recent *American Greed* episode about a phony suicide came to mind. A Mafia-type had parked his car in the middle of a bridge and dropped his coat into the river below. The answer came in a flash. Geraldo was going to fake his own death. He'd toss his kayak into the surf and fly to Australia. The kayak would turn up empty, and people would assume he'd drowned and his body washed out to sea.

Jason played out the scenario in his mind. He'd probate Geraldo's estate, and the creditors and relatives would get official notice of his death. He'd leave enough money so everyone got a little something. Who'd question it? If he did it right, even people he told about disappearing would think Fate got him before he could pull it off. *It would've been a brilliant plan, but someone killed him first. The question is, who?*

With all his other worries, he hadn't considered it until this moment. He sorted through the possibilities. Everyone said Danni and Geraldo had an abusive relationship, and she certainly was big and strong enough to kill him. But would she? Then there were guys that Geraldo owed money to, like Mack Hammersley. Geraldo screwed them financially, but would they kill him? Hammersley certainly seemed angry enough. And there was El Carnicero, who Admiral Bill said was a cartel enforcer. He could've killed Geraldo for revenge, or just to send a message.

Jason turned back to his desk and focused again on the list of banks. Due diligence required that he contact them all to request account balances. He created a new spreadsheet and began to input the information alphabetically by bank name. Ally Bank, Bank of America, Bank of the West, Commerce Bank, Farmers and Merchants, Fifth Third Bank, First Minneapolis, Grand National Bank of the Cayman Islands.

He stopped cold. "What the hell is Geraldo doing with a bank account in the Cayman Islands?" he sputtered. "People use Cayman banks to hide assets. A foreigner can't even get an account there unless it's big money. That must mean—"

Heavy footsteps banged across the deck outside Jason's office. The door slammed open, hitting the wall so hard the front window rattled. "BRINKMAN," an angry voice shouted. "BRINKMAN, ARE YOU IN HERE?" The footsteps pounded on the other side of the bookcase. "GODDAMMIT, BRINKMAN! WHERE ARE YOU?"

* * *

Tiffany Tedeski slept fitfully as the Greyhound bus lumbered south on Interstate 5. She usually slept well when she'd been up all night smoking dope, but not this time. It could've been worry or the jouncy ride, or maybe she needed more smoke. She felt terrible about ditching Victoria, her dearest, best friend, and that could be part of the problem. Tiffany knew V would be frantic. She wondered whether V would tell the police she was missing, but it didn't matter. Every teenager knew that the cops didn't consider you missing until you'd been gone 24 hours, and she'd be safe in San Diego by then.

Ditching V had been easier than she expected. Was it really only last afternoon? Victoria drove them to the House of God's Helping Hands Counseling Center in Santa Luisa, and as she'd promised, it was next door to the bus station. Tiffany added her name to the list to speak with a Spiritual Counselor and sat with V in the waiting room.

"It's going to be OK, Tiff," V said, squeezing her hand. "They can help you." V sounded so confident that Tiffany almost believed her.

"I know," Tiffany said, squeezing back. "I'm glad we came." Tiffany smiled at her. Tears welled in her eyes. "You are my absolute best friend forever and ever, and the big sister I never had." She kissed Victoria on the cheek and got up. "I gotta go pee."

Instead, Tiffany found the back door and slipped into the alley. She grabbed her backpack out of Victoria's car through the open passenger's window and hid behind a dumpster. When a bus pulled into the unloading area, she joined the passengers walking into the station.

Waiting for the morning express coach to LA and San Diego hadn't been that hard, either. She'd put on her snowboarder's goggles and pulled her stocking cap over her forehead. A dirty bandanna tied over her nose made her look scary. She sat behind a pillar with her knees under her sweatshirt and listened to her iPhone. No one bothered her. After a while, some other runaway kids came into the bus station. They'd smoked weed, laughed, and binged on vending-machine munchies all night. And now she was on her way to San Diego and Tommy, her most recent stepfather.

Tiffany thought that could be part of the problem, too. She'd lied to her best friend about her plan. But was it really a lie? Was it a lie to keep her secret plan to herself? Look what happened when she told V about Geraldo, at the beginning when it was exciting. All her friends at school found out. That taught her the only way to keep something secret was to lock it away inside and never share it with anyone.

When it came down to it, Tiffany had decided Tommy was the only person she could turn to for advice. He'd always respected her and treated her like an adult, and never hit on her, the way so many older men did. Especially Geraldo. She shuddered. She imagined his bristly beard on her cheek and his alcoholic breath. Plus Tommy's new wife, Heather, was a nurse, and she'd know what Tiffany should do.

Should I keep it or get rid of it? Keep it? Get rid of it? Keep it…? The rhythm of the words blended with the thumping of the tires and the rattling of the bus, and Tiffany finally fell asleep.

* * *

"BRINKMAN, GODDAMN YOU! ARE YOU IN HERE?" The angry voice boomed through Jason's office.

Jason scrambled from his chair and grabbed his All-Star bat from the corner behind his desk. He cocked the bat shoulder high and planted his feet firmly, ready to swing at the head that would appear any second at the end of the bookcase.

A beefy crimson face with wild eyes and a mouthful of cigar rounded the corner. Jason recognized James Paige a split second before he swung. Paige stopped abruptly, taking in the bat and Jason's power stance. The two men stood their ground, glaring at each other.

"What the hell do you want?" Jason spoke in a deep baritone to mask the quiver in his voice.

Paige was built like a linebacker who lived too well. He obviously was a brawler, despite his Tommy Bahama veneer. A sneer worked the corner of his mouth, and Jason imagined he was calculating the reach of Jason's swing, and how to take him out without getting hit.

Minutes seemed to pass. Then, like the flip of a switch, the tension left Paige. His shoulders sagged, the anger drained from his face, and his breathing slowed. He held up his hands in mock surrender. "Hey, cowboy," he said, taking a step back, "calm down. I need you to do something for me, so pounding the crap out of you will have to wait."

Jason leaned the bat against his credenza. Still standing, he said. "What do you want?"

"I need you to sue someone. Can I sit down?"

Jason gestured at the client chair across from him. Paige sat. Jason stood behind his desk.

"Here's the deal—" Paige began.

"No, here's the deal. You owe me $2,500. This conversation ends right now, unless you brought the money with you."

Paige waved his hand dismissively. He reached into the pocket of his cargo shorts and pulled out his money clip. Thumbing through credit cards, he tossed an American Express Black card across Jason's desk. Jason sat in his chair and picked up the card. He dropped it in his shirt pocket. "I don't take credit cards. You get this back when I get my money. Cash is good, but I'll take a local check."

The expression on Paige's face was half bemused, half disdainful, like he was toying with a valet hovering for a tip. He held up his hands again. "OK, cowboy, whatever you say. Come by my house this afternoon. I'll give you a check. Now can I tell you who I want to sue?"

Jason nodded.

Paige related the events of yesterday afternoon—how Slade and Hayley discovered the corpse in the storm drain, how terrified they were, and how the fat cop traumatized them with his stupid, insensitive questions. He grew more and more agitated as he described Deputy Hardesty's questioning and his kids' near-catatonic responses.

"So today, I called Ramon Sepulveda, the stupid cop's supervisor. I told him how his dumb-ass deputy terrorized my kids." Paige was shouting now, red in the face and leaning over the desk. "Nobody treats my kids like that! No cop, nobody! I told Sepulveda I wanted that idiot busted and fired. Do you know what he said?" Paige pounded Jason's desk. "He told me to file a citizen complaint! He said he'd talk to Hardesty, but couldn't do nothing 'til I filed a complaint." The veins in Paige's temples throbbed. "He wouldn't even look into it 'til I did."

Paige half-stood and planted his fists on Jason's desk, leaning so close that Jason saw the pores in his nose and smelled his stale cigar breath. "I want you to sue that son-of-a-bitch," Paige roared. "He messed up my kids. They're zombies. I want to destroy him, get him fired. I want you to sue him for everything he's got."

He punched the desk so hard that Jason's coffee cup bounced. "I want his balls!"

CHAPTER 21

Danni ran up the front steps of her house and charged through the unlocked front door. "TIFFANY, where you at, baby? Mommy's home. Where you at, honey?"

The house was silent.

Danni stood in the living room, deciding where to look first. She stuck her head in the kitchen. Dishes were piled in the sink and on the counters and island. She gagged at the reek of decaying food. Flies darted from dish to dish, buzzing like tiny jackhammers in her head. An empty plastic jar of peanut butter lay on the cutting board, pinned to the wood by a butcher knife. More flies crawled inside the jar, devouring the last brown smudges.

No Tiffany.

Danni retreated to the hallway and leaned against the wall, gulping the fresher air. Waves of nausea washed over her and she shivered with cold sweats. "Gotta dry out a coupla days," she told herself sternly. Her head pulsed in time with the ticking of the kitchen clock. "Oh, God," she groaned, clutching her stomach, fighting the heaves. "Maybe a beer'll help. Might be one in th' fridge." She took a step toward the kitchen, but the reek pushed her back. "Nuh-uh. Gotta find my baby first."

The nausea passed and Danni's head cleared a bit. "Why don' she answer me?" Danni realized the voice she kept hearing was her own. "Ohhh, I know. She's playin' hide 'n seek, like when she was little. But Mommy knows where you're at."

"TIFF-ANNN-EEE!" She ran down the hall to the TV room and pressed her ear to the door, listening for the sound of the TV or a video game.

Bursting through the door, she cried, "Found you!" The room was empty. Heavy curtains blocked the bright daylight. The air was hot and stale, and stank of cigarettes and marijuana. The flat screen above the fireplace glowed blue, casting ghostly shadows on the walls.

Danni collapsed on the sofa, moaning, "Oh, my baby." A bunched-up blanket, stained by untold liquids and fluids, lay on the cushion next to her. She clutched it to her stomach, swaying back and forth. "My baby, my baby," she wailed, "where you at? Why you do this ta Mommy?" She lost track of time, hugging the blanket and rocking gently on the sofa, the way she used to comfort baby Tiffany.

After a long while, she began to think more coherently. "When was it I seen her last?" Talking out loud seemed to help. "Must of been 'bout a week ago, at the spec house. The night all them people was there." Something happened, Danni couldn't remember what, but she'd had to get blind drunk afterward. Then she'd fucked her eyes out for a week with Bunion.

"Where'd my baby go? She run away? Wouldn' of, would she? Ain't no note, but there's gotta be a clue somewhere in this house. My baby would of hid a clue."

It finally clicked. Danni might not know the name of her daughter's best friend. She might not know if Tiffany believed in God, or wanted to go to college, or even her favorite movie. "But I do 'member where my little girl hides everythin' she don' want Mommy ta find out about. And tha's where the clue's at." Danni clumped up the stairs to Tiffany's bedroom. Opening the closet and flipping on the light, she craned her neck. "There it is. Up there on th' top shelf. Tha' pink Barbie box."

* * *

Locating the silver minivan turned out to be a simple matter of serendipity. Cable-TV installer Bradley Clark finished a job in Rock Bay and decided he needed a Krispy Kreme before his next appointment. Waiting in the drive-thru, he noticed the vehicle in front of him was a silver Honda minivan with an "IE" international sticker in the right corner of the rear window.

Bradley followed the Honda through town, hoping it would go to a house with an address he could read. Instead, the van drove straight through town and sped north on Highway 1 in the direction of Sea Cliff.

"Well, damn," Bradley swore. He made a U-turn and headed toward the marina and his favorite spot for snacking and napping. "Coulda got more reward with a address," he grumbled, "but I got the description of the van and the plate. That'll be worth a few hundred."

He took a big bite of his doughnut and called Spike on his cell phone. "Hey, Spike, how you doin'? You comin' to bowlin' Friday night? Throw coupla more seven-ten splits for the team, heh, heh. Hey, I got the license plate number."

"No shit? Give."

"It's gonna cost ya. $500."

He heard Spike cover the mouthpiece, and a woman's loud voice on the other end.

"She say $200."

"No way, dude. $400."

More heated discussion.

"She say $300, and not a dime more."

"$350. I just seen the van, man. It's headin' north on Highway 1 right now this minute as we speak."

"$300, dude. Hang on, hang on, I'm gettin' a call from a guy that don't wanna bust my balls."

"OK, OK, $300 it is. Where you at now?"

"Santa Luisa, but hey, bro, I can't get the money 'til tonight."

"OK. Meet me tonight at nine at Bootleg's in Rock Bay. Bring cash. I'll buy ya a beer with your money, heh, heh. Got a pencil? Here's the plate: RELSTAT."

* * *

James Paige's tirade against Deputy Hardesty subsided and he sank back into the chair opposite Jason's desk. Jason sat quietly until the man's face regained its normal color and the veins in his temples stopped throbbing.

"OK, Mr. Paige, I understand why you're upset. I've had encounters with Hardesty myself, so I know how dense he can be."

Paige grunted, but his eyes burned with frustration.

"Here's how I see your case. You want to sue Deputy Hardesty. But you have to think about the end game—what you're going to have to prove to a jury. Hardesty's lawyers will argue your kids were harmed by finding the corpse, not by his questioning. They'll try to put the blame on the county for leaving the storm drain open. The county's lawyers will argue that a corpse falling into the storm drain and being discovered by kids who are traumatized is not the type of harm for which the county can be held liable—that this type of harm is not foreseeable, and therefore, the county has no liability."

Paige sat silently, listening as Jason spoke. He began shaking his head back and forth, as if saying "no." He leaned forward, planting his forearms on Jason's desk. "You're not listening." His face flushed red again. "I DON'T CARE IF I WIN! I want that fat fuck fired. I wanna make his life miserable. I wanna make him such a problem, they gotta fire him."

Paige's demeanor changed suddenly. The explosive hothead was replaced by the persuasive businessman. "Look, I got lawyers in Fresno who could do this for me. But you're here. You know the judges and how things work in this county. And I know you need the money."

For the first time since he learned Geraldo was dead, Jason saw a flicker of light at the end of his financial tunnel. It would be a fun case to litigate, trying to hold the county—the deep pocket—liable for damages for negligence and the emotional distress Hardesty caused the two kids. Nonetheless, he hesitated because he was too broke to pay for discovery, investigators, and psychologists. On the other hand, he figured he could do some preliminary work, earn a few dollars, and keep his foot in the door.

"Here's how we'll proceed, Mr. Paige. Before you can sue, you'll have to file a claim with the county seeking damages. A county board reviews these kinds of claims, and it will have to deny yours before we can file your lawsuit in court. Or, who knows, the board might make an offer because the facts are so unpleasant, and your kids are so appealing."

Jason did some quick calculations in his head. Paige owed him $2,500. Preparing and filing the claim form with the county might take four hours, so that would be another $1,400. Thirty-nine hundred dollars would cover some essential expenses and buy some time. Hopefully, he could take the lawsuit when the county denied the claim. He said, "I'll prepare and file the papers with the county for $1,400, payable this afternoon when I pick up what you already owe me. I'll also drop off a retainer agreement for you to sign."

He opened his desk drawer and pulled out a stack of business cards. Sorting through them, he handed two across the desk to Paige. "This is what I want you to do. Make appointments for both kids with Dr. Eve Eden, the psychologist here in town. She's very good with children. I'll call her and explain the situation. After that, make appointments with Dr. Frank Lichtblau. He's the local pediatrician. I want him to determine whether they've suffered any physical reaction to the two incidents. Make the appointments today. Do you know a child psychologist in Fresno?"

Paige nodded.

"Good. I want the kids to have counseling for at least three months. Longer, if they need it." Jason paused. "Now, it'll take me a couple of hours to draw up the retainer agreement and deliver it to your house. Please have two checks ready for me, one for $2,500 and another for $1,400." He looked Paige in the eye. "Anything else?"

Paige was subdued. He stood and stuck the doctors' cards in his side pocket. "I guess all this crap is necessary, but don't forget: At the end of the day, I want that fat little prick fired." He jabbed a thick finger at Jason's shirt pocket. "And I want my credit card back." He shoved the chair against the bookcase, rounded the end, and walked heavily to the front door.

The air of physical tension left the room with Paige. Jason breathed a sigh of relief. He'd avoided a brawl with Paige and scored a little income in the process. It was a good short-term win, but he knew Paige would come after him if he didn't win some damages or get Hardesty fired.

Jason pushed back his chair, stood, and stretched. The retainer agreement and cover letter would have to wait a couple of minutes because he needed to keep a promise first. Long ago, grown-up Jason vowed to the foster child he'd once been that he'd do all he could to save another kid from suffering as he had. His task right now was to call everyone he could think of who might know how to find Danni.

CHAPTER 22

Ally's hand shook with excitement as she wrote "RELSTAT" in her reporter's notebook. She pulled up her phone's newest app, AnyPlateAnyState.com, typed the letters in the search box, and clicked on "California" in the pull-down menu. The screen read "Loading," then "Connecting," then "Unable to find." Ally cleared the fields and reentered the information. The screen flashed twice before the message "Unable to find" appeared again.

"Shit. There's $5.99 wasted."

"Call your buddy at the sheriff's office," Spike suggested.

"I know, I know, I just wanted to find the perp myself. But I guess there's no other way." She punched in the number.

Deputy Bobby Peters answered on the second ring.

"Hi, babe," Ally cooed. "Thanks for sending the fax. I just can't wait for our dinner."

"What do you want? I'm really busy."

"Oh, I was just wondering," she said, trying to sound seductive, "if I had the plate number for the silver minivan, would you run it for me?"

"Are you nuts? I could get fired in a minute. I'm already way over the line helping you with the incident report."

"But you do want the plate number, don't you? I've got an eyewitness ID of the van, the international sticker, and the plate number."

Peters didn't speak. Ally heard male voices in the background.

"Hey, guys, hold it down," he barked at the voices. Returning to Ally, he said quietly, "OK, here's what I can do. I'll run the plate and radio the information to the unit closest to the address. I'll tell you where the unit's at, and you can follow it."

"And I can film once I get to the location?"

"I can't say you can do that."

"I understand. It's a deal. Any more info on identifying who the corpse is?"

"Jesus, Ally, you are just too much. Why would I tell you, even if I did know something?"

"I just can't get our night at the beach out of my mind. It was so magical for me. Didn't it mean anything to you?"

Bobby exhaled into his mouthpiece, a long, slow sigh. "Damn you, Ally. You do know how to push my buttons. I can tell you this much, but you can't say any of it in your reporting. Your general manager called the sheriff this morning, wanting to know when the corpse will be identified. So did the editor of the *Daily News*. The sheriff told the coroner to pull a guy off the exploding boat investigation to do a preliminary ID and cause of death on the storm drain corpse."

"I love you, Bobby." Ally blew a kiss into the phone. "OK. Here's the plate number."

Bobby was quiet for several minutes. When he came back on the line, he said, "OK, I've got the address. It's in Sea Cliff. Now let's see who's in the area. Hang on."

Ally turned to Spike. "Start driving to Sea Cliff. We're gonna film the arrest of The Storm Drain Murderer." She added to herself, "And I'm on my way to the Big Apple!"

She pictured herself walking into Nordstrom's to meet her personal shopper in the designer purse department. *Dior? Nah, I like Tommy Hilfiger better—*

Bobby's voice broke in. "The closest unit is on Highway 1 at Milepost 45. You can follow it into Sea Cliff, but keep your distance, you hear me? Now, let's see who it is."

There was static on the phone as Spike drove through Santa Luisa and merged onto Highway 1. Ally heard Bobby's voice, but couldn't make out the words.

"What, Bobby? What did you say? I can't hear you."

Bobby's voice burst through the static. "I said, 'Oh shit!' The closest unit is Deputy Hardesty!"

* * *

Spike hustled the ungainly news van north on Highway 1, trying to keep Deputy Hardesty's flashing lights in sight. The van, loaded with transmission equipment, a rooftop satellite dish, and a retractable boom, screeched around curves and pounded over expansion joints. When the rocking and bouncing subsided briefly, Ally clambered into the rear compartment to power up the transmitter and handheld mini-camera. Finishing that, she sat on an equipment box and dialed her news director, Phil Kowalski.

"Phil, this is Ally. We're heading up to Sea Cliff. We're gonna film the arrest of The Storm Drain Murderer. I want you to stand by to cut in when we start broadcasting."

"How did you … how do you … ?" He cleared his throat. "How do you know it's the murderer?"

"I got it from my contact at the sheriff's office," Ally said matter-of-factly. In a corner of her mind, she knew that this might not be *the* silver minivan, that the owner of this van might not have been the driver on the night of the murder, and that the person they were racing to confront might not be the owner or driver. On the other hand, she just knew these little details would work out the way she wanted. *Phil likes to get hung up about crap like that. I've gotta keep him on track.* She had to move the story along, put together a gut-grabber package, and send it off to New York while it was hot.

Phil surprised her. "Well, if you got it from the sheriff, it must be solid," Phil acknowledged, although he sounded unhappy.

"That's right, it is. I want you to cut in as soon as the perp is led out of the house. I want to film the perp walk and him getting into the cop's car. You know, with the cop's hand on his head so he doesn't bump it."

"Gee, Ally, I don't know. Interrupting Dr. Phil or Ellen or Kelly, depending on the timing. That would piss off the sponsors and a lot of viewers, even if they're reruns."

Ally knew where he was going. Those were the station's most-viewed shows, and advertisers clamored for slots on them. "Come on, Phil, prove that you're bigger than your nickname for once."

She imagined Phil's face growing red—no one even hinted at his nickname, Phil Noballsski, in his presence. "Think about it. We'll get the perp's name, and you can use the film for cut-ins all day. This is Emmy material, Phil. Do this, and your evening news viewers will double for at least a week. You'll see. You can get that raise you deserve."

The line was silent. From long experience, Ally knew that Phil was alternately tugging on his greasy comb-over and fondling the gold medallion around his neck. She looked out the windshield and realized they were just north of Sea Cliff, in an area of impressive houses on acre lots. Deputy Hardesty had slowed and turned off his flashing lights. "C'mon, Phil. We're here. I need a decision."

"Send me what you get and I'll decide then."

"That's bullshit, and you know it. Remember Broadcasting 101? 'It's only live if it's live'? 'There's no greater impact than a live breaking news story'?"

Hardesty pulled into the long driveway of a large, modern house on a knoll with a sweeping ocean view. He parked near the house, at an angle that would prevent other vehicles from leaving or entering. Spike parked parallel to the curb, at the foot of the landscaped yard, about a hundred yards from the front door. He cut the van's engine.

"Phil! Now!"

"OK. Go for it. But you'll be waiting tables if this blows up."

* * *

Danni stretched on her tiptoes in Tiffany's closet, coaxing the pink Barbie box from its hiding place on the top shelf. Torn jeans and sweatshirts fell into her arms as she lowered it. Holding the glossy cardboard carton in both hands, it dawned on her that she was about to break the one trust she'd kept with her daughter. She hesitated. *T'ain't right ta do this.* She reached up to shove everything back on the shelf, but stopped. "Uh-uh. I gotta know where my baby's at."

Danni dropped the clothes and stumbled to Tiffany's bed. "Wha you hidin'?" she asked the box, clutching it to her chest. "My baby ain't allowed ta have no secrets from her mama. Wha's so 'portant she hides it from me?"

She smoothed the crumpled sheets and set down her daughter's stash of secrets. Her heart pounded as she struggled to lift off the lid. It stuck, so she pried at it with her fingernail. The nail broke, and she swore a string of sailor's oaths. "Fuck it," she barked, savagely tearing one side off the cardboard top. The bottom fell on the bed.

Danni stood hunched over the bottom, peering at its contents with fuzzy eyes. There was a layer of colored tissue, then mismatched Hello Kitty socks, and a picture of The Rock. Below that, she found a blackened roach clip, a well-used hash pipe, and four hypodermic needles. Two were brand new, with blue plastic caps.

The barrels of the other two were stained with muddy brown film. The needles were scorched blue-black.

Danni knew the signs all too well. "NOOOO!" she screamed, shaking her fists at God in his heaven. The scream became a shrill wail, wrenched from the depths of her soul. "NOOO-GOD-OHGOD-NOO-PLEASEGOD-NOOO!" She fell heavily to Tiffany's bed, clutching the used syringes. "MY BABY'S A JUNKIE!"

Danni sat on Tiffany's bed, rocking back and forth, and pressing the used syringes to her breast. She lost track of time. "Wha' happen'd ta my precious girl?" she moaned after a while. Cold sweat soaked her clothes. Shudders wracked her body. She clutched her stomach, praying for the pulsing and heaving to go away.

Staring at the hypodermic needles, Danni shivered with dread. "Lord, is she 'dicted? Please don' let her be 'dicted bad." She squeezed her arms around her waist and straightened her spine. "Gotta pull myself together right now," she scolded herself.

She looked around the room for some sign that her daughter was alright. "Oh no! Where's her laptop at?" She craned her neck. "An' her phone 'n backpack?

"The bitch ran away!" Danni shouted. "The fuckin' li'l bitch left me." She threw the bottom of the box at the wall so hard that the corner seams split. A photograph fluttered to the floor.

"Ah-ha! Tha' picture'll tell me wha happen'd ta my baby." Still, she hesitated, fearful of what it would tell her. Pushing up from the mattress, she found her feet. She tiptoed a few steps on spongy knees and rubbery legs, bent down, and picked up the picture.

A heavy black "X" had been drawn across the image from corner to corner, but to Danni's blurry eyes, the photo appeared to be of a man and woman in bed. The man held the camera at the end of his hairy, outstretched arm. As Danni's eyes focused, she followed the arm down to the man's face. "Son of a bitch! It's Geraldo!" She looked closer, and saw sleepy pink eyes and a satisfied smirk.

Despite decades of drugs and alcohol, Danni's sixth sense still sounded the alarm when another woman was messing with her man. That bell had been dinging for months in the background. Now it was clanging. Danni rubbed her eyes with her fists and tried to focus on the woman in the picture. Her eyes were pink, like Geraldo's, and she wore a half smile. "Wait a minute," she sputtered. "That ain't no full-grown woman. Uh-uh." Danni had to hold the picture close to be certain. *Oh, no. No way. It can't be!*

But there was no mistake. *Lord, how could you?*

The pink eyes and freckled face in the photo belonged to her 16-year-old daughter.

The alcoholic fog in Danni's brain lifted, and the sudden clarity staggered her. She stumbled back to the bed. "I been lookin' over my shoulder all this time, and it was YOU!"

She grabbed the used needles and stabbed the images again and again, burying the points in the mattress and dirty sheets, obliterating the faces. Then she tore the picture in pieces and stomped on it with her heel.

"You'll pay, you bitch," she screamed. She stood hunched over the fragments of paper, gasping for breath. "Ya don' never treat yer momma like that. I'm gonna skin ya alive when I find ya." She ground the scraps into the carpet. "An' you, Geraldo, dying without no mercy's too good for you."

CHAPTER 23

After the adrenaline rush chasing the sheriff's car up Highway 1, the next fifteen minutes were torture for Ally and Spike. Hardesty rang the doorbell of the big house, and was admitted by a figure who stood hidden in the shadow of the door. Spike checked the settings on the transmission equipment, and Ally rehearsed her lines in her head. She used her phone to access the county's tax records, and found the name of the owner of the house. After that, all they could do was sit and wait.

Another five minutes passed. "What's he doing in there? Having tea?" Ally demanded. She used the mini-camera to zoom in on the front of the house, and then the garage. Her breath caught in her throat. "There's the van, Spike!" She focused on the license plate. "That's definitely it. It's got the sticker and that stupid vanity plate: RELSTAT. What the hell does that mean, anyway?"

The waiting continued. Spike pounded a beat on the steering wheel. Ally chewed her fingernails. All at once, the front door opened, and Deputy Hardesty led a person down the driveway toward his cruiser. Ally and Spike bolted from the van.

The person's head and upper body were covered by a gray raincoat, and he or she stooped slightly at the waist to keep the raincoat in position. It could have been a smallish man or a largish woman. No features or telltale clothing items were visible. Spike began filming with the mini-camera. He and Ally were so focused on the figure and the cop that they didn't hear another car pull up.

Ally began her narration when the perp was a few steps away from the cruiser. "This is Ally Booker reporting live from Sea Cliff with real-time coverage of the sheriff arresting the suspect in The Storm Drain Murder." She paused so Spike could pan the imposing glass-and-redwood house, then return to the suspect. She continued. "The owner of the house we just showed you, and we believe the person hiding under the raincoat is—"

From nowhere, a man's hand covered Ally's microphone and pulled it away from her face. "That's enough, *chica*," an authoritative voice said. "And you, *mayate*," the voice growled, "shut it down NOW!" Spike bristled at the insult, but obeyed.

Commander Ramon Sepulveda stepped in front of the camera and yanked the microphone from Ally's hand. He switched it off. "You two *pendejos* are begging for an obstruction of justice charge and a major libel suit."

Commander Sepulveda leaned over Ally like a drill sergeant chewing out a new recruit. "Let me make this clear to you before I call your general manager and suggest that you're damaging the station's reputation." He was so angry that specks of spit hit Ally's face. "This subject is a Person of Interest only, and probably will be home in time for dinner. He or she is not a suspect and has not been arrested. No arrest warrant has been issued in this investigation. The cause of the victim's death has not been determined, nor has the victim's identity. That is all the news there is to report."

"But I can see the van," Ally protested, pointing. "It's right there in front of the garage."

Sepulveda jabbed his forefinger at Ally's throat. "Give it up, *chica*. This is my turf. I'll tell you anything the public needs to know."

The commander stood back and wiped his mouth with the back of his hand. Glaring now at Spike, he wrenched the mini-cam from his grip. Sepulveda found the slot that held the memory card and removed it. He held the camera out just beyond Spike's reach. When Spike tried to grab it, Sepulveda let go. The camera grazed Spike's fingertips and crashed to the pavement. A slight smile curled the corners of the commander's lips. "Now get out of here before I decide to start asking about your source in the sheriff's department, who, by the way, was just placed on administrative leave."

He turned and strode toward the deputy's cruiser about 50 yards up the driveway.

Ally gasped with a rare flicker of doubt. She asked herself the unthink-able question: *Could I be wrong?* Every instinct told her the perp was under the raincoat, and the van was the one they were looking for. "I know I'm right," she told herself. "Why's this asshole cop telling me I'm wrong?"

She paced back and forth beside the curb, wavering between crippling insecurity and righteous self-confidence. Insecurity was winning until she heard the clatter of a diesel engine. A large tow truck rumbled up the street, chains and hooks clinking, and yellow lights flashing. Ally grabbed Spike's arm. "Oh my God! They're gonna tow the minivan. They're gonna impound it!" Suddenly, she was bursting. "That means they're going to get a search warrant." *That means I was right!*

The glow of sweet vindication warmed her like the summer sun after a cloudburst. "I knew it!" she cried, pulling power fists from her shoul-ders to her knees. "I'll never doubt my instincts again, you fucker," she shouted at Sepulveda's back.

* * *

An hour after Paige left, Jason finished printing the retainer agreement, a cover letter, and receipts for the past-due and new amounts. He made file copies, slid the originals into a manila envelope, printed an address label, and sealed the flap.

His cell phone buzzed as he stood to leave. Glancing at the screen, he saw the number was blocked and the caller was leaving a message.

An idea hit him. Maybe Geraldo's voicemail had a message with a clue about who killed him or where Danni was. He was pretty sure he could hack into Geraldo's first-generation flip phone's voicemail. He remembered a story from a celebrity gossip show that explained how a British tabloid had hacked into private voicemail accounts a few years ago.

Excited by what he might discover, Jason sat down and dialed Geraldo's cell number from his desk phone. When the call went to voicemail, he dialed the same number from his cell phone. Bingo! The computerized voice said, "Hello, you have eight new messages. Please enter your password and press the *Pound* key." This was the tricky part.

Geraldo was such a technophobe, he probably hadn't changed the default password, but Jason still had to guess it. The most likely choices were 0000 and 1234.

Jason punched in 1234 and *Pound*, and waited. Nothing. "Damn it!" He clicked off both phones and repeated the procedure. This time he dialed 0000 and *Pound*. The line was silent. Then the voice said, "First new message."

Jason grabbed a pen and some scratch paper. The first was from Walter Cripps, and was matter-of-fact. "Geraldo, this is Walter. You need to put some money in the bank right away so I can pay the guys and the suppliers. Call me. I'm at the office."

Next came a woman with a bored and edgy voice: "OK, Geraldo. I'm in Sea Cliff, like you wanted. You said you needed to talk to me in person, so let's get it over with. Call my cell."

That was followed by another woman, who sounded young and angry: "That's three blue 'plus' signs in a row, Geraldo. Don't tell me to wait or try a different brand. You better call me."

The fourth message said, "Mr. O'Brien, this is Sea Breeze Cardiological Solutions calling with your test results. Please call us urgently to discuss. Our number is 1-800-STATINS."

"Geraldo had a heart condition?" Jason said, surprised. The man appeared to be the picture of robust, sexagenarian health, despite heavy drug and alcohol use. The image of Geraldo's bloated, decaying corpse flashed behind Jason's eyes. *Could he have died from a heart attack? But then how'd he wind up in the storm drain?*

Suddenly, it was too creepy. "I'm spying on a dead man. What if a stranger listened to my voicemails?" Like Erin's little love messages—sometimes sweet, sometimes erotic—or Courtney's demands in the divorce, or his father's midnight ramblings about achieving success and being a man. He held the phone away from his ear and was about to click off when the next message began to play. He listened, despite his misgivings.

It was a letdown. The call was from Pedro, saying he needed to be paid. Then came Jason's message from yesterday morning.

Message number seven sent chills down his spine. "Geraldo," a man with a heavy Mexican accent said in a deep baritone. "You got somethin' belong to me, an' I wannit." Raspy breathing filled a moment of dead air. Jason searched his memory, but couldn't identify the voice. It continued, "You don' give it to me, this time I cut off part of your body you want." A deep chuckle. "Or maybe I kill you. Don' fuck with me, amigo."

Jason stared at the phone in disbelief. "'Cut off part of your body you want'?" he whispered. The evil in the voice made his neck hairs stand on end. "Geraldo's scar," he thought out loud. "Was it this guy who cut him? Sounds like they have a history, so could be. El Carnicero? Is that a leap, just because I happen to know Geraldo owes him money?"

"Eighth new message." The computer voice broke into Jason's thoughts. A man whispered: "Geraldo, this is Jamie. At the bank. Listen. I just got notice the Feds are comin' next week to inspect the bank's books. You and Mags gotta get current on your loan for the spec house. I can't hide a $2.5 million loan without a single payment for a year-and-a-half. And I hear rumors you split town. I know you won't leave me hangin', buddy, but you're goin' down with me if you do."

Jason punched *End* and dropped the phone on his desk. The message meant Geraldo had sacrificed his moneyman. The last shred of hope Geraldo wasn't screwing the investors was gone. He rested his elbows on his desk and propped his forehead in his hands. If he tried really hard, he could rationalize Geraldo missing some payments and getting into default. But no payments for eighteen months? *He was playing all of us investors and the bank for fools from the get-go!*

The shock of loss he felt yesterday evaporated. Self-preservation took over. He stood and picked up the phone. "You screwed me, Geraldo," he said to the blank screen. "You stole my $30,000 and planned to from the moment we shook hands. You owe me another $8,750. I will get it all back from you. I'll be administrator of your estate and I'll control the assets."

He grabbed his wallet, keys, and Paige's envelope. "I'll do whatever it takes," he vowed. "I'll start checking the assets this afternoon, and the Grand National Bank of the Cayman Islands will be first."

CHAPTER 24

The air was warm and the sky bright blue as Jason walked to his car and beeped it open. From his vantage point at the top of the Charles Street hill, he could see over Main Street and Highway 1, almost as far as the coast. For once, there wasn't a cloud in sight or any fog on the horizon.

He put the top down for his trip to Bluffside Drive and James Paige's house. Cruising Del Mar Road's gentle curves and long slopes, he inhaled the scents of pine and ocean. The sun warmed his head and shoulders. The Porsche's exhaust burbled behind his ear, and Etta James sang softly on the sound system. Between the stands of pine, he saw the vast Pacific, so calm today it looked like honed blue granite, punctuated by sinuous veins of white quartz.

His business with James Paige was finished quickly. Paige opened his door with checks in hand. Jason gave him the manila envelope and his American Express card. "Sign both copies of the retainer agreement and initial both copies of the cover letter," Jason instructed. "Keep the originals and return the copies to my office tomorrow." Paige grunted and closed the door in his face.

Jason decided to go directly to his bank to deposit Paige's checks, then to his office to pay some bills and start the asset search. He was curious, however, to see what the spec house looked like on a sunny day, so he drove to the south end of Bluffside Drive, where the house sprawled across its corner lot.

He pulled over at the corner of Bluffside and Driftwood Lane, angling his car to see the front and side of the house. It didn't look as oppressive as yesterday in the fog, but was gray and foreboding, nonetheless.

Yellow crime-scene tape cordoned off the entire lot, and he saw an evidence seal on the front door and jamb. Yellow tape also guarded the dirt path along the front of the house, where he'd gotten mud all over his Guccis. He wondered whether the tape meant the sheriff's investigators had discovered the drugs, or had decided the death might be a homicide.

Jason sat in his car, studying the house. He kicked himself mentally for believing Geraldo when he said the house would sell for $4.75 million. Shaking his head, he slipped the Porsche into gear and drove slowly along Driftwood to where the yellow tape turned and ran perpendicular to the street, down the rear lot line.

Stopping again, he looked carefully at the back wall of the house, just above the ground. He'd barely caught it, but it seemed that a section of the shingle siding had moved. He felt a puff of breeze, and this time saw it clearly—a midget-sized door swung open, then closed. Curiosity piqued, he peered at the wall. He decided there must be a crawl space under the house and the door gave access to it. The door was nearly invisible because it blended into the pattern of the siding.

He drummed his fingers on the gearshift knob, asking himself what Geraldo was up to. Why would he bother to disguise access to the crawl space? Was he hiding something under the house? Drugs? Money? The safe deposit key for the Cayman Islands bank? The door swung wide open, revealing a black opening. *Did someone find what he's hiding?*

Jason shut off the engine and got out quietly. He ducked under the yellow tape and walked hunchbacked across the grass to the little door. It was about three feet square. "Hello?" he called, sticking his head into the opening. "Hello? Anyone in here?" He squeezed his shoulders into the doorway. There was only blackness after the bright sunshine, so he paused to let his eyes adjust.

Faint light filtered through the foundation vents, and a dank earth odor filled his nose. He dragged his chest and hips over the sill. Pushing himself onto his hands and knees, he crawled into the cool darkness.

His right arm and leg were swept from under him. A hand shoved the back of his head, slamming his face into the dirt. A sharp point pierced the side of his neck, and his left arm was pulled behind him past the point of pain.

"What the fuck do you want?" a man's voice growled.

CHAPTER 25

The man knelt on Jason's back, forcing the air from his lungs. Dirt clogged his nose and mouth. His arm was being torn from its socket and blood trickled down his neck.

The man bent to Jason's right ear. "You wanna die, motherfuck, breakin' inta my home?"

Jason's chest heaved and stars flashed behind his eyes. He didn't dare move his head or body, but his right hand was free. He tapped the man's thigh twice.

"You tryin' to tap out, you fuckin' piece of shit?" The man head-bumped the back of Jason's head, jamming his nose into the dirt. "So, you a pussy, too?" He giggled. "Ooo, I'm gonna have fun with you." He twisted the knifepoint back and forth.

Through his pain and panic, the raspy voice and stench of dried sweat and lived-in clothes were familiar. *I know that voice.*

"Admiral Bill," Jason croaked, spitting dirt. "For God's sake. It's me— Jason. Let me up."

"I don't think so," the voice said, but the knifepoint pulled back a little and the tension on his arm eased slightly. "OK," the man challenged. "If you're Jason you know this question. If you ain't…." He pushed the knife forward just a bit. "So here's the question: What'd you buy me for breakfast yesterday morning?"

"Shit, Bill, I don't know." Jason struggled to remember. He'd seen Bill at Bites 'n Bytes. The TVs were blaring about the boat sinking in Rock Bay. Bill wanted to trade information for breakfast. He'd ordered him a croissant, but… he wanted … an egg melt.

The man yanked Jason's arm again. "Goddammit, Bill, stop!" he yelped. He coughed up dirt. "It was an egg melt!"

Bill withdrew the knife and released Jason's arm. He slid off his back. "You ought not to do that, Counselor. You coulda got killed."

Jason rolled several feet away, out of the man's reach. "I just saw the open door. I was curious." He pulled himself to his knees, bumping his head against something hard. Twisting slightly, he saw it was a plastic pipe suspended from the joists that supported the first floor of the house. The joists themselves were about four feet above the ground. Perhaps a dozen vents punctuated the foundation, admitting rectangles of light that illuminated the crawl space just enough for Jason to make out Bill's features.

"This here's my home," Bill said indignantly. "What if I broke inta your home? You'd be pissed, you would." The last sounded defensive.

Jason touched his neck and pulled his hand away, staring at the blood. "Damn, Counselor," Bill said, "lookit what you made me do to you." He offered Jason a dirty rag. "I don't got any BandAids."

Jason took the rag and dabbed at his neck until the bloody trickle slowed. He clasped his hand over his shoulder, rolling it forward and backward. "Feels like you dislocated it," he grumbled.

The little access door swung open and closed, and the flash of daylight caught Jason's eye. The bright light outside drew him to it, like a moth to a flame. He crept toward it, favoring his left shoulder as much as possible, but stopped after a few feet, unable to ignore the little voice in his head: *Bill probably knows what Geraldo was up to, maybe even how he died.*

The Admiral and his band of homeless vets knew virtually everything about every person in Sea Cliff. Bill normally traded his information for food or favors, as he had yesterday morning. But now that Bill had hurt him, Jason reasoned, he'd want to make up for it. He turned his back on the square of sunshine and sat facing Bill in the gloom, staring at him with hard eyes and wiping his neck when the blood threatened to drip.

Ducking under pipes and wires, Bill knee-walked to where Jason sat. His grimy hands trembled as he tried to brush the dirt off Jason's silk sport shirt. Jason shrugged him away. Bill reached out again, but Jason pulled back. "I'm sorry, Counselor. It's just that I don't got any place—"

Jason glanced over his shoulder at the daylight, forcing himself to shut it out of his mind. "It's OK, Bill. I should've called out again, or waited 'til you answered. I understand. You thought I was going to attack you or steal something."

"Yeah," Bill said meekly, not meeting Jason's gaze.

The two men sat in silence. Bill stabbed his hunting knife into the dirt and retied his boots. Jason pressed the rag against his neck with his right hand, and rotated his left shoulder to ease the pain. After a while, he said, "Hey, it's not a bad deal you got here, though."

Bill brightened. "Yeah, it's dry and warm enough. I got a propane burner when it does get cold." He pointed behind him into the dimness. Jason followed his gesture and barely made out a two-burner camp stove and a five-gallon propane tank. "It's quiet, too, mostly." A hint of pride entered Bill's voice. "None a my men's got so good a place. Hey, you gotta see this." He scrambled toward the center of the crawl space.

Jason's eyes had adjusted, and now he made out four vertical posts or beams that extended up into the structure of the house. He crawled after Bill, slowed by his aching shoulder. "The elevator runs on these here," Bill said when they reached the posts. The light from the foundation vents gleamed softly on them, and Jason saw that they actually were steel girders, and that the elevator's tracks were bolted to them. The ends of the girders were set into the corners of a concrete pad that was about six feet by six feet. In the middle of the pad, buried up to its hinges, appeared to be a child-sized coffin. The top was heavy-duty metal with two compression locks.

"Is that—" Jason started to ask.

"Yep, but wait 'til you see what's inside. Your man Geraldo's got a sick sense of humor."

Bill used both hands to unscrew the compression locks. He yanked the handles, straining to raise the lid. "Hermetic seal," he grunted as he struggled. "Hard to break." Panting, he scampered around to the hinge side of the lid. He kneeled and reached over it, pulling with his back and arms. The seal finally broke with a *thwucking* sound.

Bill's face lit up with a magician's smile. He glanced to see if Jason was watching, then yanked the top open. It crashed against the concrete. "Check it out, man."

Jason leaned over the open coffin, straining to make out the vague shapes inside. "What's in it?"

Bill crawled to his camp stove and returned with a box of kitchen matches. He lit one, but the flaming head broke off and flew toward the stove, landing in a pile of charred matchsticks next to it. "Damn," Bill said, lighting another match. This one burned true, and he threw it into the opening. Jason saw the casket was about five feet long and three feet deep before the flame died. It contained a dozen bread-loaf-sized bundles wrapped in heavy-duty plastic, arranged in two long rows of six each. He smelled the strong odor of cured cannabis.

"When I found this place a week ago," Bill said, "the elevator was down and I never even seen the casket. Didn't know it was there. When the elevator went up, I opened it and saw it was full a every kinda drug. That was before the party. I didn't dare take none, 'cause I didn't wanna get found out, so I locked it up tight. But now Geraldo's dead and I got me some company…."

He scooped up one of the bundles, set it on the concrete, and tried to slit the plastic wrap with the point of his hunting knife. The point was too dull, so he wrapped both hands around the handle and stabbed the package. It spilled open. "Don't ya want some smoke?" he asked, eyes dancing with anticipation.

Jason shook his head and pointed to his neck.

"You'll feel better." The corners of Bill's lips turned down to form his upside-down smile.

"No, thanks."

"Mind if I do?"

Although Jason's body was slowed by pain, his mind wasn't. He wanted to pick Bill's brain, and Bill wanted to get stoned. Perfect. Jason shrugged. "Go ahead."

Bill searched his pockets and found a ragged pack of Zig-Zags. He rolled a fat joint and lit it with a kitchen match. Inhaling deeply, he held the smoke in his lungs. "Rippy shit," he squeaked without exhaling.

Jason sat quietly while Bill took several more hits. After a while, Bill's eyes got glazy and he began to hum "Whiter Shade of Pale." Jason decided it was time to begin questioning him. "So, Bill, what's going on here?"

"I'm gettin' spaced, man. Totally. An' you ain't, which ain't polite, seeing as how you my guest." He offered the roach to Jason. "You gotta try this, man. It don't get no better."

Jason shook his head. Bill made the peace sign and plopped the roach onto his tongue. "No, Bill, I mean what's going on with Geraldo?"

"Geraldo's your man, Counselor. You know everything 'bout him. You run his business and keep his papers. Everyone knows."

"Yeah, well, everyone's wrong. He only tells me what he wants me to know, and he keeps his files locked in his house. I don't know half of what he does. Or did. Like this," Jason pointed at the coffin buried in the concrete pad. "What's this all about?"

Bill reached into the open dope bundle and pinched out a palm-full of dried leaves. He crushed them and sprinkled the flakes into a new paper. All the while, he stared at Jason from under shaggy eyebrows. He rolled the joint carefully, tapering the ends and licking the length of it. "You don' know nothing 'bout his dealing?"

"I know he was the man to go to for an ounce, but I don't know anything about all this."

"Then you not so smart as I thought. No way." Bill scratched the back of his head and looked at Jason quizzically. "What about Tiffany and Danni? Whaddya know 'bout them?"

Jason's breath caught. "Tiffany? What's happened to her?"

"Sheeiit, man." Bill regarded him with cocked head and slack lips. His tongue licked the corners of his mouth. When he didn't speak, Jason reached for the kitchen matches and lit one. He extended it to Bill, who held one end of the joint in the flame. When it caught, he inhaled so deeply the paper burned nearly all the way to his fingers. Jason snuffed out the match in the dirt.

"Bill," he said softly. "Tell me about Tiffany."

"All a Miller Street knows." Bill's voice was thick and his words slurred. "They fought all the time, the three of 'em. All hours of the night. Breakin' dishes, throwin' pots, swearin' to blue Jesus. One time, Geraldo tried to run Danni down and took out the front steps. Left him for a week that time, she did."

"But Tiffany, Bill. Tell me about Tiffany."

"She run away with her little friend, Veronica. I seen her leave."

"C'mon, Bill. There must be more to the story. Why'd she leave?"

Bill was silent for a moment. When he spoke, it was as if his words were trying to keep up with the images in his mind. "Geraldo was such a pig, man. A ruttin' pig!" He took another hit. "I used to stand on a paint can outside her house and watch her through the TV room window. Sweetest sweet sixteen, you know? All them little freckles and girly bows. After a while, Geraldo started messin' with her. A little smoke and some kissin'. Then a little blow, and he was all over her. He showed her how to shoot up, and soon they was shootin' each other up."

"Jesus! Why didn't Danni stop it?"

"Huh? Danni?" Bill paused, far away. "I 'spect she was down at Mostly's, drinkin' and screwin' everything in pants."

Jason saw now that every adult in Tiffany's life had betrayed her, including himself. *Why did I let her shut me out? The needle tracks on her arm—it was obvious.* The story of abuse unlocked hated memories of weeks and months in foster homes, the whispered rumors, the constant fear. *What if I'd been abused like that, and no adult helped me? I couldn't have been that strong. I'd have walked into the ocean.*

Bill pulled his knees up to his chest and buried his head between them. His shoulders heaved, but he made no sound. With his head still bowed, he spoke to the dirt between his boots. "And I just couldn't watch no more, man." Another heave and a snuffle. "Breaks my heart, don't you see. So young and pure."

Jason realized he was holding his breath. He exhaled and breathed in deeply, and made a silent promise to Tiffany: *I'll do everything I can to find you and help you.* He waited for Bill to continue, watching his shoulders contract in silent spasms. Minutes passed.

Finally, Bill raised his head just enough to press his dirty palms to his eyes, rotating them like he was wiping tears. When he spoke this time, his voice boomed in the close space. "And now the man's dead. Rotted in a drainpipe. He deserved to die, and worse'n he did." Bill looked up, fixing Jason with black raccoon eyes.

"I know how Geraldo died, Counselor. And I seen who done it."

CHAPTER 26

Nikki paced the deck outside the Ocean Wave Hair Salon. She lit a cigarette, spotted the one burning on the railing, walked over to it, and stubbed it out. Taking a long drag off the new one, she crossed her arms and paced, flicking ashes and burning holes in her sleeve. From far away, someone called her name. She whirled around and saw April, the salon's receptionist, behind the window yelling at her. April looked angry. Nikki flipped her off and leaned against the railing, out of sight.

"Why today, of all days?" she ranted to herself. "I'm booked solid 'til eight o'clock tonight. I'll make a week's worth of tips." She'd just walked out on Mrs. Agnes Smithers, a really good tipper, leaving her hair full of shampoo. All because her watch *binked* just as she was about to rinse Agnes, and she'd paused to read the text message from Brenda, her big sister:

Erin and Jason broke up this morning!

Nikki left the old woman tipped back in her chair, head dangling over the sink. "Oh my God!" she'd cried. She'd ripped off her apron and run out of the salon, reading the message over and over.

"It's my time," Nikki told herself as she paced. "This can only mean it's my time." She felt a rare rush of affection for her sister. Brenda was Erin's best friend, and the two shared every confidence. Brenda always made fun of Nikki for liking Jason so much, because he belonged to Erin and was so much older than Nikki. "But look at Brenda now!" she marveled. With one text message, she'd handed Jason to Nikki, favoring her little sister over her best friend. It was totally not Brenda, and Nikki had to be suspicious. She scowled, trying to spot the unseen trap, the evil intent. A cigarette later, she gave up. "Screw it!" she said. "Who cares? He's mine for the taking."

Nikki knew just what she had to do. She'd go to Jason right now and make him give her a ride in his Porsche, like he promised. She'd make him see this is the time, and she was the one. She'd be a tease if she had to, but she'd be cool. So cool. Not desperate, though, because Brenda said men hate desperation as much as women do.

She let her fantasy play out in her head. They'd drive up the coast to Big Sur and park, looking at the ocean. She'd dig her fingers into his gorgeous hair. She'd put her head on his shoulder, and be all sweet and innocent, and they'd snuggle. The leather seats would be warm on her skin. They'd kiss. She'd give him kisses he'd never forget. She gulped and felt her cheeks flush scarlet. *We'll make love with the top down!* Red-hot heat surged through her body. She hugged herself, suddenly aching with anticipation. *Yes! Oh my God, yes! We'll get naked and do it in front of God and anyone who's watching. Anything's possible on this most wonderful day!*

Her watch *binked* again. She stopped pacing to read a new text from Brenda:

Erin's totally pissed I told you she and Jason broke up. I'll kill you if you say anything to him.

Nikki stamped her heel on the wooden deck. "Dammit!" she swore. "It *is* a plot! I shoulda known. Brenda and Erin want me to go to him, or they wouldn't of told me not to. They think I'll be his rebound girl, and when he's done with me, he'll go back to Erin. Or…or…they want me to throw myself at him so he'll see how much better Erin is."

Crushed and torn by indecision, she sank against the deck railing. If they wanted her to go to him, maybe she shouldn't. Her cigarette singed her fingers. She dropped the butt and scrunched it with the toe of her sandal. She reconsidered a second later. But if she waited, Erin might get back together with him forever, and she'd never have another chance.

She lit another cigarette. *I've gotta follow my first instinct. That's what Dr. Phil always says.*

She'd seen Jason leave his office with his briefcase and drive away in his sexy silver Porsche. "He must be at home," she figured, "so that's where I'll go." She dropped her cigarette and marched into the salon, ignoring dirty looks from Agnes Smithers and the stylists. She grabbed her keys.

"What're you doing?" April hissed. Nikki walked right past the shampoo station and out the back door. "You can't leave," April yelled. "You'll get fired!"

Nikki slipped behind the wheel of her pink Miata and twisted the rearview mirror to inspect her makeup. As she touched up her bright-red lipstick and poofed her platinum curls, she imagined the conversation with Jason. Speaking to her reflection, she said, "No matter how it goes, I know what I'm gonna say to make him mine forever." She repeated her speech until she got her facial expressions just right. Satisfied, she checked her boobs in the mirror, hiked them up, and pulled her tissue tee shirt so tight her red bra and new black-rose tattoo showed through. She blew herself a kiss. *Erin doesn't have a chance.*

She stuck the key into the ignition and turned it. Nothing happened. "Crap!" she cursed. "Did I forget to get gas?" Panicked, she tried again. This time, the engine coughed and sputtered to life. She shifted into gear and headed toward her destiny.

Daylight turned to twilight as she crossed Highway 1. Thick mist covered the landscape, dripping from tree limbs and rooftops.

Nikki was oblivious to everything but the thumping of her heart as she turned onto Crescent Lane. She'd never been to Jason's house, but was certain she'd know it from the picture on his desk. Her favorite retro band so far this week, The Cardigans, pounded in her earbuds, and Nikki sang along as she cruised the curving street:

♫ Love me, love me
Say that you love me ♫

Jason's house was in the middle of Crescent Lane's long curve, and she recognized it when she saw it. Her stomach fluttered and her palms grew sweaty on the steering wheel. All at once, her bubble of confidence burst, and she asked herself, "Am I really gonna do this?"

She pictured herself knocking on the front door. Jason answers. She pours her heart out. He slams the door. "But it won't be that way," Nikki promised herself. She imagined the scene again. This time, Jason answers the door with a big smile. He's wearing his running shorts and a muscle shirt. His biceps are as big as boulders. She tells him they're meant to be with each other forever. He squeezes her in his strong arms and they fall on the couch together....

Nikki drove past Jason's house all the way around Crescent Lane and out the west gate. Driving back up Del Mar, she turned onto Crescent at the east gate. She coasted silently to the house and parked in front of the walkway. As she pulled up, she saw a full-dress Harley Hawg parked behind a tree near the corner of the yard.

She got out of her car, staring in disbelief. "Oh my God!"

The motorcycle was like one she'd seen on the cover of *Biker* magazine, with chrome everything, leather streamers, studded and fringed saddlebags, whitewalls, ape hangers, and seats for two. "Jason got a motorcycle!" she exclaimed. "It's so cool! And sooo big!" She traced her fingers along the gas tank, tingling with excitement. She whispered, "Jason...I never knew. You are so baaad! The Porsche can wait. I want a ride on this!"

She ran her hand over the seats and touched the pointed studs on the saddlebags. Kneeling to look at the chrome engine, she felt its heat, and decided that meant he'd just gotten home.

Next, she noticed the rear license plate. "N4SR." She sounded it out several times before she got "Enforcer."

"Oh my God!" she squeaked. "He's into...what's it called? Masochism? No, sadochism?" She staggered against the big machine, terrified and aching with desire at the same time. "Well," she gulped, "maybe just a little would be OK."

Nikki climbed the steps of the house of the man she loved. A man about whom she'd just learned unimaginable, exciting, terrifying secrets. "OK, be cool," she told herself. "Here we go." She pressed the button, but heard no bell. Exhaling with relief, she composed herself and was about to knock on the door when she heard a grunt and loud crash. She went rigid. *Oh, no! Does he have another woman in there?* Another crash. *Is he being sadochistic with her?* "Bitch!" she screamed. "You can't have him! He's mine!"

For the first time, Nikki shivered in her tissue tee. Spinning around, she couldn't see her car through the mist. She tiptoed down the front steps and crouched, slinking around the corner of the house to a side window. Raising her head just enough to see inside, she peeked into a bedroom. She gasped.

The bed's headboard and frame were upside down. The box spring and mattress were slashed from end to end. The chair back and seat cushions were slit open and the stuffing pulled out. The biggest Mexican man she'd ever seen pulled drawers from the dresser, dumped them, and threw them against the wall, shattering them. "*Dónde está?*" he roared, yanking the dresser onto its back and kicking in the sides.

The big man walked by the window. He glanced down and stopped, glaring at her.

Nikki stared at his face, terrified but unable to look away. In a blink, she saw crazed black eyes and *El Carnicero* branded into his forehead. The man's lips pulled back in a snarl.

"*Espia!*" he bellowed. His fist smashed through the window, showering her with blood and glass. Knuckles the size of walnuts tattooed with DETH flashed before her eyes, missing her face by an inch. Thick fingers grabbed for her curls, catching a few strands.

"EEEKKK!" Nikki screamed. "EEEKKK! Get away! Don't touch me!" She lunged backward, landing on her butt. Scrambling to her feet, she stumbled through the fog, shrieking and running blindly for the safety of her pink Miata.

Jason's front door slammed behind her. Footsteps pounded so near she heard the man's heavy breathing. He yelled, "*Puta! Alto ahi!*"

Nikki fumbled for her keys as she ran. "Please start! Please start!" she prayed.

She pulled open the driver's door and got in just as the man reached the passenger's side. He yanked the door handle so hard the car shook. Hands shaking, she missed the ignition switch. Trying again, she jammed in the key and twisted it. The motor started but died. "Oh my God!" she cried. She twisted the key harder. The motor caught. She shoved the shifter into first at the same moment a huge fist punched through the convertible top. Bloody fingers reached for her hair.

Nikki screamed again and floored the accelerator. The man ran beside the car for a second before yanking out his hand.

She stared in the rearview mirror as she sped away. A giant man stood in the fog shaking his fist and yelling. The only word she heard was "*muerta.*"

CHAPTER 27

The crawl space under the spec house was freezing now. Moist air blew through the foundation vents, and the faint light they admitted grew more dim as the fog outside thickened. The only sounds were crashing waves and screeching seagulls.

Jason shivered in his silk shirt. "I'm really cold, Bill. How 'bout if we get some heat from your stove."

"Sure," Bill said agreeably without moving.

After a moment, Jason understood. "Don't worry. I'll give you some money for the propane."

"You know, it is kinda cold down here. Some heat'd be good." Bill wobbled toward the camp stove on his hands and knees. Jason crawled after him, favoring his painful left shoulder.

Bill cranked both burner knobs full open and searched for the kitchen matches. As the odor of propane gas spread, Jason scooted back. Bill lit a match clumsily and held it to one of the burners. Flames leapt up to the floor joists, and in the brief flash of light, Jason saw scorch marks on the wood. When the area got warmer, Bill turned down the burners. They sat cross-legged next to each other, warming their hands.

"That's better," Jason said. He sat quietly for a few minutes before he said, "You know, I'm going to be the lawyer for Geraldo's estate, so it'd really help if you told me everything about the night he died. I can pay you or get you some work if you want."

Bill stared at the flames without speaking before he crept to the propane tank. Reaching behind it, he produced a pint of tequila. "My friend Jose here'll help me remember." He wiped down the bottle with a ragged sleeve and offered it to Jason. "Might help you warm up."

Jason took a sip. "So, tell me," he said, handing back the bottle. "What's going on with the coffin and all the drugs?"

"Like I told you, Counselor, that box was full of every kind of drug when I first seen it."

"What's Geraldo doing with all those drugs?"

Bill stretched out in front of the stove. Shadows danced across his face as the flames surged and flickered. "You really don' know shit, do you? An' all this time I thought you was so smart." He took a long pull of tequila. "OK, Counselor. I'm gonna teach ya the alphabet. Your man Geraldo, he's the drug kingpin here on the coast 'tween 'Frisco an' LA. Got people coming and going, buying and selling drugs all over California. Even up into Orygun and Washington."

"Is this his storehouse? Doesn't seem big enough."

"Uh-uh. This here's just a distribution point. He got storage lockers all over. Keeps his best shit in climate-controlled lockers over the hill in the valley, I hear."

"How does it work? Do you know?"

"Man, you folks in the straight world got eyes, but don' see nothing." Bill said "straight world" with contempt. "Lemme ask you something. You ever notice the guys working on Geraldo's buildings? You ever notice they's never the same?"

Jason took a short swig of tequila and felt the warm rush in his stomach. "Well, Pedro. He's on every job."

Bill snorted. "Yeah, Pedro. He killed a man in Mexico that owed him money and now he plays it straight so he don't get deported. Shows up most every day and works his full eight. But that ain't the story. Geraldo's workers, to you, they's just a bunch a Mexicans and lowlifes and gang-bangers with tattoos, and they all look the same, right?"

"You're right. I never noticed."

"Well, you need to open your eyes, Counselor. He got runners from Mexico and Arizona, and bulldogs from Fresno. He got homeboys from East LA and San Diego. He even got some guys in little boats. One a my men saw 'em up by Simon's Cove. They all bring him his shit. They work awhile to make it look legit, you know, before they scatter up and down the coast, making deliveries. They bring the money back and work a little more, and Geraldo, he just gets fat."

Bill rambled nonstop now, as if the tequila and marijuana had flipped a switch in his brain. "He even got growers in Mendo and Humboldt sending him their dope, 'cause he's got the network and the buyers."

Jason half-listened as he processed this new information. Geraldo would have huge amounts of cash to dispose of, and that was why he had bank accounts all over the country. He probably funneled the money through them into the bank in the Caymans. His workers would launder some of the money in Sea Cliff when they cashed their paychecks. It dawned on him that he was part of the scheme because he cashed Geraldo's checks! Same for Walter Cripps and Mags. Even Jamie at the bank must've run Geraldo's dirty money through his accounts.

Bill lay on his back, talking to the joists in a slurred voice. "I knew something was about to happen on the day of the party 'cause I come back here and most of the drugs was gone from the casket. The fog was thicker'n pea-soup that night, and 'bout ten o'clock all kinds a people started showin' up. I hid behind that escallonia bush in front and seen 'em all."

Jason focused on Bill's every word now. "There was Mags Turlock, and Danni, and little Tiffany, and that big Mexican guy I tol' ya 'bout—El Carnicero—but I didn't know who he was then, and some pretty blonde thang I didn't recognize, kinda tall, but man, was she built, and Pedro, and a bunch a others I seen around town—coming and going, some of 'em totin' out shopping bags full of dope and pills."

Bill stopped abruptly. Jason looked at his face in the flickering light and saw his eyes were closed. "Bill," Jason said, touching his shoulder. "What happened?"

"Huh?"

"The party. All the people. The drugs."

"Oh, yeah." Bill raised himself onto his elbow and stared at the flames. "Well, I come back down here when they was all inside, and they was up there whoopin' and hollerin', and having a good ole time, so I had my own li'l party down here with my buddy Jose." He tipped the bottle upright and drained it. "Next thing I know, there's this big crash. *Boom!* Like a hun'erd-pound sack a potatas hitting the deck. The whole house shook." He shuddered. "I thought it's a earthquake and I'd get buried down here, so I ran outside."

Bill's voice trailed off as he pushed himself upright and nearly fell over. "I been wanting to tell this to someone for so long, but it's got all fuzzy." He threw the empty bottle at the pier post, missing by several feet. "Damn booze."

His face contorted in the firelight as if he was struggling for his thoughts. "I ran outside and hid behind the bush and waited for the house to fall down." He leaned forward, elbows on knees, covering his eyes with his palms. "I seen all them people run out a the house. Some of 'em was carrying their bags of drugs. They all got in their cars and drove away. Then…then…I must've blacked out, 'cause I don't remember nothing for a while." He wiped away tears with his fingers. "I'm sorry, Counselor. I got no tolerance for hard liquor."

The wind sighed through the foundation vents, and the flames popped and sputtered. Jason moved closer to the stove and held out his hands to warm them. They were grimy in the weak light, and he felt filthy all over. He wanted a long shower, but knew he had to deposit Paige's checks before the bank closed, and guessed it was probably late afternoon already. No matter. He couldn't leave until he got the rest of Bill's story.

"Bill," he said with as much sympathy as he could put in his voice, "I understand you're fuzzy. Just tell me what you can remember. You're outside behind the escallonia bush, and…."

Bill straightened his back and crossed his legs in front of him. "OK. Yeah. I seen the front door open and two people carrying a body. A man's body, by the size of it. One of 'em had the feet and the other had the shoulders. The one holdin' the shoulders had a baseball cap pulled low. They dragged it to a minivan and shoved it in the passenger seat. Baseball cap went 'round to the driver's side and got in, but I don' know where the other one went."

"Was he dead?"

"Mebbe. Don' rightly know. I seen lotsa dead bodies in 'Nam. This one was pretty loose. Could've been fresh dead or unconscious. Its butt kept wantin' to drag."

"Did you see who the two were?"

"Uh-uh. Never did see the one that disappeared."

"How do you know the body was Geraldo?"

"'Cause I followed the van all the way down Bluffside to Vista Point. It had ta go real slow 'cause it was so foggy and drippy. I walked an' kept up, an' I hid behind the bushes an' trees so's they wouldn't see me. I froze my ass, I tell you, and...." He paused mid-sentence.

"And?"

"Christ almighty! Hang on, will ya? I need ta try ta get my head straight." Bill banged his temples with open palms. "Alright." He flapped his hands and rubbed them together. "OK. So I followed the van on down to Vista Point. It was silver, in case you care. And when I got to Vista Point, I hid behind that big rock in the parking lot. You know?"

"I can picture it."

"Then the driver gets out and opens the passenger door, and drags out the body, and I seen 'em both. I wasn't more'n ten feet away. It was Geraldo, with all his silvery hair."

"Who was the driver? Did you see the driver?"

Bill's mouth opened, but he didn't speak. He cleared his throat. His eyes darted from the joists above his head, to the stove, to the distant pier post—everywhere but Jason's face.

"The...the...driver dragged the body over to the dirt path. Coulda been heading for the cliff or the storm drain. Looked like they tripped an' lost their balance. Anyway, Geraldo goes into the drainpipe headfirst. Now he's dead for sure."

"Did you see the driver?"

"I just tol' ya I did."

"So, who was it, Bill? Tell me who the driver was."

"I been waitin' to tell someone, 'cause it's eating me up." Bill slumped onto his side in the dirt and curled into a fetal ball. "But thing is," he whispered, "I can't tell no one."

"Why? Why can't you tell me?"

"'Cause I seen it happen!" he wailed, nearly in tears. "An' the cops'll find out and throw me in jail 'til I die 'cause they'll say I'm a accomplice 'cause I din't try to stop it and I ain't never going back to jail!"

"Bill, listen to me. That doesn't make you an accomplice. I'm the one person you can trust. I'm your lawyer, remember? All the times I've represented you and gotten you out of jail? You can tell me anything, and I can't ever repeat a word of it if you don't want me to."

"Even after what I done to you today, you're my lawyer?" he whispered from the darkness. "You'd still help me?"

"I'm your lawyer 'til you fire me. Whatever you tell me in confidence is our secret."

Bill sat up. "'Cause it's a privilege?"

"Right. Attorney-client privilege. You own everything you tell me. Forever. So, will you tell me who the driver was?"

Bill hesitated, as if the secret had been buried so long it wouldn't come out. He cleared his throat. "It was mmm…mmm…." He coughed, and coughed again, hacking up phlegm. "Goddammit!" He spat into the darkness and pounded his breastbone.

Jason reached over and touched his knee. "It's OK. Take your time."

Bill rolled his head and rotated his shoulders forward and backward. He took a deep breath. When he finally spoke, it was without hesitation.

"It was Mags." The words rushed out. "Mags was the driver."

"And Mags dumped Geraldo in the storm drain? You're sure?"

"Yup. Without a doubt. It was her. Mags Turlock killed Geraldo."

PART 3

UNEXPECTED ENCOUNTERS

CHAPTER 28

Jason left One Bluffside and drove to his bank's drive-up window to deposit James Paige's checks. With the Porsche's automatic lease payment due, he wanted to be certain the funds would be available right away. The teller confirmed they would be, and he began his drive home, feeling he'd accomplished at least one critical task that day.

The pain in his left shoulder flared as he drove, which brought his mind back to the crawl space, Admiral Bill, and his claim that Mags killed Geraldo. Jason thought of several reasons he could be right.

For one thing, she was a big woman and was strong enough to move the body and dump it.

She also had motive. Her cash was tied up in the spec house, so she couldn't make payments on her investment properties and could lose them. And there was the foreclosure of the loan on the spec house. Geraldo bragged he always cut his risk by having Mags co-sign for him, and Jason thought it likely she'd co-signed the $2.5 million note that was in default. He whistled softly. "She could lose everything!"

He switched on his headlights as he inched his way up Main Street to Highway 1. The fog swirled through the intersection, hiding and then revealing the red light. When the light turned green, he counted to ten before crossing the highway. He began threading his way up Del Mar Road toward Crescent Lane and GG's house. Just before Crescent Lane, a deer materialized in the mist ten feet ahead. He slammed on his brakes, stopping just short of the animal. The buck stood in the middle of the road, staring impassively at Jason's car before ambling across the street and disappearing into the haze.

He turned onto Crescent Lane at the east gatepost, still thinking about Mags. Despite the evidence pointing toward her as the killer, he nursed some doubts. For one thing, there was the second person dragging the body out of the spec house. There also was the block of time that was unaccounted for when Bill passed out, when he was hiding behind the bush in the front yard. Someone could've snuck into the house while he was unconscious and killed Geraldo before he got carried to the minivan.

"Even so," Jason mused, "Mags is the leading suspect at the moment."

When he reached GG's house, he pulled to the left-hand curb and stopped in front of the walkway. His first thought was to call Erin, as he always did when he got home. But not this evening. "I'm not going to call first," he said decisively. "Not after this morning. She escalated and stormed out." He set the parking brake and released his seat belt. "At last," he sighed, "a hot shower, clean clothes, and a bite to eat, then some drinks at Mostly's with the boys." The most important thing, however, was to flirt with some women Erin would hear about.

His hand was on the car's door handle when his phone buzzed. He searched the pockets of his warm-up jacket but found it on the passenger's seat. *Bet that's Erin.* He picked up the phone and checked the screen. An email from Howie Simon. "Sorry, Howie," he said to the screen. "Whatley gossip can wait." He was about to flag the message to read tomorrow when he noticed the subject line: *Regis Thelen dead at 79.*

"That *is* news!" Jason said. Regis Thelen was the firm's only surviving name partner following the deaths of Avery Whatley and Wilhelm Füchs. He was legendary for working 16-hour days at a stand-up desk, always wearing an immaculate three-piece suit. He was infamous among the junior partners and associates for demanding more and more billable hours every year while chipping away at compensation and benefits.

Jason opened the email:

Hey Jason—I know you're done with everything WTF, but you'll want to know about this. Old man Thelen died two days ago at his desk in the New York office. Heart attack. His secretary found him gasping for breath on the floor. His last words were, "Do NOT loosen my tie," per the grapevine. He was a mean old son-of-a-bitch, and he made my life and yours miserable. Good riddance.

Here's what you need to know: Gretchen wants to replace him as senior managing partner of the firm's global operations in New York. She's already making her move. Office pool odds are 50 to one she'll take Courtney with her to NYC, and I agree. Someone started a rumor, though, that one of Gretchen's big victories is about to blow up. Something about her hiding unfavorable evidence in a case with a multi-million-dollar judgment. Also, there are rumors of sexual harassment complaints going back years. Clearly the raptors are circling, trying to take her down, but she always wins.

Thought you'd appreciate a heads-up about Courtney moving to NYC.

Your friend always,
Howie

The email transported him back to the last days of his former life: his cubicle in the firm's basement, surrounded by boxes of depositions; his fight with Courtney in their loft, when she blamed him for holding her back; his desperate pain at losing her and Jason Jr.; the unbearable emptiness of being alone with his life and career in tatters.

He shook away the unwelcome memories. At least Howie's email explained why Courtney was pushing him so hard to sign the divorce papers. He clicked off his phone and opened the car door. His eyes swept up the walkway to the house, ghostly white in the fog. Something was wrong. He strained to see through the mist. Climbing out of his car, he took several steps toward the house, but stopped mid-stride.

He knew he hadn't done it, because he remembered locking the dead-bolt before he left. But there it was. *The front door's wide open!*

* * *

Erin parked her car in front of the Bites 'n Bytes Café and shuffled across the patio to the entrance. Her head was bowed and her hands were buried in her jacket pockets. Grasping the heavy wooden door's handle with both hands, she pulled it open just enough to squeeze inside.

Arlene, the barista behind the counter, greeted her with, "Erin, holy cow. You look terrible. Are you OK?"

Erin lifted her eyes and tugged the corners of her mouth into a thin smile. She trudged toward the counter, passing rows of Formica-and-chrome tables gleaming in the fluorescent light. "Thanks, Arlene. That's exactly what I needed to hear."

"Seriously—what's going on with you?"

"I was taking pictures up in Big Sur all afternoon and then the fog came in, and it took me three hours to get back. That's what."

Arlene studied her face. "Seriously, girl." It sounded more like a demand than a question.

Erin examined the tired pastries in the display case: a bear claw, two cream puffs, a long john, and a dead fly. "I've got troubles, Arlene."

"Jason troubles?"

By now, Erin realized, everyone in the village knew she and Jason broke up that morning. "Yeah," she said. Before Arlene could speak, Erin said, "Let me have a dry double cappuccino with sprinkles. I have to work tonight."

Arlene flipped on the coffee grinder and yelled over the buzz, "He's just a man, Erin. We got a town full of 'em. They all got their brains in their ass or their dick. If you ask me—"

Mercifully, Erin's cell phone chimed with her best friend's ring tone. She turned her back to the counter and dug the phone out of her jacket pocket.

"Brenda, thank God." Erin managed a half-smile for Arlene and pointed to a table near the window. She went to it and sat, slouching in the chair. "Thank God you called, I really need to talk to you."

"Hon, where you been at? I've been calling all afternoon."

"I was up in Big Sur," Erin said, staring at her reflected self in the window. Outside, a few hardy pedestrians braved the late afternoon fog and cold. "No cell service, I guess, battery's probably low." She turned her head left and right as she spoke, inspecting her image in the window.

"Listen to this, hon. You'll never guess—"

"I feel so bad, Bren, I really hurt him."

"I know, hon. You told me this morning. Listen—"

"If you could've seen his eyes, it was like he died inside. I feel just terrible, how could I do that to him?"

"It's like I told you this morning, hon. Let me ask you again. Are you letting him park his yacht in your slip?"

"You know he is, Bren, an' you know I want him to."

"So, you've got every right to tell him where the marina's at, hon. If you want Los Angeles, then that's it. End of story. Period. Now, will you get that into your thick head, girl?"

"Yeah," Erin said without conviction.

"Great. You finally get it. Now, will you listen to me!"

"I'll die if I have to stay in this shit hole the rest of my life, Bren—like my mother—even another year." Erin's eyes filled with tears and she slouched lower in her chair. Big drops, blackened by mascara, splashed on the tabletop. She wiped them with her sleeve as Arlene's blurry reflection appeared in the window. Arlene set down the cappuccino and busied herself rearranging the condiments and napkins on tables nearby.

Erin lifted the cup, but put it down without tasting. "Jason and I could make it in LA if we're together, why can't he see that? He's lost his confidence because of his bitch ex-wife. I could help him, I know it. My God, Bren, what's that noise? Is it a siren?"

"That's what I've been trying to tell you, girl. I'm in the ER."

"The Emergency Room! Are you hurt, are you OK?"

"It's not me, hon. It's Nikki. My dumbass little sister."

"Oh no! What happened, is she OK?"

"She got cut up by flying glass. They're digging out the pieces. Nothing serious, just a few stitches."

"Oh my God, Brenda! What happened?"

"Can you believe this? Tits-for-brains went to Jason's as soon as I told her you two broke up. She was gonna tell him she loved him."

Erin sat up in her chair. "What? No way! What…what did Jason say?" She tried to sound casual, but she knew her tone was urgent.

"Get a grip, girl! You're twice the woman Nikki'll ever be. What is wrong with you?"

Brenda was silent so long Erin thought she'd lost the signal. She yanked the phone away from her ear to check the battery's charge. Four percent. "Bren," she said plaintively, "are you still there?"

Brenda answered with exaggerated patience. "Now can I tell you? Some ginormous biker was inside Jason's house, tearing it apart. Destroying everything. He tried to punch Nikki through the bedroom window. That's how she got cut."

Erin jumped to her feet, knocking the table and sloshing coffee on it and her pants. Her chair crashed to the ground. "Brenda! Is Jason OK?"

"Damn, girl, will you let me finish! All your whining 'bout Jason. My sister coulda got killed."

Erin pressed the phone against her ear so hard her hand shook. The only sound was her rapid breathing.

"So Nikki runs for her car and this freak chases her and punches through the convertible top as she drives away and tears off half the canvas! She's got this big hole—"

"Brenda, you have to tell me, IS JASON OK?"

"I'm telling you, he—"

"He needs me, thank God, he needs me. He needs my help. I'm gonna go to him right now." She ran to the front entrance. "You're the best, Bren, I'll call you tomorrow!"

Erin punched *End* on her phone and shouldered through the heavy door at the same time. It hit something and stopped halfway.

"OUCH!" a woman cried. Erin peered around the door, holding it half open. Outside, a woman in running gear and a sweatshirt was bent at the waist, holding her right thumb. "Damn, that hurts. You slammed the door into my thumb." Glancing up, she said, "You need to be more careful."

"I'm so sorry," Erin blurted. "Here, let me hold it so you can...." The woman slipped through the opening. She stood in front of the door, looking at Erin while cradling her thumb.

"I was just going—" Erin stopped mid-sentence. Even without makeup and under fluorescent lights, this was the most beautiful woman she'd ever seen. Erin had a very high opinion of her own beauty, but this girl was movie-star gorgeous. A head taller than Erin and maybe a couple of years older, she had thick, honey-blonde hair pulled into a ponytail. Erin couldn't help staring at her exquisitely sculpted features, flawless skin, and pale-gray eyes.

Those gray eyes held her own much too long. Erin gulped. *Is this what the magazines call a "moment?"* It certainly seemed to be for the woman. *She's hitting on me! EEEUUWW! GROSS!* The unnerving eyes bore into her, seeking the answer to an unspoken question. *Oh my God, no! I'm not like you!*

Despite waves of queasiness, Erin returned the woman's gaze, forcing herself not to flinch. After an eternity, the woman lowered her eyes to her thumb. She flexed it tentatively and said, "No worries. I'll be OK."

"It's just…" Erin said, trying to regain her composure. "My boy-friend…I'm sorry, I have to go, I hope you're OK."

The woman laid her left hand on Erin's forearm. "Of course. Be careful out there." She smiled and stared deep into Erin's eyes again. "In the fog."

Erin's skin crawled beneath the warm touch. The woman took a half-step to the side, still partially blocking the door.

"Ummm…I will," Erin said, brushing past her, shrinking from contact, beeping her car open as she ran.

CHAPTER 29

Standing beside his car, Jason eyed the open front door of his house. His habit was to make sure all the windows and doors were locked whenever he left. It was automatic after living in Los Angeles. He remembered the key sticking in the front deadbolt this morning, so knew he'd locked it.

He opened his Porsche's hood quietly and removed the lug wrench, thinking about what he should do. The neighbors were all absentee owners. No help there. He could call 911, but it'd take an hour for a cop to get to Sea Cliff. The burglar would be gone by then. His only option was to go in and find the burglar.

Hefting the lug wrench to get its feel, he crept silently up the walkway. He tiptoed across the porch and stood in the front door, listening. There was no sound, but he felt a cold draft—probably an open window or the back door.

He stepped into the tiny foyer, which was separated from the living room by an archway. GG's china hutch lay on its side, partially blocking the opening. He squeezed through, holding the lug wrench like a club. Heart pounding, he tried to make sense of what he saw. Sofa—slashed and overturned, stuffing scattered everywhere. Recliner—slit from neck pillow to footrest. Bookshelves—empty, books in heaps. Drapes—ripped off rods. TV—tipped over. Telephone—smashed, cord ripped from wall. Mantel, where GG's beloved music boxes had been—bare, music boxes crushed.

Jason took long strides to the kitchen, breathing hard. He flicked on the overhead light. "This is worse than the living room," he gasped. Every drawer had been dumped, and every cupboard swept clean. Cabinet doors were torn from their hinges. The debris lay scattered across the linoleum, as if the burglar had thrown all the silver, canned goods, pots, pans, cereal, and dishes into a giant garbage bag, shaken it, and dumped out the broken and bent contents.

He scanned the cluttered floor, looking for a knife or a cleaver—even GG's ice pick—in case the intruder was still in the house. A pile of utensils across the room looked promising. He made his way toward it, but stopped when he saw a steak knife jammed into the wall through a folded paper towel. The blade snapped when he tried to dislodge it, but the paper came free without tearing. He unfolded it and struggled to make sense of the crude lettering:

abogado yu got somthin of Geraldos belongs me
I wan it or yor ded

It's gotta be El Carnicero, the guy Admiral Bill said was looking for Geraldo. Jason crumpled the paper towel and dropped it. *He must think Geraldo gave me his drug money to hide.*

Since El Crazy didn't find anything in the kitchen or living room, Jason figured he must've searched his bedroom next. Clutching the lug wrench with both hands, he crept down the hall.

The door to his room was half closed. He pushed it open. Cold wind hit his face. He glanced at the side window. It took a second to realize the glass and sash were completely gone, as if they'd been blown out by an explosion. Shards of glass littered the floor. Bloody handprints covered the sill and jambs, inside and out. Below the sill, a crumpled Kleenex box partially hid red-brown splotches of dried blood. More splotches trailed from the window to the closet door, which was slightly ajar. Gory fingerprints circled the knob.

Jason's stomach twisted into a knot. *This can't be happening! He's bleeding to death in my closet!*

He crept toward the door. Chills of dread ran down his spine, and the hair stood up at the back of his neck. Swallowing hard to push down the gorge in his throat, he pulled the door open with the tip of the lug wrench. "The body'll be lying on the floor," he told himself, preparing for the shock, "and it'll be bloody."

Instead, like any other day, the naked bulb dangled from the ceiling, glaring in his eyes. He held the cord aside and saw his business suits hanging neatly on the rack on the back wall. Next to them, where his sport shirts should be, twisted hangers drooped from the rod. Two shirts were wadded on the floor, bloodstained. Several were missing. At the front of the closet, the cabinets where he kept old client files were undamaged, except that their drawers were open and empty. The files were scattered on the floor, opened and rifled, and smeared with blood.

He backed out of the closet and sat heavily on the overturned dresser, relieved there was no dead body. He breathed a sigh of relief for a moment, until he saw El Carnicero's next move. These files hadn't told him anything useful because they were closed. But the files at Jason's office were full of current information. They had Geraldo's bank accounts and business deals. And partners and relatives. El Crazy could terrorize them. He could follow the money trail. He could get to the Cayman account first.

Oh my God! How long before El Crazy gets to my office? I've gotta get there before he does. Wait! Geraldo's current files are on my laptop!

He ran down the hall, through the kitchen, into the living room, eyes darting everywhere, searching for the silver plastic case.

The desk where his laptop always sat was upside down on top of the printer. The drawer where he kept his backup flash drives was splintered, the drives crushed and broken. His laptop was nowhere to be seen. He threw cushions, curtains, area rugs, anything that might hide it, out of the way. "Dammit," he swore, "he must've taken it." Glancing at the floor, he saw the power cord was severed. *He cut it instead of unplugging it? He's that clueless about computers?*

Jason sprinted down the walkway to his Porsche. He fumbled for his phone while he ran and scrolled his contacts for the Ocean Wave Salon. He hit *Call* and punched the car's *Start* button at the same time. The phone connected as he peeled away. "Hi," April, the receptionist, said, "you've reached the Ocean Wave Hair Salon."

"April," he shouted, shifting into second, "don't go outside, but try to get the license number—"

April's voice said, "For salon hours, press *1*. For directions—"

"Shitgoddammit," he swore, clicking off.

Jason tore down Crescent Lane through the fog. He screeched around the long curve, racing to get to his office before El Carnicero.

* * *

Erin's car skidded to a stop in front of Jason's house. She ran up the walkway. "JASON!" she yelled from the open front door. "It's me…Erin. Are you here? Are you OK?"

Squeezing past the overturned hutch, she stepped into the living room. "Oh my God!" she cried, wringing her hands as she took in the destruction. "Oh my God, Jason, please don't be hurt."

She tiptoed through the wreckage, trying not to step on anything sharp. "Jason?" she called again. "Where are you? Are you OK?" She decided to check his bedroom first and ran to it. Broken furniture littered the floor. Splotches of blood trailed from the empty window frame to the open closet door. "Oh my God!" she wailed, eyes wide, darting all over. "He's hurt and bleeding, and I don't know where he is." She sank onto the side of the overturned dresser and sobbed. "All I want is for him to be alright," she gulped between sobs, "for us to be together in LA."

Erin sat hunchbacked on the side of the dresser, elbows on her knees and palms over her eyes to catch her black mascara tears. She remembered him pulling the blanket over her that morning. She'd drifted back to sleep feeling warm and cared for. *But I still had to go and pick a stupid fight. And now he could be dying. How could I have been so stupid…so cruel?*

She cried tears of guilt until she had no more. Her nose dripped and black makeup streaked her hands. Lifting her head, her blurry eyes made out a smashed Kleenex box next to the baseboard beneath the window. She shuffled across the room and grabbed some tissues, blowing her nose and wiping her eyes. On the floor under the box she saw a large red-brown bloodstain. It had a pattern in it, like a boot print. Hope fluttered in her heart because Jason's Gucci loafers had *Gucci* stamped into each sole. "It's not his blood!" she cried. "He must be OK!"

Now she remembered Brenda saying it was the biker who'd punched through the window, and it was Nikki who was cut by the glass.

Erin dropped back onto the dresser. She jammed her fingers into the hair at her temples and pulled so hard it hurt. "Why did I do that?" she asked herself. "Why did I decide it was Jason who was hurt?"

Maybe I needed a reason to run to him and try to help. Maybe I wanted to make things right after this morning. Yes, he'd been her way out of Sea Cliff at first, but he meant so much more now. She'd been so worried, frantic really, about him being hurt. *Do I love him?* The thought took her by surprise. She'd always told herself she liked him, and the sex was great. "But if that's all," she asked herself, "why've I been so sad all day, and what's this wet wad of Kleenex doing in my lap?"

Cold wind blowing through the broken window brought her back to the devastated room. She realized Jason might not know about his house or the biker. Maybe she could help him and still save the day. But where was he?

The bright light in the closet caught her eye. On the floor were bloody file folders. She went to them and studied the names on the tabs, thinking the biker must've been looking for information about Jason's clients. Since she didn't recognize any of the names, she figured they must be old clients. That made sense because he kept his current files at his office.

"Oh my God!" she gulped. "The biker'll go to his office! Jason's probably there and won't know he's coming! I've got to warn him!" She pulled out her phone and speed-dialed his cell. "Come on, come on!" She willed his phone to ring, but no sound came through her earpiece. *Oh no!* She checked her screen. *My battery's totally dead!*

Erin ran out of the house to her car. She sped around Crescent Lane's curve, driving too fast through the fog. The pavement glistened in her high beams. With wipers screeching, she fought to keep her car on the narrow road. The mist grew thicker as she neared the west gatepost and Del Mar Road. She careened around the corner without slowing. From nowhere, glowing eyes appeared, just feet from her hood. *Deer!* She yanked the wheel and jammed on the brakes.

The car skidded crosswise through the intersection. It jumped the far curb, slid across the grassy shoulder, and stopped inches from a 40-foot pine tree, hissing steam.

* * *

April sat at the Ocean Wave Salon's reception desk, reading *People* and twirling her hair around her finger. She heard the steps outside creak and the front door open. Looking up, she saw a tall, blonde woman in running gear and a sweatshirt. "Oh my God!" she gulped. "Charlize Theron? *Here?!*"

Realizing that was impossible, April quickly appraised the woman's looks. *Uh-uh, this girl's younger and her eyes are gray and she has bigger tits. A lot bigger.* She recovered quickly and said, "Can I help you?"

The woman said, "I saw Jason Brinkman's sandwich board on the corner. Is his office in this building?"

April nodded. "Actually, it's the end unit on the left."

"So, that is it. I was just there knocking on the door, but no one answered. Have you seen him?"

"Actually, I saw him this morning, but he's actually been gone all afternoon."

"Do you think he'll come back?"

"You can't tell with him, actually. Why?"

"I'm looking for him," the woman said.

"Do you want to leave him a note?"

"No. I'll find him."

"What's your name, in case I see him?"

"That's OK. I'll find him," the woman said. She turned and pushed open the door. "Thanks," she said over her shoulder.

CHAPTER 30

Jason's Porsche screeched to a stop at the corner of Main and Charles. He jumped out to grab his sandwich board. El Carnicero probably knew where his office was, but just in case. Back in his car, he fishtailed up Charles, slamming on the brakes in front of his office.

He ran up the stairs with the sandwich board under his arm. Once inside, he locked the front door, pulled down the shades, and switched on his desk lamp. His desktop computer beeped and whirred as it powered up. He rummaged through his cubbies to find a thumb drive, and when the computer finally was ready, he highlighted all the directories containing Geraldo's information and downloaded them onto the drive.

The paper files were next. Two file cabinets, eight drawers. He opened and closed each one, checking the client names. A full drawer was devoted to Geraldo. *Damn! What am I gonna do with all these?*

He flashed on the two boxes of printer paper he'd stored in the quarter-bath. Working quickly, he removed the reams of paper and stacked them beside the copy machine. He carried the empty boxes to his desk, where he filled them with the Geraldo folders. That left seven drawers of other clients' materials to hide.

The only space in the office with a locking door was the bathroom. He lugged three file drawers into the little room. Swearing and sweating, he shoved them under the sink and stacked the remaining four in front of the toilet, leaving just enough clearance for the door to close. *The key, the key, where's the key?* He found it at the back of his desk drawer and locked the door. "That'll do 'til tomorrow," he told himself.

Expecting El Carnicero to burst into his office any moment, Jason tossed the personal items from his desk and the unopened mail from the secretary's station into one of the boxes of Geraldo files. He paused briefly, asking himself, "What else? Is there anything else this crazy guy shouldn't find?" Nothing important stood out, so he lugged the Geraldo boxes down the steps and into his Porsche's passenger seat. He ran back into the office and pocketed the thumb drive. "The tower," he said to himself. "Better take that, too." He ducked under his desk, unplugged the cables, and carried the tower to his car. It wouldn't fit inside with the boxes, so he popped the trunk and stuffed it in.

Jason climbed the steps and stood in the doorway, trying to see the office through El Carnicero's eyes. On impulse, he lifted the shades and pulled open the drawers of his and the secretary's desks. He turned on the overhead fluorescents and contemplated the open drawers and empty file cabinets. It looked cleaned out. He prayed El Crazy would see everything was gone, and not ransack the place.

* * *

"One-one thousand. Two-one thousand. Three-one thousand …." Jason sat in his Porsche's driver's seat and counted until his heart slowed and his breathing became normal. Thinking out loud, he decided, "I'll rent a storage locker for all this stuff tomorrow, but what about tonight? Can't leave it in the car. Havta find someplace at home." He pressed the *Start* button and drove down Charles to Main.

By now, the fog had reduced visibility to a few yards. He drove carefully through town and across Highway 1. As he pulled into GG's driveway, he noticed the dashboard clock flash from 7:59 to 8:00. "Are you kidding?" he said to the clock. "How'd it get so late?"

He parked in front of the garage and walked to the side door. Knowing that his grandfather was always prepared for any emergency, he hoped to find plastic sheeting for the blown-out window, and a flashlight in case all the lamps were broken. He unlocked the door and stood on the threshold, groping in the dark for the light switch. A single bulb in the rafters cast a faint yellow glow when he flipped it on.

The odors of dried grass clippings and motor oil brought him back to visiting GG and Grandpa Larry when he was little. His mind's eye filled with the image of his grandfather working at his lathe and humming. Shaking off the memory, Jason squeezed past GG's powder-blue Plymouth Neon, and realized it was the solution to his storage problem. He'd put the boxes and tower in the car and lock it and the garage. They'd be safe for tonight, but he needed the Neon's key. He opened the passenger door, slid in, and pulled down the driver's visor. The key dropped in his hand. "Just as I thought," he smiled. "Thank you, GG."

It took a few minutes to stash the files and tower in the little car, and another five to find a bundle of plastic sheeting, a role of duct tape, and a flashlight. He locked the car and the garage, and carried his load up the back steps to the door. A boot print above the knob and a splintered jamb explained how El Carnicero got into the house.

In his bedroom, Jason taped the plastic over the broken window. That stopped the cold breeze, but the house still was freezing. The thermostat in the hall read 65. He moved the dial to 70 and waited.

The furnace was in the crawl space under the center of the house. Normally, the burner igniting and the fan blowing could be heard in the hall, but there was no sound. He turned the temperature up to 75, then 80, but the furnace still didn't come on.

He remembered this happened sometimes during his childhood visits, and Grandpa Larry had to go under the house to get the burner to work. Jason always stayed upstairs because he knew Grey Widows hid down there in the dark, but he asked his grandfather how he fixed the problem. Larry explained he just unplugged the power cord and plugged it back in.

Shivering in the hall, Jason decided he had to have heat, so he'd have to go under the house and find the cord and socket.

He grabbed the flashlight and walked down the back steps. Opening the crawl space door, he swept the bright light back and forth. He saw cobwebs, pier blocks and posts, floor joists, and bare dirt. The furnace sat on a concrete pad in the center, about fifteen feet away. A thick electric cord stuck out of a socket box on a nearby post. But something next to the furnace caught his eye.

Jason shined his light into the blackness and squinted, straining to make sense of what the beam showed. "What in the hell?" he sputtered. He stuck his head into the opening. "It can't be!"

A two-burner camp stove and a large propane gas canister sat next to the furnace.

"Bill, you son of a bitch," he swore. "After all the help I've given you, this is how you repay me? Living under my house!" Jason was so angry it took a second for the next thought to form. He pictured Admiral Bill lighting the stove under the spec house and the flames shooting up, singeing the floor joists. *He could've burned it down. Holy Christ! He could burn my house down!*

* * *

Jason secured the crawl space as best he could. He walked around the house to check whether El Carnicero had damaged the front door before breaking in the back. The door looked OK, and he shut it behind him after pushing the lock button on the knob.

In the foyer, he dropped wearily onto the overturned hutch. His Gucci loafers hurt his feet after a long day, so he looked for his Ugg scuffs, and saw them sticking from under the back of the hutch. He pulled off his shoes, pried the Uggs free, and slipped them on. He decided to leave his Guccis by the door so he could find them easily in the mess.

Turning to face the living room, he surveyed the wreckage with a heavy heart. Every piece of furniture was ruined, and it was clear he'd need some basics so he could live in the house. That meant filing an insurance claim, which required getting a sheriff's report. Patting the pockets of his warm-up jacket, he found his phone and punched in the sheriff's non-emergency number.

"There's been a burglary at my house," Jason told the bored young dispatcher who answered. He rattled off his address and phone number.

"Is the intruder on the premises, sir?" the dispatcher asked.

"No, but he left a lot of blood."

"Sir, are you injured?"

"No."

"We'll send an officer out as soon as we can. Wait. You're in Sea Cliff? Hmm … it probably won't be until sometime tomorrow morning. Could be after lunch."

"I'm reporting a burglary," Jason said sternly. "It's a felony, and some-one was injured. You need to get an officer out here right away."

"Yes, sir, I'm aware of that. We only got one deputy in your area, as you probably know. We'll do our best."

"See that you do," Jason said, clicking off. "Goddamn podunk county," he grumbled. "They'd get someone here in an hour in LA. Well, when there's an injury and it's not the *barrio*."

Given the uncertainty, he decided to leave most of the mess in place until the next day. He took cell phone pictures of the devastation in each room before sweeping the kitchen debris into a pile and clearing a space for his slashed and gutted mattress on the bedroom floor.

The TV lay on its side in the living room. It flickered to life with *Jeopardy*. No other channel worked, so he decided *Jeopardy* was perfect. He turned up the sound for company.

The announcer's soothing voice and the commercials made the house seem a bit more normal. He took pictures of GG's broken keepsakes and straightened up a little. One of the living room lamps lay on the floor, and he set it upright and turned it on. The light revealed a half-dozen fist-sized holes in the plaster walls. "This guy's using the wall as a punching bag?" he gasped. "That's crazy scary." In the corner, he saw the smashed display case where GG kept her Cabbage Patch dolls. The head had been cut off each of the six dolls, and they were slit from neck to thigh. "Make that psychopathic."

He couldn't avoid the obvious question any longer. "What if El Crazy comes back here tonight?" he asked himself.

His sensible side said, *I should go to a motel.*

His practical side countered, *I really don't want to spend $250. He won't come back here.*

Yeah, his sensible side argued, *but what if he sees the office is cleared out and comes back?*

He won't do that. Look at all the blood. He searched every square inch of the house. It's late.

He is crazy, though. Violent crazy.

He won't. I'm positive.

But if he does, what am I gonna do?

Well, I should find some kind of weapon. Maybe in the kitchen.

He sifted through the debris pile in the kitchen searching for a butcher knife, but decided that wasn't enough protection if El Crazy had a gun or a switchblade. He decided to look in the garage.

Jason clomped down the back steps and across the lawn to the garage. Inside, he pushed past the Neon and surveyed Grandpa Larry's worktable. Only an X-Acto knife and a handsaw came close to being weapons.

He knelt to examine the jumble of bins and containers under the table. His grandfather's tackle box caught his eye, and stirred a faint memory. He leaned closer to make out the faded handwritten label above the clasp:

Larry's tackle box. Keep out. Get your own damned tackle.

He pulled the box free and opened it. The odor of machine oil filled his nostrils. Inside was an oil-soaked cloth wrapped around a heavy object. He pulled on the cloth, and then he remembered: This was where Grandpa Larry hid his .45 from Vietnam.

Searching the tackle box, he found a box of cartridges and the magazine. He slipped seven cartridges into the magazine, ran it home, and chambered a round. He cocked the hammer and flipped on the thumb safety, then laid the pistol on the cloth in the box.

Jason carried the tackle box into the kitchen and set it carefully on the counter. *What was that?* Something clattered in the living room. "Did I really hear that?" he asked himself, holding his breath. He listened. "There it is again. I know I closed the front door. Did I lock it?" An icy chill ran down his spine. Goosebumps prickled his arms. "Someone's in the house," he said without meaning to speak out loud. "Oh my God! It's El Carnicero!"

CHAPTER 31

Jason opened the tackle box as quietly as he could with his shaking hands. He removed the .45 and eased off the safety.

The kitchen was separated from the living room by an archway. He tiptoed up to it, pressing himself against the stub wall and peering around the jamb into the front room. Nothing except for demolished furniture.

A *clink* that sounded like keys came from near the front door. The overturned hutch blocked most of his view of the foyer, but he made out the top of a balding head. He leveled the weapon and steadied it with both hands, the way he'd seen TV cops do it. He stepped into the archway. "Stand up slowly and show me your hands," he growled deeply to keep his voice from quavering. "I've got a gun."

A man rose to his feet with a grunt, dropping one of Jason's Gucci loafers. He held out his palms, showing they were empty. "Whoa there, Dirty Harry," Deputy Hardesty said calmly. "I'm just answering your call. Dispatch said you demanded an immediate response."

Jason lowered his weapon. "Sorry, Duane—uh, Deputy," he said sheepishly. "I'm a little edgy." He gestured toward the broken and overturned furniture.

Hardesty glanced around the room. "You got a permit for that?" he demanded, pointing at the .45.

"For Chrissake, this is my home, my residence."

"Uh-huh. Penal Code 26505, I 'spose. Still, you shouldn't be threatening a law enforcement officer."

"And you shouldn't be sneaking in here without announcing yourself!" Jason turned and walked to the mantel, laying the pistol on it carefully. Voices chattered on the television. "Look, I called you here to take a report on this burglary. Can you please do that without giving me a hard time?"

Hardesty maneuvered around the hutch. "Those your shoes?" he asked, jerking his thumb over his shoulder. "Them fancy-ass Gucci loafers sittin' by the front door?"

"Yeah, but what's that got to do with you taking my report?"

The deputy's expression said, "Gotcha." Jason didn't understand but squashed the urge to ask. Instead he said, "Will you just do your inspection and write your report so I can clean up this mess?"

"OK, can do. But first, let me ask you something. Everyone in Sea Cliff knows you're broke and that Gerald O'Brien was your best client, which leaves you without any source of income. How do I know you didn't stage this to collect the insurance money?"

Jason's jaw dropped. "Goddamn you, Duane! You are way out of line. Just take the report and get out of here, will you?"

"So you don't deny it?"

"Of course I deny it. It's the stupidest thing you've ever said to me."

"OK. So, who did it?"

Jason and Hardesty glared at each other from across the room. The deputy straightened his posture, as if striving to project authority. He pushed his utility belt below his paunch. The belt creaked and clinked in protest. He hooked his thumbs behind the buckle. "So, who did it?" he repeated.

Jason punched his fist into his palm, imagining the satisfying *thump* of a hard right to Hardesty's jaw, followed by roundhouse to his doughy stomach. He smacked his fist again, this time grinding his knuckles into his palm. Then, he remembered something his father told him after a winning night of blackjack: "If the table's running against you, create a distraction and break the rhythm."

With great show, Jason unclenched his fists and stuck his hands in his pants pockets. He smiled the most genuine smile he could manage. Hardesty's beady eyes clouded with confusion. At that moment, a chorus of voices on the TV yelled, "WHEEL OF FORTUNE!" Both men's eyes flew to the television in the corner.

The tension broke.

"To answer your question, I heard there's a cartel enforcer in town looking for Geraldo," Jason said. "Calls himself El Carnicero. I think he did it. He's looking for something of Geraldo's he thinks Geraldo gave me to hide." He noticed the words "cartel enforcer" seemed to get Hardesty's attention, and figured arresting El Carnicero would be a very big deal for a twinkie cop like Deputy Duane.

"Any description?" the deputy asked.

"Just big and mean. Rides a Harley. Cut himself pretty bad when he tore up my house."

"OK. Whatever you say."

Jason said, "Come in here and look at this." He led the deputy into the kitchen. Kneeling, Jason found the crumpled paper towel with El Carnicero's scrawled message. Hardesty read it. He pulled a plastic evidence bag from his pants pocket and slid the paper into it. Walking back to the entry, he retrieved his clipboard from behind the hutch. He began to inspect the house and the damage, taking notes on his form.

When Hardesty finished writing, he said, "That's it. We'll mail you a copy tomorrow, and I'll send forensics out for the blood. It may take a while, 'cause they're still working on the exploding boat."

Jason said, "Not good enough. I can't live like this. I gotta clean up this mess." He paused, thinking. "Come with me."

He led Hardesty to the bedroom closet. "Here are some fingerprints," he said, pointing at the bloody doorknob. He nodded at the shirts wadded on the floor. "Get some pictures and take one of the shirts. You'll have your blood sample and your chain of evidence."

The deputy pulled out another evidence bag and slid it over the doorknob. He stuffed a shirt inside a third bag and headed to the front door. Jason called out to his back, "You know, this cartel enforcer guy might decide to search my office, too. I already checked, but would you mind swinging by to take a look?"

Hardesty stopped and turned to face him. His eyes lit up. "Can do. Maybe I'll contact the hospitals, too." He lumbered down the walkway.

"Creepy little man," Jason muttered, watching him. "And incompetent." He locked the front door, testing it this time, and retrieved the .45 from the mantel. The gun's solid heft and cold metal gave him a feeling of security as he carried it back to the kitchen and placed it in the tackle box.

Leaning against the sink, he surveyed the mess on the floor. His eyes stopped at the Marlboro pack he'd set on the table this morning. It was torn open, and most of the cigarettes were gone.

He felt his shoulder for the nicotine patch before walking over to pick up the remains of the pack. The smell of tobacco and the feel of the crisp paper stirred a longing in him. He told himself he could smoke just one if he crushed the rest first.

Rolling a cigarette between his palms, he held it under his nose and inhaled the tobacco aroma. Immediately, he pictured Courtney the first time they met in the Whatley conference room. A second later, the constant stress and seething frustration of his years at the firm came rushing back. "Nope," he said. "That was my old life. I was an addict and a slave. I don't want any part of it." He dropped the pack on the counter.

He realized he was ravenously hungry. El Carnicero had muscled the refrigerator away from the wall, but hadn't tipped it over or swept out the contents. In the freezer, Jason found a Home Style Meatloaf Dinner Entree and stuck it in GG's Radar Range. He found a fork and knife in the debris pile and washed them in the sink.

With the microwave whirring and the TV murmuring in the living room, he stood at the sink and stared out the dark window. His mind wandered. He wondered briefly what Erin was doing. He remembered he'd forgotten to look at Courtney's divorce papers, now scattered all over the living room. With some bitterness, he thought about her and asked himself for the hundredth time, "Could we have made it, if not for Gretchen? Working 18-hour days to try to please her? So we'd get assigned high-dollar cases, and maybe both make partner? Would Courtney have been satisfied then?"

The microwave dinged and the smell of dinner filled the air.

Jason leaned against the sink, devouring the meatloaf, stuffed potatoes, julienne carrots, and thick brown gravy. Despite all his problems, he felt at peace. He had some money in the bank, he could pay some bills, and there was more money on the horizon. He was living where he wanted to live, in a beautiful place. He was practicing law, not trapped in a cubicle shuffling papers. Better days had to be ahead.

Suddenly, his father's drunken voice barked in his head: "You failed, boy. You threw away all that money and prestige for some lame moral code no one cares about. Everyone fucks their boss on command. You coulda kept your penthouse and wife and kid."

Jason recoiled in disgust. He shot back, "Maybe in your world, Barry Brinkman, but not in mine. I'm nobody's sex toy, ever." The next thought, however, popped into his mind from some hidden corner: *Three hundred thousand a year was nice, though.*

"NO!" he shouted. "No one owns me anymore. I'm a free man!"

He grabbed the Marlboro pack from the counter and crumpled it and the remaining cigarettes. "I can make it on my own," he said more calmly, "on my own terms." He threw the pack into the pile of debris. "And I sure as hell don't need these!"

As the day and night had gone from bad to worse, the idea of blowing off steam at Mostly's Saloon sounded better and better. "OK, Jason," he told himself, "compartmentalize, like you were taught. No more moralizing or worrying. It's time for a few drinks and a little flirting that the gossip mill will tell Erin about. Then, get to bed early and be ready for tomorrow."

He rinsed the plastic plate and headed to the bathroom for a quick shower.

CHAPTER 32

Forty-five years ago, young Gretchen Fautz wrote this caption for her college yearbook picture:

I will be the richest and most powerful lawyer in California.

Like many with great ambition, Gretchen never counted the bodies as she clawed and slashed her way to wealth and power. When she finally reached the pinnacle, she never looked back at the ruined lives and careers she left in her wake, and in her arrogance, never considered that some of those broken people might seek revenge.

Harlan Redaway was one of them. Fresh out of law school, he and Gretchen were first-year associates at the Goldbloom insurance defense firm in Los Angeles. He fell in love with the glamorous and fiery Gretchen the moment they met. Fate put them on a team of lawyers defending a series of big-dollar lawsuits. Their combined knowledge and skills made them a formidable pair, and they began to work together constantly. In time, she said she loved him, and he proposed.

Fate changed its mind, however, as it will do. Gretchen and Harlan were lead trial counsel defending different clients against million-dollar claims in separate trials. She won, he lost. And so it went for the next half-dozen cases. She broke off their engagement. When asked why, she told him, "I got smart." She began an affair with Avery Whatley, the oldest partner at Whatley, Thelen & Füchs. She left Harlan and Goldbloom for Avery and the Whatley firm, and soon became a senior partner.

Harlan was devastated by her betrayal, and vowed revenge. After years of building his own high-powered firm, Redaway and Associates, he personally opposed her in court whenever she sued one of his clients.

To his incredible frustration, she won every time. He knew she was doctoring evidence and bribing witnesses, but could never develop enough proof to seek a reversal. His anger grew, and he became obsessed with destroying her.

On this particular June evening, Harlan poured himself three fingers of Pappy Van Winkle and returned to his desk. The lights of Century City and Santa Monica Boulevard glowed out his office window behind him. He lowered the shade to block out the annoying sparkles. After a day of dealing with mundane litigation matters, it was time to open the envelope that had arrived by private courier at nine o'clock. The envelope, marked *Hand and Eye of Addressee Only*, bore the despised WTF logo.

Harlan drained his whiskey and slit the flap. He removed an unsigned cover letter and a copy of a handwritten note. As he read, his chest tightened and his stomach burned with 40 years of pent-up hatred. Pouring himself another three fingers, he studied both documents to be sure they left no room for doubt.

He pounded his desktop in elation. "Got you at last, you bitch!

"Loretta!" he barked into his intercom. "Get your bony ass in here, and bring your dictation pad."

* * *

From the quiet darkness of Main Street, Jason pushed through Mostly's swinging doors into glaring lights and a wall of sound. The throbbing beat pounded in his ears. Voices roared over the din. A woman's drunken laugh trilled above the rush of noise. Flat-screen TVs blared in each corner. Inhaling deeply, he relished the smoky air, the odors of stale whiskey and beer, and the scent of too many warm bodies.

Stopping a few steps inside, he scanned the room to see who was there and where he wanted to sit. A rough-looking man in a cut-off Raiders sweatshirt and ripped jeans bumped him hard as he passed by. "Excuse me?" Jason shouted at his back.

The man turned around and staggered back, stopping chest-to-chest with Jason. His biceps and paunch were the size of bowling balls, and his breath smelled of beer and marijuana. He said, "Fuck you an' fuck O'Brien."

"You got a problem with me or Geraldo?"

"You both the same, far as I'm concerned," the man said thickly. "Fuckin' O'Brien owes me two weeks' wages. Three thousand, two hundred dollars and change, and he ain't paid me, so I figure you owe me."

Jason moved back a step and said, "Stand in line, bud. Geraldo owes a lotta people money, and I'm looking for it, but I have nothing so far."

The man said, "It ain't Bud."

"What?"

"My name ain't Bud. It's TJ."

"Look, TJ. I don't know you. I need a copy of your timecard and your contact info, and I'll add you to the list. Send it to my P.O. Box—"

"Fuck that shit, man. I know your car, and I know where your office's at, so you'll be hearin' from me, 'less I get my money 'fore my rent's due." He lurched toward the door, stopping long enough to turn and shout, "Asshole."

Jason exhaled and unclenched his fists, which he hadn't realized he'd clenched. If it wasn't obvious before, TJ made it clear everyone who wanted a piece of Geraldo now considered his lawyer fair game for their claims. He told himself again he had to start watching his back. *Tomorrow. I just want to chill right now.*

Looking around, he spotted Christina, his one-time secretary, at a table across the room with a girlfriend and two guys he didn't recognize. She waved and he waved back. He noticed Mandi Jo and Cindi, the gossip queens, texting and taking pictures of everyone who entered. Several other people he knew smiled or nodded.

"J-Man! Yo, Jason! Over here." He heard his name and followed the sound halfway down the bar, where two red-haired, barrel-shaped men waved to join them. The Cody twins, Roady and Brody, were the owners of We Kill Kritters Pest Service, and the go-to guys for village gossip, but weren't the kind of company he had in mind. Hesitating, he looked over his shoulder, as if he'd heard someone else call his name. He didn't see anybody he wanted to sit with, and decided to join the twins to get the latest on Geraldo.

Jason pushed his way through the crowd. "Dang, bro," Roady said, high-fiving him. "Thought you was gonna ignore us."

"Dude," Brody said, slapping his palm on the down swing. Turning to Mostly, the bartender, he said, "Hey, dude, a brewski for our buddy here. And some matches."

Mostly set a bottle of Firestone Double Barrel Ale in front of Jason and flipped a book of matches at Brody, who pointed at the beer and said, "Tab, dude." Mostly nodded and moved to the next customer.

Jason took a long pull of beer and set down the bottle. "So, what's new, guys?" he asked. He moved closer so they could talk without yelling. The twins slid their stools over, bringing a cloud of Old Spice body wash with them.

Roady said, "New ink, bro. Check 'em out."

Jason couldn't believe either twin had a square inch of flesh left for another tattoo. As it was, each was covered from wrist to neck to waist, and from knee to heel, with a phantasm of shapes and colors—spider webs, iron crosses, Madonnas, Star Wars scenes, naked women, crèches, swastikas, crucifixes, lightning bolts, cartoon characters—swirling and blending together. All were on display beneath their matching muscle shirts and basketball shorts.

Jason knew from a chance encounter at a job site that each also had his name emblazoned on his chest in bold, gothic letters. "So's our clients can tell us apart," Brody had explained, "'cause most folks can't." Jason understood. As far as he could tell, the twins were truly identical, with the same wiry copper hair and beards, ruddy round faces, barrel bodies, and tattoos.

His curiosity was piqued. "Let's see 'em," he said. Both men held out beefy left arms. "This here's a termite," Roady pointed above his wrist and then up the length of his arm, "an' this here's a queen termite, 'cause most people can't tell 'em from a lace wing. An' this one's a black widow, and this is a boring beetle...." Jason had to look closely, but made out the new tattoos against the background of other shapes. Roady continued pointing at images until he reached his biceps. "An' this here's a Norway rat," he said proudly. He flexed his muscle, and the rat's back arched and its belly bulged.

The brothers looked at him expectantly, but he was at a loss for words. Finally, Brody said, "We figured it'd help our customers understand their pest destruction needs and the solutions we offer if we could illustrate what the pests actually look like."

Jason nodded. "That's good thinking, guys. Brilliant marketing. Great artwork, too."

The twins smiled. "Inky Dink," Roady said.

"The best," said Brody. "Even gives us his two-fer discount."

Brody picked up the book of matches and lit one. "So, J-Man," he said, watching the flame burn down to his meaty fingertips, "things ain't so good for you right now." He swore and dropped the match on the bar. "You broke up with Erin, and your meal ticket's dead. You ain't got no other payin' clients right now that we know 'bout. Admiral Bill sure don't pay you nothin'." He chuckled.

"I'm OK," Jason protested, but quickly changed the subject. "Hey, whaddya know about Geraldo?"

Brody lit another match. "You know he was seein' a heart doctor?"

Jason remembered the voicemail on Geraldo's phone from a cardiologist, but said, "No."

"There's some say he died of a heart attack 'fore he was dumped," Roady continued, "but we don't believe that."

Brody shook his head and dropped the match into his empty beer bottle. It sizzled. "Why else would the police take in Mags Turlock?"

"They arrested Mags?" Jason asked, surprised.

"Person of interest, they say," Roady replied, "but she's still in lockup—been there all day—and they towed her van."

"I'll be damned," Jason said, thinking Admiral Bill might be right.

"'Course any number of people hated the man," Roady said. "Coulda' been any one of 'em." Instead of continuing, he waved at Mostly and pointed at the three empty beer bottles.

"Like?" Jason prodded.

"Anyone he did business with. He just up and stopped payin' his bills a few months back. Everyone's after him for their money."

"Mack Hammersley?" Jason asked.

"To name just one. Geraldo owed him fifty grand, and Mack's wife's got cancer and needs a big operation."

Jason whistled. "Didn't know that part. Any other ideas?"

"Danni," Brody said. "The way he treated her, and she's crazy anyway. And a mean drunk."

Roady nodded. "Not to mention Tiffany."

"Now that's interesting," Brody said, striking another match. "You know, she disappeared—"

"Right after Geraldo died—" Roady interrupted.

"An' she was knocked up—" Brody said.

"Are you sayin … ?" Roady asked.

"Everyone knew Geraldo was ballin' her. She coulda killed him just for touchin' her, if she'd any sense." He lit a second match and watched the two flames race toward his fingertips. "Yup, that's what happened. Mark my words."

"Yeah, but you're forgettin' that that li'l fuck Jamie the bank manager disappeared the same time—" Roady argued.

"Tiffany and Jamie? Dude, you been breathin' too much copper naph-thenate. Jamie split 'cause the Feds was comin' to town to check his bank records. You know, the $2million-plus loan to Geraldo? I heard he never made a single payment."

"Oh, yeah," Roady acknowledged. "The Federals. Sorry, bro. You right on that one."

"Don't you forget it neither, little brother," Brody said firmly. He dropped the flaming matches to the floor and scrunched them.

"Wait a minute," Jason said, making a "time-out" sign with his hands. "Tiffany's pregnant?"

The Cody twins stared at him with wide eyes.

"Dang, bro."

"Dude," they said in unison.

"You never gonna make it in this town if you can't find out basic shit like that," Brody scoffed.

Jason stood facing the twins with his back to the room while they sat on their stools, facing him and the entrance. They were looking at him with pity and amusement when Roady's eyes swept to the front entrance. "Holy shit, bro." He slapped Brody's round belly with the back of his hand. "Will you check out what just walked in?"

"Ho-ly Christ!" Brody whispered.

Jason pivoted to see what was happening. Standing just inside the swinging doors was a tallish, blonde woman wearing a skintight black jumpsuit. Her hair was pulled back at the nape of her neck. She scanned the room as if she was looking for someone.

"The blonde runner!" Jason breathed. He tried to remember what Nikki's note said. She's from Beverly Hills? It did say she's gay.

He admired the woman from across the room. It had to be her. She looked like Beverly Hills, with her clothes and poise. No townie had that kind of style.

After five years of watching Courtney build and perfect her wardrobe, he guessed the jumpsuit was Tom Ford and the sandals Jimmy Choo. He stared at her and felt his heart pound rapidly. "No one from this town looks like that," he whispered to himself. "She is beautiful." He took a deep breath to calm his pulse.

"Bro, dang it, check out them chalopies," Roady whispered throatily.

Brody leered. "Nah, ain't top heavy 'nuff for my taste," he said. "I'm strictly a double D man. Can't settle."

"You don't never get none, neither," Roady mumbled.

In truth, Jason thought she had a fabulous body. And was proud of it, judging by her skintight outfit and all that cleavage. She stood at the door a few more moments, looking for someone or something, before walking along the far wall toward the rear.

"Must be goin' to the can," Brody grunted.

"Bro, you got shit for brains," Roady said. "A woman that fine don't never need to go to the bathroom. Their bodies works diff'rent."

Jason swallowed a chuckle and turned back to the bar, thinking he'd have to talk to her and be seen by the gossip queens. But first, he had to remember what Nikki said her name was.

Mostly set down three beers and the twins swung around to them. Jason slipped his Visa card from his wallet and handed it to Mostly. "For this tab, and you see Christina over there?" Mostly nodded. "A round for them, too." Jason asked the twins, "So, you guys, where do you think Tiffany went?"

Brody replied, "Someone seen her an' that li'l sweet thang, Victoria, drivin' in Santa Luisa."

"Nuh-uh, bro. I'm tellin' you, I heard she left with that Jamie fella."

"Dude." Brody slid off his stool. He planted his feet and shoved his belly into his brother's. "Forget about Tiffany and Jamie. I'm tellin' you that ain't how it is."

The two men locked eyes. Jason said, "Hey, guys, it's not that important. They're both gone. End of story."

Brody mumbled, "He gots to remember who the older brother is, that's all." He hoisted his bulk onto his stool.

"Just by five minutes," Roady grumbled sullenly.

Mostly stopped in front of them, holding Jason's credit card. "Sorry, Jason, but your card's been declined. Got another?" Mostly set the card on the bar, and the three men stared at it as if it was broken and they could figure out how to fix it.

Jason was reaching for his wallet when a woman spoke behind him. "Let me get it."

He turned and met the pale-gray eyes of the blonde runner.

CHAPTER 33

Jason did a double-take. *The blonde runner! Where'd she come from? Is she looking for me?*

She placed a Visa Black card on the bar, snapping the edge with a blood-red fingernail. Mostly picked up the card and hurried to another customer. The twins' eyes grew wide, and they shrank back on their stools. Jason's heart fluttered, stopped, started again. He searched his memory frantically for her name. It was in Nikki's card. Rebecca? Roberta? Rhonda? Ronnie? Rory! That's it. He was about to say, "Is it Rory?" when the woman stuck out her hand and said, "Aurora O'Brien. And you're Jason."

"Aurora *O'Brien*?" he stammered. He held out his hand reflexively. She shook it firmly and held it for several extra seconds. His hand tingled. Her gray eyes appraised him for an uncomfortably long time.

"Geraldo's daughter. My friends call me Rory."

"Geraldo's *daughter*?" He heard his voice shaking. To cover, he picked his credit card off the bar. He slipped it into his wallet, brushing her hand accidentally. The tingle raced up his arm.

An alarm bell dinged in his head. Geraldo didn't have any children, as far as he knew. Studying her face, he looked for some resemblance, but found none. This woman's fine features were nothing like big-boned Geraldo's. *But those eyes.* He found himself staring into them, unable to pull away, try as he might. The noise, the people around him disappeared, leaving only the *boom-boom* of his heart and the rushing blood in his ears. He told himself to get a grip. "Geraldo never mentioned a daughter."

"I've been looking for you, because everyone in town says you're my father's lawyer."

"You know, normally I'd say 'Yes, I am,' or 'No, I'm not,' but I don't know who you are or what you want. Geraldo doesn't have any kids."

"Everyone in town says you're his lawyer," she repeated, as if that settled the matter. Jason shrugged. He stepped closer to the twins on their stools with their backs to the woman. Brody lit matches and Roady tore his napkin into little pieces, but their eyes were glued to her reflection in the mirror behind the bar.

"That's not the reaction I expected," Rory said, standing close to Jason so she could be heard.

Her perfume filled his head. *Is it Chanel?*

"Everyone else I've met in Sea Cliff has been so friendly. Why would I tell you I'm Geraldo's daughter if I'm not? You're so suspicious."

Jason turned halfway to face her. "Think about it from my side. You show up here the day after his death hits the news. You say you're his daughter, but you could be anybody. You're not showing me any ID, let alone anything conclusive—"

"Like?"

"A birth certificate would be conclusive."

She stepped back and stood with perfect posture. "If you don't see it," she said sarcastically, "I don't have it."

Jason had to admit her jumpsuit left nothing to the imagination. He also noticed it didn't have any pockets.

"Anyway," she continued, "I'm supposed to carry my birth certificate around with me? That's ridiculous."

"If you want to make a claim against Geraldo's estate, you'll have to provide proof he's your father, no matter who's handling it. Plus, how'd you know it was me sitting here?"

"So you're paranoid as well as rude? Don't you realize you're pretty well known in Sea Cliff? I asked some girl in the bathroom if she knew you, and she said you were sitting at the bar. It's not like I expected to find you here."

It was a good answer, but her timing was way too coincidental. He figured she must think Geraldo had significant assets. Legally, if she was Geraldo's child, she'd be first in line to inherit whatever he had, since he wasn't married. Geraldo never mentioned any kids, however, and he didn't list her in his Next of Kin worksheet. Jason decided to change tack. "For sake of argument, let's say I am Geraldo's lawyer. What do you think I could do for you?"

"There are some family mementos, and there must be some assets. I've seen him driving a Cadillac Escalade."

He thought for a moment. Geraldo's personal items were garage-sale knickknacks. He owned the house on Miller and some land, and he owned his Escalade and tools. But he owed more than $2 million on the spec house. Admiral Bill thought there was cash, and there was the Cayman account, but that was all speculation at this point. "I don't know anything about his assets."

"I heard he owns a couple of houses in town."

"I couldn't say," he said, thinking she was fishing and it was time to end the conversation. "Look, I don't mean to be unreasonable, but my relationship with Geraldo, if I have any, is privileged. That's the end of the story, unless something changes, like you can prove you're his daughter. Now, will you please excuse me?"

He leaned closer to Roady and Brody. They seemed to be studying the bottles behind the bar, but were turned enough to hear the conversation. "So, boys, who do you like better this year? Giants or Dodgers?"

The man on the stool to Jason's left was head down on the bar, drooling. Rory squeezed between the man and Jason, pressing her breast, pelvis, and thigh against him. In spite of himself, the pressure of her body took away his breath. *It's definitely Chanel.* He tried to focus on the twins' opinions of the two teams' pitchers, and ignore the soft warmth of her breast and her firm thigh.

She whispered in his ear. "Look, we got off to a bad start. Even if you can't help me, you're a good-looking guy, and everyone says you're nice, so I'd like to get to know you better. And this sweet little town. Maybe you could show me around Sea Cliff? Can't we go somewhere more private to talk?" Her tone challenged him to refuse.

He hesitated. His head told him to say, "No," but his body pulsed with sexual energy each place she touched him. He told himself that was crazy because she was gay. *At least that's what Nikki said, but does she even know what "gay" means? Didn't her note say "gaye"?* He was certain she was playing him because she thought he knew more than he actually did. But, he asked himself, what's the risk? He could do some fishing, too. If she was Geraldo's daughter, she might know something that could lead to his money, if there was any.

Torn between caution, the need for information, and the sensation of her body, he reached an uneasy decision: He could play her just as well as she could play him. "Well, when you put it that way. There are some booths in the back, near the restrooms."

"Bartender," Rory called to Mostly, "will you bring my card and receipt? We'll be in the back." Her tone reminded Jason of Courtney ordering her secretary to fetch coffee. She slipped from between Jason and the drunken man and began walking toward the rear of the bar.

As she walked away, Roady sighed, "Sweet Jesus." He clapped his sweaty hand on Jason's shoulder. "You go, bro. Get some for the rest of us."

* * *

Jason and Rory sat across from each other in a booth near the restrooms, where it was quieter and less smoky. With the table between them, Jason was able to look at her more objectively.

She probably was around thirty. Everything about her appeared to be natural. Her skin was flawless and lightly tanned. Her features were exquisitely feminine—a model's brow and cheekbones, complemented by sensuous lips. But it was her gray eyes and long lashes, he decided, that gave her face its particular beauty. He remembered Courtney describing an actress' eyes as the color of rain, and that was the perfect description of Rory's.

She leaned forward, laying her forearms and hands on the table. An intricate filigree pendant dangled in the hollow of her throat. Its movement caught his eye, but he couldn't make out the design. Curiosity got the better of him, and he stared at it, hoping it might reveal something about her. It appeared to be platinum with two red stones. He looked again, trying not to be obvious. He decided it was some kind of insect. A dragonfly with ruby eyes. He thought that was actually sweet. *No ... it's a ... it's ... a ... praying mantis.* With recognition came a forgotten fact. *The females eat the males during sex. Is that the message? Christ, that's creepy. But fair warning, I guess.*

The tension between them was like a third person in the booth. Her expression seemed to say, "I want your help," but the set of her jaw said, "I'm not going to take any crap." Jason rested one arm across the back of the booth and the other in his lap, trying to appear relaxed. He forced himself to ignore her uncanny allure and focus on getting as much information from her as he could. When they finally spoke, they interrupted each other.

"I wanted to talk to you—"

"Why don't you tell me—"

"I didn't mean to—"

"No, go ahead—"

"I wanted to talk to you," Rory said, "because I thought you'd know more about my father's death and his property."

"Why don't you tell me some things that would help me believe you're Geraldo's daughter?"

"For God's sake, I am his daughter!" She slapped the table so hard the napkin holder jumped. "He married my mother, Ingrid Johanssen, his first wife, in 1984. You must know this."

There wasn't anyone named "Johanssen" in Geraldo's Next of Kin worksheet, Jason thought. He said, "Go on."

"She died the year after he left us. I was fourteen when he left, fifteen when she died." She bowed her head and her blonde ponytail swung forward, caressing her neck. After a moment, she looked up at him through incredibly long lashes. She blinked away a tear.

He knew she was working him, but he couldn't help feeling a wave of compassion. He told himself to ignore it. Even if he bought her tears, it didn't mean he could trust her. He decided to try changing direction slightly. "You have to realize, it's quite a coincidence you show up here the day after his death is the lead story, and claim to be his daughter and only heir. Dressed to cause a heart attack, I might add."

Rory jerked like he'd slapped her. The gray eyes narrowed, and pink crept into her cheeks. "So now I'm a slut as well as a grave robber? This is how people in Beverly Hills dress when they go to bars. You're from LA, you should know that. Would I be having more luck if I was a frump in a sweat suit?"

Ah-ha! She checked up on me. She didn't run into me by chance. He said slowly, "Just how do you know I'm from LA?"

Her eyes darted to her blood-red nails before coming back to his face. "I don't know. Maybe the girl in the bathroom told me. Or one of your chatty townspeople. Maybe it's your Canali shirt and Zanella slacks and Guccis. I don't know how I know, I just do. What's the big deal?"

She pushed herself back and crossed her arms under her breasts, tightening the fabric around them, revealing another bit of taut, tan skin. The mantis's red eyes glowed. "My father called me, to answer your question. He asked me to come up to Sea Cliff so we could talk. I've been here more than a week. You can ask the rental company. I thought he wanted to say he was sorry, maybe make peace with me." She sniffled, and tears escaped the corners of her eyes. "Damn," she sobbed, "I told myself I wasn't going to cry."

Jason pulled a napkin from the holder and handed it to her, watching as she dabbed her eyes.

It was possible she was the woman on Geraldo's voicemail, he thought, the one who just said, "I'm here. Call me." He waited until she crumpled the napkin. "OK," he said, softening his expression. He smiled a smile he hoped was soothing. "I don't want to be unreasonable—"

"Look, Jason Brinkman, I want three things from you." She half-stood, glaring at him, leaning over the table, her cleavage inches from his face. He focused on the delicate pendant instead of her smooth skin. The mantis bounced and swung toward him as she moved, raking at his cheek with spikey claws. Her pale-gray eyes bore into him, cold as ice. "First, my father had some pictures of me I want back. Second, I'm his only heir, so I want all the money he had. Third, I want to get out of turnip town and back to my life."

"I don't know about any pictures," Jason shot back, pushing himself up and forward so his face was even with hers. He willed away the sensations of her warm breath and perfume. "And I haven't found any money yet, so you might as well go back to Beverly Hills. Leave your email and phone number, and I'll contact you if I learn anything I think you're entitled to know about."

He expected her to get up and storm out, so her reaction took him completely by surprise. She sank back to her seat and reached across the table, taking his hand. The corners of her lips lifted into a sad smile. "I'm sorry, Jason." Her hand was soft, but her touch was electric. "It's just that...." Her eyes became luminous, and he noticed the faintest hint of freckles on her cheeks. She took a deep breath, stretching the black fabric tighter across her breasts, briefly exposing another half-inch of skin. "It's just that this is very hard for me. I didn't really know my dad, and I never saw him again after he left. We had a lot of issues that can't be resolved now that he's gone. I never thought you wouldn't be willing to help me and I'd have to argue with you."

Jason's ethics and resolve crashed in flames. He withdrew his hand and sat up straight, inhaling deeply to calm himself. "Alright, Rory," he said as evenly as he could. "Why do you think Geraldo had any money to leave you?"

"It's complicated," she said, glancing at her hands and shifting in her seat, "but the simple answer is he promised me, and that's the one promise I was sure he'd keep."

She stopped. Jason waited for her to continue, and when she didn't, he said, "Go on."

"He'd bring home duffle bags full of money when I was little." Her expression was far away. "I was too young to understand, but now I think he was making drug deals. He'd dump all the money on the floor of my bedroom and we'd roll around in it together. We'd throw it in the air and laugh." She wiped her lower eyelids. "Then he'd hide it somewhere in the house where I couldn't find it. He'd tease me about where he hid it, and I'd look all over for it. One time I found bundles of hundreds stuffed between the... what do you call them... the wood in the garage wall... the studs. When I was about twelve, I found a safe set into the concrete basement floor, and after that, he stopped teasing me."

"But that doesn't mean there's any money now," Jason said gently.

"You don't understand," she said, suddenly angry. "That was the deal he made with me. He promised me that if I … do you know what he said to me when he left for good? The very last thing he ever said to me?"

"How could I?"

"He said, 'It's all for you, sweetie. It's my payback. One day, it'll all be yours.' And then he closed the door and I never saw him again." She began to cry, and Jason melted. He pulled some napkins from the holder and put them in her hand, squeezing it gently.

Mostly appeared beside the booth, startling them both. He placed Rory's credit card and charge slip on the table in front of her. "Sorry to interrupt you two," he said with an envious glance at Jason, "but you need to sign, miss. It's more'n $50." She scrawled an initial on the slip and pocketed the card without looking up.

"Thanks, Mostly," Jason said. He dug a ten-dollar bill out of his pocket and laid it on the table.

"Sure thing, Jason." Mostly picked up the $10 and the charge slip and headed back to the bar.

When Mostly was out of earshot, Jason said softly, "Tell me about the pictures, Rory. I've never seen anything remotely personal in Geraldo's house, but maybe when I go through his stuff … you know, so I'll know what to look for … ."

"They were family pictures," she said in a voice he thought sounded strained. "Polaroids in a shoebox."

"You, your mom, and Geraldo?"

"Well, no. Not really. They're of me, mostly."

"Birthdays and Christmas? Baby in the bathtub?" he asked. "That sort of thing?"

She shifted in her seat. For the first time, she avoided looking at him. "Not exactly." She examined her nails, gouged a cuticle, picked at it. "They're kind of childhood pictures. You know, growing up. Things like that."

Jason was at a loss. "I don't understand. Like what?"

"Well … yeah, like me in the bathtub. But when I was young."

He thought she sounded defensive. Then he decided he was imagining it, so he asked, "Doesn't every parent take pictures of their kid in the tub?"

"Not like these." Her voice was cold. "I don't want to talk about it anymore." She paused. "Look. Are you making fun of me? You must have them. You must've seen them. You know what they're like. *You must want them.*"

"What are you talking about?" Jason held up his palms in protest. "I don't have anything of Geraldo's. I've never seen...." A sick realization suddenly clicked. Geraldo was a creep, obsessed with young girls. He could've invented that *Jail Bait* magazine. But his own daughter? That was too sick, even for him.

Jason's stomach twisted. "Wait a minute! If you're saying what I think you're saying...you are seriously out of line to suggest...to think that I... you'd better tell me exactly what you're talking about."

"For Christ's sake, I know that you know." Her voice shook with anger. "He must've bragged to you, shown them to you. I want them back. End of story."

Jason stared at her in amazement. Her composure was completely gone. Her eyes were pink, her cheeks red, and her breathing ragged. Circles of sweat darkened her jumpsuit under her arms.

"I'm sorry. You're talking about something that's obviously very important to you, but I can't help you. Geraldo never gave me any pictures of any kind. Period." He checked his pockets for his cell phone and wallet. "This conversation is over." He pushed himself to edge of the booth. As he rose, she pinned his arm to the table with surprising strength, knocking him off balance. He sat heavily on the seat cushion.

"Now you listen to me, Mister Hick Attorney. Those pictures of me are pornographic. Don't you get it? He was a disgusting pervert, a pedophile, and I was too young...." She trailed off. "Do you know the penalty for possessing kiddie porn?" she continued a moment later. "I want them back. The Polaroids—all one hundred of them. And I want all his money. I earned every penny of it."

"And you listen to me," Jason growled, rising on his fists and glaring down at her. "I don't have your pictures and there isn't any money. Forget about it and go back to Beverly Hills."

"You're lying." She planted her fists on the table and stood so their faces almost touched. "He'd never get rid of them. He treasured them. I was the prettiest one, his favorite. But he would've given them to you for safekeeping because you're his attorney. You could protect them because they'd be privileged."

"You're out of your mind." Jason slid to the end of the bench and started to stand, but she grabbed his arm again, digging her nails deep into the back of his hand.

"I've got a friend in the FBI who'd love to bust you for possessing kiddie porn."

"That's extortion, babe. That's a crime and an expensive tort, not to mention libel, slander, false light, and about a half-dozen others."

"And stealing your client's assets." Her voice was raw. "The police and the FBI—"

"More extortion, more slander and libel. Very expensive."

"Try me." She breathed in his face.

They stood forehead to forehead. Her perfume intoxicated him. He inhaled her breath, felt her warmth, saw the flush in her cheeks. Nothing in the world mattered but those tiny freckles. Her luminous gray eyes. The deep V of her cleavage. The mystery of the mantis pendant. Her eyes captured him, pulling him closer. He leaned toward her lips, hesitated. She tilted her head ever so slightly, brushing her lips against his. His breath caught. He bent forward, seeking the rest of the kiss. Her lips were soft and full, inviting—

"Jason! Look at you!" a woman's voice rang out. The spell broke. They pulled away from each other. His anger surged, drowning all other emotions. He looked around and saw Mandi Jo filming them on her iPhone. "Timing really is everything when you have to go to the bathroom." She strutted toward the women's room.

"Mandi Jo!" Jason shouted. "Dammit! Come back here!"

"Like I always say," she called over her shoulder as she walked away, "gossip is for everyone."

Jason stood beside the booth, looking down at Rory. "We're done, you and I." His voice was so harsh it surprised him. "Don't bother me again, unless you have proof of relationship and a lead on assets." He strode out of the smoky bar into the cool night.

CHAPTER 34

As sometimes happens in June on the Central Coast, the day's thick fog had given way to nighttime high overcast. The sky was pitch-black beneath the dome of clouds, save for a full moon that peeked through now and then. When the moon found an opening, it beamed pools of silvery light on the pavement as Jason drove north on Highway 1 toward the village of Simon's Cove.

After leaving Mostly's, Jason decided he needed some driving-thinking time to sort through his toxic encounter with Rory O'Brien. Simon's Cove—20 miles up the narrow, winding road—was a favorite midnight drive, and the right distance for tonight.

He'd stopped at his office on his way out of town. A quick look told him El Carnicero hadn't broken in. Waiting for the light at Main and Highway 1, he wondered about Mandi Jo's iPhone video. He scrolled through his phone's directory looking for her blog, GossipGoddessBlog.org, and opened it.

The first link was to the video of Rory and him. From the phone's angle, it looked like they rose simultaneously and shared a long kiss. Mandi Jo had edited the scene to make it look longer, and had dubbed in passionate groans to cover their angry words. He checked her other social media channels and found the video on all of them.

"Goddammit!" he swore. His scheme to generate a little gossip was a disaster. He'd wanted a minor buzz about him chatting with a couple of women at Mostly's, perhaps a still shot or two on the GossipGoddessBlog. Just enough to make Erin jealous. But the video looked like he and Rory were making out in a dark corner. Erin would be crushed. He peeled around the corner before the light turned green.

Highway 1 snaked and undulated along the coastline. Just below him, the Pacific crashed against the bluffs, occasionally soaking his windshield.

Alone on the dark road with just the peek-a-boo moon, the only sounds were the growl of the Porsche's exhaust, the pounding of the surf, and the clanking of Grandpa Larry's .45 in the tackle box in the passenger's footwell. He felt free of his cares as he drove, downshifting, cutting the apex of a curve, hitting the power at exactly the right moment.

He shifted into third and accelerated into a long, straight stretch. His thoughts wandered back to his fight with Erin. She'd always been so sweet, at least until this morning when she announced she wanted to move to LA. Out of the blue, as far as he could tell. She seemed happy in Sea Cliff, and he thought they were in good shape, spending as much time together as they could. They'd never talked about the future, and she'd never pressed for more commitment.

Thinking about the video and how Erin would react to it, he punched the wheel in frustration. He told himself he had to swallow his pride and call her tomorrow. He had to explain the video and apologize for getting so angry about LA. *But it shows anyone can have a hidden agenda.*

"So," he mused out loud, "what's Rory O'Brien's agenda? No secret, really. She thinks there's money and she's entitled to it. Doesn't care how she gets it." He pictured their faceoff in the booth at Mostly's. "Flirtation, threats, seduction, sex, tears—it's all fair to her. She's out for number one; nothing else matters. She's manipulative and passive-aggressive and very twisted behind all her beauty."

If all that was true, and he was certain it was, why was he so attracted to her? He jabbed the accelerator. With a roar, the car jumped to 75. He'd felt it the moment he saw her, like an animal in heat—wild and primitive. He remembered being intensely attracted to Courtney at first. But that was different, because they had an intellectual connection and they were learning how to survive at Whatley. Erin was completely different. She was so fresh and pretty, beautiful really, he just wanted to get to know her.

His thoughts turned back to Rory. She was stunning, but it was more than that. It was rip-each-other's-clothes-off, up-against-the-wall lust, based on...what? Chemistry? Raw sex appeal? Some cosmic connection? And there was the praying mantis. Made her seem dangerous—mysterious.

He lifted off the pedal as the car hit 85. "Is it because you want most what you can't get?" he asked himself. "Because she's gay? It doesn't make any sense. She's damaged goods. Bad news in every way. A nightmare packaged like a dream. She thinks the world owes her 'cause she had a tough childhood." He barked a laugh. "Like she's the only one."

Stabbing the brakes, he slipped the gearshift into second and set up the next curve, but his mind was on Rory. He almost believed she was Geraldo's daughter. Why would she tell that sick story about the pictures if she wasn't? He tried to convince himself it didn't matter because he'd never see her again.

Still, like the fleeting memory of an erotic dream, he couldn't shake the feelings she created in him. He remembered the soft touch of her hand and his surprising surge of tenderness when she cried. Not to mention the explosion of passion when they threatened each other, head to head, deep inside each other's aura. *She would've kissed me for real if we weren't interrupted. She definitely feels it, too.*

Reliving the moment of the half-kiss, he misjudged the curve and had to slow to 40 to keep from skidding. Out of nowhere, a single high-beam headlight glared in his rearview mirror, coming up so fast he feared the motorcycle would crash into his rear bumper. The glare blinded him as he fumbled for the mirror's "night" setting. He slowed to 30 and pulled right so the bike could pass, but it remained dead center, a foot back. He slowed even more, but so did the cycle, riding just behind the Porsche and flooding the cabin with its bright-white light. At this speed, Jason heard the distinctive *thump-thump-thump* of a Harley engine. He had a panicky thought: Didn't Admiral Bill say El Carnicero rode a Harley?

The next straightaway appeared in Jason's driving lights, and he floored the accelerator. The Porsche shot to 90 in a heartbeat. Two beats later, the Harley roared up. It was so close, Jason was certain it would hit his rear bumper. He tapped his brake pedal. The cycle fell back a car length.

The moon broke through the clouds. Glancing in his rearview, Jason saw the rider sitting tall on his bike. *Jesus, he's huge!* The man reached back to his saddlebag. "What's he...?" Jason wondered aloud. "He's pulling something out of the bag." Eyes back on the road, Jason judged the next curve was far enough ahead to speed up. He pushed it to 95. A flash of light in his mirror caught his eye. He looked again. This time, he saw a long trail of sparks on the pavement. "He's dragging... a chain?"

With a snarling *brrrraapppp*, the cycle leapt ahead. Jason checked his rearview quickly. The Harley nearly kissed the Porsche's bumper. The sparks disappeared. The man leaned forward, whipping his arm over his shoulder. *KAHH-THUNNKK*. Something heavy and metallic hit the Porsche's engine cover. Startled, Jason jerked the wheel. The car swerved toward the bluff. He yanked it back into his lane.

The Harley pulled even closer. Jason tapped the brake pedal again. The cycle held its position. *KAHH-THUNNK*.

"Alright, I'm intimidated," Jason whispered. Bitter acid burned his throat and churned in his stomach, and cold sweat dripped down his sides. He knew he could lose the Harley on a long enough straight run, but also knew that wasn't to be. North of Simon's Cove, the highway became more twisty and hilly, giving the advantage to the motorcycle.

The little village blew by at 105, with the Harley inches from the Porsche. Jason checked his mirror again. The rider whipped his arm. *KAHH-THUNNKK*.

OK. What am I gonna do? He tried to think clearly. It might not be El Crazy. It could be a meth-head or a PCP freak. Didn't matter. The guy obviously was dangerous, and Jason wasn't going to confront him, even with the gun. But if he couldn't confront him or outrun him, what else was there?

The seconds ticked by without an answer. Just when he was about to lose hope, he remembered a long-ago *Dukes of Hazzard* episode. He pictured luring the motorcycle closer, then standing on the brakes in a tire-smoking panic stop. He imagined the rest. The cycle would slam into his rear bumper and throw El Crazy. Traction control and ABS would keep the Porsche on the road. The car would be damaged, but they'd survive. Probably.

The last straightaway was in sight. Jason prayed the *Dukes* scene wasn't just Hollywood make-believe. He eased back to 100. The Harley was right behind him, engine roaring and headlight glaring. Jason gripped the wheel tight with sweaty hands, ready to slam on the brakes. He looked in his mirror to be sure the bike was close enough. It was. *Wait! What's that?* Many curves behind, red and blue lights flashed. The sight nearly brought tears to his eyes. "Thank God," he breathed, "but will I run out of straight road before the cop catches up?"

Time slowed to a crawl at 100 miles per hour. The first of several hairpin bends appeared just ahead. The cop was still far back, but closer. The curves rushed up at him. The cop gained a little. *Time to slow down to set up the corner.* He downshifted into third. "Find the sweet spot," he whispered. "Don't lose too much speed. Where's the fucking cop?"

Like wishing away a nightmare, the Harley's headlight went dark. The *thump-thump* of the engine dropped back. *What's he doing?* Jason checked his mirror, catching the gleam of chrome in the moonlight as the motorcycle veered to the shoulder and sped up a lane into the hills east of the highway. The flashing red and blue lights were about a half-mile behind.

Jason slowed and pulled into a turnout. A minute later, the cruiser skidded to a stop, lights flashing, headlights pulsing, and spotlight on Jason in his car.

"Put your hands on the wheel where I can see them and do not move," a metallic voice boomed.

Jason did as he was told. He squinted against the glare in the driver's side mirror. The cruiser's door opened. A heavy man in uniform walked slowly to the Porsche, holding an eight-cell flashlight like a club. His other hand rested on his weapon in its holster. He stopped at Jason's window, blinding him with the flashlight's white-hot beam. "Exit your vehicle," he commanded. "No sudden moves."

CHAPTER 35

Jason squinted into the bright light. He couldn't see the cop's face but was sure he recognized the voice. "Duane?" Jason's heart pounded wildly. He ordered himself to calm down and deal with the situation. *This nightmare isn't over yet.*

"That's Deputy Hardesty to you, Brinkman. Now get out and give me your ID."

Jason opened his door and climbed out in slow motion. Hardesty swept the flashlight's beam over him from head to toe. The flashlight shook in his hand. His face was covered with sweat, and his breath was short and rapid.

Jason removed his license, registration, and insurance from his wallet with trembling hands and handed them over. Hardesty jerked his thumb at his cruiser. "Get in." He shined his light in the Porsche's side window. After scanning the interior, he walked back to his car, opened the driver's door, and dropped heavily into the seat.

Jason sat in the passenger's seat. Fast-food containers littered the back, and the cabin smelled of grease, onions, and sweat. The interior was lit dimly by the dome light and the screen of the onboard computer. Outside, the landscape was pitch-black, except for the arc of blue-white light cut by the cruiser's headlights and spotlight. Jason's Porsche sat ten feet ahead, glinting in the cold beam. The engine cover was battered and dented, and silver metal gleamed through jagged tears in the paint.

"You lease that vehicle?" Hardesty asked, handing Jason his registration certificate.

"So?"

"So, you ain't such a LA big shot if you can't afford to buy it."

"May I have my license and insurance card back, please?"

Hardesty handed both to him. "How much does it cost to lease a vehicle like that?"

"What do you want? Why am I sitting in your car?"

Hardesty pointed at the dash-mounted radar gun. Red numbers flashed *105*. He asked, "What's in the metal box?"

"What metal box?"

"The one on the floor of your leased vehicle."

"Fishing tackle."

"Mind if I take a look?"

"Got a warrant?"

The deputy tapped the flashing red numbers. "Here I am trying to decide whether to write you up. Why you wanna piss me off?"

"Because you have no legal justification to look in the box."

Jason tried to guess Hardesty's next moves. Hardesty knew that was the law, but was the type who'd open the box anyway and find the loaded gun. He'd say Jason had it in his waistband and arrest him for carrying a concealed weapon. That'd probably be a $1,000 fine, maybe jail time—

"I got me this dilemma," Hardesty broke in. "I could charge you… with violating…Vehicle Code section 22348(b)." He spoke haltingly, as if thinking out loud. "That's operating a motor vehicle at a speed in excess of one hundred miles per hour. Five-hundred-dollar fine and thirty days suspended license for you, and for me—I'd win the office pool this week. Might even earn some points with Commander Sepulveda, which I could use."

"You could drive up that hill over there and find El Carnicero. You wanted to find him when you were at my house a few hours ago."

"Yeah, well, it's just me patrolling this sector tonight, and there's all them little side roads up there, and there's paranoid pot farmers with shotguns, so I don't think so."

"The guy ransacks my house, threatens to kill me, chases me at a hundred miles an hour, beats the crap out of my car with a chain, and you're not gonna do anything about it?"

"Not tonight. You're like catnip to him, so he'll be back. I'll get more chances." Reaching into the console, Deputy Hardesty removed his ticket binder. He tapped the edge against his chin.

"Oh, damn," Jason groaned silently. "Here it comes. Five hundred dollars, points on my license, probably double my insurance."

Hardesty opened the binder and clicked his Bic pen. Holding the ticket form where Jason could see it, he wrote the letters "B," "r," and "i" in the first boxes. He clicked the pen again, then clicked it rapid-fire. After a long silence, he said, "Here's my dilemma." He turned in his seat to look Jason in the face. "Commander Sepulveda's pissed at me, and I need him not to be. Something about a lame-assed complaint about me by some civilian."

"Why do I care, Duane? What's it got to do with me?"

The deputy reached into his shirt pocket and removed an evidence baggie containing what looked like little clumps of dirt. He shook the bag in Jason's face. "Everything."

Jason raised his eyebrows, as if to say, "So?"

"This little baggie of dirt means you're gonna help me get on Sepulveda's good side."

"Tell you what." Jason dropped his license in the cop's lap. "Write your ticket and let me go home. I've got a lot to do tomorrow."

Hardesty tossed the license back. "Lemme spell it out for you. That dirt? I got it off your fancy-ass Gucci shoes when I was at your house this evening. Now, you might ask why that's important." He paused, his beady eyes full of anticipation.

Jason ignored him. He opened his wallet and put his license and registration back in it.

"OK, I'll tell you why it's important. It's because of footprints. Footprints outside Gerald O'Brien's house on Bluffside Drive, which the sheriff's department now considers a crime scene. *Capisce?*"

"No, I don't *capisce*. I think you've watched too many *CSIs*. Now I'm going to get out and walk back to my car and drive home. You know where to find me if you decide to give me the ticket. Otherwise, leave me alone." Jason reached for the door handle, but Hardesty's finger was resting on the power-lock button. The locks clicked, trapping Jason in the car.

"Uh-uh. You stay here 'til I say you can go." Hardesty continued, speaking with exaggerated patience. "There's a dirt path along the front of O'Brien's house. The fog and ocean air make it muddy, and there's two footprints in the mud, very clear ones, that say the word 'Gucci.' I got pictures if you wanna see 'em." He pointed to a cell phone in the console. "Show me the bottom of your right shoe."

"Take a hike, Duane." Jason spoke firmly, but he felt a trickle of worry in his stomach. He'd forgotten the Gucci logo was engraved in the soles of his loafers. He remembered walking the muddy path yesterday and could've left footprints.

"No matter, I know it says 'Gucci.' I seen it at your house. Now do you understand?"

"Do you have any idea how many millions of Gucci shoes there are in California?"

The deputy sighed. He leaned back against his headrest and ran his hands through his short buzz cut. He wiped his palms on his pants. "I see you still ain't with me." Fumbling in his other shirt pocket, he produced a second evidence baggie containing clumps of dirt. "This here is dirt from inside O'Brien's house. Now, if I was a bettin' man, I'd bet that if forensics analyzed this dirt and the dirt from your shoes and the muddy path, they'd all match."

Jason saw where this was headed. He'd left muddy footprints on the foyer floor yesterday and a lot of fingerprints upstairs, so Hardesty could show he was in the house. Hardesty would contend that implicated Jason in Geraldo's death. But Hardesty didn't know *when* Jason was inside—it could've been weeks ago. He decided his best move was confrontation. "Alright. That's enough. You're harassing me, and this is false imprisonment. I'm telling you one last time to unlock this door—"

"Here's how I see it. I can prove you was in the house where O'Brien was killed. He owed you, let's see, is it $40,000? You're big enough to dump him in the storm drain. So I got me motive, means, and opportunity."

"You want to be careful. You're heading toward a serious accusation that's wrong and based on illegally obtained evidence."

"What's illegal? We hadta look in O'Brien's house before we sealed it as a crime scene, didn't we? Would a good ol' boy judge say one of the sheriff's own can't take a little dirt sample off the floor when the rest of it's still there?"

Jason pushed himself over the console so he was inches from Hardesty's face. "Go ahead and arrest me if you're so certain. I'll sue you and the sheriff within an inch of your life. You'll be lucky to be a security guard at Walmart when I'm through with you."

Hardesty leaned back against the driver's door, smearing an oily scalp print on the window. He spoke more softly. "Calm down. I ain't gonna arrest you. Yet. But you are definitely a person of interest. So I got me one ace showing, which is you being a person of interest, and another in the hole, which is you being a likely suspect."

The trickle of worry in Jason's stomach became a fist-sized knot. What if Hardesty got the investigators to focus on him? He could tie Jason up for months with investigations and court hearings. He wouldn't be able to earn a living, and the bad press would ruin his practice. A moment later, he kicked himself mentally. It was something Hardesty said. Something to do with Sepulveda. *Hardesty doesn't want me—he's pressuring me to do something for him.*

Hardesty interrupted his thoughts. "Here's how this is gonna go if you don't want to become a actual suspect." He grabbed the steering wheel and pulled himself upright in his seat. "You're gonna help me find O'Brien's killer. And when I deliver the killer, Commander Sepulveda'll owe me, and it'll be payback time."

"But you've already got a person of interest—Mags Turlock."

"Nah. My cop sense tells me she ain't the one. Well, she could be, I guess. If you find out she did it, then it's her, and I lose this round."

Jason sank back against the passenger's door and considered his options. Bizarre as it was, he decided cooperating with Hardesty, or at least pretending to, could work to his advantage. He reasoned it would keep Hardesty from ruining his life, and if he found the killer, he might find money for Geraldo's estate. He could get his $38,000 back, and there might be more. Plus the 'lame-assed' civilian was probably James Paige, and he might get some intel for Paige's case.

He decided to agree, provided that… "OK, I'll play along, but only if you promise to tell me everything the sheriff's department knows as soon as they know it. And for the record, I had nothing whatsoever to do with Geraldo's death. Do you agree?"

"Why should I tell you shit? You got no juice here."

"It's to your advantage. Think about it."

"How's it to my advantage to disclose confidential investigation information to a civilian?"

"You want to earn points with Sepulveda, right? This is a high-profile case. You don't want to serve up the wrong suspect. You do, and he'll bust you to foot cop in the *barrio*. The more information I have, the better leads I can develop, and the quicker we'll find the right guy."

Hardesty shifted in his seat. He tapped the steering wheel, cleared the radar gun, closed the ticket binder and slid it into the console. "OK, partner," he shrugged. "You got it. We're a team."

Only then did the deputy's peculiar phrase hit him. Jason asked, "You said, 'Lose this round'? What does that mean?"

"Damn, you are slow. This is all about me getting promoted to sergeant. If I bring Sepulveda the killer, he'll have to give me the promotion. Why else'd I care about who killed a scuzzbag like O'Gerald Brien?"

CHAPTER 36

Jason pulled into his driveway, dog tired and still fuming from his confrontation with Deputy Dumbass. He glanced at the Porsche's dashboard clock before climbing out. 2:00 a.m.

His cell phone rang as he unlocked his front door. He didn't recognize the number but answered anyway, hoping it was Erin.

"Brinkman?"

"Who's this?"

"Mags Turlock."

His heart sank. "What do you want, Mags. At this hour?"

"You've gotta help me."

"Why?"

"I'm in jail."

"Why're you calling me? Isn't Charles Chalmers your attorney?"

"He's in Barbados deep-sea fishing, and his associate is sick. He said to call you, that you could handle it 'til he gets back."

"I'm flattered. I love to carry another attorney's briefcase. Why are you in jail, Mags?"

"They're saying I killed Geraldo."

Mags normally conveyed no emotion when she spoke unless she was browbeating another real estate agent or a client. He heard panic in her voice now.

"They're gonna charge me, and my bail hearing's tomorrow morning. Please! I need your help."

"Bail hearings are at ten a.m. Can't this wait 'til eight tomorrow?"

"Tomorrow? No way! I'm freaking out. I never even had a parking ticket. I'm gonna lose it. I need you to … you've gotta … I'll pay you double to come down here right now."

Jason had a short list of people he never wanted to represent, and Mags Turlock was at the top. They'd despised each other from the moment they met. He disliked her overbearing personality and thought her business tactics were sleazy. She acted paranoid about his confidential relationship with Geraldo and was jealous of the time they spent together. Nonetheless, this was an opportunity to score a few thousand dollars representing her until Chalmers returned, plus a chit with the county's top trial lawyer.

Jason imagined himself falling into his bed. He felt the pillow under his head and the soft warmth of his down comforter. A moment later, he pictured Mags handing him a check for $3,000. He sighed. "OK, Mags. Don't say anything else. Are you in the main lock-up in Santa Luisa?"

"No. Rock Bay. You know, the sheriff's office."

"I'll be there in a half-hour. Keep your mouth shut."

* * *

Thirty minutes later, Jason handed his business card to Deputy Flack, the night duty officer at the sheriff's Rock Bay office. "Jason Brinkman to see Mags Turlock."

"You got ID to go with this?"

Jason produced his driver's license and State Bar card. Flack examined them under the light of his desk lamp. "Wait here," he said, yawning and handing back Jason's ID. He pushed away from his desk and shoved through the metal door from the lobby to the bullpen. "Manny," he called, "the detainee's got a visitor."

Before the door swung closed, another male voice said, "It's fuckin' two-thirty in the morning."

Flack said, "Goddamn lawyer."

Jason sat in a plastic chair in the lobby and tried not to doze off. The bullpen door clanged open a few minutes later, startling him awake. Flack stood in the opening with a clipboard under his arm. "Mr. Brinkman. Follow me."

The officer led him into the bullpen, a windowless room about 40 feet by 30 feet painted prison-gray. A dozen halogen fixtures hung from the ceiling, flooding the space with brilliant white light. Dented and chipped beige metal lockers lined the walls, and scarred wooden benches were bolted to the floor in front of them. Another deputy, presumably Manny, sat on a bench reading on a tablet.

In the corner closest to the door was a glassed-in cubicle with a desk and a phone. A plastic sign taped to the cubicle's slider said *Commander Ramon Sepulveda*. Below it, a handwritten sticky said *DO NOT BOTHER ME NOW*.

A holding cell—actually, a steel cage about eight feet square and six feet tall—filled the center of the room. Mags Turlock sat on a cot inside the cage, rocking back and forth with her arms wrapped around her torso.

"This your attorney?" Flack asked her. She glanced at Jason and nodded weakly. Jason caught her eyes before she looked away. He saw panic instead of her normal arrogant self-assurance.

"May I see the charging documents, please?" Jason asked the deputy.

"Don't have 'em," Flack said. "Just a summary." He removed a computer printout from his clipboard.

Jason arched his eyebrows as he scanned the sheet. "You can't be serious," he muttered. "All that's missing is the kitchen sink." He folded the sheet and stuck it in his pocket. "I'd like to talk to my client in private. Where's a room we can use?"

"Well, now, that's going to be a problem, sir. We don't usually get attorney visits at this facility."

"So you're denying my client her right to consult with her attorney in private?" Jason said with measured menace. "What do you think the judge will say about that at the bail hearing tomorrow?"

Deputy Flack looked over his shoulder at Manny. He closed the cover on his tablet with exaggerated care and jerked his head toward the bullpen door. Flack said, "You can stay here, sir. Just knock when you're done." The two deputies circled the room, checking the padlocks on the lockers. When they finished, they walked to the door and pulled it open.

"Hey!" Jason barked at their backs. "You wanna let my client out?"

Flack grunted and strode back. He sorted through the keys on his belt caddy and unlocked the cage.

"Thanks," Jason said as the deputy walked away.

"No problem."

The bullpen door slammed shut.

"Mags," Jason said encouragingly, "why don't we sit on the bench out here and talk about things."

"Umm...no...." Mags's voice was tentative, unlike her usual combative tone. "I'm too scared. There's only mean people and things I don't understand out there. I'm safe in the cage. You come in here."

That was the last thing Jason wanted to do after his afternoon under the spec house. He said, "Small spaces bother me. Come out here. It's more comfortable."

Mags resumed her rocking. He waited several minutes before shoving the door open enough to slip through.

Sitting next to Mags on the cot, he was surprised at her appearance. She was a large, robust woman, who used her stature to intimidate competitors and clients. Her usual outfit—an oversized gray or black sweat suit—made her even more imposing. At three in the morning, after spending the day in custody, she appeared shrunken and broken. Even her gray sweat suit, always crisp and fresh, was dirty and sweat-stained.

"You gotta get me out of here," she said after a long silence. "I can't go to jail."

"I will, but we have to get some things settled first." Jason explained his fee and went over the terms of his representation. "Chalmers will handle any negotiations, your plea, and the trial, if there is one," he summarized. "Tomorrow I'll have a retainer agreement with these terms, and you will sign it. Agreed?"

"What? Sure."

"And there's one more thing. Deputy Hardesty, the cop in Sea Cliff... you know who he is?"

"Hardesty? Oh yeah, him."

"He considers me a person of interest in Geraldo's death. Not the sheriff's department, just him. You need to understand it's possible, but unlikely, that a conflict of interest could arise. I'd have to withdraw from your case if that happened, but anything you tell me will continue to be privileged and confidential. Understood?"

"Uh-huh."

"Good. Alright. Now, they're really throwing the book at you, so why don't you tell me everything that happened the night Geraldo died."

Mags spoke as if describing a dream. "It was Geraldo's retirement party. He invited everyone he knew to One Bluffside to buy all the drugs they wanted at wholesale. He promised me he'd pay off all the debts on the house, and give me money for Jamie to bring the mortgage current. He said he'd sign the house over to me, and we agreed I'd send him his share of the profits when I sold it. Same with his house where he lived with Danni and Tiffany."

That surprised Jason because it suggested Geraldo didn't plan to screw the investors after all. But he knew that Geraldo was better at making promises than keeping them. Focusing again on Mags's story, he asked, "Who was at the party? Can you remember?"

"I didn't know a lot of them. There was Pedro, and most of the workers. Some of his material suppliers and subcontractors. A bunch of scroungy guys who must've been runners. One huge Mexican with a tattoo on his forehead—I never got close enough to read it—but he was one scary-looking dude."

"Huh. Did you see him and Geraldo together?"

"No, but I wasn't paying attention, either. Why?"

"I heard Geraldo owes him a lot of money."

Mags snorted. "Geraldo owes everyone a lot of money, including me and you. Anyway, let's see. Danni and Tiffany were there for a while, and Jamie, and some of the Mostly's crowd, and a real pretty blonde, but I'm sure she was a les. Funny how you can just tell sometimes. And some others. I'll have to think about it."

"Do that. Do you know where he was going to go?"

"Probably Australia, but he wasn't sure. Maybe Fiji. Any place with sun and good surfing and beach babes. You know, I did see him and Jamie arguing. Jamie got all red in the face, and stormed out."

Jason decided he should add Jamie to the list of people he wanted to find out about. He asked, "What about Danni and Tiffany? Was he going to take them with him?"

A hint of the real Mags returned. "Get real. No way. He was done with them." She paused. "I could give a shit about Danni, but Tiffany's just a kid. He should've done better by her. I feel bad about that. Always have, since I met her."

Jason had to agree. Danni chose her life, and it was a train wreck, but Tiffany was paying the price. He made another silent promise to Tiffany to do everything he could to find her.

Mags fell silent.

"So, what happened?"

"Huh? Oh. Well, there was a big crowd by about eleven o'clock, and everyone was having a good time. People were buying the shit they wanted. Geraldo was drinking and snorting and smoking, and I even saw him shoot up once in the kitchen. Then everyone was standing in a circle in the great room and Geraldo was in the middle, and we were going to toast him and wish him good travels, but...." She stopped.

Jason looked at her face. Incredibly, tears ran down her cheeks. "Mags," he said gently. "What happened?"

"The son of a bitch died. He fucking fell flat on his face and died." She let out a single sob and wiped her eyes with her sleeve. "The whole spec house shook, like in an earthquake. *BAWHAM!* And that was it. He was dead."

"And? What happened next?"

"Everybody ran out of the house. Like cockroaches when you turn on the light. It was just me alone with him in the empty house."

"How do you know he was dead?"

Another glimpse of the real Mags showed through. "I felt his pulse, dumb shit. How else would I know for sure?" She wiped her nose with her cuff.

"Did you call 911? I mean, he could've just passed out from all the booze and drugs."

"What part of 'dead' don't you understand? There was no pulse! He was dead! Why would I call 911?"

"What happened next?"

"I sat with him a few minutes. He had a heart problem, you know. He was taking some kind of meds for it. And he and I had a thing for a while. You've probably heard that. We weren't in love, but we were close to each other, and there was all the business stuff. We were like a couple when it came to business." She trailed off and stared blankly through the cage bars.

"Mags?"

"Then I left. He was lying on the great room floor in a pool of blood from his nose. I got in my car and drove home."

"Did you lock the spec house?"

"No. I just closed the front door."

"Was the house empty?"

"I think so. Don't know for sure."

"Can anyone vouch for when you left or when you got home?"

"No. I guess that would help." She paused for a minute. "Anyway, I got home and started thinking. That son-of-a-bitch died, leaving me holding the bag for the mortgage on One Bluffside, plus all the money I put into it, which was all of my liquid cash, and now I can't even pay my own bills."

The color returned to Mags's cheeks. She stood and began pacing the cage. "And how am I supposed to sell a home when someone's just died in it? Will you tell me that? Nobody wants to buy a home where someone's just died. Six months from now, I could sell it. Buyers aren't so squeamish after six months or a year. But I don't have six months, do I, 'cause the bank's gonna foreclose and my whole leveraged life's gonna collapse."

She stopped at the far end of the cage and spun around to face Jason. "That's when I started getting pissed. 'Calm down,' I told myself. 'The Lord tells us every problem's got a solution, and His divine wisdom and guidance will show us the way.' So I prayed. I got down on my knees, did the whole bit. I thanked the Lord for bestowing His blessings on me for so long, and I reminded Him how I'd given Geraldo all my money. I told Him how I can't sell the fucking spec house and how I'm going broke 'cause I don't have any free cash, and I asked Him what I should do. And I prayed and prayed really hard."

She paced to the cot, back to the other end, forward again, finally stopping just short of Jason. "Jesus, it's way too close in here. I've gotta go outside and sit on the bench."

CHAPTER 37

Mags pushed her way out of the holding cell and straddled the closest bench. Her cheeks burned red with anger. Jason followed and sat facing her. He asked, "So, what did the Lord tell you to do about Geraldo and the mess at the spec house?"

"You know, I couldn't believe it," Mags said, her expression full of wonder. "He said to move the body and clean up the blood. Problem solved. I asked Him twice if He was sure that's what I should do, and He said yes. So I took my insulin kit, 'cause I was about due for a shot, and got in my van and drove back to One Bluffside."

"How long were you at home?"

"I don't know. Half-hour. Forty-five minutes maybe."

"What'd you do when you got back to the spec house?"

"I took the elevator upstairs. I was so tired, I trusted it not to get stuck. All the time, I was trying to figure out what to do with the body."

"Were you alone? Was anyone else in the house?"

"You know, that was strange. Danni just appeared, like magic. Said she saw my van and came up the stairs. *Poof*, there she was."

"Was she the only other person?"

"Yeah, I think so."

"And then?"

Mags was on her feet, pacing again. "We cleaned up the blood together. That was a mess, let me tell you. It stinks and it's sticky. Disgusting! After that, we got the body into the elevator and dragged it out to my van. I carried the head and she carried the feet. It wasn't so bad with the two of us."

"How did Danni react? To Geraldo being dead."

"She was hard to read. Could've been drunk or stoned, I suppose. Seemed kinda numb, moving in slow motion." Mags circled the outside of the bullpen, talking as she paced. "I told her to clean up all the drugs that were lying around and put 'em away. Told her I could take it from there." She walked faster, speaking louder with each step. "I drove the body through the fog to Vista Point. I wanted to push him over the edge at the end of the Point, so it'd look like he'd jumped—"

"For God's sake, lower your voice! You don't want them to hear any of this." He gestured at the door behind him. "Come over here and sit."

Mags completed her circle and straddled the bench, facing him. She continued in a stage whisper. "I wanted it to look like suicide, but his boot caught on the lip of the storm drain, and he fell into it instead. Threw my hip out dragging him across the parking lot. I wanted to get him out of there, but he was way down and I couldn't reach him. Wouldn't have had the strength anyway, I guess. There was nothing left to do, so I went home. I prayed he wouldn't get found, and all week long I thought it was gonna be OK, but the cops showed up this morning."

She started to stand, but Jason pushed her down. "OK, listen to me. Everything you've said and will say to me about the case is privileged and confidential. Now, as your attorney, I'm asking you: Did you kill Geraldo?"

"For the love of God! Have you been listening? How could I kill him if he was already dead? I only moved him so I could sell the damn spec house."

"It's a yes or no question. And keep your voice down. Did you or didn't you?"

She shoved herself toward him on the bench. "You want 'yes' or 'no'? OK. The answer is 'no'! But let me ask you something. Why do you care if I did?"

"Because you threatened to kill him when you and I were at the spec house. You said, 'If I lose even one property because of him, I'll kill him twice.'"

Mags was in his face now. "Yeah, but what difference does it make? Isn't your job to get me off, even if I'm guilty?"

Jason pushed her away. "No, that's Silver Throat Chalmers's job. But for sake of argument, my ethical duty is to represent you to the best of my ability, even if you are guilty. I need to know whether you killed Geraldo so I can evaluate the evidence while I'm responsible for your case. Now, are we done with this?"

Mags nodded, but her eyes smoldered.

"One last question: Do you know who killed him?"

Her eyes darted over his shoulder before wandering back to his face. "No, goddammit! He was already DEAD! How many times do I have to say it? He was DEAD!"

Jason was certain she was holding back, but felt that was all he was going to get for now. "Alright. Let's look at the charges they're filing against you." He unfolded the summary of charges sheet and smoothed it on the bench between them. "Here's what I think is going on: The picture of Geraldo's body hanging from the crane went viral. This became a high-profile case overnight. The district attorney and the sheriff must be under a lot of pressure to solve it. That's why they're throwing the book at you." He handed her the summary sheet. "Looking at the charges, their theory must be that Geraldo was unconscious when he keeled over in the spec house. They must think you drove him to Vista Point to kill him, and you did it by dropping him on his head in the storm drain."

Mags picked up the summary sheet and read it. "How do you get all that? It's just a list of words and numbers."

Jason pointed at the first line. "They're charging you with kidnapping. That means they think he was alive when you moved him to Vista Point. Felony murder, because he died during the commission of a felony—in this case, kidnapping. First degree murder, because they'll argue that you acted with premeditation. They can also base the first degree murder on the kidnapping. Conspiracy… probably because they think you couldn't move the body without help. Elder abuse—because he was sixty-five—as well as battery and false imprisonment of an elderly person. And, destroying evidence. That must be because you cleaned up the blood. It's a misdemeanor, but it'll have to be dealt with."

Jason blew out a long breath. "What did you tell the sheriff? Why did you talk to them at all?"

The color drained from Mags's face. "Can they do that to me? How can they say those things?" She crumpled the paper and dropped it on the bench. "All I told them was I moved the body. I told them he died in One Bluffside and I drove him to Vista Point in my van. I thought if I cooperated and told the truth, they'd leave me alone. Boy, was I naïve."

"Did they want to know why you moved the body?"

"I told them I had an appointment to show the house the next morning. It was a lie, but just a little one, 'cause I did show the house a week later, the day I found you there. It was the elderly couple from Beverly Hills, the ones who want an elevator. I'm expecting they'll make an offer, actually."

"Did the cops ask why you didn't call 911 to remove the body?"

"They did, and I told them I didn't know you could call 911 for a dead person. Honest, I didn't. I thought 911 was only for like car accidents and heart attacks, you know, emergencies with living people. I guess I should've."

"Did you tell them they could search your minivan?"

"Sure I did. Why wouldn't I if I had nothing to hide?" She drummed her fingers nervously on the bench. "So what happens next?" she asked.

"Well, I'd say old Silver Throat's going to earn his fee. Your bail hearing's at ten o'clock, and I'll be there to represent you. If the DA agrees to bail at all, I'd guess he'll ask for $1 million because the charges are serious. I'll try to get less, given your ties to the community, but I don't know. If it's a million, you'll have to put up $100,000."

"A hundred grand?" she squeaked. "I told you I don't have any cash! I can't get that kind of money! All my properties are leveraged already." She grabbed both his arms. "I can't be in jail with a bunch of lesbians. I'm diabetic. I'm a vegetarian. I have claustrophobia. I'm a germaphobe. I'll die in there. Some bull dyke will rape me. You've gotta keep me out of jail! Please! You havta do something!"

Jason pried her fingers off his arms one by one. "I'm sorry, Mags, but I think that's how it's gonna go. I'll argue for the lowest possible bail, but…wait a minute." He uncrumpled the summary of charges. "You know what's missing here?" He ran his finger down the lines of type. "Possession. There's no charge of possessing drugs. Huh." He explained his thinking. "When you moved the drugs out of the kitchen, the law says you took possession of them. If the cops knew about that, you'd have been charged with possession. Did you tell the cops about moving the drugs?"

"No."

"Did you tell them about the drugs at all?"

"No. Why would I?"

"Well, where are they? Hardesty said he and the cops were in the spec house before they sealed it as a crime scene."

Mags looked over his shoulder, seeming to gather her thoughts. "There's a hole in my memory of that afternoon. Happens when I black out like I did. So, let's see…. After you left, I took my injection and had some candy. I remember getting boxes and garbage bags from the kitchen and packing the rest of the pills and shit in them and stacking them all in the master closet. There's a lock on that door, and I remember locking it. The house was clean when I showed my clients yesterday afternoon, so it was clean when the cops were inside."

Jason felt a bit of hope. "That's the first smart thing you've done. You kept a bargaining chip."

"I did?"

"You did. I'll tell the district attorney I have important information about the case he doesn't know about. I'll offer to trade the information for lower bail. Maybe I can negotiate it down to something more manageable—say, $500,000, or even $100,000."

"Do I need cash?" Mags asked, wringing her hands. "I might have $10,000 equity in my rentals. I could sign them over."

"Good. Yes, they'll usually take property instead of cash. Now listen to me. Don't blow this. Don't say anything about the drugs to anyone. Let me bring it up to the DA before the bail hearing."

"You won't tell him I moved the drugs, will you?"

"Of course not. I'll just say you saw them in the closet."

Mags's face relaxed and the corners of her mouth twitched up. "I guess I underestimated you. Thanks."

"You're welcome, but I still have to make the deal happen."

* * *

The moon was beginning to set as the KHYP news van crept down the alley next to the sheriff's office in Rock Bay. Spike stopped at the corner of the building before nosing forward just enough to see the floodlit entrance in the middle of the block.

Ally craned her neck. "Move up. I can't see the door."

Spike swore under his breath. He inched ahead.

"More! I still can't see."

Spike cut the ignition. "Chill, girl! We plenty close for the big lens, not that there gonna be anything to film."

Ally bristled. "You just refuse to understand my vision, don't you! Whatever we get will be a integral part of the whole story! You've got no faith in me and you're not thinking big! I…we can ride The Storm Drain Murder all the way to New York. I know how—"

"You say, but we don't know it be murder or who the perp is, and you got me here at five in the mornin' when I should be home lyin' with my warm woman."

Ally punched his shoulder. "Will you open your mind and listen to me! In the first place, you're wrong. It *is* murder, or they wouldn't be holding someone. Secondly, we definitely need video of the perp being escorted from the lockup here. That's why we're here at five a.m. Then we'll follow the sheriff's van down to Santa Luisa to get the guy being perp-walked into the main jail. In the third place, we need to film the bail hearing and the arraignment, if we can get in with a camera. Even a cell phone would be OK. That's half our story!"

"Nuh-uh, girl. That ain't news. Some dude in a orange suit starin' at his feet."

"Of course that's news! I know what I'm talking about. I'm getting an 'A' in my online journalism class. The story is the whole package, and the whole package is the story. We've gotta have every piece of it recorded. Even if we don't use something in the package, we'll use it in the documentary we'll sell to *48 Hours*."

"You do talk some shit, girl."

They sat in the dark van. Spike beat a rhythm on the steering wheel. Ally checked her Twitter, Instagram, and Facebook feeds, but everything was boring. She scrolled through the other TV stations' feeds to see the stories they were running. There was nothing on The Storm Drain Murder. Good news for her.

"I'm thirsty," Ally complained. "Where's the water bottle? Or did you drink it all again?"

Spike ignored her.

"You're a selfish man, you know that? You never leave any for me. You don't even wipe off the mouth. I'm gonna get a case of water at Costco just for me—"

"Who that leaving the sheriff's?"

They watched a man walk toward them under the bright streetlamps. He stopped in a cone of light 20 yards away and checked his phone.

"Don't know," Ally replied. "He looks so LA. I mean, his clothes and hair." She gulped. The guy was gorgeous! So gorgeous, she could eat him up. His silk shirt screamed *money*, and he was built like he worked out every day. She forced herself to focus on her mission. "I'll bet he's the perp's lawyer. Who else'd be leaving the sheriff's at five in the morning? Get the camera ready."

Spike powered up the camera and adjusted the light and lens settings. "I think I seen him in Sea Cliff."

"He's getting into the Porsche!" Ally cried excitedly, thinking they guy was a ten, and the car was a twelve, except for the dents in the trunk. She wanted to know his story. Why was he doing the lawyer bit in Podunk when his face could be making him millions in LA?

"Lordy, that be one sweet ride," Spike sighed, hoisting the camera and fine-tuning the focus. "Gotta be $150 grand. Too bad the back end's all beat to shit."

"Can't be many cars like that in these parts," Ally said thoughtfully. "If we can find him, we can learn everything about the perp and the case." She added silently, "And him."

The Porsche's lights came on as it backed out of its parking space.

"Get the license," Ally ordered.

The camera's red light reflected in the van's windshield. "Got it, babe," Spike whispered, squinting into the eyepiece. "Vanity plate. Buncha letters." He filmed until the Porsche turned the corner at the far end of the block.

"What does it say?"

Spike sat silently, smirking. Ally fidgeted while her mind spun. The guy was totally hot. She'd build her story around him—the hunky young lawyer. She definitely could use him. *Who am I kidding? He can use me all weekend and twice on Monday morning.* Her core demographic was women 18 to 35. They'd love him. He'd sell her story like that Peterson guy who was convicted of killing his prego wife. Forty-two percent of women in her demographic watched the stories about him just because he was so cute.

"Spike! What does the license plate say?"

He didn't answer. He checked the camera's power level, dug a cleaning cloth out of his kit, and wiped the lens. The dashboard clock ticked.

Ally let her imagination go. Maybe he took the case so he could make a name for himself, same as her. They could be a team, and they could solve The Storm Drain Murder together. He could be her agent when she sold her story. She'd take *him* to New York with her. They'd be a power couple and make shows about solving crimes. He'd syndicate them and they'd be rich. But they had to find him first, and Spike still hadn't told her!

"Dammit, Spike! What does it say?"

Spike set the camera on the console between them. He reached behind him and took a pack of cigarettes from his jacket. He shook one out and patted his pockets until he found a book of matches. He offered a cigarette to Ally. She batted it out of his hand.

"Spike!" Ally shouted. "Tell me!"

Spike's smile crinkled his eyes. "That little ol' license plate? Why, it say BRNKMAN. That his name. You right. He be a lawyer. I seen his sign in Sea Cliff," he said triumphantly. "Be no trouble finding him. No trouble 'tall. You Google him, and we go find him after we film the hearing in Santa Luisa."

Ally stretched over the console and kissed his cheek. "You're awesome, Spike! That's why I'm taking *you* with me to New York. You'll always be on my team!"

She settled back in her seat, lost in thought. *BRNKMAN. Must be Brinkman. Hmmm. Brinkman. Ally Brinkman. Allison Booker Brinkman. ABB Productions Inc. I like it! Girl, you go for it!*

PART 4

BAD BARGAINS

CHAPTER 38

Whatley, Thelen & Füchs was known throughout California as the law firm that never sleeps. Twenty-four hours a day, 365 days a year, the Whatley Tower's lights blazed against the downtown Los Angeles skyline—a 45-story beacon of wealth and power summoning the corrupt and greedy.

At 6:30 on this foggy morning, like any morning, every lawyer, paralegal, investigator, and secretary was already hard at work. The rest of downtown Los Angeles was beginning to come alive as Gretchen Fautz, senior managing partner and preeminent Southern California super-lawyer, ended her first conference of the day.

Gretchen met weekly with her two top lieutenants for briefings on the major lawsuits she managed. This morning, every lamp in her corner office burned brightly against the gray mist that shrouded her windows. She wore a white Chanel business suit that offset her leathery tan skin and coal-black eyes. A 4-carat diamond pendant and a 10-carat tennis bracelet completed the day's ensemble.

Sitting behind her massive rosewood desk, Gretchen wrapped one leg around the other, coiling herself like a snake ready to strike. Andrew Weathersby and Courtney Brinkman sat quietly in client chairs across from her, balancing stacks of red-back litigation binders on their laps. They waited for her next question or reprimand.

Gretchen scowled at Andrew, her black eyes burning with displeasure. "Your team's spending too much time on the refinery explosion litigation. I shouldn't have to tell you that. It makes me question my faith in you." Reaching for her jeweled Cartier lighter, she lit a cigarette and inhaled deeply. "I want the complete liability analysis and evidence summary on my desk by next week's meeting." She paused to cough, then coughed again, setting off a frenzy that wracked her thin body. "Lock your people in their offices if you have to," she rasped. "I want it done!"

Safely out of harm's way for the moment, Courtney opened a file and pretended to read it while she silently pondered the question that consumed her day and night: *How does this osteoporotic little woman wield such enormous power?*

Andrew stiffened in his chair. "OK, Gretchen," he replied hesitantly. "Two of my people are out sick, but I'll do my best—"

Gretchen raised an eyebrow.

"It'll be done by next week."

Gretchen said, "Good. Now, Courtney and I need the room."

Andrew looked at the red-backs on his lap and then at Gretchen. "But—" he began.

"Now!"

Andrew gathered his binders and stood. "Right. Have a good day, Gretchen. And you, Courtney." Arms bursting, he shuffled across the antique Bokhara carpet and nudged the door closed with his elbow.

Courtney closed her file. "What's up?" she asked. Her face was a mask of composure, but she tensed with anticipation. *Is this it?*

Gretchen opened her desk drawer. She handed Courtney a letter from Redaway and Associates, signed by Harlan Redaway. Courtney knew his reputation as a cutthroat litigator almost as vicious as Gretchen. The subject line read: "Demand for Return of Monies Paid."

"Jesus, Gretchen. When did you get this?"

"Last night at ten-thirty. I ran into the messenger as I was leaving. We've got to be sure no one finds out about it until I decide what to do."

Courtney smiled to herself as she read Redaway's letter—the first step in her coup. Soon, Redaway would pound a stake through the bitch queen's heart. The firm would be in chaos. The partners would turn to Courtney to restore order because only she knew everything Gretchen knew.

The letter announced that Harlan Redaway had been retained by the heirs of the late Everett Granquist, Jr. to recover $40 million won by Gretchen from his estate in the case of *Lancaster v. Estate of*

Granquist. The letter demanded return of the money plus interest, and accused Gretchen of withholding material evidence and perpetrating a fraud on the court. It threatened to inform the judge about Gretchen's malfeasance and gross violation of ethical duty, and to seek significant monetary sanctions against her and the Whatley firm. It also threatened to refer the matter to the State Bar of California for disciplinary action, which could result in Gretchen losing her license to practice law.

Courtney thought the letter was perfect. Better than she could have written it. Her satisfaction was marred, however, by an annoying nostalgic memory: The Granquist case was one of Jason's and her first cases together. Back when she thought she loved him. Before she saw her true potential if she wasn't encumbered.

She remembered the facts of the case like it was yesterday.

* * *

Fifteen years ago, Lucas Lancaster—teen heartthrob, turned leading man, turned reality show host—paid environmental philanthropist Everett Granquist, Jr. $10 million cash for 40 acres of northern Alaska mountaintop with stunning views of the Brooks Range. The Granquist family had owned the land for 100 years, and 50 years ago, Everett Sr. built a rustic lodge at the summit. The family stayed at the lodge from the Fourth of July through Labor Day every year, even though it was accessible only by mule or helicopter.

Lancaster spent $30 million razing the old lodge and building a new luxury retreat on the site. Following several unusually hot summers, the permafrost beneath the summit melted. This caused the building to settle unevenly, and finally, to slide down the mountain.

Lancaster's architects and engineers had certified the structural integrity of the building and the stability of the land, but they went bankrupt early in the Great Recession. Granquist, the only remaining deep pocket, was killed by the 2008 Gap wildfire in Santa Barbara County, which also destroyed his home and burned all his records.

Gretchen sued Granquist's estate on behalf of her Hollywood buddy Luke Lancaster. She argued that Granquist had a duty, and failed, to disclose that the entire mountaintop sat on permafrost and could become unstable due to warming summer temperatures. She cited the Granquist family's knowledge of the property gained over 100 years of ownership and 50 years of regular use. The estate's lawyers argued that Everett Granquist, Jr. had made proper disclosures, but were not able to produce any written proof because of the fire. Gretchen steamrolled her way to a $40 million verdict.

But Courtney knew Gretchen had a big problem. Before the sale, Granquist had prepared a handwritten note relieving him and his estate of all liability arising out of the sale if global warming melted the permafrost and caused the land to give way. He required Lancaster to sign the note and agree to its terms as a condition of completing the transaction.

While reviewing Lancaster's records in preparation for the trial, Jason discovered the original note crumpled and crushed in the bottom of an expanding file folder. He showed it to Courtney, and they decided Gretchen had to be told about it. Then, and now, Courtney knew it was the right thing to do. It would've been malpractice if they didn't tell Gretchen, and they would've been fired when the case blew up, which Courtney knew would happen someday.

Jason included the note in the evidence summary he prepared for Gretchen, and emphasized his conclusions that Lancaster was not entitled to any recovery and that the case was unfounded. The Granquist estate's lawyers didn't know about the note, however, so Gretchen ignored it in her march to victory.

Still pretending to study Redaway's letter, Courtney gloated silently. Gretchen didn't know that Jason kept copies of the note and summary. Courtney kept her own copies, of course. Jason didn't know. Now that the time was right, now that Gretchen was about to become the firm's most powerful partner, Courtney sent a copy to Redaway.

Courtney frowned to show her concern, and handed Redaway's letter back to her boss. "This could be serious, Gretchen."

"I don't need you to tell me that," Gretchen snapped. "Here's what you need to remember: Regis Thelen is finally dead and out of the way. I will be named the firm's senior managing partner of global operations in New York. It's all but certain, but it can still get fucked up, so you're going to fix it. Find someone to blame for not telling me about the note, someone expendable, and get rid of them. I'll plead ignorance to Harlan and try to negotiate a compromise. Harlan and I go back a long time. I'm sure he won't be too unreasonable."

For the first time, Courtney saw a flicker of doubt in Gretchen's eyes. "Doesn't Redaway hate you because you beat him every time you try a case against him?" she asked innocently. "And weren't you engaged to him once?"

Gretchen waved her hand, as if to dismiss the idea she couldn't bend Redaway to her will. "Get on it, Courtney. Keep me posted, but no electronic communications. Only face-to-face."

"I'll take care of everything." Courtney smiled reassuringly, but her eyes remained stone cold. "Trust me, Gretchen. Things will work out."

* * *

Jason slumped face-down on his desk, dead to the world.

He'd left Mags in her cell at 5:30 a.m., driven home, taken a cold shower, and changed into a suit. The drive to the courthouse in Santa Luisa took 45 minutes. He and the deputy district attorney entered the courtroom at the same time, minutes before the bail hearing. Jason asked him to confer in the hall, and they'd stepped outside.

They'd reached an agreement after some dodging and feinting. Jason promised to disclose the existence and location of the drug cache at One Bluffside. The deputy DA agreed to ask the judge to set Mags's bail at $200,000, with the condition that she not leave Sea Cliff. The judge approved the agreement without comment.

When Jason left the courthouse, a pushy young reporter tried to interview him about what she called "The Storm Drain Murder." Fearing his sleep-deprived brain would trip him up, he'd brushed her off. He'd driven back to Sea Cliff with the top and windows down so he wouldn't doze off.

Instead of going home to sleep, he'd decided to work on Geraldo's estate at his office for a few hours, and stopped to get the files from GG's garage. As soon as he sat down at his desk, however, he fell into a deep, dream-filled sleep.

The dream was as real as life. The sun was hot on his shoulders and back, and the odor of burned wood filled the air.

"Jason!" his grandmother cried. "My roses are dying. Look at them. They're all sticks and brown leaves. You killed them!"

"I've been trying so hard, GG," Jason pleaded. "Please let me… I'll make them better. You'll see. They'll be beautiful. You'll be proud of them. And me."

But she wasn't looking at the roses anymore.

"There's nothing left!" GG shrieked. "What have you done to my home?"

The house was completely gone. Only the foundation remained, a rectangle of cinder blocks framing raw dirt.

"No, GG, that's not true," Jason said, trying to soothe her. "You see the foundation? It's not damaged. I can build us a new house, just as soon as Mags pays me. It'll be just for the two of us, like when I came to live with you. You'll see."

GG picked up her cane and climbed clumsily over the foundation wall. She tottered to the concrete pad where the furnace used to be, dragging her IV pole through the dirt.

"What's this?" she demanded. She tapped her cane on a metallic surface. Tap, tap, tap. Jason stood on the foundation and saw the door to the safe. It was buried up to its hinges in the cement.

He was jubilant. "I found it! Rory said Geraldo's floor safe was in the basement. And there it is."

Tap, tap, tap. GG leaned over the safe's door, tapping on the heavy metal.

Tap, tap, tap. "Open up," she cried.

Jason awoke with a start, disoriented. He looked up and saw he was in his office. *How…?* It took a minute for the events of the morning and last night to come rushing back.

Tap, tap, tap.

He mumbled, "There it is again. It's real."

"Hey," a woman's voice called. "Open up in there."

Jason stood and stretched. "Alright, alright," he muttered, "I'm coming." He padded around the end of the bookcase and down the hallway in his stocking feet. The tapping grew louder and more insistent as he got closer to the door. The window shade was drawn, so he couldn't tell who was outside, but he was certain it wasn't anyone he wanted to see.

Tap, tap, tap. Tap, tap, tap.

"Jesus Christ," Jason growled, opening the door. "What is it?"

Rory O'Brien stood on the porch in a tank top, jogging shorts, and a black baseball cap. She held out a white paper bag and an envelope, as if they were peace offerings.

"I thought," she said with a friendly smile, "we can help each other."

CHAPTER 39

Deputy Hardesty sat on the bench in the bullpen of the sheriff's Rock Bay office scanning the morning paper. The coffee pot sputtered in the background, spitting final droplets into yesterday's grounds. Waiting impatiently for the last blast of steam, Hardesty turned to the Employment ads. He scowled when he read:

Exotic dancers wanted. Must be 18. No experience needed. Loving and caring employer will train. Fulfill your fantasies. Call 1-800-POLEDANCE, ask for Rod.

Duane threw the paper on the floor. When he became sergeant, he promised himself, he and his squad would run every last prevert out of the county. He imagined himself in SWAT gear drawing a bead on Rod with his laser scope while the rest of his team helped naked 18-year-old girls cover themselves with blankets. *Wrong. I'll help the naked girls and let someone else take down Rod.*

The ringing telephone on the dispatcher's desk interrupted his fantasy. The sheriff recently ordered that all phone calls be answered by the fourth ring, and everyone knew that the sheriff himself sometimes made test calls. The phone had already rung four times. Hardesty heard loud voices coming from Commander Sepulveda's cubicle and saw the boss dressing down the dispatcher. On the sixth ring, Hardesty leaped to his feet and dashed for the phone.

"Sheriff's office, Rock Bay," he answered, trying to sound professional and not gasp for breath. "Deputy Hardesty here. What do you ... how can I help you?"

A timid voice said, "I want to report a missing person."

Hardesty cringed. He knew missing person reports were a waste of time because the person always showed up in a day or two. They were lots of paperwork, and he wouldn't get any credit when the case resolved itself. He told himself he was stupid for answering, and vowed he wasn't going to get stuck with the case.

"Speak up," he said gruffly. "How long's the person been missing?"

"Since yesterday afternoon." The voice sounded like a young girl's.

That made him smile. She wouldn't know when a report was supposed to be taken, so he could get rid of her. He said, "I'm sorry, little lady, but we can't take a report 'til the person's been missing for seventy-two hours."

"But it's my friend. She's only sixteen. Please, you've gotta help...."

"So, get her parents to call. Someone legally responsible."

Duane heard sobbing on the other end. "Please...she needs help. She's pregnant and all alone. I don't know what she'll do."

The thought of a lost and pregnant 16-year-old struck a chord deep within Deputy Hardesty. He raised his eyes to heaven and made a silent promise to this girl, and every other underage girl in the county, that he'd be their personal protector when he got his sergeant's stripes.

"OK. Why don't you go ahead and tell me about it." He tried to sound encouraging. "What's your name?"

"Victoria."

"Victoria what?"

"Viviano. I'm her best friend. I drove her—"

He interrupted. "What's your friend's name?"

"Tiffany. Tiffany Tedeski. She lives in Sea Cliff."

"Address?"

"317 Miller Street."

"OK. And her parents? What're their names?"

"Her mother is Danni Tedeski. I don't know her father's name, but she lives with a man named Geraldo O'Brien. At least, she did—"

Deputy Hardesty felt the earth move beneath his feet. Dumb luck he'd answered this call, and now he was going to get key information about the O'Brien murder that no one else would have.

"OK, Valerie—"

"Victoria."

"Right. Whatever." Hardesty sat in the dispatcher's chair and found a pen and a piece of paper. "I can't take a official report 'cause it ain't been seventy-two hours. But I can take a informal one, so why don't you go ahead and tell me everything you know."

Victoria explained that Tiffany really was a good girl, but that Danni drank and was always gone on binges. She described how Danni and Geraldo fought terribly when they were both at home. She told him about driving Tiffany to the God's Helping Hands Counseling Center in Santa Luisa, and how she'd snuck out the back door. "I feel so guilty," Victoria sobbed, "letting her run away. I'm terrified she'll get hurt."

Duane half-listened, doodling images of sergeant's patches on his paper. Army, Air Force, Marines, Highway Patrol, Sheriff's Department. They were all different shapes, but they had one thing in common together: the third stripe.

When Victoria stopped talking, he refocused and asked, "Any idea where the girl might've gone to?"

"No," she sniffled.

"Do you think she might've been abducted?"

"What do you mean?"

"You know, kidnapped or taken against her will."

"Oh my God! I never thought of that!" Victoria began sobbing again.

"Calm down, missy, will you? Does Tiffany have any relatives you know of?"

"I don't know," Victoria wailed. "Oh my God! What if she's kidnapped? I'll never forgive myself!"

The deputy asked every follow-up question he could think of. He was about to hang up when he had a thought that made his private parts throb. *Some zit-faced teenager scored a home run with a 16-year old. That's statutory rape in violation of Penal Code section 261.5, and I wanna know who.* It was his duty to ask, after all, if he was going to be the protector of young girls.

He cleared his throat and spoke in his most official voice. "Do you know who the father of the baby is?"

There was a long pause. "Why do you want to know that? Why's it any of your business?"

She's covering for some pimply-faced jerk-off. "Because," he replied, lapsing into cop talk, "the perpetrator could be charged with statutory rape in violation of Penal Code section 261.5, and because we find that the perpetrator may be implicated in the victim's disappearance in a case like this, if she in fact doesn't reappear of her own personal volition."

Silence again. When Victoria spoke, her voice was tiny and flat. "It's Geraldo O'Brien. Tiffany's sure it's Geraldo."

Deputy Hardesty swelled up like a grouse. He jumped to his feet, crashing the desk chair into the wall behind him. That was it. Case solved. The Tedeski girl killed O'Brien. She had the biggest motive. She killed him, and that moose-woman Turlock dumped him down the storm drain.

Duane punched the *Mute* button and dropped the receiver. He high-fived the wall. "I'm gonna find this girl," he crowed, dancing an end-zone jig, "and when I do, I'll get my stripes."

* * *

Rory stood in Jason's office door, beaming as brightly as the morning sun that warmed the village. She pulled off her baseball cap and fluffed her ponytail with her fingers. "Rough night?" she asked cheerily. "You look absolutely terrible."

Jason was still half asleep. His mouth said the first thought that popped into his head: "What do you want?"

She took a step forward, but he stood where he was, blocking the door. "I was driving to the bluff trail for a run," she said, "but decided to stop here first. Like I said, I thought maybe we can help each other."

Despite his stupor, Jason noticed how her lavender tank top and running shorts complemented her gray eyes, golden hair, and light tan. The overpowering physical attraction he felt last night at Mostly's nearly buckled his knees. The rush was followed by warning bells:

I can't trust her for an instant. A second later, he thought, *she might be right.*

He decided his best move was offense. "I remember telling you not to bother me unless you can prove you're Geraldo's daughter."

"Here," Rory said, opening the envelope and unfolding a piece of paper. "Look at this." She jabbed it at his hand.

He examined the page. It was a photocopy of the birth certificate for Aurora Dawn O'Brien—seven pounds, six ounces, born to Ingrid Johanssen O'Brien and Geraldo Gomez O'Brien, in Los Angeles on March 21, 1993. "Huh. How'd you get this?"

"I had Alex scan it and text it to me."

"Who's Alex?" he asked as he inspected the document for any obvious sign of alteration or forgery.

"My significant other."

A twinge of jealously surprised him as much as her answer. She's in a relationship, he thought, and she likes men? If she was such bad news, like he kept telling himself, why did he care? He pushed his confusion aside. "Got a picture ID to go with this?"

She removed a driver's license from the envelope and handed it to him. The picture looked like her, and the name and date of birth matched the birth certificate. The license told him she was five foot eight, which he would've guessed, and weighed 130 pounds. He handed it back to her.

"OK. I believe you. You are Geraldo's daughter."

"Thank you, finally," she said with heavy sarcasm. She slipped the document and license into the envelope and folded it in half. Lifting her tank top a couple of inches, she stuck the envelope in her waistband, revealing a flat, tan stomach in the process. "Are we going to stand in the door, or can I come in?"

Jason stood aside. She brushed by, trailing a hint of classic Chanel. "Follow me," he said after closing the door. He led her past the long bookcase. Reaching his desk, he motioned for her to sit in the client chair. She plopped the paper bag and her baseball cap on his desk and sat back, hands in lap, one slender leg crossed over the other. He sat on his side, grateful for the three feet of oak between them.

"I thought—" she began.

"Why do you think we can help each other?"

"Well, I know things about Geraldo that you don't. Personal things. Since you're his attorney... are you still going to deny that?"

Jason shook his head. "No, I don't. But what about you? Do you believe me when I say that I don't have any pictures of you?"

She nodded. "Yes," she said sadly, "I do."

He thought that was a tiny step toward trust, maybe. He asked, "What kind of personal things?"

"Like how his mind worked, who he trusted, relatives who might be helpful—that sort of thing. He was a creature of habit, never liked to change the way he did things once he figured it out, and I know his habits back then. And you, you must have files about his business dealings and properties, and maybe finances?"

The thumb drive with Geraldo's computer files lay on Jason's blotter, and the two file boxes from GG's garage were in the footwell under his desk. "A few," he agreed. He casually straightened a pile of papers on his desk, covering the thumb drive with them.

Rory said, "You know, I haven't eaten yet. I brought some pastries from Bites 'n Bytes. Want one?" She stood and leaned over the bag, so that her cleavage filled his view. "Let's see. There's a bear claw, something they call a mini cannoli, a Long John, and a creampuff. I want the bear claw."

In spite of himself, his heart skipped a beat as he took in her pink bra and tan breasts, and the faint freckles that dotted the V between them. He chided himself for being a fool for freckles. Leaning back in his chair to create some space, he found himself looking into her pale-gray eyes. He noticed almost invisible freckles on her nose and cheeks. The pendant—a praying mantis, he reminded himself—swung at the hollow of her neck.

"And you?" she said, licking a drop of frosting from her upper lip with the tip of her tongue. "I don't think you're a creampuff kind of guy. Not after last night." She flashed a mischievous grin. "No, I'd have to say you're a mini cannoli guy." Her eyes were completely innocent beneath her long lashes.

"Well, when you put it like that," Jason replied dryly, "the Long John is all me."

They ate the pastries in silence. Jason finished first and wiped his mouth with a Kleenex from the box on his desk. "Thanks," he said, "I guess I was hungry." He handed her a tissue. "Alright. Let's get to it. What are you suggesting?"

"I can help you go through the files and tell you which relatives are dead and which properties are worth anything, at least the ones in the LA area. I know the banks he liked to use."

"That's not much of an offer. I can get all the same information myself, it'll just take longer."

"But I'm his child, his heir. I have rights. I need to see his files. I'm entitled to what he had. I looked it up on the Internet. "

"Maybe, maybe not. The size of your share depends on how many heirs he has and how they're related to him. I have to notify all his relatives. He has debts that'll have to be paid. I have to get a list from his accountant and publish a Notice to Creditors. Bottom line, Geraldo's files are confidential and covered by his attorney-client privilege, and I have an ethical duty to protect them and treat all the claimants fairly. I could be sued or lose my law license if I don't."

Her bottom line, he thought, was to get into Geraldo's files because she figured they'd lead her to his money. If there is any. He shrugged. "I can't give you any preferential treatment just because you're his child."

Rory leaned forward, exposing a pink bra strap and tan shoulder. "Maybe I can sweeten the offer."

"How's that?"

"I can give you a list of his drug-dealer associates."

"How would that help me?"

"He dealt with the same people, year after year. I knew them all. They were always at our house before he left. There's a good chance one of them killed him."

Jason scooted back his chair, thinking that might be useful. Her list would be years old, but he could give it to Hardesty to investigate. That would keep him busy for a while, and it would give Chalmers time to do his own investigation, and maybe even turn up the killer. But was it really enough?

He sat up straight and locked eyes with her. "So, your proposal is to give me a list of Geraldo's associates, which is probably fifteen years out of date, and I disclose to you all of his personal, attorney-client protected files?"

"Exactly."

"Well, if that's your best offer, this conversation can end right now."

"But if you find the killer, you'll find the money."

"Look, Rory, you might as well know. The legitimate assets I know about are modest. If there is any drug money, it's ill-gotten gains, and the cops will seize it."

Rory's eyes narrowed and her cheeks reddened. She yanked a Kleenex from the box. "I hear what you're saying." She wiped her hands and wadded up the used tissues, pastry wrappers, and paper bag. "We can't help each other. Or you won't let us help each other." She stood and threw the wad in the wastebasket beside Jason's desk. "I'll find another way, so screw it, and screw you. I'm going for a run."

She strode angrily around the end of the bookcase. Her rubber soles squeaked down the hallway toward the door. It opened, but didn't close.

"Goddamn you, Jason Brinkman, attorney at law," she yelled. "There was always money. Bags of it." The door slammed and footsteps pounded toward him. The pounding stopped and she stood at the corner, breathing hard, eyes blazing. "He could never get enough," she shouted, red-faced. "He stashed it in a hundred hiding places, a hundred banks, and he promised it to me. Do you hear me? TO ME!"

Jason expected an explosion of anger, but instead, she seemed to crumble in front of him. Her shoulders trembled and her eyes brimmed and overflowed. She slumped to the chair and fell into it. Tears ran down her cheeks. "I earned it—his little porno princess whore. I earned every fucking penny of it. Every costume, every bath, every time he clicked the shutter."

She clutched her face and wept into her hands. "He never said, 'I'm sorry,' or told me he loved me. Not even 'Goodbye.'" Her voice trailed off. "And then," she said in a whisper, "and then he goes and dies."

Jason sat silently, watching her shoulders heave, not knowing what to say or do. He fought to steel himself, but his resolve faded with each gut-wrenching sob.

"He owes it to me!" She looked up, her face puffy and pink. "I can find it. I know it's there. But I need your help. You have to help me, Jason. You're the only one who can. Will you please help me? Please?"

A voice in Jason's head said, *She's pushing your buttons, man.* Despite that, despite his mistrust, despite his ethics, his heart opened to her and he gave in. "How can I help, Rory? We still don't have anything to work with."

The tears slowed, and a tiny smile lifted the corners of her lips. "Yes, we do," she sniffled, blowing her nose and wiping her eyes. She slid her hand into her bra and pulled out a worn, folded piece of notebook paper. "We have this. This is the key."

Rory dried her tears with a tissue and blew her nose. Her eyes were still puffy from crying, but the pink was fading slowly from her cheeks. Even though her face was splotched and swollen, Jason was struck by her beauty. She forced a weak smile. "Where do we start?"

"Why don't you show me your paper? The key, you think, to finding Geraldo's money."

She handed him the folded square of paper. It was warm from her skin. He smoothed the paper on his desktop, taking care not to tear it along the deep top-to-bottom and side-to-side creases.

He saw a page of notebook paper filled with schoolgirl cursive. An adult hand had changed some of the letters. He read:

1 h<u>E</u>n
<u>2</u> ducks
3 squawking geese
4 limerick o<u>y</u>sters
5 corp<u>u</u>lent porpoises
<u>6</u> pairs of Don Alverzo's tweezers
7,000 Macedonia<u>N</u>s in full battle array
<u>8</u> brass monkeys from the ancient, sacred cr<u>y</u>pts of Egypt

9 apathetic, diabetic old men on roller skates with a mArked propensity toward procrastination and sloth

10 lyrical, spherical, diabolical denizens of the deep who hall and stall around the **Q**uo of the corner of the qua**y**

Easterday

Kingston

"I don't understand," he said, trying not to sound irritated. "What is this? What does it mean?"

"It's a memory builder for kids. It's nonsense, so you have to memorize it. My father made me learn it when I was ten, and write it over and over until I never forgot it. He made a game of it. He'd say, 'Three ducks and seven porpoises,' and I'd say, 'No, Daddy, it's two ducks and five porpoises.' Then he'd say, 'Nine brass monkeys,' and I'd say, 'Nuhh-uhh, it's eight brass monkeys,' and he'd tickle me until we both laughed so hard we had to stop." Tears brimmed over her lower eyelids. "He could be sweet and fun sometimes," she said wistfully. "I did love him, when he wasn't being mean." Her voice was so soft that Jason barely made out the words. She tried to catch her teardrops with a used tissue, but they splashed dark circles on her lavender top.

In that moment, Jason knew there was no artifice or calculated sensuality, just the pain of a little girl whose father had betrayed and deserted her. Watching her cry, every strand of Jason's being wanted to hold her in his arms and kiss away her tears. Instead, he sat rigid in his chair, gripping the arms with white fingertips.

"Anyway," she sniffled, "that's how I learned it by heart."

"But how will it help locate Geraldo's money?"

"When my father left me and my mother forever," Rory replied, dabbing at her eyes, "the last thing he said to me was, 'It's all for you, Goldie. It's my payback. One day, it'll all be yours.' Remember, I told you that last night at Mostly's?"

Jason did remember, but today the statement struck a chord it hadn't before. He tried to make the connection as he listened to her. There was something about the name "Goldie." He'd seen it in something he'd read.

She continued, "He gave me this paper and told me, 'Do you see the numbers and letters I changed? It's a secret code. Only you, me, and a couple of other people know about it. Someday, when you're older, someone will ask you for the code, and you tell them. If you get it right, they'll give you all the money I want you to have.' He folded the paper and closed my fist around it and told me to keep it safe forever. And now he's dead, and here I am, trusting you with my precious secret."

Jason picked up the paper and studied the changes Geraldo had made. "Any idea what the words 'Kingston' and 'Easterday' mean?"

"I don't know," she said, her composure beginning to return. "Could be names, I guess, but I don't really know."

The poignant moment was gone, and wariness replaced Jason's tender feelings. The code might be her precious secret, he thought, but she was still holding something back. *It's like peeling an onion, dealing with her.* He slipped the top of the sheet under the base of his desk lamp, hoping he could make a photocopy of it.

"So," he summarized, "we've got a ten-digit alphanumeric code, which is," he glanced at the page, "E2yu6N8yAQ." Picking up a pen, he asked, "May I?"

She nodded, "Sure, I guess." He wrote the string of letters and numbers across the middle of the page below the ten lines of text.

"We also have two key words that could be names. How do we use all of this? Who do we give it to? Did Geraldo tell you that?"

"Don't you see, Jason, that's where your files come in. They'll tell us." She spoke with such certainty Jason almost believed her. "He'd have left me a clue. I know he did."

CHAPTER 40

The KHYP news van lumbered north on Highway 1, heading to Sea Cliff. Spike drove, slapping the wheel in time to a beat rapping in his earbuds. On the left, 30 feet below the roadway, frothy whitecaps crashed against jagged sandstone bluffs. On the right, rolling pastures and gentle hills glowed golden-brown.

Ally Booker sat at the video console in the back, cuing up her report on The Storm Drain Murderer's bail hearing. As usual, she'd had to browbeat Phil Kowalski into letting her run her story. "It's great coverage, Phil," she'd argued. "Live from the courthouse steps, the latest on The Storm Drain Murder. Details on the number-one suspect. Viewers will eat it up. Sponsors, too." Phil waffled so long she'd nearly missed the midmorning newsbreak.

She found the report and punched the *Play* button. The monitor flickered, and she saw herself standing on the sunny courthouse steps. Throngs of people streamed in and out of the building. Spike's camera focused on her face, and she stared deep into the lens. Thrilled as always to see herself on the screen, she watched and listened to her report:

"This is Ally Booker live in Santa Luisa with exclusive coverage of The Storm Drain Murderer's bail hearing. Just minutes ago, Judge Lyle Ferguson ordered bail set at $200,000 for Mags Turlock, the leading suspect in the gruesome murder case. Turlock is a well-known real estate agent in Sea Cliff and a business partner of the deceased, Geraldo O'Brien."

Jason Brinkman appeared in the picture, descending the steps quickly with briefcase in hand. Ally positioned herself directly in front of him.

"Mr. Brinkman, you're Ms. Turlock's attorney. Can you tell us, what's her state of mind?"

He walked straight at her. She stood her ground, moving aside only when he was about to bump into her. He continued down the steps.

As he reached the sidewalk, Ally called out to his back, "Can you tell us why Judge Ferguson set such low bail in a first-degree murder case?"

He ignored her.

She shouted, "Why did your client kill Mr. O'Brien?" He stopped in his tracks.

Ally hit the *Pause* button. *Damn, I'm good!* She swelled with pride. *The network loves a ballsy girl reporter.* She pressed *Rewind* and played the scene over again a couple of times before pressing *Play* again.

Brinkman waited until Ally and her microphone clambered down the steps to where he stood. He said, "Mags Turlock is innocent of all charges unless she's found guilty by a jury of her peers."

"But why did she kill him?" Ally insisted.

"Ms. Turlock is innocent unless she's found guilty. I have no further comment." He turned abruptly and walked toward the parking garage.

"You heard it here," Ally beamed smugly. "The attorney for the accused Storm Drain Murderer doesn't deny she killed the victim." Ally paused for a count of five so her viewers could absorb the import of what they'd just heard.

"This morning's other major development," she continued, "is the Coroner's Office just issued a statement concerning an announcement that they're finished identifying the victims of the exploding boat in Rock Bay, and will begin an in-depth analysis of the cause of death in The Storm Drain Murder case. So, pretty soon, we'll know how she did it."

Ally paused again to set up her close. "This is Ally Booker reporting live from the courthouse in Santa Luisa. I'm tracking every lead in The Storm Drain Murder case, and I'll bring you developments throughout the day, so keep your TVs and devices right here, with me, Ally Booker, on KHYP."

The camera zoomed in until her head and shoulders filled the screen. Ally pressed *Pause*, freezing the picture. She swiveled her chair so Spike couldn't see her face in the rearview mirror. "You go, girl! I am one amazing, awesome woman!" she crowed under her breath. Her feet danced over the cables cluttering the van's floor. Grinning from ear to ear, she knew her story turned out better because the prick attorney tried to ruin it by walking away, and because she got him good. So good. She blew her screen image a kiss. *Move over, Lester Holt, 'cause here I come!*

As pleased as Ally was with the content, however, she was distressed by her appearance in the piece. Her clothes... well, she had to admit she looked small-town. Not up to network standards. She made herself a solemn promise: When she got to New York, she'd get a personal shopper and go to Bloomingdale's and get herself a whole new wardrobe. She'd make Norah O'Donnell look like a bag lady.

Ally maneuvered into the passenger's seat. "I Googled that prick Brinkman. His office is on Charles. I'm gonna nail his ass to the wall."

"Say what? After all yo' talk 'bout how fine he be, with his cute butt, an' his LA clothes an' car an' all? An' you gonna marry the man an' have his child?"

"He tried to ruin my story. He walked away from my interview. No one walks away from Ally Booker. No one, no way. He's goin' down."

"OK, babe," Spike sighed. "Whatever you say. I seen his sign, and can't no one miss that car. We find him. No worries."

* * *

"When I was driving to your office this morning," Rory said, standing up from the client's chair, "I told myself a hundred times I wasn't going to cry. I guess talking about my father dredges up a lot of things I never want to think about."

She walked the length of the bookcase, looking at the titles of the law books and the framed pictures of Jason with his high school teams. A photo of Jason and his grandmother held her attention longer than the others. She picked up the unopened Marlboro pack, spinning it in her fingers and glancing at him quizzically before replacing it.

"I'm good at reading people," she said with her back to him, "and I sense you don't trust me completely. I don't know why. Everything I've told you about me is true, and I'm telling you the truth about Geraldo's files. They will tell us how to use my secret code."

The business side of Jason's brain snapped to attention. Tearful revelations to the contrary, there was no question all she cared about was the financial files. He was beginning to think, however, she might have some insights, and he might benefit by letting her look at them. After he peeled away a few more layers of onion. Two tactical diversions came to mind.

He said, "I'm supposed to be finding suspects in Geraldo's murder. How 'bout if you give me your list of his drug-dealer associates?"

"So now you want my out-of-date list? Maybe I've reconsidered. What do I get in return?"

"To make a long story short, I get to stay out of jail. You've got nothing if I'm locked up."

"I don't understand."

"There's a deputy sheriff threatening to arrest me if I don't help him find the murderer. Like I said, it's a long story. I want to give him your list to keep him busy, and me out of jail."

He handed her a pen and a piece of paper. She took them grudgingly and sat in the client chair, pulling it closer to his desk. While she wrote, he checked his phone for messages. There were three: texts from Courtney and Deputy Hardesty, and an email from his father.

"Here," Rory said before he could read any of the messages. She tossed the list on his blotter. "Geraldo dealt with these guys for years."

Although he didn't expect to recognize any of the names, Jason scanned the list:

Stephen de Grande, aka "The Stallion"
Brycen "Bunco" Baldwin
Guido DeChecco
Grover Frederick, aka "Two Fingers"
Hector "Hellboy" Hector
Luis "Loco" Robles

Guillermo Escobar
Vic "Hacker" Thacker
Parker Bolander
Yuri Yukovich

"That's helpful," he said. "Thanks." He folded the list and stuck it in his shirt pocket, thinking it would keep Deputy Hardass busy for a while. "I also need your help identifying next of kin, and—"

"Why not financial institutions?"

"Next of kin first. Everyone has to be notified and have time to respond before I file papers with the court. Otherwise, the whole process gets delayed and can drag on forever."

He pulled a folder from under his desk. "I had Geraldo fill out these Next of Kin worksheets for his estate plan, but he didn't include any relationships. Some of these people may be dead for all I know."

"So he was thinking he was going to die? That's not like him, at least when I was young."

"No, I don't think so. He was always bragging about all his money and property, so I kept bugging him to think about an estate plan. He finally told me to start working on it, but it never got finished. And I haven't found much in the way of assets."

"Explain why I should help you identify relatives if one of them could take my share."

"Like I said, everyone has to be notified, or the distribution of assets can be challenged. It's best to notify all the living relatives now, so they can't make a surprise claim later."

Cocking her head, she searched his face. She seemed to reach a decision. Her eyes narrowed and she leaned over the desk, into his space. Her tank top gapped, revealing pink bra, tan cleavage, and tiny freckles. "Look, let's cut to the chase. I've done my homework. He wasn't married when he died, and he didn't have a domestic partner, so we don't need to worry about what's community property and what's separate. It's all his separate property. Since there's no spouse or partner, I'm entitled to it all because I'm his... what does the law call me... his issue."

Jason was surprised and impressed. She was right, if it was all Geraldo's separate property, and if he didn't have a wife or other kids somewhere. But these days he knew Geraldo better than she did, and a wife and kids were possibilities. For that matter, Tiffany's baby would be entitled to half her share, if Geraldo really was the father.

"As the lawyer for the estate, I can't assume Geraldo doesn't have any wife or domestic partner, or other kids," he countered. "The probate court'll have to rule that you're his sole heir and specify what you're entitled to before you can collect a dollar." He paused to let his words sink in. "So let's get next of kin out of the way. We'll look at financial records after that."

She still hesitated. He nudged her toward the decision he wanted. "I'd think you'd want to see who he listed, just so you have an idea if you've got a problem."

Rory held out her hand for the sheaf of worksheets. She thumbed through them with an annoyed expression. Scanning the first sheet, she exclaimed, "Look at that! There's Uncle Emilio in Taos! I haven't thought about him for years." She turned to the second page. "And Auntie Barbara!" She glanced at a couple of more pages. "All these people I've forgotten about! I can tell you who they are, but I don't know if they're still alive. Is there a desk I can use?"

He pointed to the front of the office. "There's a table by the window. Just put the books on the floor."

While Rory made notes on the worksheets, Jason returned to the messages on his phone. As he expected, Courtney berated him for not returning the divorce papers. He couldn't help noticing that an angry text from Courtney sounded just like angry Courtney in person.

The message from Deputy Hardesty announced that he expected Jason to respond immediately to all texts, "or else." The "or else" meant Hardesty would get an arrest warrant if he didn't cooperate.

The message from Barry Brinkman was odd because he never initiated contact. Jason nearly fell out of his chair when he read it:

Jason: I know my mother wanted you to have her house, but things aren't going well here in Frisco. I need to move into the house immediately. I expect you to vacate by the end of the week. Leave all my mother's furniture and possessions. This is not negotiable. If you'd followed my advice, you'd have plenty of money to buy a place of your own.

Very truly yours,
Barry Brinkman

Christ almighty! My own father! How can he do that to me? Where am I gonna move?

He jumped when Rory spoke. "Oh my God! He did remember me. I knew he would. Look at this." She scurried to his chair, clutching the worksheets opened to the last page. She slapped them on his desk and leaned over it beside him, her cheek touching his and her breath warm on his neck.

"See?" she said pointing. "'Goldie O'Brien.' He called me 'Goldie' when I was little 'cause my hair was so golden. He did remember. Now you have to believe me. He does want me to have his money."

Rory draped her arm playfully over Jason's shoulders and pressed her cheek against his. He saw the words and heard what she said, but could only focus on her smooth cheek and her arm across his back. Her body was warm, and her soft breast pressed against him through the thin fabric of his shirt. "Rory, listen, this can't…" but she leaned even closer, pushing her breast into him.

He willed himself to ignore the passion building inside him. "Why's she doing this?" he asked himself silently. "Is it real or is she just manipulating me? What about her Alex?"

The sensations of her body overcame him. He slid his free arm around her waist and tugged her toward him. She nuzzled her nose into his neck and squeezed him against her hip. "Oh my," she murmured, "I do love strong shoulders." All at once, she seemed to melt into him. He thought he heard a muffled moan deep in her throat. *I can turn my head and kiss her, pull her into my lap* …. His lips found her earlobe and nibbled it. Her breath caught.

"Rory!" he blurted, shoving his chair away and shaking his head to clear it. "It has to be strictly business between us. I don't know what that was, but it can't be."

She jolted upright and stepped back. Turning so he couldn't see her face, she said lightly, "It's always been just business, Jason." She walked around the desk nonchalantly and sat in the client's chair, completely composed, except for the fading red in her cheeks.

Jason struggled to get his mind back on track. Now he made the connection he couldn't make before. Goldie O'Brien was the name he'd found amusing in the Next of Kin worksheets.

To give himself a minute, he reached for the sheaf of papers and flipped through them page by page. When he reached the end, he said, "It does make sense that you're *the* Goldie O'Brien. But that doesn't mean Geraldo wanted you to have his entire estate. There are seventeen other relatives here also, so we still have to go through the probate process."

"Oh my God!" She pounded the arm of her chair. "You're such a Boy Scout!"

"So? Look at it from my side. Say that I let you take all the money we find. The other heirs will sue me. They'll accuse me of having an affair with you. The State Bar will take away my law license, and the district attorney will charge me with fraud, and aiding and abetting grand theft. That's exactly what happened to a lawyer I know in Palm Springs, and I'm not going down that road."

He slipped the worksheets into their folder and set it aside. When he looked up, she was staring across the office at the front window. He tried to read her face, but it was a mask.

"This is what's going to happen," he said. "We're going to jump through all the hoops, and the first step is to list you on the Notice and Petition for Probate that I'll file with the court."

"Gee, you'll do that for me?"

"So let me get the information I'll need."

"Then the financial files?" she demanded.

"Then the financial files."

After an hour of verbal fencing with Rory, her rating on Jason's trust meter had moved from zero to five—out of a hundred. He figured they needed information from each other right now, so she'd work with him. But he also figured she'd disappear the moment she learned where the money was. He needed to get her personal information while he had the chance, so he could find her later if he or the court needed to.

His client intake sheet would do the trick. He'd pretend the information from it was necessary to complete the Notice and Petition.

He printed out an intake sheet and filled in the lines for her name, birth date, and relationship.

"Alright. What's your address?"

She told him the number and street of a condominium in Beverly Hills, which he recognized as a prime neighborhood.

"Driver's license and Social Security numbers?"

She rattled them off.

"Phone numbers with area codes?"

"Just a cell phone." She recited the number.

"Education?"

"Why does the court need that?"

Jason shrugged and pointed to the intake sheet.

"Associate degree from Cal. State Northridge, followed by two years of professional training."

"Training as a … ?"

"I'm a licensed esthetician."

"Really? I've never known what that is."

"I make average people look beautiful. You know, facials, makeup, massage, custom lotions and potions. Mostly I give my clients Botox and collagen injections with tiny micro needles." She studied his face. "You'll age well," she said in a professional tone, "but you'll need some work …."

Smiling mischievously, she walked around his desk and perched on the edge in front of him. Jason shoved back until he hit his credenza, but their knees still touched. Sitting on the desktop in her short-shorts and tank top, she held his chin and turned his head back and forth. She leaned forward, touching his forehead and cheeks gently. "Yes, you'll need injections here, and here, and here."

Despite his many misgivings, he longed to slide his hands up her tan thighs, grab her hips, tug her onto his lap. Her fingers were cool, and each place she touched tingled with electricity. Lavender haze and Chanel overwhelmed his senses, smothering thoughts of anything else. Her breasts were inches away, round and full beneath the thin silk, rising and falling tantalizingly. He gripped her wrists to yank them away, but pulled her toward him instead.

Raising his gaze, he expected those cool gray eyes to mock him for the effect she knew she was having. Instead, to his amazement, they were filled with tenderness. Her hands now cupped his face, trembling, and she bent her head forward to brush her lips against his. He drew her closer, pushing himself up to claim the kiss she promised. She fluttered her eyelashes against his cheek and brushed his lips again.

His cell phone buzzed, shattering the spell. Rory sprang to her feet and busied herself straightening her top. Jason sat upright. *Oh, shit! It must be Erin!* He pushed himself forward, searching his desktop for his phone. Sharp pangs of guilt stabbed his stomach. But, he reminded himself, she hadn't called, so she must be really angry. Or… she was with her new guy who was going to take her to LA.

Rory retreated to the client's chair on the far side of the desk. Jason found his phone and tapped open the text message. "For God's sake!" he swore. It was from Deputy Hardesty:

SgtDH to Wingman: Mt @ Simon's Cove pier prkng lot 1 hr or else.

He deleted the message and set the phone on his desktop in a spot without clutter. He waited 20 heartbeats.

"Rory," he said firmly, "this has to be business."

"I know. You're right. It does."

She stood and walked to the window, pulling the curtain aside and looking out. "I could really like you, Jason Brinkman. A lot. I never expected that." Each word seemed to be torn from her soul. He held his breath, waiting for her to continue, not knowing what to expect.

She stared at the sunny street. "Everything's so complicated right now." Her hand sought the praying mantis pendant at her neck. She ran her fingers over it and squeezed until her knuckles turned white. "Another time…other circumstances…I don't know…." Her voice trailed off and she bowed her head. Her shoulders slumped.

When she bent her head forward, silky golden strands escaped her ponytail. He imagined kissing them and the nape of her neck. Wrapping his arms around her slim waist, pulling her to him, kissing her throat, her cheek, her lips. His trust meter soared to ten.

But what about Erin? a little voice in his head demanded. He answered indignantly. Where is she? What's right and what's wrong here? Where's the line I'm not supposed to cross if she's with her other guy?

He wanted to ask Rory, "Why is it complicated? Because of Alex? Geraldo? The estate?" The question was on his lips when he remembered a playground rhyme from fifth grade:

> If she pretends she likes you,
> And you think you like her, too,
> Then she can do
> Anything she wants
> To you.

The meter sank back to three. He told himself that she was playing him like a fish, just like last night, and that her only purpose was to get Geraldo's money.

Jason searched his briefcase for nothing and straightened the papers on his desk. He adjusted his desk lamp and wiped dust off a framed picture of GG and him. Rory continued to stare out the window. "Can we continue with these questions for the court?" he said after a few minutes. When she didn't respond, he asked, "What's your income?"

She spoke without turning her head. "I make a comfortable living." Abruptly, she squared her shoulders and walked back to her chair, and by the time she sat down, her composure had returned. "That's all you need to know."

"Ballpark?"

"Well, I'll tell you this much. I'm half owner of my salon on Rodeo Drive. I've got a contract with Disney, which means I have to race over the hill to Burbank every time one of their snotty starlets gets a zit. I do beauty maintenance for a half-dozen actresses you'd recognize. I always work the Academy Awards and the Emmys. I'm comfortable."

"So why're you so intent on getting Geraldo's money, if it turns out there is any?"

"How many times do I have to say it?" she bristled. "It's mine by right. Besides," she said in a milder tone, "I don't want to work forever. I want to enjoy life while I'm young."

His cell phone buzzed again.

CHAPTER 41

Danni lugged a stack of dirty plates to the kitchen sink and lowered them gingerly into the soapy water. "OUCH!" she exclaimed. "Damn, that's hot!"

After many pots of coffee and twelve hours of nonstop cleaning, the house she shared with her daughter and Geraldo was nearly fit for human habitation. The dryer hummed in the laundry closet down the hall, and plastic garbage bags full of decaying food were piled at the back door.

Danni fished the sponge out of the steaming water and began scrubbing a plate. "I'd ask you to help out, but it ain't your mess, and you look like shit, anyway. But you better be listenin' to me, Guillermo, 'cause I don't usually got no one to talk to."

She propped the plate in the drying rack and started on another one. "It's not that Tiffany's a bad girl," she said, gazing out the window behind the sink. "No, she's a good girl, really. 'Specially when you think about what she's been through. I never had much time to spend with her when she was growing up. Well, I never took the time, to be honest. Me and her dad—Danny was his name… I know, I know, Danni and Danny—it's too precious. Everyone said. I was a nurse in a hospital, and he was a contractor, and we were working all the time to get money for our own house. Tiffany was in daycare, I guess that's where her troubles began. The aide told me she was 'acting out,' not that I knew what that meant."

Danni wiped her hands on her jeans. "More coffee, Guillermo? You look like you could use some. Shakin' off oxy in the morning can be tough, 'specially after all you had last night. You did cut up your hand pretty bad. It feeling better today?" Without waiting for answers, she crossed to the kitchen table and poured. "Men are such pussies about pain. You wanna know real pain? Try childbirth."

"*Leche,*" Guillermo growled.

"You mean, '*Leche, por favor.*' All I got's Creamora, 'cause it don't never spoil." She opened and closed cupboards until she found the plastic container. Dropping it on the table, she said, "Here. Make do."

"So," she continued, returning to the sink, "one day the charge nurse forgets the key to the drug closet and tells me to fetch it. That was the worst day of my life, it turns out, 'cause I sneaked into that closet, and I saw all them vials and bottles and pills of every color. I just had to know what every one of 'em felt like, so I tells her I can't find the key, and I get a copy made 'fore I 'find' it and give it back. One of my rehab counselors said I got a 'dictive personality, and I guess it's true, 'cause I started stealing every kinda sample. What I couldn't swallow or snort, I'd shoot up. I got pretty good at sticking needles in me in places where no one could find. But I was high all the time, and fucked up at the hospital and got fired. Pretty soon, Danny and me split up. Well, he left me, to be honest, not that I blame him now—and I been goin' from one man to 'nother ever since.

"By the time me and Geraldo hooked up, I just wanted a roof for me and my kid and steady meals. I met him at Mostly's—go figure. Thing about Geraldo is … was … he can be really charming when he wants. And the best sex I ever had, when we could stand the sight of each other. He's just mean and ornery the rest of the time. Tiffany sweetened our deal with him, I guess, but I didn't see it until just yesterday.

"Yup. Yesterday. The day I finally come to my senses. Saw the light. Now, I gotta find my baby and be a mother to her. She needs me, and I ain't gonna let her down again. That means no more drugs or booze. So you take all your pain pills and shit with you when you go. Don't leave none of it here, 'cause this is a clean house from now on. I don't want any part of your drugs, but I do want $100 for the damage you done to my house last night. The nursing care for your cut-up hand is free.

"I'll miss drinking, to be honest. I think the Eagles said it best, something 'bout some people drinking to remember, and some to forget. You recognize that? No, I guess you wouldn't, being from Mexico and all. Well, I drink to forget. I can drink so much I forget months, but it all comes back when I sober up. I ain't proud of what I done the past coupla weeks, but it is what it is, and I can't change it now. You think you can maybe help me with them garbage bags later?"

The dryer buzzed from the laundry closet. Danni jumped at the sound. "Whoa," she said, pressing her hands to her heart. "I guess my nerves is still jagg'd." She held her fingers in front of her eyes and watched them tremble. "That'll pass in a few days. Usually does. Tell you what. Lemme look at your hand, see how it's healing up. Then we'll see what we can find on Brinkman's laptop." She picked up a basket of dirty laundry and lugged it down the hall. "If you want," she said over her shoulder, "later on, we'll go searching for Geraldo's money. Oh shit, Guillermo, now don' get pissed, you know I meant your money. Lemme get this load of wash going, then I want to see that hand."

She unwound layer after layer of bandage, each more bloodstained than the last. "Christ, you shoulda gone to the ER last night. You need stitches to close them cuts. I can keep it from gettin' infected, but that hand won't never be the same." Lighting a cigarette, she inhaled deeply and blew the smoke over his head. "Stupid fuck. I said you wouldn't find nothin' at Brinkman's house, but no, you gotta be the big tough guy an' go tear the place up and try to kill that little Nikki."

Danni cleaned the bloody cuts with cotton swabs and alcohol, lost in her work. Guillermo grunted and popped an oxy.

"No, Geraldo wouldn't never trust no one with his money," Danni said, "not even a bank, least not for long. Always hid it in one of his secret hiding places. I know you say it's your money, but it ain't yours 'til you get your hands on it. It ain't here, neither. You known Geraldo twenty years, and you think he'd stash it here with me? You're one crazy wetback, you think that. Didn't stop you from trying to break in here last night, though, did it? You're just lucky I was here to stop you bleeding."

She tore open a new roll of bandages and handed it to him. "Hold this," she instructed, pulling on the free end, "and don't let none of it touch nothin'." She wound the long gauze strip around his right hand, gradually encasing it in a soft white cloud. "If you ask me, which you ain't, 'cause you're too macho to ask a woman nothin', Geraldo hid the money in the spec house. Yup, that'd be just like him. I bet it's piled in the stud bays and covered over with dry wall. Or maybe in the crawl space. We'll go over there this afternoon, take a look-see."

Lighting another cigarette, she offered the pack to Guillermo. He shook his head. She took a deep drag and blew smoke rings at the ceiling. "Too bad we can't get into Brinkman's laptop," she mused, watching the rings dissolve. "Might have some clues. Figures a lawyer would have a secret password."

The doorbell rang. They both jumped. "Shit, Guillermo, you can't be here. You go hide in the TV room while I see who it is." The big man rose to his feet and sauntered down the hall, cradling his damaged hand in the crook of his left elbow.

On her way to the front door, Danni caught a glimpse of herself in the entryway mirror. She stopped, remembering how meticulous she'd once been about her appearance and the impression she made. That was decades ago, before alcohol, cocaine, and every other kind of drug took over her life. The face she saw gave her a start—hollow black eyes, broken nose caved in by cocaine, porous skin, craggy wrinkles, white roots beneath silvery-gray hair. She scarcely recognized the pretty young mother she'd been, whose angelic little girl looked so much like her. "I can fix a lot of it," she vowed. "My baby'll be proud of me again."

Danni opened the door to find an Express Mail envelope resting against the jamb. As she bent over to pick it up, she had a vision of the telegram under the front mat of her childhood home, announcing her father had been killed in Korea. She closed the door and leaned against it. "Oh God," she whimpered. "Please don't let this be bad news." With shaking hands, she ripped open the envelope. A single piece of notebook paper fell to the floor.

A dark shape filled the hall doorway, drawing her eyes across the living room. Guillermo towered there, an eight-inch switchblade in his left hand. "*Que?*" he growled.

"It's no one. Just a letter. From Tommy Reynolds, my third ex-husband." She slid down the door until she sat on her butt. Picking up the paper by one corner, she read:

Dear Danielle,

I hope this finds you. I got your address from Google, so it probably will.

I'm writing to tell you that Tiffany is with me and Heather. She said she ran away when you didn't come home for a week. She took the bus down here, and we're going to take care of her during her pregnancy. But I'm afraid there's bad news.

This is hard for me to write, because I loved her like my own daughter. Tiffany was crossing the street and got hit by a car. She died two days later in the hospital. It was terrible, but she was suffering so much.

I'll take care of all the arrangements, you don't need to worry none, or come down here to San Diego.

I swore I'd never speak to you after the divorce, but I thought you should know.

I'm sorry.

Sincerely,
Tommy

"Guillermo!" Danni screamed. "I need a needle an' a dime bag, right now. Please! Right now!"

CHAPTER 42

Jason's cell phone buzzed a third time, breaking the silence in his office. He picked up the phone, thinking it had to be Erin this time. He tapped open the message:

SgtDH to Wingman: Mt @ Simon's Cove pier prkng lot 1 hr or else.

"God, what an idiot. He's sent the same message twice. It's the cop who's making me help him find Geraldo's killer. I'm going to have to leave to meet him."

"What about the financial files?" Rory demanded.

"We'll get there, I promise, but it'll have to wait 'til I get back."

Rory frowned. "There must be something in them you don't want me to see."

"Not at all. I really do want your help with that, but this cop will throw me in jail if I don't throw him a bone. I'm going to give him your list of Geraldo's druggie associates to get him off my back."

As annoying as meeting Deputy Hardesty was, it did provide an opening Jason welcomed. He unfolded Rory's list and smoothed it on his desk. "I've got another idea maybe you can help me with." He drew a line across the paper under the final name. "I'm going to add possible suspects from around here, to keep him busy longer."

"That's it," Rory said, standing. "I'm going for a run. Call me on my cell when you get back. And don't you dare start the financial files without me, after all the BS you've put me through."

"Wait. Hang on a few minutes. You've been in town a week. You might've heard something useful."

"I need to move around. I came straight here this morning, so I didn't get my run." She walked to the front of the office and stood silhouetted by the sun shining through the window. Bending at the waist with knees locked together tightly, she pressed her palms against the floor. She held the position for a full minute before wrapping her arms around the backs of her thighs and holding her head against her knees. After another minute, she uncoiled her arms and stretched them to the ceiling before slowly bending her back into a semi-circle. Standing straight again, she pulled one heel, then the other, to the hem of her running shorts.

Jason's desk phone rang as she began a set of leg lunges. He picked up and swiveled to look at the bookcase instead of the show she was putting on. The call was from the court clerk in Santa Luisa to confirm Jason's fax number before sending the orders with Mags Turlock's bail and arraignment date.

Rory's movement caught the corner of his eye. He wondered if she was teasing him, or actually trying to exercise. Either way, it wouldn't get her into the financial files any quicker. He couldn't help noticing, however, the grace of her movements and the suppleness of her body. A fantasy body, he thought as he hung up. Like a gymnast-centerfold.

Rory began pacing the length of the bookcase, walking the fifteen feet from the front to the far end—once, twice, three times. On each pass, she glanced toward the Marlboro pack on the shelf at his eye level, directly across from his desk. She finally stopped to examine it, picking at the cellophane wrapper with a blood-red fingernail. "Never opened," she mumbled. She replaced the pack on the shelf. Turning to face him, she asked, "Why do you keep an unopened pack of cigarettes in your office? Where you can see them all the time?"

Jason ignored her and began writing on the suspect list: "Mags Turlock." He said the name as he wrote it. "She's the leading suspect. Did business deals with Geraldo and had an affair with him. Says she's broke now because he took all her money for the spec house. He left her holding the bag on a $2.5 million mortgage that's in default. Are you with me?"

"I'm not going to help you, or even pay attention, until you answer my question."

"I was a smoker, am a smoker," Jason said, tapping his pen against the edge of his desk. "It's like a thirteenth step for me, keeping cigarettes around. I figure if I can face down nicotine every day, I can take any punch life throws at me. Or any temptation." He looked her in the eye. "Now can we get on with this?"

He wrote: "Danni Tedeski." Glancing up to see if Rory was watching, he explained: "Geraldo's live-in woman. Hated him, by all accounts."

Rory sank into the client's chair and scooched it closer to the desk. She craned her neck to see, exposing her pink bra strap and tan shoulder.

Jason continued to write: "Tiffany Tedeski. She's Danni's daughter. Lived with her and Geraldo. Disappeared when Geraldo's body was found." He decided not to mention she was pregnant by Geraldo.

"Next is El Carnicero. Supposedly a badass Mexican cartel enforcer. He's in town, looking for Geraldo. Says Geraldo owes him a lot of money. Tore up my house last night."

"Wait!" Rory exclaimed. "El Carnicero means 'the butcher.' That's Guillermo Escobar! One of the names on my list. He's very violent."

"See, you *are* being helpful."

"He killed one of his dealers over a hundred dollars that turned out not to be missing. I remember Geraldo telling me about it when I was twelve or thirteen," she said with a shudder. "And you know that scar on Geraldo's left cheek? Guillermo did that. They got into a big argument, and Guillermo pulled a knife. They made up, but I don't think Geraldo ever forgave him. Anyway, Guillermo could be the one."

"Yes, he could," Jason said, thinking he was at the spec house the night Geraldo died. He circled the name. "That's good information.

"OK, just to be complete...." He added two more names to the list, explaining as he wrote: "Jamie McDougal. He's the manager of the local bank, and Geraldo's go-to man for getting mortgages and loans. They say he disappeared after Geraldo defaulted on the $2.5 million mortgage on the spec house, and the Feds announced they were going to audit his accounts. And finally, Pedro Rodriguez. He's Geraldo's foreman. Lost all his money on Geraldo's spec house."

"My money's on Guillermo," Rory said, "but it sounds like they all had motive to kill Geraldo. Are we done? Can I go?"

"In a minute. There's something I want to ask you first." Jason hesitated, not sure where his question would lead, or what kind of reaction he'd get. "You know," he said as casually as he could, "a couple of people told me you were at One Bluffside the night of Geraldo's party, the night he died. Were you there?"

She looked surprised, but said evenly, "Yeah, I was there. For a couple of minutes."

"And?"

"And, what? He asked me to come." Her gray eyes left his face, flitted to the wall behind him, finally settling on her hands in her lap. "He looked so old, I barely recognized him." She gouged a cuticle, drawing a bright-red drop of blood. "He was totally smashed—stoned, worse than I'd ever seen him. We didn't talk at all. He said he'd call next week, and I left right away."

"So, you lied to me. You told me last night at Mostly's that you never saw him after he left you and your mom. Why did you lie?"

"It wasn't a lie. Last night, I didn't think it made any difference. I'd just met you. I was going to tell you if it seemed important later."

"You really don't understand. Everyone at the party's a potential suspect. A smart person would see that and want to avoid suspicion by being open about being there. Can anyone vouch for the time you left?"

She looked up from her hands and cocked her head. "You mean, do I have an alibi?"

"I didn't use that word, but yeah."

"Of course I don't. I didn't know anyone there. I don't even know anyone in town. Besides, only guilty people make sure they have alibis."

"You've been watching too many cop shows. You'd be more believable if you could verify the time you left."

The gray eyes narrowed and bore into him. He imagined he saw the wheels turning in her head.

"So, are you suggesting ... ? You must think that I ... C'mon, Jason," she scoffed. "You think I could've killed my own father?"

"You were there, and you've got plenty of motive. You look strong enough to move him."

Rory jolted in her chair. The color drained from her face. "I did hate him for a long time—years. I don't deny it." Her voice was completely flat and emotionless. "It's hard to understand, but he could be very sweet and fun. I loved him when I wasn't hating him. He never touched me—I guess that was a line even he wouldn't cross. If it weren't for the pictures and him leaving.... Oh God, I don't know!" She trailed off, focusing on her bloody cuticle.

He studied her, trying to decide if she was hiding genuine pain or playing him once again. The room was quiet, except for the cars passing by on Charles Street. Dust sparkles danced in the sunlight streaming through the front window. Slowly, she came back. "I wasted so much energy hating him. For years! My last foster mother finally got through to me. She told me to turn that negative energy around and channel it into a positive force; to use it to make something of myself, to prove I'm better than him, better than what he did to me. And I did. I put myself through school, and found a profession and a soulmate. My life was going great, until he called."

As she spoke, Jason flashed back to his last foster father, red-faced and yelling at him because he failed woodshop. "You worthless faggot," the man had roared, "you'll starve if you can't work with your hands."

"You were lucky, in a way," Jason said, still deep in the memory. "I never had a foster parent like that."

"*You* were in foster care? No way."

"I never talk about it, but yeah. Six homes in six years when both my parents were in rehab at the same time. Some homes for a few weeks, some for months. Each one worse than the last. For me, it was my grandmother who turned me around. I don't know where I'd be if it wasn't for her."

"Uh-uh. No way. I've known guys like you. You grew up in Palos Verdes. Your dad was the CEO of a bank and your mom was president of the Junior League."

"Nope. Both were drunks. Still are. My grandmother took me in when I was twelve."

She looked at him like she saw the whole person for the first time. "I guess we've got more in common than I imagined," she mumbled. "And we both had to overcome big odds to make something of ourselves."

The moment of painful kinship passed. He said softly, "You still haven't answered the question. You were at the spec house. You had the motive and opportunity. Did you kill Geraldo?"

Rory flew out of her chair, red-faced and wide-eyed. "No, goddammit! You bastard! How can you say that after I opened myself up to you?" She slammed both her fists on Jason's desktop. "I did not kill my father! Get it? It took him sixteen years to call me! I thought he wanted to make amends, but he fucking died. I thought he wanted to apologize for all the horrible things he did to me, but now he's dead, and I have to live with the turmoil forever, so he owes me, and I want what's mine. All of it!" She glared at him until her breathing slowed and the red faded from her cheeks. "Anyway," she said more calmly, but still defiantly, "you should put yourself on your little list, too."

"And why should I do that?"

She sat in the client's chair, a smug look spreading across her face. "Fair's fair, Jason. Since you're accusing me, you've got your own motive. Geraldo took your last $30,000. And, as you say, you're big enough to move him. Can you prove where you were the night he died? You're definitely a suspect."

"You're accusing *me*?" Jason's blood pressure jumped to 180. Through the pounding in his ears, he spat out, "You've been in Sea Cliff for five minutes. You don't know anything about—"

"It's a small town. Everyone knows you lost your nest egg to Geraldo. They know you prefer silk boxers, too."

Like bloodied boxers in their corners waiting for the bell, they eyed each other across the desk. Jason looked away first, checking the time on his cell phone.

Rory stood up. "I'm going for my run. Is there a bathroom?"

Jason pointed to the door in the rear corner of his office. As she walked away, he forced himself to ignore his anger and blood pressure and get focused. He had to leave for Simon's Cove this minute, but first had to make a copy of the suspect list to give to Deputy Dumbass. He debated adding Rory's name to it, but decided to make that decision after he'd cleared his head. Picking up the list, his eye fell on the sheet with Rory's secret code, half hidden under the base of his desk lamp. He wanted a copy of that also in case he needed it when she wasn't around.

The lock clicked on the bathroom door. Just as he tipped back the lamp to pull out the secret code sheet, footsteps clacked across the front deck. The office door opened and closed.

"Jason?" Erin called, "are you here?"

CHAPTER 43

"Jason?" Erin called again from the door of his office. "Where are you?"

Jason stood at his desk, suddenly paralyzed. Half of him was relieved. She'd come to him, and that had to mean she wasn't angry anymore. The other half was worried. She hadn't returned his calls. She must've seen the video by now. She'd find Rory there with him.

It took a moment for relief to trump worry. Even so, he couldn't make himself move. He told himself to get a grip. He'd been about to do something. Looking down, he saw the list of local suspects in his hand. He needed to copy it and Rory's secret code, but they'd have to wait. He dropped the list on his desk, walked around the end of the bookcase, and stopped, hands in pockets.

Erin stood inside the front door, a black silhouette against the sunlit window. He willed himself to be cool, but his heart beat double-time when he saw her. The bright light shone through her auburn hair, creating an aura of gold, brown, and red around her head while shadowing her face. He tried to read her. Her posture said "confidence," but there'd been a catch in her voice when she called his name.

He took a step in her direction. She took a step, hesitated. He stopped, hands still in pockets, and leaned against the bookcase. Erin moved forward just enough for him to see her face. Their eyes met. He smiled and strode toward her, arms half-open. She ran to him, throwing her forearms around his neck and wrapping her leg tightly around his calf. She pressed her body against him, and he tugged their waists together. She kissed him on his lips, cheek, neck.

Jason absorbed every sensation of her embrace. The hungry pressure of her pelvis against his groin, her breasts crushed against his chest, the herbal scent of her shampoo, the urgent probing of her tongue. She felt so natural in his arms, so right. *This is what I want—to be with her. No more games, no more being teased.* He leaned back just enough to stare into her blue eyes. He whispered, "I'm so sorry, sweetheart."

"It's my fault," she murmured into his neck. "You're more important than Los Angeles."

"I should've been more patient."

"It's OK. It's really OK."

"No, we could've talked. I tried to call you."

"I know, I know, my phone's dead." She kissed him passionately. "Oh my God, Jason, I was so worried about you. All the blood and smashed furniture at your house. I was afraid someone was trying to hurt you, or kill you." Tears ran down her cheeks.

"You went to my house?" He hugged her even tighter, kissing away the wet streaks.

"I wrecked my car trying to warn you," she choked with a half-laugh, half-sob. "I walked all the way here from Shorty's Garage."

The warmest rush of affection he could remember filled his chest. *She really does care for me. It's not just about sex and getting out of Sea Cliff.* In the emotional intensity of the moment, he knew he could say, "I love you." He pressed her cheek against his chest and kissed the top of her head. "Sweetheart," he began, "you mean so much to me. I haven't felt this way forever. I never thought I'd say it again, but I … I …."

While Jason struggled to actually say the "L" word, the sound of the toilet flushing broke the silence. Erin stiffened in his arms and bent back at the waist. "Is someone else here?"

Rory stepped out of the bathroom, closing the door behind her. With a bemused expression, she considered Jason and Erin, now in a half-embrace. "What an interesting conversation. And I thought *my* life was a soap opera."

Erin broke free from Jason's arms. The blue eyes that had been so loving just a moment ago burned with anger. "I saw the video, Jason. Mandi Jo's video of you kissing that woman."

"I did not kiss her! It was just the angle where Mandi Jo was standing."

"Don't lie to me! I made myself believe you didn't, convinced myself you'd never, even told myself it wasn't you, because you were in the hospital, but now I know what I saw. You did kiss her, and here she is with you in her underwear, almost."

"You'd rather that I'd been injured?"

"Than have you betray me? Yes, I would. That's how much I care about you. Used to care."

Jason stood midway between the two women. He glanced over his shoulder at Rory and was shocked. Her eyes were locked on Erin, like a jungle cat ready to pounce. They raked her figure up and down, stopping at the open button that revealed an inch of cleavage.

Erin buttoned herself to the neck and glared back. "She tried to pick me up last night!"

"That's what I'm trying to tell you," Jason said. "She's gay. She doesn't like men. She's Geraldo's daughter, and … and she's here … to help me … with his estate—"

"Hey, you two," Rory interrupted. "I'm not a potted plant. I'm right here." She stalked toward them, ogling Erin.

Jason was surprised to see Erin cringe. She retreated until she hit the side wall of the office. He quickly stepped back, standing between her and Rory.

Stopping inches from Jason, who was inches from Erin, Rory reached around him to caress her cheek. "Yes, I do like girls," she purred. Erin batted her hand away. "But sometimes," Rory's hungry gaze shifted to Jason, "I fall off the wagon for a while." With that, she kissed him full on the lips. "And when I do," she grabbed his hand and clamped it to her breast, "I get what I want." Jason jerked his hand to his side, but Rory bumped him backward against the wall and pressed herself against him. She smiled sweetly at Erin. "We've got a connection you'll never understand, since the moment we met. Just ask him. He's all mine, so run along, little girl. You're way out of your league."

"Erin! Don't listen to her." He pushed Rory away. "There's nothing between us. Nothing!"

Erin looked from one to the other, mouth agape. Her voice was icy when she spoke. "You know, Jason, how you tell me to trust my instinct when I take pictures?" She paused. "I see this picture, and my instinct is,

'You betrayed me and I hate you.' You're both disgusting. You deserve each other." With her head held high, she walked defiantly to the front door. "To think I was so worried about you that I wrecked my car!" She slammed the door behind her.

"God damn you, Rory! Why did you do that?" He shoved her against the bookcase so hard she had to grab it for support.

"Admit it. We've got a connection like I've never had with anybody. I know you feel it. Anyway, she can have you when I'm done."

"That's where you're wrong. It's just business." He didn't add, "From now on." "We're done—really done this time. Get out of my office. I'll email you if I need anything for the estate."

"OK, business it is. Show me the financial files."

"Later."

"Now!"

"I've gotta go meet the cop."

Rory darted around the bookcase. He heard her rustling papers on his desk. She returned a moment later holding up the page with the alphanumeric code. "We still need each other," she said, folding the paper and slipping it into her bra. "You know where the banks are." She tapped her breast. "And I've got the key to get into them."

CHAPTER 44

Jason drove slowly up Highway 1 to Simon's Cove and his rendezvous with Deputy Hardesty. A leaden dome of fog was settling over the ocean and village, and Jason's mood was just as dismal.

Erin and he were ruined, probably forever. He wanted to tell Rory to go to hell, but needed the secret code. Geraldo's banks would require it for access to his accounts. He kicked himself for not making a copy when he had the chance, and grudgingly accepted she was necessary for now. There was one positive thing—the attraction was gone. Completely.

Beyond that, his financial situation was even more rocky than usual. Thanks to his father kicking him out of GG's house, he'd have to come up with a security deposit and pay rent.

If he listed the positives and negatives in his life, as GG always told him to do when he was depressed, the only positive thing right now was his escape from Rory's force field of sexual energy.

Turning off Highway 1, he drove across the parking lot to the foot of the Simon's Cove pier. He hoped this meeting with Hardesty wouldn't take long because Rory had demanded to meet at four to go through the financial files. Coffee and a sandwich were essential before he met with her.

Simon Cove's pier jutted a quarter mile into the Pacific. He parked as close as he could to the entry gate and watched the whitecaps crash into the pilings before they surged against the rocky shore. The ocean spray and moist salt air soon clouded his Porsche's windows. He sat numb and motionless in the cool of his metal-and-glass cocoon, oblivious to everything but the rhythmic roar of the waves.

Deputy Hardesty's headlights brought him back to the present. He parked next to Jason and lowered his side window. Jason opened his a crack. "Get in here," Hardesty bellowed over the surf.

The interior of the cruiser smelled of stale grease, onions, and dirty body. "So, what've you got for me?" Hardesty demanded.

"It's a two-way street, if you remember our deal. What do you have for me?"

"You're a pissant. Tell me something useful, or we'll take a drive down to Rock Bay and the cage."

"Screw you." Jason opened the cruiser's door. "You want your sergeant's stripes? I've got some good leads, but you'll have to trade me some information."

The deputy was silent. He stared out the windshield and chewed his lip, apparently considering Jason's ultimatum. Jason stuck one foot out the open door and began to stand.

"The coroner's reexamining the body," Hardesty blurted.

Jason edged his shoulder through the opening.

"And he's revised the cause of death."

Jason lowered himself into the seat and closed the door. "And?"

"Now they're saying it wasn't blunt force trauma to the head. He was dead before he got dumped in the storm drain. They were working on the bodies from the exploding boat when O'Brien came in, so I guess they saw the crushed skull, figured that was it, and stuck him in a drawer. They're finished with the boat now, so they're looking more closely at O'Brien. They ain't sayin' it was natural causes, mind you. They still think it's homicide."

So Mags could be right, Jason thought. Geraldo did die from a heart attack during the party. He asked, "When'll they make a final determination?"

"That stupid girl reporter's got her station manager hounding the DA, and he's all over the sheriff, and the sheriff's ragging at the coroner, so soon, I 'spect. This afternoon? Tomorrow morning?"

"And you'll let me know?"

"Depends. What you got for me?"

Jason pulled Rory's list of Geraldo's drug-dealer associates from his shirt pocket. Before leaving his office, he'd torn off the bottom half with the local suspects. He handed Hardesty the top part. "These are Geraldo's known drug-dealing associates. Some of them are pretty big names. They all could have motive to kill him."

The deputy read each name aloud, excitement building in his voice. "This is gonna be helpful. I'm gonna collar me a dealer and solve the murder." He draped his arm over the steering wheel, releasing a burst of sour odor. With his other hand, he traced a V on his sleeve where his stripes would be sewn. "Woo-wee! Sergeant Duane Updegraf Hardesty, here I come!"

Jason leaned away, pressing himself against the passenger's door. "Anything else? I've got work to do."

"Yeah, since you been so helpful. We got a search warrant for O'Brien's house on Bluffside where he stashed his drugs. The forensics guys're there right now." He paused. "You know that girl, Tiffany Tedeseki? We got a tip she might be a suspect."

"I don't think so. I know her, she's a good kid. Stick with the drug-dealer list."

"You done good this time, but we ain't done. You get your ass back up here whenever I say."

"Sure thing, Duane. Anytime you've got something for me."

He slammed the cruiser's door behind him.

* * *

Jason grabbed a large coffee and a roast beef sandwich at Bites 'n Bytes and went back to his office. Sitting at his desk eating and thinking, he decided to start contacting the banks without Rory.

He spent an hour Googling, and came up with email addresses for the 24 banks in Geraldo's financial worksheets. He composed a letter to send to each of them:

Greetings:

I represent the late Geraldo Gomez O'Brien, who was a depositor at your institution. I am preparing the initial probate filing for Mr. O'Brien's estate, and require information regarding account balances for that purpose.

Please provide as complete information as possible, including account numbers, status, and balances (or range of balances). Also, please state the date and nature of the last transaction on the account.

It would be most helpful to receive this information within 10 days.

Here is Mr. O'Brien's identifying information:

Social Security number: 999-27-6830

Date of Birth: November 30, 1951

Driver's license number: CA337451A

Thank you for your cooperation. Please contact me if I may answer any questions.

Sincerely,

Jason Brinkman, Attorney at Law

California Bar Number Q309451

812 Charles Street, Suite A, Sea Cliff, CA

805-760-3670

Jason@BrinkmanLaw.com

He attached the letter to each of the emails and sent them.

Being realistic, he knew he'd probably need an Order for Probate before the banks provided any useful information, but he hoped the rural ones might be less strict. Anyway, he told himself, he had to start somewhere.

Totally exhausted, he checked the time on his phone. It was 3:15, and Rory wouldn't get there until 4:00. He'd done everything he needed to do for the moment, so he decided to blow off their meeting until tomorrow.

Before he could leave, however, he had to deal with the possibility El Carnicero would search his office that night. Jason summoned the last of his energy. He trudged his computer tower and Geraldo's file boxes to his car, then went back to gather the folders of his best-paying clients from the files in the bathroom. He locked all the doors and carried the folders back to his Porsche. The car rumbled to life, and he drove slowly through the fog.

Despite being half-asleep, he couldn't get Hardesty's words out of his head: "O'Brien was dead before he got dumped in the storm drain."

Jason considered this new fact as he drove. Geraldo could have died of a heart attack, but that wasn't the only possibility. Somebody at the party could've spiked his drink or the cocaine he snorted, or substituted the pure heroin for the cut stuff he thought he was shooting. Somebody with a grudge, like Jamie, or Rory, or even El Carnicero. Or someone could've snuck back into the spec house while Bill was passed out and Mags was at home, and killed Geraldo while he was unconscious. Then there was the second person carrying the body to the van. Mags said it was Danni, but was Mags telling the truth?

When Jason finally reached his wrecked house, he piled the files and tower in the corner of his room. He dropped into his bed without undressing and fell asleep in an instant.

CHAPTER 45

Jason jogged along the bluff trail at first light the next morning. The sun peeked through the pines that dotted the hilltops to the east, casting gnarled black shadows down the rocky slopes. He was breathing hard, but his stride was steady as he passed the mile-and-a-half point—the bench where he'd burned out three mornings ago. That was before he'd learned Geraldo was missing, and moments before Rory sprinted by so effortlessly, with her long legs and bouncing ponytail. "I'm gonna make my two miles today," he puffed, ignoring the searing pain in his lungs and thighs.

After leaving his office yesterday afternoon, Jason slept ten fitful hours. Now, as he ran, snippets of his dreams popped into his mind's eye: Tiffany slamming her front door in his face. Deputy Hardesty bellowing, "You're gonna help me find O'Brien's killer, or else." Mags pacing her cell and begging him to get her out of jail. The last one—the look of betrayal on Erin's face when Rory walked out of the bathroom—haunted him. He made himself a silent promise he'd never lose her.

At eight o'clock, he was sitting at his desk with a large coffee and a breakfast burrito. It occurred to him he'd never confirmed with Charles Chalmers that he'd represent Mags until Chalmers returned from Barbados, so he texted a message agreeing to the arrangement.

Two bites into the burrito, he began to fret again about the automatic lease payment on his Porsche, and decided it was time to find out whether it had cleared. He set his food aside and found the number for his bank's robo teller.

To his surprise, a person answered—a young woman. She explained the system was down for maintenance all morning. "I'm answering the phone for my mother. She's the branch manager, and she's out back with the network support guy having a smoke."

Jason told her why he was calling.

"Service is our number one priority," the young woman said. "I can check for you, so you don't have to call back this afternoon,"

He told her his name, and recited his account number, security code, and the amount of the debit.

"Alrighty. Let's see if I can tell what's going on."

He heard the tapping of a keyboard. "What's your account number again?" she asked. He repeated it slowly. After more tapping, she said, "It looks like a debit in that amount was rejected, but a deposit was made before it was resubmitted, and it was paid the second time it came through."

"Thanks," Jason said, breathing a sigh of relief.

"No worries. Have an awesome day, sir."

He hung up, thinking today was going to be a better day. Finally.

Jason sipped his coffee, ate his burrito, and thought about the day ahead. Rory would be furious because he'd stood her up yesterday afternoon. He expected her to bang on his door first thing. Before that happened, he wanted to see if any of the banks had responded to his inquiries. He finished eating and went outside to his Porsche to retrieve the computer tower and his files.

Many of the banks were in eastern time zones, so he thought he might get preliminary responses from them. He swallowed the last of his coffee as his computer powered up. He was surprised that his email icon showed 15 new messages.

One by one, he opened the emails. Three were from Rory, blasting him for not keeping their appointment. The responses from the banks were what he'd feared—polite refusals to disclose any customer information without a PIN or evidence of consent or court authority.

Jason searched his desk drawers until he found a new legal pad and a pen. Returning to the emails, he began to list each bank and its requirement for accessing Geraldo's account:

Commercial Bank—power of attorney or certified copy of order from probate court

Farmers & Mechanics Bank—password or power of attorney
Fifty-Third Street Bank, Chicago—password or court order
First Bank of Pottstown, Iowa—notarized power of attorney
First National Bank of Greater Minneapolis—password
Grand National Bank of the Cayman Islands—password
Bank of Saginaw, Michigan—court order and certified copy of death certificate

He was about to open the email from the Totten Trust Bank of New York when he heard pounding on his front door. He went to it, flipped the lock, and stood aside.

Rory stormed in, eyes burning and face flushed. She ripped off her baseball cap. "Brinkman, you fucker, you're trying to screw me out of my father's money!"

"I'm not trying to—"

"My partner's an FBI agent—"

"I don't want your—"

"And the FBI will hit you like a ton of bricks if you steal a dime!"

Rory was four inches shorter than Jason, but stretched on her toes, she was very much in his face. Her whole body shook and her cheeks turned scarlet as she raged at him. "Goddamn shyster lawyer... stealing my money... I trusted you... I earned it... you can't imagine what I went through... he owes me...." Specks of spittle flew from her mouth. Her breath, normally sweet, reeked of stomach acid.

Jason let her rant until she ran out of steam. When she finally took a breath, he said, "I was dog-tired yesterday afternoon. Up all the night before, and then had an early court appearance in Santa Luisa. I went home and slept." He put both hands on her shoulders and pushed down hard, until she stood flat-footed. Holding her at arm's length, he said, "Anyway, we both hold the keys to the puzzle, as you point out."

The tension ebbed slowly from her body and her usual air of self-confidence began to return. "Like Frodo and Gollum in *Lord of the Rings*," she muttered. She wore a black warm-up suit and running shoes, and unlike the other times he'd seen her, seemed unconcerned about her appearance. Although he was certain he was free from her spell, he couldn't deny she was stunning even in drab athletic gear.

He beckoned her to follow him around the bookcase to his desk. "I did start to contact some of the banks," he began as they walked.

"What?" she shrieked. "You just told me—"

"Christ, Rory, will you let me explain! I wanted to see what kind of responses I'd get." He turned to face her, speaking patiently. "Banks have so many privacy restrictions these days, and we don't have anything to prove we're entitled to access Geraldo's accounts."

"Uh-huh," she said with an edge in her voice, "so what'd you find out? Anything useful?"

"Pretty much what I expected. We need a password or some kind of authorization. Here. See for yourself." He gave her his handwritten list.

"Your writing's too hard to read."

"Alright, I'll translate. The first one is Commerce Bank, and they require a power of attorney or a court order. The next is Farmers & Mechanics.…" He read the rest of the list.

"There's no way Geraldo gave you power of attorney or any kind of authorization."

"You're right. No way."

"How long will it take to get a court order?"

"A couple of weeks after I file the papers."

"Why so long? I can't…don't want to wait forever."

"It may be longer," he said. "I heard the Probate Judge just retired."

"Well, why can't we figure out the passwords? We have Geraldo's alphanumeric code."

"That's ten characters," Jason said, thinking out loud. "Passwords can be any length, but they're usually six or eight, and we don't know which six or eight he'd have used for any particular bank. Or whether he'd have mixed numbers and letters, or capitals and lower case. Or used fewer characters."

"Can't we just try different combinations?"

"Yeah, we could try that ... maybe on one of the banks that doesn't seem important ... but you probably get just one bite of the apple in this kind of situation."

"You mean where strangers are trying to get information about a dead person's account?"

"Exactly."

Rory pointed to the list of banks. "What are the rest of them, again?"

"Well, the next one is this bank in Iowa, and they want a notarized power of attorney. Boy, he sure did spread his money around."

"Yeah, he was always paranoid someone would find it and steal it from him."

"Sounds familiar," Jason quipped.

"Screw you," she shot back, but her tone was light. She took the legal pad and ran her finger slowly under each name. "I'm getting the picture. We're SOL," she mumbled. Her finger moved down the list line by line. "Wait a minute. Grand National Bank of the Cayman Islands. This one's important. Why does it ring a bell?"

She reached for the client's chair and sat, staring at the paper. "Cayman Islands ... Cayman Islands. Geraldo went there on vacation, I remember. It was just before he walked out on me and my mother. All he talked about before he went was how great the surfing was going to be." She paused, tapping her foot impatiently. "I've got it! When he got home, it was all about how great the banks were, and nothing about surfing. I thought that was so strange. I mean, who goes to a tropical island and gets excited about their banks? That's why it stuck in my mind ... ."

She trailed off at the sound of the office door opening and closing. "Jason?" a girl called out. "Are you in here?"

"Nikki?" Jason shouted. "What is it? I'm with a client."

High heels clacked on the other side of the bookcase. Nikki's platinum curls appeared around the end. "It's Deputy Hardass again, Jason. He's giving you another ticket."

"Oh, for God's sake! Thanks, Nikki." He shoved back from his desk and stormed out the door.

* * *

Nikki stood at the end of the bookcase. Rory remained seated, studying Nikki from her curls to her makeup to her outfit to her stilettos.

"Who are you?" Rory asked after a long silence. Her smile was both amused and friendly.

"Umm… I'm… umm… Nikki. I'm… uh… the shampoo girl from the salon next door."

"Hi, Nikki, I'm Rory." She held out her hand, and Nikki walked over and shook it.

Rory held onto Nikki's hand and stared intently at her face. Nikki's eyes grew wide and she blushed. "I'm just the shampoo girl now," she blurted, "but I hear all the gossip, and I tell Jason a lot of it, but I really want to go to cosmetology school someday and be a stylist."

Nikki pulled her hand free from Rory's grasp. She retreated to the bookcase and stood stiffly. Her eyes roamed all around the office, not stopping on Rory until she finally said, "You're… you're the beautician from LA, aren't you?"

"Esthetician from Beverly Hills."

"Esthetician? So you give injections?"

"Yes, mostly. How do you know who I am?"

Nikki sighed. "A girl can't get a zit in this town without someone blogging or tweeting about it. And, well, looking the way you do… you're so pretty. I never saw a girl as…. Jason asked me to find out about you."

"Did he, really? And what did you learn?"

"Mostly what I just said, and you're renting a house on Bluffside for the rest of the month."

"You have such beautiful skin. So clear and fresh. Do you mind my asking what happened to your face?"

"I got cut by a broken window," Nikki said matter-of-factly. "It's so stupid, but it's all Jason's fault, really. If he wasn't so dreamy, I wouldn't of gone to his house, and none of this would of happened."

"Dreamy," Rory repeated. "Yes, that's a good word for him. And beyond sexy."

Nikki cleared her throat. "Umm … the other thing I heard about you … I mean aren't you … I mean I thought you wouldn't like, well, someone like Jason because he's a, you know, not a—"

"Listen. You're too pretty to have scars. My salon sells a cream. Visage Exquis." She reached into her pocket. "Here's my card. Call and tell them I said to give it to you at our cost. And use it! Twice a day."

The office door opened and closed, and Jason walked to his desk, holding a fluorescent-green ticket envelope and a scrap of paper. He said, "Thanks for telling me, Nikki, but Rory and I have some work to do." He looked at the paper in his hand. "And I have to meet Deputy Dumbass in Simon's Cove in forty-five minutes."

* * *

As soon as Nikki left the office, Jason said, "Let's look at the Cayman Islands email." Rory walked around the desk and stood next to him. They leaned close to the screen as he opened the message and read:

Welcome to the Grand National Bank of the Cayman Islands. Access to accounts is governed strictly by the password chosen by the account holder. Please enter your password in the box below.

WARNING! Two incorrect passwords will close this portal permanently. It may be reopened, at the Bank's discretion, upon providing in-person authentication of identity acceptable to the Bank.

"I guess we better be careful with this one," Jason said.

"Yeah. But how're we going to figure out the password? Do you think it's the ten-digit code?"

"Probably not the whole thing. That's the problem. We don't know which six or eight characters he'd have used. He could've used the first six, or the last six, or every other one, or something random." Jason picked up a pencil and tapped the empty box on the screen. "Maybe we should try a different approach first. Did Geraldo have a favorite saying, or maybe play the same lottery numbers all this time?"

"I was so young. I just don't remember anything like that."

"Did you have one of those really long addresses, you know, like in some parts of LA, where they're six or eight digits long?"

"For a little while, but he'd never have used something so obvious."

"True when I knew him, too. That lets out phone numbers, birthdays, names, and things like that."

Heads together, they bent over the screen, staring at it glumly.

"I've got to get ready to meet Hardesty, which means I have to give him something to keep him busy and away from me." He rummaged through the papers on his desk until he found the list of local suspects. He tore a clean sheet from his legal pad and rewrote the names, leaving out Tiffany Tedeski.

"Why didn't you include her?" Rory asked.

"Because I know her and just can't believe she'd kill anyone, even Geraldo. She's only sixteen, and a good kid, and Hardesty has his sights set on her for some reason." He folded the sheet and stuck it in his pocket along with his cell phone. "I have to go. Meet me here at four, and we'll see what we can come up with."

"Can I trust you that long?" she said, looking at him sideways.

"Think Frodo and Gollum."

"Who's who? I mean, Frodo had the ring at the end."

"Doesn't matter. We're joined on this quest, and neither of us can reach the end without the other."

"And at the end?"

"I'm sure there will be a bond of trust between us by then." He said it with a smile, hoping he sounded more convincing than he felt. His computer dinged to signal a new email. "Guess we should look at it before I leave, but I really need to get going." The email was from ke@gnbci.com. "Doesn't ring a bell. It's probably a business deal that's too good to pass up."

"Or you won a lottery."

Jason opened the message. The screen was blank, showing only a pdf attachment. He clicked on the icon. The image was blurry at first. It slowly resolved into a document on pastel letterhead. "Holy shit. Look at this."

"Oh my God."

The letter was from the Office of Kingston Easterday, President and General Counsel to the Grand National Bank of the Cayman Islands.

"Kingston Easterday. It's a person," Jason said.

"How about that? It is a man's name, after all."

Together, they leaned over Jason's desk to read the letter:

Dear Jason Brinkman, Esq.:

For 150 years, the Grand National Bank of the Cayman Islands has guaranteed the absolute anonymity and confidentiality of its deposi-tors, whilst assuring the safety and liquidity of their funds, and their immediate availability anywhere in the world. I hope, therefore, you will appreciate that this letter represents a profound breach of this institution's most sacred principles, which I am moved to undertake in this extraordinary circumstance.

I am deeply grieved to learn of Geraldo O'Brien's passing. He and I became close personal friends during the fifteen years he was a client of this institution, sharing the Islands' natural and man-made pleasures.

Mr. O'Brien also was a highly valued client. It is a tribute to this institution's integrity that he chose to consolidate with us all his hold-ings from numerous banks in the United States.

Since Mr. O'Brien designated you to represent his estate, I trust he provided you the 10-digit alphanumeric code required to access his accounts. If not, I regret, for the sake of his heirs, that his assets will inure to the benefit of this institution after five years.

In these premises, I remain,

Your obedient and humble servant,
Kingston Easterday, LLM
President and General Counsel

"That's it!" Rory cried. She pulled the paper with the code out of her pants pocket. Unfolding it, she smoothed it carefully on Jason's desk, trying to flatten the deep creases without tearing them. "Let's plug it in and see how much there is. You type. I'll read the numbers and letters." When Jason didn't move, she said sharply, "Well?"

"We can do that, but you have to remember whatever's in that bank belongs to Geraldo's estate, not to you. At least, not until the probate court says it's yours, if it does."

Jason saw the flush of anger building in her and tried to head it off. "There may be other heirs, or taxes he owes, or creditors we don't know about. I told you that before. There may be complications because it's offshore money. It's probably drug money, and the Feds might claim it."

"How long will probate take?"

"Depends. If no one challenges or files a claim, maybe six months. If someone creates problems, maybe a year."

She shook her head, as if she didn't want to hear what he was saying. "And if I just take it?"

Jason spoke sternly. "You don't want to do that. You could be prosecuted for grand theft or perpetrating a fraud on the court. The other heirs could sue you."

Her eyes narrowed with suspicion. "And if *you* took it?"

I could solve my money problems. The thought survived a nanosecond— just long enough to be recognized and banished. He said, "I wouldn't do that. No way. I have a fiduciary duty to Geraldo's estate. But the consequences would be the same, plus I'd lose my law license."

Rory took a deep breath and exhaled slowly. "Alright. We'll have to trust each other. I'm not going to bite off your finger, and you're not going to throw me into the fiery pit." She bit her lower lip. "Besides, the account might be empty. Let's see what it says."

Jason closed out the Easterday email and reopened the one from the Grand National Bank. "Ready," he said, placing the cursor in the box.

She read the numbers and letters slowly. "Don't make a mistake!"

Jason typed:

E-2-y-u-6-n-8-y-A-Q

He scrolled down to the *Submit* button and pressed it. The screen went blank. An error message appeared. "SHIT!" they both exclaimed.

"Try it again," Rory ordered, "and be more careful this time!"

Jason wiped his palms on his pants and realized his hands were shaking. "OK. Read it slowly."

He typed:

E-2-y-u-6-N-8-y-A-Q

"Say it one more time, to be sure," he said. She repeated the code, and he compared each character against what he'd typed. He pressed *Submit*. Shoulder to shoulder, they bent over the desk. The screen went blank. It flashed, went blank again.

"Why's your computer so slow?"

"It's not my computer. The village doesn't have high-speed Internet yet."

The screen flashed again. *Welcome, Geraldo O'Brien* appeared at the top. Small-type warnings, notices, disclaimers, and an Agreement to Terms of Use filled the rest of the page. Jason scrolled down until a button appeared that said *Check Account Balances*. He clicked on it.

Nothing happened. Another error message materialized:

You must agree to the Terms of Use in order to proceed.

Jason closed the message. At the bottom of the *Welcome* screen, in the far left margin, he saw a faint box that said *I agree to these terms*. He checked the box and clicked on the *Submit* button. The screen froze. Then it went blank. Seconds ticked by. Finally, a list of accounts appeared, each with a balance.

"Add them up," Rory ordered harshly.

Instead, Jason scrolled to the bottom of the page and the line, *Total of all accounts*.

"There it is," he said, trying to sound calm. "$781,382.89."

Rory stared at the numbers silently. When she spoke, her voice was so cold that Jason stepped aside to look at her. "So, that's it. All this time

I wanted to know, and now I wish I didn't." Her face was a stone mask, hollow-eyed and grim. "That's my value, what I'm worth to him," she said in a monotone. "That's what it cost him to tear out the soul of a little girl and leave her dead inside."

She pressed the "+" button on the keyboard until the figure filled the screen. "Seven hundred eighty-one thousand, three hundred eighty-two dollars, and eighty-nine cents," she said, her voice trembling. "You probably think that's a lot, but it isn't. Not for what he did to me, for what I've had to live with all these years."

Splotchy color crept into her cheeks as the mask began to crack. Her eyes glistened and overflowed. She wiped them with her fingers, leaving streaks of wet. "*I'm* the one who's had to pay for it, and he...he gets off scot-free, goes on his merry way, and finds someone new when he's tired of me...us, me and my mom."

She faced him with quivering lips and tears flowing down her cheeks. For a moment, he saw the frightened 14-year-old girl whose father walked out after betraying the bond between them.

"You can't imagine the humiliation," she choked. "He'd say, 'C'mon, Goldie, let's see how the apple of my eye is ripening. Go get in the shower,' and he'd load up his Polaroid with film. You know it's wrong, but he's your father, and you want to please him so he'll keep loving you." She traced the numbers on the screen with a wet finger. "Daddy," she whispered.

Teardrops splashed on the keyboard. "I hated him so much for so many years. More than I hated myself. I swore I'd kill him, but now he's dead, and what else can I do? He never apologized, never said he was sorry, never even tried to explain. He kept his word to little Goldie at least, but it's not enough...there can never be enough." She fell into Jason's chair and crumpled onto the desktop, burying her face in her elbow. "God," she sobbed, "where is the closure? When does it end?"

Jason's heart swelled with pity for the abused and abandoned girl. He came to his senses a moment later. *That's not who's sitting in my chair. She'll stop at nothing to get what she wants, and sex is her weapon.* He swore he wasn't getting sucked in again. Even so, he walked to the bathroom and grabbed the Kleenex box, and placed it next to her arm.

Minutes passed. The office was silent, except for Rory's sobs. Finally, they slowed. She sniffled and wiped her tears. "Still," she said, looking up at him, forcing a weak smile, "it's enough to make a fresh start somewhere. To get away from everything that's dragging us down." She placed her hand on top of his. His skin tingled at her touch, in spite of his resolve. "Somewhere warm and carefree," she continued in a dreamy tone. "Someplace where two people can spend all day in bed together—if they want—and lie naked in the sun, and make love in the surf in the moonlight."

She squeezed his hand, and fixed him with her pale-gray eyes. Shy. Imploring. Demanding.

Jason pulled his hand away.

CHAPTER 46

The instant Jason pulled his hand from under Rory's, she grabbed the corner of the paper with the 10-digit code. Jason grabbed the other corner. They both yanked. The paper had been folded so many times over the years that it tore down the middle. He glanced quickly, and saw half of the code on each piece.

With a savage cry, Rory lunged against his side, knocking them both to the floor. Jason landed flat on his back, smacking his head.

"You will not steal my money!" she screamed, straddling him. She punched him in the jaw and clawed with her other hand for his piece. He held it just beyond her reach, stretching his arm as far as he could.

Her strength and solid body surprised him—more like a lightweight wrestler than a beautiful young woman. She grabbed his extended arm and dug her fingernails into his wrist, drawing blood as she fought for the paper. Jason crumpled it and flipped it backward across the floor. Wrenching his arm free, he slapped her hard across her cheek. She punched wildly at his head, but he caught her fist in his palm. "Stop it!" he shouted. "I don't want the money. I need the code. For the estate." He captured both her wrists, pinning them by her side.

She jerked and twisted her arms and tried to knee him in the groin. He released her wrists to block the blow. Her fingernails raked at his eyes. He caught her hands just in time and twisted her fingers back until she yelped. "Rory, enough! Stop this!"

Panting, she sat back on her haunches. The fury drained from her face, and her eyes focused on the purple bruise spreading along his jawline. "Oh my God, Jason," she whimpered. "I'm so sorry." She loosened his grip on her hand and gently touched the ugly welt. "I didn't mean to. I'd never hurt you."

They both struggled to catch their breath, Jason on his back, and Rory straddling his hips. She bent forward, resting her palms on the floor above his shoulders. He reached up to push her back.

"It's OK," she whispered softly. "I'm not angry anymore." She stared into his eyes and smiled affectionately. "Feeling you like this," she murmured, "I know we'd be great together." She kissed him on his bruise, and again on his cheek. With a sigh, she brushed his lips.

"Can't you feel it?" she whispered into his ear. She kissed his mouth, slowly and deeply.

Jason felt it in every neuron and synapse. Tasting her lips, breathing her breath, feeling her firm body on top of him, he gave in to the passion he'd fought since the moment they met. He wrapped his arms around her neck and pulled her to him, kissing her long and hard. She moaned deep in her throat and kissed him hungrily. Her tongue tickled his lips, teasing him until his tongue caressed hers in an eager dance. His breath became short gasps. He heard another moan, and realized it had come from him.

Rory pressed herself against his groin, rubbing gently. He gripped her hips, guiding them back and forth. Aching, throbbing, blood-boiling lust surged through him. Her moist warmth electrified him. He thrust himself up to meet her and they rose and fell together as one. She kissed him on his lips and cheeks, and he pushed her hips down his body until her breasts pressed against his chest. She crushed them into him and unbuttoned his shirt, kissing his bare flesh. He slid his hands slid up her sides and under her breasts. She moaned and raised herself so they filled his palms. He caressed one, then the other, and gently squeezed her hard nipples. Nibbling his ear and nuzzling his neck, she murmured, "I knew it. I knew we were made for each other."

Her words brought him back. His mind filled with the image of her ogling Erin and caressing her cheek. "Jason and I have a connection you'll never understand," she'd said, pressing herself against him and kissing him. "He's all mine."

Her kisses and the intoxicating sensations of her body turned bitter. *WHAT AM I DOING?* He grabbed her biceps and pushed her upright.

He said coldly, "You deliberately destroyed Erin and me, and you had no cause to do that. Erin's my future. She's my future, right here in Sea Cliff."

The she-demon returned in a flash. Rory fought to free her arms from his grip, and it took all his strength to hold them. Swinging her forearms from her elbows, she slashed at his face with claw-like fingers. When she came too close, he'd had enough. Using the momentum of her swing, he bucked his hips and twisted his arms and shoulders, throwing her off him. She crashed into the side of his desk, dazed.

"I don't want to hurt you," he said, gasping for breath. Without taking his eyes off her, he crawled a few paces to where the crumpled paper lay on the floor. He jammed it in his back pocket.

Rory sat limp for so long, he worried she'd injured herself. The expression returned to her face slowly. She tore at the neck of her warm-up suit, ripping the fabric and gashing her chest with her nails. Bowing her head, she clasped her praying mantis pendant, caressing and kissing it. "Lexy, Lexy, my sweet Lexy," she whispered, "I'm so confused."

Jason sat where he was on the floor, studying her, trying to guess where her mind would jump next.

All at once, the life returned to her body and she focused on his face. Steel doors slammed shut behind her eyes. "I'm taking the money." She spoke without a trace of emotion. "There's nothing you can do to stop me." He started to speak, but she interrupted him. "I know what you're going to say. There are relatives who may claim it. Why should I give a shit about them? They did nothing for me when my mom died after my father left. Six foster homes, and not even a birthday card from any of them. All I ever had to rely on was myself, and this body God gave me after He saw fit to take away my family. And Lexy, my precious Alex, my dear Alexandra, who showed me how to become the woman I am."

Rory kissed the pendant again and tucked it inside the torn neck of her warm-up suit. "But Alex is getting restless." Her voice became bitter. "I've learned how to tell when people are about to hurt me, and I can feel it in her. I gave her my heart and eight years of my life, but she's leaving. She's been my anchor forever and now my life's in total chaos." She wiped the corners of her eyes with her fingers and climbed to her feet, steadying herself against the desk. "I got what I stayed here to get. It's always been the money. You would've been a nice bonus, but that kind of money can buy a lot of happiness."

Jason stood slowly. "Rory, listen. Let the probate process run its course. There may be more money. Besides, you don't want to be looking over your shoulder the rest of your life because you stole this money from the estate."

"You don't understand what I'm saying," Rory exploded. "The only people who know about the $780,000 are me, you, and Kingston Easterday. I'm not going to tell anyone about it, and Easterday isn't going to jeopardize his bank's reputation. So if anyone comes after me, it'll be because of you, and I'll ruin your life. Look at these scratches." She pointed to her ripped neckline and the bloody gouges across her chest. "I'll take selfies to prove you tried to rape me. I'll say you tried to steal the money for yourself. And Alex will do me one last favor. She'll turn the FBI loose on you. Did I tell you she runs the LA office? They just love to bust child pornographers, and if they can't find the pictures I know you have, they'll dig up something else. Nobody's so clean the FBI can't find something to crucify them with. So don't even think about fucking with me."

They locked eyes, each waiting for the other to blink or waver. A lifetime seemed to pass before Jason said, "So be it. At least we finally understand each other. Now get out."

* * *

The scene with Rory replayed on an endless loop in Jason's mind as he drove to Simon's Cove to meet Deputy Hardesty. He told himself that he shouldn't be surprised by her viciousness; that she was a survivor and had been since she was a kid; that she'd do whatever it took to get what she wanted.

Lost in thought, he missed the turn-off for the pier parking lot. He pulled onto the shoulder and realized there was something important he should do right now. The first lesson he'd learned at Whatley was to preserve every bit of information and evidence in a case, because he never knew the twists and turns it might take before it ended. That lesson applied to Geraldo's estate. He stopped and set the hand brake. Digging into his pocket, he pulled out the crumpled sheet containing the last half of Geraldo's code:

N-8-y-A-Q

Staring at the paper, he willed himself to remember the first five characters. He'd typed the whole code an hour ago. Twice. He visualized his fingers striking keys on his keyboard and tried to relive the moment when Rory read him the code correctly. He heard her voice.... *Got it!*

E-2-y-u-6

He found a pen in the glove box and scribbled the letters and numbers on the paper before folding it carefully and sliding it into his pocket.

When the traffic cleared, he made a U-turn and drove to the pier's parking lot entrance. He spotted Deputy Hardesty's cruiser backed into the corner at the far end of the lot.

The familiar odors of greasy food and stale onions greeted him as he climbed into the cruiser. "Don't you ever air this thing out?"

"What've you got for me?"

"You called this meeting."

The deputy chuckled. "Yeah, I'm just jerkin' yer chain, Mr. Bigshot LA Attorney." He continued in a more serious tone. "Who's the blonde hottie I seen going into your office a coupla times?"

"Blonde hottie?"

"You know, the tall Barbie doll with the awesome hooters and ponytail."

Jason took a minute to consider his answer. After Rory's threats, he had no personal or ethical obligation to her. It made sense to reveal some tidbits about her to keep Duane busy. That would help him, and maybe Mags while he was responsible for representing her. He'd save the Client Intake sheet information about Rory and the list of local suspects for use later if he needed them. "Her name is Rory O'Brien."

"O'Brien?" Hardesty lit up like a Christmas tree. "As in Gerald O'Brien, the dead guy?"

"It's Geraldo, and yes, she's his daughter."

"Jee-hoss-ahh-phatt! Maybe *she's* the one that killed him."

"Says she didn't."

"She'd say that—'course she would," Hardesty mumbled, staring out his windshield. "Imagine if I prove a filly that looks like that killed her own father. I'd be front-page news all over the state. I'd be number one on Twitter and Facebook and all them things. I could have Commander Sepulveda's job! That's sexier than the Tedeski girl killing him. Way more sexy."

As soon as Jason heard Tiffany's name, he chastised himself for not having done anything to find her. "Any news on her?"

"'Tween you and me, I'm kind of keeping that one to myself, 'cause I wanna get all the credit for solving the case."

"Uh-huh, but you haven't answered the question."

"I did some research. Her friend Victoria says she took her to a place called God's Helping Hands in Santa Luisa. I Googled it and it's right next to the Greyhound station. The Tedeski girl could've got on a bus. I was gonna go question both places this week, but now this O'Brien babe's got more sergeant-making potential."

Jason thought that was actually useful information, and promised Tiffany to follow up the lead. He decided it was time to end the meeting. "So, I drove all the way up here. What've you got for me?"

"Coroner and DA are chasing shadows, far as I'm concerned, 'cause my gut says the Turlock woman didn't kill O'Brien. Coroner says O'Brien's body's loaded with pure heroin, and it's the same as what they found stored in the house. They're certain it was injected—they can't see how that much could've got into him otherwise. Theory is, he must've been unconscious and someone injected him. But they can't find needle marks, even in the usual places people think are secret, like under a toenail or between the toes. Anyway, they're saying the heroin killed him." He fell silent. "I shouldn't say any more, 'cause you're representing Turlock."

"Uh-uh. That's not our deal. It's a two-way street, remember? I help you, you help me. What else do you know?"

"Where can I find that O'Brien babe?"

"She's renting a house on Bluffside. That's all I know."

"Got an address? A cell phone number?"

"For God's sake, you're a cop. Do some detective work. Now tell me what else you know!"

"You said her name's Rory. That her real name, or is it a nickname?"

Jason lifted the cruiser's door handle. "You going to tell me the rest, or do I leave you guessing about her name?" He pushed the door open.

"Fingerprints."

Jason let the door swing closed. "What about them?"

"They found Turlock's fingerprints all over O'Brien's house. And on a bunch of the drugs."

"So? She was Geraldo's real estate agent. The house was her listing. Of course you'd find her fingerprints."

"Yeah, but here's the kicker. They found a cap for a hypodermic needle. The cap has her prints. Now they're looking for the hypodermic, 'cause they think that's how she injected the heroin."

Jason flinched mentally. He remembered stepping on a plastic cap for a disposable syringe under the breakfast bar the afternoon he'd gone to One Bluffside searching for Geraldo. That must be the cap the cops found. They would identify the brand of syringe using the cap, and try to match the diameter of that brand's needles to the diameter of the hole at the injection site when they found it. If the diameters matched and the prints really were Mags's, it would be bad news for her, although not conclusive. It was a little more worrisome that the plastic caps on the syringes in Mags's insulin kit matched the one the cops found. The cops didn't know that yet, but could find out easily enough.

"That worry you, Mr. Defense Attorney?"

"Not at all. It's all circumstantial at best, especially since they don't know if the heroin was injected."

"Well, here's something that oughta worry you. They found your fingerprints in O'Brien's house and on the drugs. And they don't even know about the footprint and dirt sample I found. You'll be a official suspect before long, I reckon."

The thumping thunder of motorcycle engines interrupted them. A dozen chrome and candy-apple Harleys roared south on Highway 1 toward Sea Cliff. All the riders wore beany helmets and black leathers, and had long, white hair and beards that flowed in the wind.

"Whoo-wee!" Hardesty crowed. "Lookit all them Vehicle Code violations just waiting for me to write up. I won't have to work the rest of the week! Get outta my car, Brinkman."

CHAPTER 47

Guillermo Escobar swore a mighty oath in Spanish. He hunched over Danni's breakfast bar, pounding the keyboard of Brinkman's laptop computer with his left fist.

"S'matter, babe?" Danni called from the living room, where she lay sprawled on a recliner. Her voice was slurred and muffled. The shades were drawn against the bright sun, and the room was dark and cool. A disposable syringe, a baggie of heroin powder, a rubber tube, and the rest of her drug paraphernalia cluttered the table beside her.

"*Chingado!*" he roared.

"I tol' ya, babe, Brinkman's a smart lawyer an' he's got a smart password on his computer. You won't get nothin' out of it."

Guillermo pounded the keys until they flew off. "*Mierda! Pinche mierda!*" He grabbed the laptop and hurled it to the floor, stomping on the case until it shattered.

"Lissen ta me." Danni sat up in her chair. "Brinkman wouldn' of put nothin' important 'bout Geraldo's money on his computer. He'd keep it in his head, jus' like Geraldo. I'm tellin' ya, the money's hidden in the spec house. How's your hand? Does it hurt?"

He stalked into the living room and sat in the chair next to Danni.

"Lemme see the hand."

He held his bandaged right hand in front of her face. She pulled it closer, then pushed it away, struggling to focus on it.

"Dressing's clean, no new blood. Does it hurt?"

"*Sí.*"

"So you need some a my frien', Mr. Smack, *mi amigo.*" She held up the baggie. "You lissen ta Nurse Danni. Think I'll have me some, too. An' mebbe s'more of yer oxy ta take the edge off."

Guillermo snugged the rubber tube around Danni's upper arm and pushed her back into the recliner. "*Duermte un poco*," he growled.

"Tha's right," she said, letting her body go limp. "A li'l peace 'fore we go inta town. We find Brinkman, an' go search One Bluffside."

* * *

June gloom was the norm on the Central Coast, so on a sunny afternoon like this, the townies flocked outdoors in their shorts and tee shirts. At the Bites 'n Bytes Café, a crowd of locals filled the patio. They drank sun tea and iced coffee, and chatted about the fine weather and surf conditions.

Parking on Main Street was never a problem, but today Jason was lucky to find a place at all, let alone directly in front of the patio. He grabbed the spot, darting across the lane of oncoming traffic and nosing into the space front-end first.

The parking space was convenient and also served a purpose. The thumping Harleys in Simon's Cove reminded him of El Carnicero, and now he couldn't get the man out of his head. He'd concluded, reluctantly, that a confrontation was inevitable, and that a crowded public area was the best place for it to happen. He guessed El Crazy would take advantage of the good weather to search for him in one of his usual haunts. By parking his car so conspicuously in front of the café, he hoped to draw El Carnicero into the patio to look for him.

Standing in the entrance, Jason saw two empty tables—one in the far rear corner, mostly screened by lattice, and another in the middle. He headed toward the one in the middle. Winding his way through the crowd, he made a point of saying "Hello" to people he knew.

He stopped to chat with Christina, his former secretary. She was now the manager of the Law Offices of Saul Shapiro, whose four attorneys and one paralegal made it the biggest firm in town. "How's it going?" she asked with concern, as she always did when they ran into each other.

"It's been a tough couple of days," Jason admitted, "but I'm keeping my head above water."

"I was sorry to hear about Geraldo. I know he's an important client."

"Yeah, he leaves a big hole. You still happy with old man Shapiro?"

"You know I'd rather work for you, but yeah, it's OK. He's still looking for an associate if you ever—"

"I know, but I spent five years in Whatley's moral cesspit. Now I'm free, I have to make it my own way, on my own terms. No reflection on Saul—he's a gentleman and a good lawyer."

"Always so stubborn and ethical," she said with a smile. "That's a tough road." She slid her sunglasses down her nose and looked over them at his face. "How'd you get that bruise? I saw the video of you kissing some woman at Mostly's. Bet her boyfriend did it." She reached up and touched his jaw gently.

"Nah. It's stupid really. I ran into the bathroom door in the dark. Guess I should've turned on the light." He squeezed her shoulder and walked to the table.

Once seated, Jason let the warm sun relax him. He listened to the buzz of conversation and began a mental list of things he needed to accomplish that afternoon. The first thing was to text Erin to try to fix the mess Rory made.

He ordered a turkey club and a large coffee, and decided it was time. He tapped open his phone. Out of habit, he checked his email and scrolled through the unread messages. One caught his eye—from Courtney. No subject, so he skipped it for now.

He thumbed a text to Erin:

You mean too much to me to end it like this. Please let's talk.

Message sent, he figured she was at work and wouldn't reply right away, so he opened Courtney's email:

Major changes coming. I need to get you out of my life and the divorce finalized. Sign the damn papers now! You've already pushed me too far.

Her message gave him grim pleasure because he knew it drove her crazy when she couldn't check things off her list in the proper order. He was giving her fits, although it was the events of the past couple of days that deserved the credit.

His phone buzzed with a new message, from Erin:

Leave me alone. I'm really hurt. I've got nothing to say to you.

"There's a bit of promise," he muttered, "because she responded and didn't tell me to go to hell. And she cares enough to be hurt."

He replied:

Sweetheart, this all started the other morning when I was upset about Geraldo dying and Courtney's divorce papers. We never had the chance to talk. I care about you too much.

He'd barely pressed *Send* when she shot back:

Do you care, Jason? You never say it. You never say you love me.

Jason was dumbstruck. He typed:

But you said you want a casual relationship. You don't want to be tied down. I thought that meant we had an understanding about saying things like that.

Erin responded a moment later:

You don't understand women very well, do you? Didn't I tell you I want to live with you? Do you love me? I've a right to know, because, well, I just do.

He stared at his phone. Could he honestly say he loved her? He hadn't said those words since early in his relation with Courtney. He was about to say it yesterday before Rory interrupted them, but was that just in the moment?

He pondered for a moment before taking a deep breath and thumbing slowly:

I do love you and I want to be with you. I'd rather be here in Sea Cliff, but if you insist on LA, then we can go there.

There was a long pause. Her message finally appeared on his screen:

My break's over. I have to go. I've watched Mandi Jo's video a hundred times, and I can see you're telling the truth. You probably didn't kiss that awful woman. But she was with you this morning at your office.

He felt a flutter of hope.

Only because of Geraldo's estate. Honest. Come over tonight?

She answered:

Yes.

A moment later:

No.

A moment after that:

Maybe.

Finally, she typed:

I don't know. I have to think about it.

Her words left an ache in his heart. But, he told himself, at least the door's half-open.

CHAPTER 48

A Tows Я Us Vehicle Recovery Service truck turned off Highway 1 onto Main Street and stopped next to the *Welcome to Sea Cliff* sign. The driver checked his location on his GPS and radioed his dispatcher to confirm his next work order.

The KHYP news van turned onto Main 50 feet behind the truck. In the passenger's seat, Ally was in full combat mode. She raged, "Why are you arguing with me? I want to find Brinkman and hand him his nuts! Live, on air!"

Spike replied, fuming, "An' I say it mo' 'portant now to find witnesses 'n clues than comin' down on the lawyer. You gotta follow the story, girl." He leaned over the wheel and swiveled in his seat, looking her in the eye.

"Damn you, Spike, watch the road!" She gripped his jaw and twisted his head toward the windshield. "No one walks away from an interview with Ally Booker! I'll bet Lester Holt doesn't respect a reporter who loses an interview."

Spike turned his head again and glared at her. "How you know so much 'bout Lester Holt?"

"LOOK OUT!" Ally cried. Spike stood on the brakes and yanked the wheel. The van careened around the stopped Tows Я Us truck.

"Crazy bitch."

"If you'd just do what I tell you," Ally purred in her I'm-the-most-reasonable-person-in-the-world voice, "I just know we wouldn't have these problems. Now, drive down Main into town. Let's find the dickhead. Go past his office first."

* * *

Danni and El Carnicero staggered down the front walk from her house to his Harley. Zipping up their vests, they climbed onto the big motorcycle. He punched the *Start* button. The V-twin engine roared to life, rattling the windows in Danni's house and sending waves of vibrations through the two riders.

"Woo-wee, babe," Danni shouted in his ear, "yer big, hot, throbbin' machine sets my girly parts tinglin'." She licked his earlobe. "Maybe we have a li'l party tonight, after we find the money."

"*Sí, porque no?*" he growled. He tied a purple silk do-rag around his head, tugging it down to cover the brand on his forehead. He slipped on his Terminator shades and dropped the bike into gear.

They rumbled slowly down Main Street into the business district, checking each side for Jason's Porsche. A block from Bites 'n Bytes, a delivery truck double-parked, stopping a dozen cars in front of them. El Carnicero blipped his throttle impatiently as they waited. Danni leaned forward between blips and spoke in his ear. "Brinkman likes that café. Look for his car. If it ain't there, take a right on Charles, an' we'll check his office."

The traffic inched forward. After a few more minutes, a van several vehicles in front of them pulled over to drop off passengers at Bites 'n Bytes. Danni tapped El Carnicero's shoulder and pointed at the silver Porsche in front of the café. He nodded and backed his Harley between two parked cars.

El Carnicero eyed the crowded patio. "We wait here. Too many people. If he no come out, we go get him."

* * *

The KHYP van crawled past Jason's office. "No lights and no car," Ally grumbled. "Let's check the main drag."

Reaching the bottom of the hill, Spike craned his neck to look up and down the street. "Left? Right?"

"Left. No, right. Shit, how am I 'sposed to know?"

"You the boss, an' this be your goose chase."

Ally rolled down her window, looking both directions. "I don't know. Go left, then we'll turn around and check what we missed." Spike peeled onto Main and immediately jammed on his brakes, just missing a half-dozen tourists jaywalking across the two lanes of traffic.

"C'mon, c'mon," Ally fumed. "I've got a deadline to meet."

The pedestrians chatted and laughed as they ambled across the street. They finally made it to the far side, squeezing between a blue pickup and a silver car. A plump woman wearing an *I'm with Stupid* shirt dropped a Kleenex by the bumper of the silver car. She bent over to pick it up.

"There it is!" Ally cried. "That's the Porsche and there's the license plate—BRNKMAN. Park the van, Spike. Let's get this jerk."

The van lunged into a handicapped spot across the street from the Bites 'n Bytes patio. Spike clambered over the console and yanked his camera out of its padded carrying case. "Right with you," he called out.

Ally scooped up her reporter's notebook and a pen. Spike checked the camera's charge and settings. He grabbed a microphone. Ally pulled the door handle. Her cell phone rang. "What the fuck!" The phone rang again. Ally glanced at the screen. "It's the station. It's Phil No-balls. What the hell does he want?" She debated whether to answer, thinking he'd probably make her do some happy-shit story, like a dog's birthday party. She punched *Decline*.

* * *

Jason finished his sandwich and wiped his hands on his napkin. His cell phone rang. No name or number appeared on the screen, so he decided to let the call go to voicemail. After two rings, he reconsidered, thinking it might be a new client. He answered, "Jason Brinkman."

"Jason?" a staticky voice whispered.

"Yes. Who is this?"

"It's Howie. Howie Simon."

Jason felt a rush of friendship for his co-worker and fellow sufferer at Whatley. At the same time, he tensed because this out-of-the-blue call could only mean something was seriously wrong.

He said, "Howie, it's great to hear from you. Is everything OK? Can you speak up? You didn't show up on my Caller ID."

"I know," Howie whispered. "I'm on a burner phone. I can't talk long. I've got a trial strategy meeting in a couple minutes. I told them I had to go to the men's room."

"I can barely hear you. Where are you?"

"In the janitor's closet on the sixteenth floor, you know, around the corner from your old cubicle. I'll stand closer to the window. Can you hear me better now?"

"Jeez, Howie. A burner phone and hiding in the janitor's closet? Why so much drama? Tell me what's going on."

"Look, man, an avalanche of shit's about to hit you, and I had to warn you because you're my friend, but you have to swear not to tell anyone I told you. I could get fired just for calling you."

The paranoia that ruled Jason's life for five years at Whatley came flooding back. He shuddered, but forced himself not to give in to it.

"OK, I promise. What's so important?"

Howie whispered, "Do you remember *Lancaster v. Estate of Granquist,* one of the first cases you worked on here, I think?"

"The facts were so bizarre, how could I forget? Lucas Lancaster builds a mega-lodge on a mountaintop in Alaska. Global warming melts the permafrost, and the lodge slides down the mountain. Gretchen wins $40 million for him, arguing the seller didn't disclose the mountaintop could become unstable."

"Yeah, that's the one, but it turns out Lancaster *did* know. He signed a waiver of liability, and Gretchen knew, too. Only she kept the waiver a secret. Didn't tell the judge or the other side."

Jason remembered it all. Gretchen assigned him the file as punishment for rejecting her demands for sex. It was a dog of a case because he had to spend weeks of his own time reading reports on global warming and learning arcane areas of geology—subsidence, shear factor, slope stability, bearing capacity, and the like—in order to evaluate and summarize dozens of conflicting structural engineers', climatologists', and geologists' reports. The case turned out to be a loser because Lancaster had signed a waiver of liability, which Jason found crumpled at the bottom of one of Lancaster's many file folders of documents. In it, he acknowledged the mountaintop could become unstable if the underlying permafrost melted due to global warming, and accepted all financial responsibility for any resulting damage. Gretchen won the huge judgment anyway by not disclosing the waiver.

Howie continued, "Well, now the shit's hit the fan. You know Harlan Redaway's been gunning for Gretchen for years. He got ahold of the waiver. He's accusing Gretchen of withholding evidence, ethical violations, defrauding the court, and on and on. He's threatening to report her to the State Bar and the judge who heard the case unless she repays the $40 million immediately. With interest. He's threatening to seek sanctions against her and the firm."

Jason whistled softly. "So, he settles his score with Gretchen, plus he gets $40 million."

"Be quiet and listen! I've gotta get going. Gretchen could lose her license to practice law and even get fired. She'll never be elected senior manager of global operations in New York now because she's damaged goods. Of course, that opens the door for Courtney, her trusted and ruthless protégé."

Jason shook his head in wonder. Gretchen Fautz, a pillar of California's power elite for decades, whose cunning and viciousness crushed every would-be rival, was about to crash and burn.

Howie's voice grew louder and his words tumbled out of Jason's earpiece. "Here's why I'm risking my neck. Gretchen needs a scapegoat, and it's going to be you, my friend. She's going to say you deliberately didn't tell her about the waiver so she'd win the case and you'd get back in her good favor."

"How can she say that?!? I told her in the cover memo. I gave her the note."

Howie talked over him. "She's going to refer *you* to the State Bar and demand they revoke your license to practice law. She and Courtney are working on the complaint right now, and they're going to file it this afternoon. You can bet the Bar will do what they want, given Gretchen's and the firm's clout. You'll be lucky to be a janitor when they're done with you."

The line was silent for a moment. Jason fidgeted, thinking he had to go look for his copies of the waiver and memo right now. He said, "You're a good friend, Howie. You probably saved my life. Watch your back...." A cell phone buzzed on Howie's end.

"Damn," Howie said. "They're paging me for my meeting, so listen up. It gets worse." He spoke so rapidly he was hard to understand. "Rumor is, Courtney's behind all of this, that she told Redaway about the waiver. The smart money here's betting she's going to take Gretchen down. Everyone knows she wants to be senior managing partner. People say this is her big chance."

Howie raced on. "One more thing: Courtney's engaged to Benedict Sloan in the New York office. He's president of the firm now, domestic and international. They're gonna be king and queen of Whatley, Thelen & Füchs, running the firm's offices worldwide. People think she'll announce the engagement and move to New York as soon as she gets Gretchen out of the way. You could probably not care less about Courtney by now, but she's taking your son with her, according to her secretary."

All at once, the pieces fell into place. Courtney was pressuring him to sign the divorce papers so she could marry Benedict Sloan immediately and take custody of Jason Jr. If it came to a custody battle, she and Sloan were models of stability and affluence, while Jason lived in a borrowed house and had scant income. Plus, she was setting him up to lose his law license so he couldn't make a living at all. She'd win without breaking a sweat.

He heard Howie's phone buzz again. Howie said, "They're paging me. I gotta go. One more thing. There's a new rumor that Gretchen has really bad cancer. Don't know any more. Gotta go, man!" He ended the call before Jason could say "Thanks" or "Goodbye."

* * *

Howie's bombshells left Jason in turmoil. Images from his life at Whatley flashed behind his eyes: his cubicle stacked high with boxes of documents and evidence to review and summarize, always by tomorrow. Gretchen backing him against her desk, rubbing her leathery body on him, kissing him on the lips and pulling down his zipper. His final fight with Courtney after Gretchen blocked his promotion to partner.

It took all his willpower to blot out the bitter memories. He told himself there was one bright spot—he had copies of the waiver and the cover memo telling Gretchen about it. *She can't win. It'll be a fight, but I'll be OK.*

The frantic weeks preparing for the *Lancaster* trial were a blur. He remembered making pdf copies of the documents just in case he ever had to prove he wasn't negligent. It seemed an idle precaution at the time, nearly seven years ago. That was before the Cloud, and he wouldn't have trusted anything so important to it anyway. He'd probably loaded the pdfs onto a flash drive and taken it home to copy the documents to his desktop, which was now his office computer. That had to be what he'd done, and that's where they were, in a password-protected file.

On the other hand, he might have transferred the pdfs to his new laptop when he cleaned out his desktop's memory, and copied them to a flash drive as backup. He decided to look on his laptop first, and the flash drive if the pdfs weren't on the laptop.

"No, wait!" The words burst out. "El Crazy stole my laptop and smashed my flash drives!" Icy fingers wrapped around his stomach and squeezed with all their might. "I've gotta go check my office computer right now!"

Dear God, let the copies be on my desktop! He started to stand, but froze when he glanced at the patio's entrance. His knees buckled and he dropped back into his chair.

An enormous Mexican biker blocked the entrance. Danni Tedeski staggered up behind him.

CHAPTER 49

Danni and El Carnicero stood in the entrance to the patio, swaying slightly and surveying the tables. Jason slumped in his chair to avoid being spotted while he checked them out.

The man was at least six-four and 350 pounds, with a barrel chest and biceps the size of hams. He radiated savage power, like a linebacker pumped on steroids in a skull-splitting rage. His bandaged right hand was stained with dried blood. The edges of his purple headscarf were dark with sweat, and drips ran down his forehead.

Jason's breath caught and his heart hammered against his ribs. His fear was more instinct than rational thought—a silent, primal scream of danger. El Carnicero looked every bit the killer Admiral Bill and Rory said he was. For a split second, Jason pictured escaping out the patio's back gate. *No!* he commanded himself. *Gotta do this now.* He pushed his fear back into its dark hole.

But what to do? El Carnicero believed he was hiding Geraldo's drug money. Jason had to convince him he didn't have it or know where it was. Jason wanted his laptop back, but had nothing to trade for it. His only advantage was they were in a very public place with lots of witnesses. Only then did Jason realize no one was paying attention to El Carnicero and Danni. After staring at them when they entered, the curious ones returned to their conversations and food.

Jason's only move was to confront the man, but he needed a safety net. He looked around for Christina and saw her sitting with her back to the entrance. He quickly texted her:

> Don't look. Bad dude behind u w/Danni Tedeski.
> Must talk w/him, maybe 5 mins. He stole my laptop.
> Pls watch, call cops if trouble. OK? Thx.

She replied a few seconds later:

OMG. Of course. Be careful.

He stood up. Danni pointed at him and El Carnicero took off his sunglasses. He fixed Jason with death-mask eyes, black as night and cold as ice. His fleshy lips curled at the corners, revealing metal teeth. He grunted and lumbered across the patio. Danni followed a step behind.

Jason walked toward them with as much confidence as he could muster. El Carnicero planted himself directly in front of him, arms crossed, blocking his path. "We talk," he growled hoarsely.

Up close, the man's brute physicality was overwhelming. He dwarfed Jason, standing four inches taller and weighing twice as much. His bulging pecs stretched his shirt to the point of bursting. He dropped his arms to his side, and Jason heard a metallic click. Glancing down, he saw an eight-inch switchblade in man's left hand. El Carnicero cuffed the knife's handle and most of the blade, and linked his free arm through Jason's.

"*Vente conmigo, mi amigo,*" he said loudly enough for people nearby to hear. Danni pressed her shoulder against his other arm.

"Hey, Jason," she slurred, "how ya been?"

With El Carnicero on one side and Danni on the other, they steered him toward the far rear of the patio, to the table screened by lattice.

The space behind the lattice was about eight by ten, and was enclosed on three sides by a brick wall, a wood fence, and the building next door. The lattice closed off the fourth side, except for a narrow opening between its edge and the building. The table was in the center, with a bench against the brick wall and two chairs on the side closest to the opening.

El Carnicero shoved Jason onto the bench, then sat across from him, partially hidden by the privacy screen. Danni sat in the other chair and turned it so she viewed the patio.

"*Abogado,* I finally catch you," El Carnicero growled in understandable English. "Now we talk business." The switchblade gleamed in his left hand, its tip angled toward Jason's neck.

He pressed his bandaged right hand against his heart. "Geraldo—he was my friend, *mi compañero*. I visit his *casa*. I know his *familia*. I tell stories to his *niña bonita*. We ride our *motocicletas* in the desert. We do—how you say—business together for many years…."

Jason studied the two as the man spoke and concluded both were completely stoned. One dubious benefit of his years in foster care was that he recognized the signs. Danni was sweating and weaving back and forth in her chair. Her hands twitched. He decided it was probably heroin, given her reputation. El Carnicero's mouth seemed to be dry and his voice hoarse. His face and purple do-rag were wet with sweat, and his cruel eyes were red with pinpoint pupils. Jason figured it was oxy. That meant he could have abrupt mood changes, which was doubly concerning because he was violent to start with.

"I bring him merchandise," El Carnicero continued, "he sell it, give me the money. For many, many, many years." Each time he said "many," he flicked the knifepoint back and forth before Jason's eyes. "But now, Geraldo break the bond of trust between us. *Se rompió la confianza*." He pronounced each Spanish word precisely, slamming the butt of the switchblade against the tabletop after each one for emphasis. "The trust is gone!" he snarled. "*La confianza se ha ido!*"

With lightning speed, El Carnicero hooked Jason's neck with his bandaged hand and jerked him forward. The knife point glinted an inch from his face. "Two million dollars, *abogado*. *Dos millones de dólares!* You know where it is." The cold steel point pressed against Jason's cheek, just below his left eye.

* * *

"Spike! You ready to hang Brinkman by his balls?" Ally demanded.

"Yo."

"Follow me." She trotted up the sidewalk.

Spike trudged behind with his camera and microphone. "How you know where he at?"

"'Cause his car's in front of that café like a big neon sign, and where else can he be … ? Just shut up and follow me." She stopped behind a tall bougainvillea bush outside the patio entrance. "They're in there. I know it. Reporter's intuition. How's my hair?"

"You a honky princess."

"Remember what I told you. Don't make it look shiny and don't make my nose look big."

Spike rolled his eyes.

"I mean it. This is gonna be part of my … our … package to NBC. Ballsy girl reporter goes after the story and all that crap." Ally stood stock-still behind the bougainvillea. "Breathe in, breathe out," she whispered to herself. "Focus."

She threw her shoulders back and charged into the crowd of tables. Spike followed right behind, camera running. Every customer, waiter, and busboy looked up in surprise. Silence filled the patio. She stopped when she didn't see the attorney. Looking confused, she scanned the faces. "Where the hell? Spike! Where is he?"

Spike lowered his camera. "You one crazy bitch."

Thirty pairs of eyes watched the ballsy girl reporter deflate like a punctured balloon. Her shoulders slumped and she nearly dropped her notebook. The hum of conversation and the clink of dishes resumed. "It can't be," Ally muttered. "He's gotta be here somewhere. His Porsche's outside screamin', 'Come find me.'"

"Maybe you an' your intuition was wrong," Spike said with a smirk.

"Yeah, maybe I jumped the gun," she said dejectedly. "OK. Let's go. But let me take one last look first. You wait here. I guess we already made fools of ourselves."

"We?" Spike muttered as she strode to the center of the patio.

Ally scrutinized every table and admitted defeat. She returned to where Spike was standing. "We'll check up and down the street, see if we see him. Let's go."

He ignored her, staring at the back of the patio.

"Spike! What's wrong with you? Come on!"

He shouldered his camera, looked through the viewfinder, and adjusted the focus. "I got 'em."

"Where?"

"Close by."

"I *knew* I was right. My intuition's never wrong. Where is he?"

"Not far."

"Where? Goddamn you! Where? Why are you torturing me?"

"'Cause you so easy."

"Where? Where is it? TELL ME!"

"There you go, girl." He lowered his camera and pointed to the rear of the patio. "Way in back, behind that lattice. See the purple and them three people? That be where he at."

* * *

The cold knife pressed against Jason's cheek. El Carnicero twisted the point just enough to prick the skin below his left eye.

Jason jerked back in panic. Bitter acid burned his throat. Every muscle tensed with dread, but his mind seized this new information. El Crazy had just told him how much money Geraldo stole. Exhaling from deep within, Jason said in the calmest voice he could muster, "*Señor*, you know Geraldo well. He was a man of many secrets. He told me only what he wanted me to know. He never mentioned you or your business dealings. He never told me about your $2 million. I don't know where your money is. As far as I know, Geraldo used all his money to buy land and build houses."

Without moving the knife or releasing the pressure on the back of Jason's neck, El Carnicero half-stood and bent over the table. He glared down at him. "Then I want the land and houses," he snarled in a blast of hot breath that reeked of decay. "You will prepare the deeds for me, the *títulos de propiedad*."

The demand surprised Jason. He'd anticipated questions about Geraldo's bank accounts, but this opened an unexpected door. Riveting his eyes on the man's tiny black pupils, Jason said, "My laptop computer. All of Geraldo's information's on it. You've got it."

Jason sensed the tension in El Carnicero's arms slacken ever so slightly. "Laptop computer? There is no laptop computer."

"You took it from my house. Where is it? What did you do with it?"

The man's eyes widened with confusion. Slowly and carefully, Jason pushed the hand with the knife away from his face. He cautiously unhooked the other hand from around his neck. El Carnicero sank into his chair. With a mighty blow, he stabbed the knifepoint into the tabletop. "*Pinche mierda!*" he bellowed, pounding his fists on either side of the blade.

Indecision danced across El Carnicero's face for a split second, and in that second, Jason thought it might be over. Suddenly, the man roared, "NO!" He lunged across the table, yanking the knife free and thrusting it at Jason's face. Jason jerked back, slamming his head against the wall behind him. Cold steel pricked his skin. A drop of warm liquid rolled down his cheek. *That can't be blood!* He instinctively touched his finger to it. When he glanced down, his fingertip was bright red.

The big man towered over him, pressing the sharp blade against his throat. "You will give me *los terrines y las casas!*" he roared. Jason struggled to pull the arm away while his panicked mind tried to find the words to explain that it was impossible, that all of Geraldo's property had to go through probate, and that a judge would have to sign off.

Danni spoke first. "Hey, Guillermo," she said, tugging his sleeve. "Sit down an' hide yer knife away." He spun toward her, blood-lust in his eyes. "Now! We got company." She wagged her head toward the patio.

El Carnicero followed her gaze. He sat and was sliding his switchblade into his cuff just as Ally burst around the lattice. Spike followed a step behind, camera to his eye.

CHAPTER 50

Heart pounding double-time, Ally rounded the lattice. She saw Jason Brinkman sitting behind a small table with his back against a brick wall. An enormous man and a woman with silvery hair sat across from him. Ally stopped mid-stride to avoid colliding with them. Spike, viewfinder glued to his eye, crashed into her, knocking her into the woman. The woman jerked, startled.

"Hey!" the woman shouted in a slurred voice. "Step back, ho!"

Ally ignored her. "Spike, you idiot!"

"Nasty honky bitch," Spike whispered under his breath. He adjusted his eyepiece and resumed filming.

The distraction broke Ally's adrenaline rush. She quickly checked her surroundings. The space was enclosed on three sides and was barely large enough to hold the five people who filled it. The only exit was immediately behind her and Spike.

She looked at Brinkman and his two companions. The attorney looked scared and the man looked angry. He radiated savage menace, which now was directed at her. A glint of light reflected from his left shirt cuff. *A knife?!?*

The attorney caught her attention by wagging his head toward the patio. He wagged his head again and began to stand up. The big man half-stood and jammed his forefinger into the table. "*Sientate!*" he snarled. Brinkman slid down the wall to his bench.

Ally shuddered at the violence the man projected. She examined him as he glared at Brinkman. The man looked like a video-game version of a Mexican drug dealer. His tight silk shirt barely contained his biceps and pecs. The shirt was open to his stomach and was covered with skulls, cobra snakes, dice, snarling dogs, and naked women. A heavy gold neck chain and crucifix dangled in his sparse chest hair. His chin sprouted a wiry three-day growth and studs pierced his heavy brows. Sweat soaked his purple headscarf. Sharp steel stuck out of his cuff, and the handle bulged in his sleeve.

She had to admit the guy was scary. Her smug confidence faltered, and fear crept into the void. But just for a minute. There was a story here, and she told herself she'd never see New York if she walked away. Her head filled with the calming voice of her online journalism teacher: "The camera rules. Trust it. As long as the camera's running, no one misbehaves."

With renewed courage, she grabbed the microphone from Spike and stuck it in the attorney's face. "Mr. Brinkman, I'm Ally Booker from KHYP News in Santa Luisa." She glanced at Spike to be sure the camera was on the subject. "I want to ask you some questions about your client, Mags Turlock."

"I'm happy to talk to you in private," the attorney replied. He jerked his head again toward the patio.

She understood he wanted to get away from the guy with the knife, but she needed the whole story, so everyone had to stay put. Her viewers would want to know who these people were, and why they were here. "Alright. In a minute. First, who are you with?" She bent down and held the microphone in front of the woman, who was weaving in her chair. "Ma'am, what's your name?"

The woman's face glistened with sweat. "Me? I din't do nothin'. Wha's it to you who I am?"

"You're gonna be on the news, ma'am, on TV. Station policy says you havta tell me your name." Instead of a name, Ally got a blank look. "Hello, ma'am?" she said, bending close. "Can you hear me?"

"Station policy?" the woman mumbled. "Umm-humm. Tha' sounds impo'tant." A smirk flitted across her lips, and she sat up in her chair. "OK, then, my name is … umm … Mrs. Stoner."

"And your first name, ma'am?"

The dazed look returned. After a moment, she said, "Ima. Ima Stoner. Yup, that's me. Mrs. Ima Stoner."

"You gotta be kidding! No one's really named—"

The woman jerked to attention. She leaned close to the microphone. "You makin' fun a my name, ho?" Specks of spittle flew from her lips.

Ally's teacher's voice came to her again: "Never lose control of the interview! Move on!" Ally said, "No, ma'am, not at all. It's just, well... OK, Mrs. Stoner it is. So, is this your husband?" She turned to the man. Spike's camera followed.

"Mr. Stoner, what's your first name?"

He growled, "*No hablo Inglés.*"

"WHAT IS YOUR NAME?"

The man's tiny black pupils bored into her eyes. Ally fought the gorge rising from her stomach. Her cell phone rang. She stepped back and checked the screen. "It's goddammed Phil!" she swore. Her thumbs hovered over *Accept* and *Decline* before she pressed *Decline*.

Spike stopped filming and lowered his camera.

The man pushed back from the table and stood slowly, towering over her. He yanked the dazed woman out of her chair and lumbered toward the exit. As he passed Ally, he spat at her feet. Spike lowered his camera and moved aside as much as he could. The man slid the knife into his hand and swiped it at Spike's stomach, slicing his shirt. "*Gusano,*" he laughed.

Ally's first reaction was immense relief. A second later, she was angry at losing part of her story. She ordered herself to get focused and be a reporter—she'd come here to get Brinkman, and she still had him.

She counted to ten to compose herself. Throwing her shoulders back, she turned and nodded to Spike. He resumed filming. "Alright. I'm here in Sea Cliff with Jason Brinkman, the lawyer for the accused Storm Drain Murderer." She paused for dramatic effect. "Mr. Brinkman, why do you believe your client, Mags Turlock, is innocent?"

With the camera focused on Brinkman, she imagined how he'd look to her viewers. She was disappointed. The tall, handsome lawyer in the expensive suit, who strode so confidently down the courthouse steps yesterday morning, was gone. In his place sat a tired, disheveled, 30-something man with a yellowish-purple bruise on his jaw, and a trickle of dried blood on his cheek.

A bemused expression spread across his face. He said, "I'll give you about a minute, 'til those two leave the patio. Ms. Turlock is innocent in the eyes of the law, as I told you last time you asked me. It's up to the district attorney to prove beyond a reasonable doubt she's guilty."

"It sounds to me," Ally replied sternly, "like you're hiding behind legal mumbo-jumbo because you think your client is actually guilty." She paused to formulate the question she knew would make Jason Brinkman crumble and make her a star. She puffed herself up, and laced her voice with all the righteous indignation she knew her viewers shared with her. "How can you, as a lawyer, defend someone you know is guilty?" *There. I've twisted the knife. Anything he says will sound insincere and evasive.* She expected Brinkman's face to contort with panic or desperation.

Instead, he laughed at her. "That's the best you've got? Every first-year law student gets asked that question a hundred times."

Ally's mouth dropped and her brain went dead as her moment of triumph turned to dust. She told herself to say something! The camera was running! Bust his balls! But for once in her life, she had no cutting rejoinder. Spike switched off the camera and lowered it.

Her cell phone rang, breaking the silence. *Thank God!* She scowled at the screen and shouted into the mouthpiece, "Dammit, Phil! Again? What do you want? I'm really busy here."

Phil's voice came through the speaker. "You still in Sea Cliff? There's a five-alarm fire. I want you to go cover it. Right now."

Ally said, "Fire? Where?"

Jason said, "Where is it?"

She switched off the speaker and pressed the phone to her ear. "I don't know where that's at." She looked at Jason. "You know where Conifer Hill's at?"

"Yes. I live there. What's the address?"

Phil said in her ear, "We're the only station that has it. It'll be our exclusive! Go get it!"

Ally walked to the far corner of the enclosure. "I don't care if it's an exclusive," she yelled into her phone, "I'm doing the biggest story of the year here."

"Come on, Ally," Phil pleaded. "This is big. We never scoop the other stations. We could get an Emmy for this."

"Yeah, yeah, yeah. Like The Storm Drain Murder isn't Emmy material. I'll do it, but only on my conditions: It's my exclusive and I'm the lead story at five, six, and eleven. That's my deal. Take it or leave it. Send the directions to Spike's phone."

Jason walked around the table and grabbed Ally's shoulder. "Where is the fire?"

She turned her back on him. "Phil, you're sure no other station has it?"

Jason shook Ally's shoulder. "Where is the fire? What's the address?" She wriggled free and turned away.

Jason's cell rang. He dug it out of his pocket.

"Christina? What is it?" He listened. "My car? What's happening to it?"

Pushing past Ally and Spike, he bolted into the patio.

* * *

Jason dashed through the patio to the street and saw his Porsche on the back of a flatbed tow truck. A tattooed young man in a cutoff Tshirt and dirty overalls was ratcheting down the safety chains.

"Wait!" Jason shouted breathlessly. "What are you doing?"

"Yes, sir. My name is Cooper, and I'm the team leader on the Tows Я Us Vehicle Recovery Service repossession team. I'm repossessing this vehicle on behalf of…" he pulled a work order from his pocket, "…on behalf of Newport Exotic Leasing."

Jason felt his face burn bright red. He clenched his fists and stepped toward Cooper.

The young man pulled a blackjack from his back pocket and waved it at Jason. "Sir, I need you to stay at least three feet away. No closer 'n three feet, sir." He smacked the leather and lead weapon in the palm of his hand. "Me an' my frien', Mr. BJ, we don' want no trouble, sir." He smacked his palm again.

Jason stopped in his tracks. "You can't do this. I'm current on my payments. There must be some mistake."

"Can't help ya, sir. Jus' doin' my job. They tells me what ta pick up an' I goes out an' gets 'em."

"Can you call Newport?"

"No, sir, I ain't got their number. I 'spect they'll get in touch after they get their vehicle back."

"But I just checked with the bank this morning. My last payment cleared."

"I been a repossession perfessional fer five years, sir, since I was eighteen, an' all I can tell ya is that with a car this expensive, they don' let it go long when a payment's been missed."

"Goddammit! I am not in default. My payments are current. This is not a legal repossession!"

Cooper slapped Mr. BJ into his palm. "I got the repo order from Newport, an' that makes it legal, sir." He slammed the blackjack against his truck's metal fender. *THHWUNNK!* "You want, we can call the sheriff an' he can tell ya it's legal."

Jason glanced over his shoulder at the people on the patio watching. "No. No need to get the sheriff involved."

"That's a good decision, sir. That'd only create a scene. I seen it happen that way before. Besides, it looks like you're gonna be on TV." He pointed to Jason's left.

Jason looked over his left shoulder. Ally Booker and Spike stood about ten feet away, just outside his peripheral vision. The red light on Spike's camera glowed and Ally grinned malevolently. Jason's first instinct was to confront them, demand they stop, but he thought better of it. *No need to create more of an embarrassing spectacle.* He turned back to Cooper, forcing himself to be calm, and said, "OK, then. What's next?"

Cooper said, "I'm gonna inventory the vehicle's contents on this here form, sir." He climbed onto the flatbed and sat in the Porsche. Through the side window, Jason saw him searching the interior and writing on the form.

Cooper got down a few minutes later. "This form lists the contents of yer vehicle, sir. Ya need ta sign it. It's for yer pertection, so there's a record a what's inside when I tow it. There's two cardboard boxes with the name 'Gerald O'Brien,' and a metal box that says 'Larry's tackle box.' An' a Valentine radar detector an' a power cord in the glove box. There anything else?"

Jason fumed inwardly but spoke in a friendly voice. "OK, I understand you're just doing your job, but I need to do mine too, and I need all those boxes."

"No can do, sir. What's in the vehicle stays in the vehicle. Ya havta get yer pers'nal prop'ty back from Newport in a coupla weeks, but tha's why ya need ta sign the inventory form, so's there's a record."

"Look, bro, I'm a lawyer, and I've got a trial next week. I need those boxes for the trial. Just let me have them and the tackle box, 'cause it belonged to my grandpa. You can have the Valentine. It's less than a year old. Take it and the power cord. No one needs to know."

Cooper seemed to be thinking about it. Jason tried to look relaxed. He turned his head when he felt someone take his arm. It was Christina, tanned and radiant, in a halter top and short-shorts. She slipped her arm around his waist and kissed him on the cheek.

Cooper's jaw dropped. He stared at Christina with wide eyes. She smiled warmly. "I overheard your conversation, Mr. Tow Truck Driver, and it's true. I'm Jason's assistant, and he's got a trial next week and he needs those boxes. You don't want him to lose, do you?"

Jason thought Cooper looked like he was wavering. Christina added, "I really like your clown tattoo on your arm. Is it new? It's totally awesome. Where'd you have it done? I'd like to get one just like it."

Cooper's cheeks turned rosy pink. "Umm..." he mumbled. He thumbed through his wallet and pulled out a discount card for Rusty's Piercing and Skin Art in Tarzana. Handing her the card, he said shyly, "I ain't never had such a purty lady like one a my tattoos." His fingers brushed her hand and his cheeks burned scarlet. "Dang it! I shouldn't, but I'll do it for you, darlin'. He can have them boxes." Cooper climbed back onto the flatbed, opened the Porsche's door, and lowered the boxes and tackle box down to Jason.

Jason set them on the curb. Out of the corner of his eye, he saw the reporter and cameraman trot across the street and climb into their news van.

"You tell Rusty that Cooper the repo dude sent ya," Cooper said, swinging into his cab. The diesel engine clattered to life and "Highway to Hell" blasted from the open windows. The truck rattled and roared down Main Street, trailing a stream of black smoke.

* * *

Jason and Christina watched the truck drive away with his Porsche. She leaned into his side. "I'm so sorry you're having this rough spell."

"It has been tough," Jason admitted, "but I see some daylight."

She took his arm. "I know you want to do it your way, but remember what I told you. There's an office for you at old man Shapiro's if you want it. It'd be a steady paycheck until you're on your feet. I'd love to work with you again."

"Thanks, Christina. I'm sure I'll get through this. I will think about it, though."

"What are you going to do now?"

"I really don't know. I need some time."

"Do you want a ride?"

"No," he replied wearily. "I'm gonna carry this stuff up the hill to my office and try to figure out my next move."

She gave him a peck on the cheek and left him standing at the curb with his stack of boxes.

PART 5

TIPPING POINT

CHAPTER 51

Nikki was sitting on the salon's porch with a cigarette when Jason came huffing up Charles Street, lugging two cardboard boxes and a metal case. She knew the story because she'd seen the Twitter feed of his Porsche getting towed and him arguing with the tow truck driver. Her heart broke to see her dreamy, sexy Jason get put down by a tow truck driver—even such a cute one—and wrestle with the boxes like a UPS delivery guy.

And now, the man of her fantasies sat in the passenger seat of her Miata, so close she could hear his heart beat. She wished there was an app for recording emotions because she wanted to download and replay the next fifteen minutes over and over, no matter how it worked out.

Normally, just being in a car with him would push the imaginary emotion needle up to 100. The trouble was, it was her icky pink Miata, not his Porsche, and she was driving, and they were going to his grandmother's house, not Big Sur, like she'd always dreamed. That dropped the needle down to about 50.

Fighting disappointment, she searched for something to supercharge the score, something to make this moment as magic as she'd imagined so many times. She decided to free her senses to embrace his aura of masculinity, like her magazines talked about.

She felt his heat, he was so close. She could touch his hand. She could even touch his thigh. With a quick glance, she checked out the mysterious soft bulge in his lap. She could put her hand right there.... Every inch of her body tingled with his sexy vibe. Those feelings should be worth at least 110 out of 100, but, well, not today.

Peeking sideways as she drove, she noticed just a couple of gray hairs in his sideburns and temples. She could get rid of them in a minute at the salon, returning all his hair to the fabulous chestnut brown she'd always adored. But she just couldn't help asking herself if she really wanted to be with a guy who was old enough to have gray hair. Then there was the bruise on his jaw and the red spot on his cheek that looked like a popped zit. And his clothes. He was usually so cool-looking, with his LA casuals, but his shirt and pants were dirty and scruffy, like he'd been in a fight. The needle slipped to about 25.

Even worse, he wasn't paying complete attention to her. Now that she finally had him all to herself, she expected him to be thinking only about her, but he was edgy and seemed impatient. She decided he was nervous, too.

They drove up Main Street toward Highway 1 in unbearable silence. Nikki tried to think of something to say, some way to begin the conversation about "US," but Jason spoke first. "So, why did you go to my house yesterday?"

She wanted to scream, *Isn't it obvious? I went there to tell you I love you and want to be with you!* She blushed at the memory, hoping he wouldn't notice. Losing her concentration, she slammed on the brakes when the light turned red at Main and Highway 1.

"Well, um, I heard, um, well, that you were in trouble, and just wanted to be sure you were OK," she blurted. She felt herself getting even redder.

"And that's when your face got cut by broken glass?"

"Yes!" she said, relieved he didn't question her lie. "That crazy man punched through the window, and I got hit by some pieces." She poofed her platinum curls and wanted desperately to check her makeup. Instead, she fiddled with the ventilation controls, adjusting the vents and the fan. She turned the radio up, down, off, and on again. "And then he chased me to my car and tore that hole in my top." She pointed to the duct-taped patch above Jason's head.

"Nikki, I'm so sorry," Jason said softly. He put his hand over hers on the gearshift. His touch sent pins and needles racing up her arm and set off a shower of flutters in her stomach. "Did you need stitches?"

"Just a couple. Most of the cuts, they closed with just tape."

"Does the doctor think you won't have scars?"

"Yes! Oh my God! Thank goodness!"

"You have such pretty skin," Jason said absently. She melted inside. "Now that I think about it, it was my bedroom window he broke. Were you outside my bedroom window?"

All the blood in Nikki's body rushed to her cheeks. How could she tell him she peeked in the bedroom window because she heard grunting and banging inside the house and thought he was having kinky sex with another woman because she saw the "N4SR" license plate on the Harley out front and thought the noises meant he was into masochism and sadochism?

Before she could answer, a KHYP news van screeched to a stop at the light on the other side of the highway. "Huh," she said, changing the subject. "I wonder why they were on Conifer Hill."

"There was a fire."

"Oh yeah, I saw a coupla Tweets. Didn't say where it was at, an' I didn't hear any sirens. Wait! I didn't think before—your house is on Conifer Hill. I hope it's not yours!"

Jason craned his neck to look up at the signal. "Damn, that's a long red." After a moment, he said, "It probably is my house, after the day I've had. I need to see if it is. That's why I wanted to get a ride home as quick as I could, soon as I put my files back in my office. And there you were, sitting on the porch." He drummed his fingers on the armrest. "Thanks for ditching work on the spur of the moment," he said, checking the light again.

"No worries, Jason, anytime." She wanted to shriek, *How can you be so stupid? Why can't you see that I've always been ready to do anything for you?* That had been true forever and ever, until right now, when her fantasy was beginning to fade.

The light turned green. The news van turned right and sped south on Highway 1 toward Santa Luisa.

"OK," Jason said. "Let's go!" They crossed the highway and began the climb up Del Mar Road. Pine trees and glimpses of blue ocean flashed by, but Nikki couldn't be distracted. The needle on the emotion meter was hovering dangerously near zero, so she had to ask the most important question of all. "Jason, do you think you'll get your Porsche back?"

"What? I was thinking about the fire. Everything that's important is in my house. My car?" He sighed and looked out the window. "Honestly, I don't know. I thought I was current on my payments, but the leasing company thinks not. I guess it'll depend on whether we can work out some kind of deal."

"But you need a car. How'll you get around?"

"I can use my grandmother's, if I have to."

"Isn't your grandmother's car a Plymouth Neon?" she asked, trying not to sound like she was putting it down.

"Yeah, it's the perfect grandma mobile. Powder blue and four doors."

The needle crashed to zero.

Nikki knew what her mother would say. "Don't be superficial! Jason has a profession! Lawyers make good money! He's handsome and has other good qualities." But she also knew that Jason without his Porsche just wasn't Jason, or at least not the one she wanted to be with. She faced the truth. She wouldn't be caught dead in a powder-blue Neon, even if Austin Butler or Timothée Chalamet or The Rock was driving it.

No Porsche, a powder-blue Neon, gray hair, a zit, and he's obviously not into me like I'm into him. She sighed. *Used to be into him.* That was it. She'd made the decision that was unthinkable even fifteen minutes ago. She stopped on Del Mar to turn left onto Crescent Lane, missed her shift, and stalled the car. "Jason," she said, grinding the gears and struggling to keep her poise, "we'll always be friends, won't we?"

"Friends? Of course, Nikki. Why do you say that?"

"Well, you know I think the world of you, would do absolutely anything for you, but...."

"But?"

"Well, this is hard for me to say, because I've always liked you sooo much...." She gathered her courage. "I met this boy at the hospital, an' he's an orderly an' I think he's twenty." The hurtful words tumbled out and tears blurred her vision. "He held my hand while they were doing the stitches, an' he was so tender an' his name is Caleb, an' I really, really like him. He has chestnut-brown hair, like you, an' a Jeep Wrangler. Can you ever forgive me?"

She completed turning onto Crescent Lane. Realizing she could barely see the road through her tears, she stopped next to the east gatepost. Jason still hadn't answered. *Oh, no! I've broken his heart on this day that's already the worst one of his life.* She wiped her eyes and cheeks and turned to stare at him, silently begging and imploring him to see that it was for the best. But he ignored her. Following his gaze, she saw he was focused down Crescent Lane, on the flashing red and blue lights of fire trucks and sheriff's cars parked in the middle of the street. "OK if I just drop you here at the corner?" Nikki asked, her voice still thick with emotion. "I think the street's blocked down there. I hope it's not your house."

"Looks like it is, but maybe it isn't. Thanks for the ride."

"Friends forever?" Nikki asked, dabbing the corner of her eye.

"Of course, Nikki. We'll always be friends."

Smiling sadly, she blew him a kiss as he closed her car door. She made a U-turn and headed back up Del Mar toward Highway 1.

* * *

Jason walked around Crescent Lane's curve to the cluster of emergency vehicles in front of GG's house. He squeezed between a water tanker and a paramedic van, ducking under their side mirrors and stumbling over high-pressure hoses. When he stepped into the open, the scene was like the set of a disaster movie. Fire engines crowded the front yard. Red and blue lights pulsed in his eyes. Men in yellow slickers and helmets huddled near their trucks. Static crackled and voices barked from walkie-talkies. Acrid, gray smoke hung in the air and burned his throat.

He stopped at the curb, trying to make sense of what he saw. His grandmother's house was gone. All that was left was the cinder-block foundation and a few charred studs. The lawn was littered with jagged wood splinters, roof shingles, broken china, bits of glass, and scraps of clothes. Tufts of insulation clung to the pine trees like Christmas ornaments. Overspray from the fire hoses dripped from pine boughs, splashing into muddy puddles like raindrops.

The feeling of loss hit him like a roundhouse punch to the stomach. *This was my real home.* GG's cozy bungalow was his refuge from his crazy, alcoholic parents and their constant battles to possess his body and his soul. Here, GG gave him the love and security he needed to cope with the bitter chaos of his childhood. Here, she made him understand he was smart and strong enough to make his way in the world. If he'd been alone at that moment, he'd have sat on the curb and cried. Instead, he just wiped his eyes with the backs of his hands.

Another feeling nudged his consciousness. He'd lived this scene before in his dream. The feeling of *déjà vu* was overpowering, but the gauzy sense of familiarity gave him little comfort. If *déjà vu* showed some version of what had already happened, it didn't show what was yet to be.

An official in a black slicker crossed the back yard carrying rolls of yellow tape and bundles of wooden stakes. The man dropped the tape and one of the bundles on GG's planting table beside the garage. Walking to the foundation wall, he began to pound stakes in the ground at intervals along the rear edge. Jason summoned his courage and strode up the brick walkway to the front of the foundation, as he'd done in his dream.

The man tapped a stake into the ground with a hammer. *Tap, tap, tap.* He moved on, tapping in another. *Tap, tap, tap.* The tapping noise took Jason deeper into the memory of his dream. There was a cement pad in the middle of the foundation where the furnace used to be. GG tapped on the pad with her cane. It hit something metal. "What's this?" she'd cried.

Tap, tap, tap. The man's hammer and GG's cane pounded simultaneously in Jason's ears. His sense of *déjà vu* told him to focus on the concrete pad. He remembered GG found the metal door to the floor safe that was buried up to its hinges.

In a flash, he understood. The dream wasn't about the house being destroyed. It was about discovering a secret hiding place. The floor safe must've been in his subconscious because Rory said Geraldo hid his drug money in a safe he'd installed in their basement floor.

Jason stared at the actual concrete pad, ten feet from where he stood. Its surface was covered with ash and debris. He understood the safe was just in the dream. But what if Geraldo hid the $2 million he stole from El Carnicero? He was a creature of habit, so wouldn't he hide it like he'd done before? Like Rory described, in a floor safe somewhere? Some secret place that he controlled? Maybe…like one of the houses he built?

A voice in his ear made him jump. "Brinkman. How convenient to find you here."

Jason whirled around to face the voice. "Holy Christ, Duane! You could give a guy a heart attack."

"My name is DEPUTY HARDESTY!"

"What happened to my house?" Jason asked, struggling to recover his focus. "Why are you here?"

"You got insurance on this place?"

"You know I do. I told you when you inspected my house after it was trashed. Two days ago."

"What we got here," Hardesty said in an officious tone, "is a five-alarm fire. We got engines and men from all over the county. Do you want to know why?"

"Obviously."

"Where you been at this afternoon?"

"With you, at Simon's Cove."

"After that?"

"I was at Bites 'n Bytes having lunch…on the patio."

"People see you there? Lots of witnesses?"

"People, of course. What do you mean by witnesses?"

Hardesty grabbed Jason's upper arm and shoved him forward, forcing him to step on top of the foundation. The deputy hauled himself up beside him.

"You see them mangled chunks of white metal in the yard and them shards stuck in the studs?" He pried a jagged piece from the nearest stud and tossed it at the cement. "What happened here, according to Forensics, was you had a old gas stove and a leaky gas line. Someone left a burner on, and when the gas collected, the stove exploded. The stove was sittin' in close proximity above the furnace, and it exploded, too. Then the gas supply line caught fire, and *BAW-WHAM*!"

Hardesty gripped Jason's bicep again and swung him around so they faced each other. He stood on his toes, making himself tall enough to look Jason in the eye. "The whole neighborhood coulda blowed before the fire got reported, you got so many empty houses 'round here. Every house on this hill coulda burned down. THAT'S why I wanta know where you was at this afternoon."

Jason jerked his arm free. "I don't like where you're heading with this, so back off. I was at Bites 'n Bytes all afternoon. I was even interviewed by a TV reporter. You can check."

"You got a alibi. 'Course you do. It's only innocent people that don't got alibis. But, you don' know what else we found."

"This is bullshit. Stop playing games. Just spit it out."

Hardesty focused his beady eyes on a canvas tarp lying on the ground at the far rear corner of the foundation. Jason followed his gaze. The canvas was so dusty it hadn't registered before, but now he saw it was wrapped around something about six feet long.

The deputy stared at the tarp. He seemed to be thinking—maybe even calculating his next move. Jason grudgingly admitted this doofus cop could be cunning, and chided himself for never bothering to get gossip and dirt on him from the gossip network.

"OK, Brinkman. Cards on the table." The deputy pulled a clear plastic evidence bag from his pants pocket. "You know what this is?" He held it close enough for Jason to examine.

"Looks like dog tags."

"Uh-huh. And what do they say?"

Jason took the bag and smoothed it so he could make out the letters on the metal tags. "Let's see. They're Navy tags." He pulled on the plastic to make it tighter, turned so the light was better. "It says...William... Wallace...Williams, III. Oh, Jesus, no! It can't be! Admiral Bill?"

CHAPTER 52

Jason didn't think of Admiral Bill as a friend, although they'd known each other for two years. They chatted easily about the weather and village gossip, but Bill shut down if anything serious came up. Their conversation under the spec house was the longest and most personal one Jason could recall. In Jason's mind, Bill was a Vietnam generation guy who'd survived the war but whose psyche was mortally wounded; someone he could never really understand.

Still, learning Bill was dead shook him deeply. Bill was the second person he knew who'd died—been killed—in three days. Two people he saw all the time who'd been snatched away in the blink of an eye, with no warning. Literally, here one minute, and gone the next.

"Hey, where you at?" Hardesty poked Jason's arm. "I'm talking to you, and you better listen up." He paused, but got no reaction. "The way it looks to me, and I 'spect the way the district attorney'll see it, is we got arson here. You burned the house down so's you can collect the insurance 'cause you're broke. I know how you did it, 'cause I saw it on one of them true crime shows. You closed all the windows, unloosened the connection where the stove hooked up to the gas line, and turned on all the burners. The gas flowed for a few hours, and didn't explode 'til you was down at Bites 'n Bytes having your lunch with all them people to be witnesses."

Hardesty jabbed Jason's shoulder with his finger. "You got the motive and the means, Mr. LA Attorney. It's Penal Code sections 451(b) and 548, pure and simple. That's arson of an insured structure with intent to defraud, in case you don't know it."

That finally got Jason's attention. "You're crazy. I did not burn down my house."

"Shut up and listen to me. Now, I don't know if you knew that the victim was under the house, but it don't matter, 'cause he was, and he died in the fire, so we also got felony murder. Arson's a felony, and a human being died while you was committing the felony, so we got felony murder. That's Penal Code section 189. You with me? Following what I'm saying?"

"Yeah, it's Crim Law 101, but cut to the chase. What do you want?"

Hardesty grabbed Jason's upper arm again and dragged him to GG's front steps, away from the other emergency personnel. "You stand here," he instructed, pointing at the brick walkway. Climbing to the first step, the deputy made himself the same height as Jason. He spoke quietly, inches from Jason's face. "The only way I'm gonna make sergeant is if I find O'Brien's killer. Your little felony murder here is pissant stuff. Any jerkoff can figure it out. It ain't got no 'wow' factor, like solving The Storm Drain Murder. But it does give me more leverage over you. We're talking nine years for arson, and the death penalty for killing the bum."

"You've got nothing. I didn't set the fire, and I didn't kill Admiral Bill. All you've got is a lot of 'could haves' and 'might haves.'"

This close, Hardesty's breath smelled of onion and coffee acid. Jason turned away and studied the debris inside the foundation. His eyes roamed to the dusty tarp in the far corner and back to the concrete pad. A scrap of metal next to it caught his attention. The remains of a red-and-white label stood out among the ash and fragments. Squinting, he made out the letters OPANE.

The propane tank! Of course! That explains the explosion. Jason said, "I'll tell you what did happen, if you're interested in facts instead of harassing me. See that piece of metal with the label? It's from a propane tank. Admiral Bill had it and a camp stove in the crawl space. I discovered them a coupla nights ago. He slept under my house, and used the stove for heat. He liked to turn the flames up high, to get warm faster. He got drunk and stoned and passed out after he lit the burners, and they got so hot they blew up the tank and the furnace."

The deputy waved his hand like he was shooing away a mosquito. "Yeah, yeah, and monkeys might fly outta my butt. I ain't convinced, and

I doubt the DA would be neither. You don't appreciate it, but I got you in a major headlock."

Jason struggled to keep his face neutral, but he seethed inside. It was obvious he'd never win an argument with Hardesty, so he decided it was time to force the issue. "OK. You think you've got grounds, go ahead and arrest me. Otherwise, I've got work to do. I'm going."

Hardesty grabbed his forearm. "Uh-uh. No way. I will haul you down to Rock Bay right now, unless you start providing information I can use to arrest someone in The Storm Drain Murder. I'll make your life a holy hell, spending all your money and time defending yourself. I got insurance fraud, arson, felony murder, reckless endangerment, and I'm sure I can think of more while I'm driving. One of 'em will stick. It's your choice."

Jason's every instinct told him not to give in, but he knew the fat cop had the upper hand. Between fighting Courtney, saving his law license, getting a new place to live, and tracking down Geraldo's stolen money, he had no time or resources to defend frivolous charges. "Alright," he sighed. "What do you want from me?"

* * *

A battered Range Rover sputtered to a stop two houses up Crescent Lane from the emergency vehicles. The car's engine steamed and its brakes screeched. Stacks of boxes and piles of bedding and clothes blocked the back and side windows. A rusted vanity plate and frame dangled from the rear bumper, trolling for the naïve and unwary:

$ Barry B $
MONYMAN
Call 1-800-2B-RICH2

The driver, Barry B., shouldered open his door with a sharp metallic *scrunch*. Stepping out, he drained a can of Red Bull and tossed it on the lawn in front of him. He took a last drag off his cigarette and flicked the butt into the wood-chip ground cover.

The man was skinny and average height. His clothes—a faded Lacoste polo shirt and calf-length cargo shorts—looked slept in. Gray stubble covered his scalp and pockmarked cheeks. Tattered Birkenstocks squeaked on the wet pavement as he walked toward the fire engines. "Jeezzus," he muttered to himself, "the boy really fucked up this time."

Picking his way through the high-pressure hoses, he spotted several firemen huddled near a truck. He tapped one of them on the shoulder. "Hey, bro—oops, I mean—Captain…Ramirez," he said pleasantly, glancing at the man's badge, "what's the story here?"

Captain Ramirez looked the man up and down. "What's your interest in the property, sir?"

Barry B. waved in the direction of his vehicle. "I'm supposed to be moving in."

"Well, sir, I can't say anything because there's an investigation under way at the present time, but you can call the Public Affairs Officer tomorrow."

"I understand you need to follow protocol, but I have a right to know because, you see, this is my house. My name is Barry Brinkman. My mother, Grace Brinkman, just died and left it to me."

The captain's radio crackled and he unclipped it and held it to his ear. An annoyed expression crossed his face. "I'm sorry, sir, I have to take care of this call. All I can tell you is it looks like an appliance leaked gas and exploded. That compromised other sources of combustion, and the entire structure became involved. We were lucky we could confine the incident to a single structure."

Barry Brinkman's face crinkled into an engaging salesman's smile. "I'm much obliged, Captain Ramirez." He shook the captain's hand warmly, placing his left hand over their clasped hands.

"No problem, sir. Sorry 'bout your house. Nothing we could do to save it."

"I know you and your men did your best. Please tell all your crew how much their efforts mean to me." He squeezed the captain's hand firmly, and then ducked between the emergency vehicles. Stopping to survey the charred studs and debris, he spat, "I'm gonna kill that little cocksucker."

* * *

The official in the black slicker finished pounding stakes around the burned-out foundation and began attaching yellow crime-scene tape to them. As he worked, the firemen hauled hoses back to their trucks and retrieved equipment. The static and chatter of walkie-talkies faded. Paramedics wheeled a gurney carrying a black body bag across the yard to the rear of a waiting ambulance. They closed the doors, and the van crept through the maze of emergency vehicles.

Deputy Hardesty and Jason stood locked in silent confrontation. Hardesty said, "Your move. Give me something that'll get me my third stripe."

"Uh-uh. Our deal is, you have to tell me the latest on the O'Brien murder if you want me to help you. So give."

The cop looked behind him and to each side. "The coroner finally found the injection site," he whispered. "So now they know it was pure heroin that killed O'Brien, and the location where it was injected at."

"And? You going to tell me?"

"Right upper eyelid," Hardesty exclaimed, raising his voice a little. "A tiny hole, barely noticeable. It's right out of *CSI* or *24*. The heroin hit his brain, and *POOF*."

"That's interesting," Jason mumbled absently, processing this new information. *Danni, Tiffany, Mags, and Rory were there the night Geraldo died, and they all know how to use a syringe.*

"There's more," the deputy whispered. "Commander Sepulveda was in his cubicle talking on speakerphone when I was in the bullpen, so I listened. I know what the sheriff and district attorney are thinking." Hardesty stopped as a fireman walked behind him. "Too many ears here," he growled. "Move over there."

He led Jason away from the emergency vehicles, across the front yard, to the driveway apron. "Forensics and the coroner've been busy," he continued in a low voice. "They found that the diameter of the injection hole matches the kind of needle that comes with the little plastic cap we found at the scene. That's the cap that's got Turlock's prints on it, you remember?"

"So?"

"So? You should be able to connect the dots, Mr. LA Lawyer. The DA says he can convict Turlock because the hole and the cap with her fingerprints match the kind of needle she uses for her insulin shots. He says that evidence ties the whole case together."

Jason made a time-out sign with his hands. "Hold on. That proves nothing. There's probably two hundred people in this county who use needles just like that. Doctors, nurses, diabetics, estheticians, veterinarians. No way that coincidence proves Mags is guilty."

"Alright, then whadabout this? The crime scene guys found O'Brien's driver's license in Turlock's van, slid down between the passenger seat and the console, like it fell outta his pocket. And his hair's all over the seat."

"All easily explained. Mags used to drive him home when he was too drunk to drive himself."

The deputy moved so close his shoulder touched Jason's arm. "See, me and you's finally on the same page. The DA thinks the injection site and the evidence 'bout the needle gives him enough to prove first degree murder. I think he's crazy."

"I agree," Jason replied, thinking it was all circumstantial. Even so, he worried about the totality of the evidence—the things Hardesty knew about plus some things he didn't know. The DA could show premeditation because the heroin had to be prepared before it was injected. He could establish motive by showing Mags was in deep financial trouble because of Geraldo. He could say she wanted revenge because of that, and because Geraldo broke off their relationship. She told the cops she moved the body and dumped it down the storm drain. The DA could say she was trying to destroy evidence of her crime, and her actions show her guilty conscience. Finally, Mags's fingerprints were all over the spec house. It all added up to a credible case, and the jury just might buy the package as a whole.

Jason decided to change direction. "So why's the DA going for murder one, instead of something easier to prove, like murder two or elder abuse?"

Hardesty looked over both shoulders and behind him. "Truth is, he wants to take down Silver Throat Chalmers in a big murder case with lots of media coverage. Knock him off his pedestal. That's the scuttlebutt. He's pissed 'cause Chalmers wins too many acquittals. Him and Chalmers've hated each other for decades, so the story goes. Since they was in law school. Something about Chalmers and the DA's wife. The DA's gonna try the case himself so's he can nail Chalmers's ass."

"The district attorney would risk losing a high-profile case just to settle a personal score?"

"Guess so. DA's got you in his sights, too, since you're helpin' Chalmers. Gives me more leverage over you. That, plus the arson and felony murder here, and the dirt and footprint evidence that ties you to O'Brien's murder." Hardesty smiled malevolently. "So, you got to ask yourself what you're gonna do to help me get my sergeant's stripes. Or, do you wanta go right now down to the Rock Bay lockup?"

Jason felt himself being pushed into a corner, but knew he had a few moves left. He said, "Here's my most important tip for you. Mags Turlock did not kill Geraldo O'Brien."

"Like I told you, I'm inclined to agree. I still think it's that Tedeski girl that killed him. She's got motive, being knocked up by him. Why else'd she get her friend to drive her to the bus station and then run away?"

"You have any luck questioning the ticket clerks at the Greyhound station?"

"Nah, I ain't got down to Santa Luisa yet. It's kind of a far drive, there and back to Sea Cliff. I did put out a BOLO, though. Might get a hit or two from it." His face drooped with frustration. He shifted back and forth on his feet and wiped his forehead with a dirty gray handkerchief. "Come on. Help me out here. Whaddya got for me?" He jingled the handcuffs clipped to his utility belt.

Jason reminded him about El Carnicero and the list of Geraldo's drug-dealer associates. Hardesty shrugged and said nothing had panned out. "Come on," he demanded. "What else you got?"

Jason was about to pull the list of local suspects out of his pants pocket when Hardesty blurted, "Hey, what about O'Brien's daughter? That would be awesome, proving a hottie like that killed her own father. I'd get my stripes and a spot on a true crime show. Maybe even a book deal."

Sensing an unexpected opening, Jason jumped at it. If he gave up Rory, he could leave this minute because all her information was at his office on her client intake sheet. He said, "I'll give you everything I've got on her, but it's at my office." The snap decision was followed by a surprising wave of regret. Yes, she'd destroyed any obligation he had to her, but her uncanny allure lingered. He pictured her beguiling gray eyes and their many moods: playful, challenging, seductive, angry. He tasted her lips from their long, passionate kiss on his office floor. He felt her pain when she cried for her father. He kicked himself. *Am I crazy? She nearly broke my jaw. She tried to destroy Erin and me. She's probably taken the $780,000 already. No, I don't owe her a thing.*

The fire trucks' diesel engines clattered to life. The noise startled him and Hardesty. Glancing, Jason saw the firemen, paramedics, and investigators had stored their equipment and were leaving. Soon, quiet prevailed. A gentle breeze rustled the pine trees, swaying their boughs, shaking loose droplets of water that splashed softly into puddles. Forest birds chirped and squirrels scolded. Far in the distance, ocean surf roared.

Hardesty's radio crackled. He cocked his head, listened, and nodded. "OK, Brinkman, you go to your office and I'll swing by later for that info." He jingled his handcuffs again. "But if you flake out, I will hunt you down like a hound on a rabbit and throw your ass in the cage at Rock Bay." He swaggered in the direction of his cruiser.

Jason breathed a sigh of relief. At last he could go back to his office to search for the pdfs ... but he didn't have a car. His shoulders slumped. He told himself it was just another hurdle to get past today. An Uber or a Lyft would do for now.

Pulling out his cell phone, he turned to take another look at the remains of his house. The garage, set back at the end of the driveway, appeared undamaged. Inside it was GG's Neon. With a glimmer of hope, he trudged up the slope of the drive. He was pondering how to get the car started when a man's voice shouted: "Jason Brinkman! Do not dare to walk away from me!"

CHAPTER 53

Jason stopped on the driveway and looked in the direction of the voice. A skinny man with an angry expression stood on the sidewalk. As soon as Jason stopped, the man began striding across the lawn.

It can't be my father. He wasn't supposed to arrive until Friday, and the anorexic man hustling toward him looked nothing like the towering tyrant in his memory. But it was Barry Brinkman, and despite Jason's fervent wish not to see him, there was no avoiding him now.

Twenty-five years ago, Barry Brinkman was the go-to man for real estate deals in San Francisco. If a speculator wanted to build a retail complex, convert a hotel to condos, or purchase land for a high-rise, Barry knew the officials to squeeze and pots of money to plunder. Cocaine, alcohol, prostitutes, and enforcers—all were Barry's business tools, as handy as the telephone and as familiar as the calculator.

In those days, cash flew into and out of Barry's accounts so fast he couldn't keep track of it. He purchased a mansion on Belvedere Island, with views of the San Francisco Bay and the Golden Gate, Bay, and Richmond bridges. He threw parties for his clients and cronies that were legendary for their excesses. Barry, wife Lola, and little Jason were rich beyond their dreams.

And leveraged to the hilt.

Barry's pyramid of properties began to collapse when a tenement in Hunter's Point burned down and the insurance refused payment because arson was found. Without that revenue stream, the next property up the line defaulted, and then the next, and the next, until the Belvedere mansion was in foreclosure.

A year later, the Brinkman family found themselves living in two rooms above a sandwich shop in the Tenderloin. Cocaine and gin became Barry's and Lola's tools for survival, and blame and recriminations filled their days. At night, the mixture of drugs and hate became combustible.

Jason tried to recall the last time he'd seen his father. It must have been two years ago, just before he quit the Whatley firm. Before that, it was five years ago, when Jason Jr. was born. In all that time, the only communications from Barry were midnight voicemails with drunken lectures and his email yesterday announcing he was moving into GG's house.

He couldn't be a worse father, but he is my father. Jason steeled himself and reached out for a manly, father-son handshake. "Dad, how are you? It's good to see—"

Barry Brinkman slapped his son hard across the face. "Where am I supposed to live?" he bellowed. He pointed at the charred remains of GG's house. "That was my hideout 'til my deal comes through and I get back on my feet."

Stunned, Jason clapped his hand over his cheek and turned away to hide the hurt and pain he knew his face showed. He tried to imagine recent events in Barry's life that led up to this moment. One seemed most likely, so he asked, "Did another business deal go south?"

"I don't tolerate impertinence, boy," Barry snarled. He focused on the empty space where the house used to be. "I have never been so profoundly disappointed in you. It's one thing to fuck up your life, but for you to drag me down with you—"

"Drag you down? I don't understand. What're you talking about?"

Barry glared at him from under angry, hooded brows. His pupils were fierce black dots. "Don't play dumb with me, boy. You know what you did and how it'd affect me."

"Dad, honest, I don't have any idea."

"That old broad at your firm. The letch that wanted sex, the one you blew off. What's her name?"

"Gretchen. Gretchen Fautz."

"That's the one. She sicked the IRS on me this time."

Jason winced, thinking his father had gone completely off the deep end. He said, "Dad, that's crazy."

Barry's eyes narrowed into slits and the veins in his temples pulsed. He grabbed Jason's shirt with both hands and pulled until they stood chest to chest. "I know women like that. Powerful, vindictive women past their prime. They want a bit of straight pipe from you, you give it to 'em. Keep 'em happy. No big deal." His words tumbled out in a slurred jumble. "Refuse, and they're obsessed with destroying you. They'll chase you to the gates of hell and still want more revenge."

Standing so close, Jason caught the familiar scent of gin on his father's breath, saw the telltale specks of white in the creases of his nose.

"Why didn't you just shtoopf the old bitch?" Barry bellowed.

"Because I have ethics and morals. Things you know nothing about."

"And what did your ethics and morals get you? She ruined your career and busted up your marriage. But destroying you wasn't enough for her, was it? No way. A woman like that, she needed more vengeance, so she called the IRS on me."

"Don't you see that's totally crazy! How would she know—"

"My name's in your personnel file, or your Facebook page, or the god-damned Internet," he shouted. "I don't know how, but she got it, and she gave it to those bastards, and they took my last twenty grand. I know it was her. And now I've got no place to live, all because of you...."

Barry spun around and stared at the burned-out foundation. The longer he stared, the more agitated he became, until he shook with anger. Suddenly he turned and grabbed Jason's neck with both hands, shaking him violently. "How could you burn it down?" he shrieked. "That was my last secret asset! It's raw land now. Worthless." His thumbs twitched as a shrewd look crossed his face. "I see it now. There's insurance, and you're broke." The thumbs dug into Jason's windpipe. He shook him again, hard. "The insurance money's mine, you little fuck."

A lifetime of rage erupted in Jason. He rammed his arms up between his father's, bursting them apart, breaking his grip. Barry didn't cover his body core. Jason slammed one fist, then the other, into his father's stomach and solar plexus. Barry grunted and bent over, gasping for air. Jason aimed his knee at the man's nose, coiled to deliver a blow that would smash his face, but pulled back just before connecting. "I did not burn down my grandmother's house," he shouted at his father. "I loved her! I'm not scum like you!"

Barry sank to the curb, wheezing. "You hit ME! What kind of son strikes his father? After all I did for you."

"Like six foster homes?" Jason roared at the slumped figure. "Like summer vacations and weekends in your crash pad in San Francisco watching you drink all day and pass out in front of the TV?"

"At least I had you with me, instead of Lola getting her hooks in you."

"How 'bout hitting me every time I made a mistake? And locking me in the closet when I was in the way?"

"I fought for you, son. You were too young. You don't know all I did to save you from her clutches. I spent every dime fighting her, sending my lawyers to every damn court hearing in LA."

"Yeah, you're a real hero. That's why I told the judge I wanted to live here with your mother, to get away from you. Both of you."

"You came up with that?" Barry sat up straight. "Lola told me it was her."

That surprised Jason. It meant Lola had protected him from his father's rage if he'd learned his son didn't want to live with him. Or she and her lawyers had simply sandbagged her husband and deprived him of custody.

Barry struggled to his feet. "You deliberately deserted your own father? No, that can't be. I could never forgive that." Barry thrust his face an inch from Jason's and bore into his eyes. "We've had our differences, I know," Barry said, menace growing in his voice, "but that is unforgivable, for a son to abandon his father. You tell me right now, boy. Tell me it was Lola, that she told the judge, or I disown you forever."

Jason blinked. "Dad, that was more than twenty years ago. You didn't even bother to attend the hearing. I'm not going to apologize, but can't you see it was for the best?"

"Right now, boy. Lola or you? Think carefully. Do you want a father or not?"

Jason's stomach turned to water. He staggered back, like it was he who'd been punched in the gut. But in that moment, he felt freed from guilt he never knew he carried. "It doesn't have to be either/or, Barry, and I'm not going to lie to you." He forced his voice to be flat and without emotion. "But if that's the way you want it…. It was my idea. You would've destroyed my life and I'd probably have killed myself. Your mother saved me."

Barry slumped and staggered, as if Jason had punched him again. "You are no son of mine," he moaned softly.

"Dad, you don't have to…," Jason began, but reconsidered. With a sigh, he accepted this was the end. The frayed and tattered cord that bound them loosely for so long had been severed. Jason searched his pocket for the key to GG's front door. He ran his thumb over it before unhooking it from its ring. "Goodbye, GG," he said sadly, kissing the key. He flipped it at his father's feet. "Here you go, Barry. You get the asset. And lose a son."

CHAPTER 54

Jason got the Neon started without too much difficulty, despite the battery being dead. The key was in his pocket because he'd stored Geraldo's files in the back seat. Pushing against the driver's doorjamb, he got the car rolling down the driveway, jumped in, and turned onto Crescent Lane's long slope. The Neon gathered momentum. When the speedometer hit fifteen, he switched on the ignition and popped the clutch. The motor sputtered, coughed, then caught.

With the engine running fairly smoothly, the little car puttered up Del Mar Road toward Highway 1. Jason drove slowly, brooding. He told himself that he'd made an effort to be a good adult son, and that Barry, always a terrible father, had become so paranoid there was nothing left to work with.

Jason pictured his worn and haggard father as he trudged back to his Range Rover, tossing GG's key into the neighbor's bushes. Knowing they'd had their last brutal fight brought relief, but also guilt because he felt relieved. In his LA days, he'd have given his father the $20,000 just to buy some peace of mind. Now it was all the money in the world. He barked a harsh laugh. *Here I am, broke on my ass, and I know where there's $780,000.*

He rolled down the window for some fresh air. The car's interior was dusty and cluttered with the day-to-day debris GG had let accumulate. Wedged into the ashtray was an unopened pack of Newports. He eyed it warily, imagining a deep drag of smoke filling his lungs and the rush of nicotine hitting his brain. He reached for the pack, but touched the patch on his shoulder instead, thinking if he could beat the urge when he was this upset, he could kick the habit forever. Reaching for the pack again, he crushed it and flipped it under the driver's seat.

Glancing around the interior, he saw his grandmother's floppy-brimmed sunhat and a blanket. Jason Jr.'s sand pail and shovel rattled on the floor—a sad reminder of his son's only visit. Her lumbar support pillow lay on the passenger's seat. He grabbed the pillow and dropped it in his lap, recalling that her bridge club gave it to her when she turned 80 and began complaining about back pain. They'd had it monogrammed with her initials. She'd said she was "tickled pink."

Jason ran his fingers over the letters. "GGB." Gwendolyn Grace Brinkman. He'd always called her "GG," but couldn't remember if it was because of her initials or because he couldn't say "grandmother." He clutched the pillow tight against his stomach, releasing scents of her hairspray and talcum powder. They brought back warm memories of her hugging him when he was sad about his chaotic life before the judge let him live with her. She'd say, "What's the matter, dear boy? Won't you tell me?"

"Oh, GG," he said as he drove, "my life's not going so well right now."

"Now, Jason." Her imaginary voice soothed him, and he smiled despite his sour mood because she always began with "Now" when she wanted to say something important. "Now, Jason, it can't all be bad. There must be some good things in your life."

"I can't think of anything."

"Well, you do have a place to sleep, even though my house burned down. You can sleep at your office."

"Yeah, that's what I'm going to do."

"And you have some clothes. Don't you keep a suit and shirts at your office in case you get called to court unexpectedly?"

"I think they're still there."

"You have your files on Geraldo O'Brien, don't you?"

"Yeah, luckily."

"How much money do you think he has?"

"El Carnicero said $2 million. Almost $3 million, with the money in the Grand Caymans. I keep forgetting about the $2.5 million construction loan for One Bluffside that he got without telling the investors. So it's more than $5 million he's got stashed away somewhere."

"That's a lot of money. Enough for a lifetime."

"Yes, it is, if it exists. But it belongs to the estate, although Rory would say it's hers."

"My boy—always taking the high road. I guess I taught you too well." Jason drove a few minutes in silence before his grandmother's voice continued. "You have a car. You can drive my little Neon as long as you want. But you will have to put gas in it."

"Thanks, GG. I promise I'll take good care of it."

"And you have enough money for the rest of the month, don't you?"

"Probably."

"And some income from Mags Turlock and that James Paige fellow to tide you over?"

"Most likely. If I don't lose my law license."

"I'll bet you'll find the paper you need to fight Courtney and Gretchen. What is it?"

"Lucas Lancaster's waiver of liability and my cover memo to Gretchen highlighting it. I think I've got pdf copies somewhere. I'm gonna check my office computer's hard drive as soon as I get there."

"My heavens, I have no idea what all that means, but you see how a few positive thoughts lead to others? You can solve all these problems if you put your mind to it."

"I guess, GG, it's just that there's so much at once."

"I know, dear boy. You have been under a black cloud. You know, I believe bad things always happen in threes, and you've had at least four. Your luck will change soon, believe me. The moon will move into the Seventh House in no time, and things will be better. You'll see."

Jason was so deep into his mental conversation that he was surprised to find himself at the intersection of Del Mar and Highway 1. He stopped for the red light. "I wish I could talk to you for real, GG. I miss you so much. You always helped me see things more clearly."

"I know, my darling. I wish I could be there to help you, but you'll get through it. You have to keep being strong. I have to go now, but I want you to think about something."

"What's that?"

"Don't be too tough on your father. Grandpa Larry and I always pushed him to make a lot of money. Our lives were so hard for so long, we thought it was the right thing to do. I know I've told you that before. Your poor father's spent his life chasing pots of gold he can never find."

"Why're you telling me this?"

"It's too late for him," she whispered, "but not for you."

* * *

The light turned green, and Jason crossed Highway 1 to take Main Street into town. His phone rang, but the screen read *Unavailable*. He was about to let the call go to voicemail, but decided it could be a new client.

"Jason Brinkman," he answered, trying to sound professional.

"Brinkman?" a staticky voice said.

"Yes, this is Jason Brinkman. Who's calling?"

More static before the voice said, "Brinkman, it's Mags Turlock. I need to talk to you. Right now."

"Mags, I'm driving. Hang on 'til I get better reception."

When he reached the business district, the static stopped. She barked, "I need to talk to you right now."

"Alright, alright. Where are you?"

"Still in my cell in the Santa Luisa lock-up, no thanks to you."

He started to say, "Thanks to me, you only need to post $20,000 bail," but held his tongue. Instead, he asked, "How'd you get a phone?"

"Huh? Oh, it's Yuri's. He's the night janitor here at the jail. He's Russian. He's my buddy, now. Hey, Yuri," she called out. "We're friends, uh, *tovarisch*, right?"

"*Da*," a man's voice said in the distance.

"He's a hard worker, him and his wife. They've been working two jobs, saving their money since they got to California. I'm gonna sell 'em one of my homes, soon as I get out of here."

"But how can you be in your cell calling on someone's—"

"It's between shifts." Mags spoke like the explanation was obvious. "Afternoon guards are in the locker room, evening crew's putting on their uniforms or at coffee. It's the same every day 'bout this time. I've got a few minutes to talk 'til they come in. Now, will you listen?"

"Alright. What's so urgent?"

"I've been thinking 'bout my case. Lots of time to think in jail. What've you found out?"

"Anyone else within earshot? This has to be between just us to preserve attorney-client privilege."

"Nope. I'm the only prisoner in this wing, and Yuri's just gone out back to empty the trash."

"OK, here it is. I know the district attorney's plan. They're going to go for first degree murder. They found your needle cap with your fingerprints on it, and they found the injection site. It matches the diameter of the needle you use for your insulin. Your fingerprints are all over the spec house, and you admitted you moved the body and dumped it. They'll say you had motive, because Geraldo took all your money and now you're broke and losing your properties. And even more motive 'cause he ended your relationship."

"That can all be explained. I've already explained most of it. And the stuff about the needle—that's pretty circumstantial, isn't it? I mean, can't Chalmers poke holes in it?"

"He can try, Mags, but you have to understand how serious this is. You're looking at twenty-five years to life in prison at best, and the death penalty at worst, if you're convicted."

"Isn't he the best defense attorney in the county?"

"Without a doubt."

"Didn't he get that bank robber off last month? The guy who shot four people and stole a car?"

"He did."

Mags was silent. She changed direction when she spoke. "So, I've been thinking 'bout Geraldo and me. We were like cats in heat, fucking our brains out one minute, and trying to kill each other the next. He was a mean son-of-a-bitch—didn't care who he knocked around. He picked me up and threw me across the room one time when he was drunk, and I'm no lightweight.

"Funny now, but I actually thought I might love him, for about five minutes. I was really pissed when he dumped me for Danni. Wanted to kill him. I tried not to hold a grudge against her. It's a sisterhood thing—you wouldn't understand. I mean, here's a decent-looking guy with money to spend, he opens his home to her and her young daughter, and all she's gotta do is put out and swing a hammer when he needs it. I couldn't hardly blame her, but I never liked her. I cut her a lot of slack, though, 'cause of Tiffany. They had a pretty rough road to travel, and I always felt sorry for the girl. No fault of hers that her mother's life's so fucked up." Mags sighed before adding, "A girl that age needs her mother. Even a bad one."

Jason followed the traffic, half-listening. When she paused, he said, "What about Geraldo? You were talking about him."

"Geraldo? Oh, yeah. We got along great when he was sober. We kept doing business deals together after he took up with Danni, and that became our relationship. But sitting here in jail, it's the bad in Geraldo I'm remembering. I talked to Danni 'bout it once. He treated her the same way he treated me, beating her when he wasn't screwing her. Only she had nowhere to get away from him, 'cept for Mostly's. She'd crawl into a bottle and disappear for a week." Her voice grew louder and shook with anger. "And leave little Tiffany alone with him. A sixteen-year-old girl alone with that pig! I'm thinkin' now he'd pick fights with Danni so she'd leave and he could get at the girl."

A long silence followed. Jason imagined Mags pacing her cell, like she did when he interviewed her at the sheriff's office in Rock Bay. "I talked to his other women, too," she began again. "Same story. Charming, great sex, money to spend, but always abuse. I wrote down a list of his women I knew about. Came up with nine just in Sea Cliff. I told each one of 'em, 'We've got this in common. We've got to stick together, be ready to help each other.' I even made up a name for them—us. 'WAGs—Women Abused by Geraldo.'"

When Jason didn't react, Mags continued. "So, here's what I'm thinking…." She paused.

"Go on, tell me what you're thinking."

"I'm thinking that someone killing him is sort of a public service."

The implication hit Jason with a thud. He jerked the car into a parking spot so he could focus fully on the conversation. "Are you saying you killed him?"

"What if I did? I'd be kind of a hero, don't you think? You know, saving the women of Sea Cliff from being abused by a drunken, macho letch. He deserved it, and I might as well get the credit."

"Did you kill him, Mags? You told me before you didn't. Did you?"

"Yeah, I did it." Her voice was far away. "The night of the party, I got a baggie of the pure heroin from the kitchen, cooked it in the spoon lying on the counter, filled up my hypodermic, and injected it in his eyelid. He was dead in seconds."

Is she really confessing? Jason turned off the engine and rolled down the windows. No, he decided, she's playing some kind of head game. Maybe she thinks she's the savior of the women Geraldo abused, or maybe all women who are abused. Maybe she's covering for Danni and Tiffany, or maybe just Tiffany? But that definitely was not the Mags he knew. "OK, where did you inject the dope?"

"His eyelid, like I said."

"Which eyelid? Left, right, upper, lower?"

She hesitated. "Umm...lower...left."

"I want to be sure I understand you. You're saying Geraldo's lower lid on the left side of his face? Is that correct?"

"That's what I said. Why are you making such a big deal about it?"

"'Cause that's wrong and it proves you're lying. Why're you pretending you killed him? Who're you covering for? You told me Danni and Tiffany were at the spec house the night he died, and the tall blonde—the pretty one you said must've been a lesbian."

"I don't give a shit about her, and I'm not pretending. OK, so I don't remember all the details perfectly. There was a lot going on that night, or maybe I know something I'm not saying—"

"What? If you have exculpatory evidence, tell me, for God's sake, so I can try to get the charges thrown out or reduced."

"Just chill out. You know everything you need to know. For now, anyway. Let me ask you. You think Chalmers can get me off if I plead not guilty to first degree murder and go to trial?"

"Why would you do that? You're crazy not to tell me everything that aids your defense. Are you on some kind of mission?"

"There'd be TV from everywhere. I could tell my story, shine a light, and send a message. Kinda like the Fox special I saw last night in the mess hall, on abused women that can't break free."

"I didn't know you were so altruistic," Jason said, trying not to sound skeptical.

"It might even be good for business. 'Mags Turlock—the Realtor you don't want to mess with.' Seriously, I've had lots of time to think, and I've prayed really hard on it. The Lord told me to try to make something positive out of this whole experience. He said I'm the person who can tell the story. He told me it's my duty as a Christian woman, on behalf of the WAGs and all women."

"Alright, now you listen to me. This is a really bad idea, and as your attorney, I'm telling you don't. The DA wants to destroy Chalmers, and he's gonna use your trial to do it. Even though we think the evidence about the needle is circumstantial, and your prints and moving the body can be explained away, you never know how a jury will view it. You'd be playing Russian roulette with your life."

The sound of a metal door opening and slamming shut came over the phone. "The guards are coming in," Mags said. "I've gotta go. So, you really think I could get the death penalty?"

"Absolutely. It's a very real possibility."

Jason heard heavy footsteps approaching. Mags didn't speak.

"Mags? You still there?"

"Hey!" a man said. "How'd you get that phone? Give it here! Now!"

Jason heard grunting and beeps from the keypad as hands grabbed at the phone.

"Get away from me, pig," Mags shouted.

Jason said, "Tell them you're consulting your attorney."

"I'm … I'm talking to my lawyer," Mags shouted again.

"Tell them it's privileged and they have to give you privacy."

"Attorney-client privilege," Mags yelled. "You've gotta give me total privacy. Get away from me!"

The sounds of struggle stopped. "Alright," the man said. "You got five minutes 'fore I come back to confiscate that device."

Jason heard footsteps retreating and the metal door slam.

"Brinkman?" Mags whispered breathlessly. "You still there?"

"I'm here."

"I need to ask you. If I lose…when they execute you, how do they do it these days?"

"You get your choice of gas or lethal injection."

"Which is…umm…better?" Her voice quivered like a child's.

"Well, the gas can cause convulsions. With the drugs, sometimes they get the mix wrong, so you don't die right away. I've read you're in terrible pain for a long time."

"So, it's not like flipping a switch? Alive one minute, dead the next?"

"No, it isn't."

Mags was silent. After a long pause, she said, "Tell you what I think." The familiar edge returned to her voice. "Fuck those bitches in the WAGs, and Danni and Tiffany, and all the rest of 'em. No way any of them would take this rap for me, and I'm not gonna risk dying for their sake, no matter what the Lord says."

"That's the right decision."

The metal door slammed open again in the background. A deep male voice called out, "Changed my mind, Turlock. That phone's mine, right now, or your ass is grass."

"Here's something for you and Chalmers," Mags whispered hurriedly. "I've got the hypodermic needle. I hid it where no one can ever find it. And it's got Danni's fingerprints all over it."

CHAPTER 55

Jason trudged to his desk and fell into his chair. He clutched his head in his hands, feeling powerless to stop his life from crashing around him. His son, his marriage, his father, his law license, his car, his house. Everything important was slipping away.

He prided himself on keeping a level head whenever he faced hard times. Beginning with his foster home placements, he'd taught himself not to get too depressed when things were bad, or too high when life was going well. As a teenager, he'd learned exploding in anger didn't help after a couple of moments of feeling good. Through all the ups and downs, the dead-ends, the occasional triumphs, his philosophy had served him well. After the events of the past couple of days, however, the dam was close to bursting.

His eyes wandered across his desk, stopping at the picture of his grandmother and him with her favorite rose bush. He knew what she'd say: Make a list, and then decide what to do first. He picked up a yellow legal pad and flipped to a clean page. Taking a moment to compose himself, he wrote in no particular order:

- Look on Craigslist for a new place to live
- Check Grand Cayman account balance
- Draft papers for Geraldo's estate and Paige children's emotional distress claim
- Call Newport Exotic Leasing to negotiate return of my Porsche
- Ask around for a good divorce lawyer
- Check desktop computer for copies of Lucas Lancaster's waiver of liability and my cover memo telling Gretchen about it
- And, tantalizingly,
- Figure out Mags's hiding place for the hypodermic needle

Of these, the copies of the waiver and memo were most important right now. Gretchen and Courtney would file their complaint with the State Bar that afternoon. If he didn't have the copies, he couldn't prove he disclosed them. He'd lose and be disbarred. He wouldn't be able to earn a living or fight Courtney for custody of Jason Jr.

Hoping against hope, he woke up his computer. The obvious place to look was his password-protected personal file. He typed in the password. The document list appeared on the screen. He scanned it. Nothing was obvious, but he might've given the documents fake names out of an abundance of caution and paranoia. He tried a word search: "Lancaster," "Granquist," "waiver," "liability," "Alaska," "permafrost," "geology," "slope stability," "shear factor," "subsidence"—every keyword he could think of.

No results.

That wasn't good. Maybe a global search of the entire hard drive. Closing out the personal file, he opened the *Find* program. He tried each keyword again.

Nothing.

"Well, shit!" he swore. He pushed his chair back so hard it hit the credenza behind him. "I cannot catch a break! I'm screwed!"

He paced from one end of the office to the other, and back again. "OK, Jason," he said to himself through clenched teeth, "let's see how long it's gonna take to lose your law license. Maybe you can make some money before it happens."

He sat and Googled the State Bar's website. Searching screen after screen of regulations, he found Rule 5.102—the trial would be 125 days after he was served with the complaint. That was a break. It gave him four months to earn fees from Mags and James Paige, and maybe even Geraldo's estate if he could get it filed.

Just before he closed the website, however, Rule 5.225 caught his eye. He read it in disbelief. He could be suspended immediately if the Bar showed he posed a threat of harm to the public. In an instant, he saw Gretchen's strategy. She'd go straight for the jugular, like she always did. She and Courtney would get him suspended immediately, even if they had to make up facts. They'd get what they wanted, because it was Gretchen and Whatley, Thelen & Füchs.

"I can't take it anymore!" he yelled at the monitor. "Goddammit! Courtney's gonna take my son to New York and I'll be disbarred. There's nothing I can do because I have no money!" He laughed harshly. "She'll be making a million, and I'll be flipping burgers."

His blood pressure skyrocketed and his heart hammered like it would burst. He jumped from his chair, knocking it over. Rage pounded behind his eyes, blurring his vision. *I need to destroy something right now—smash it into a million pieces.* He clenched and reclenched his fists, imagining a weapon in them. His high school All-Star baseball bat stood in the corner. He grabbed it. The smooth metal was cool in his hands—its heft so very satisfying. What to hit first? The flat-screen monitor was at waist level, the perfect height for his swing.

He cocked the bat, ready to swing for the bleachers, but a little voice in his head said, "Don't lose control. Count to 100. Jog around the block. Do something to get a grip." He forced himself to take deep breaths. "One one-thousand, two one-thousand, three one-thousand." He spat the numbers. Then, more calmly, "Four one-thousand, five one-thousand, six one-thousand…." His eyes fell on the yellow legal pad. The words *Grand Cayman account* jumped out at him.

"That's it!" he cried shrilly. "My salvation! The $780,000! I can buy a superstar divorce lawyer and another one to fight the State Bar." He propped the bat against the side of his desk and patted his pockets, feeling for the crumpled paper with Geraldo's code. He pulled out everything: wallet, keys, the list of local suspects, business cards, a ballpoint pen, and finally, the half-sheet of Rory's notebook paper with the code.

He smoothed the page on his desk with trembling hands. The top was filled with Rory's schoolgirl writing. At the bottom, part of the alphanumeric code was printed neatly, and part was scribbled. Cold doubt prickled his spine. He and Rory both had half the code. She could reconstruct the part she was missing from memory, just as he had. What if she…? He shook away the doubt, telling himself it had to be there.

Jason Googled the Grand National Bank of the Cayman Islands and clicked through to its website. The screen filled with the bank's pastel homepage and the link to the portal that would open the account. If he typed the 10-digit code correctly. He clicked on the link and smoothed the paper again. *Don't blow it. The portal will close forever.* He typed with one finger:

E-2-y-u-6-N-8-y-A-Q

The screen went blank. It seemed to take minutes for *Welcome, Geraldo O'Brien* to appear at the top. Jason hissed, "Yesss!" He scrolled down to the *Check Account Balances* button and clicked on it. An error message popped onto the screen: *You must agree to the Terms of Use in order to proceed.*

"Dammit!" He hit the back arrow. At the bottom of the page, a faint box appeared in the far left margin. He checked it and clicked on the *Check Account Balances* button again.

The screen froze. It went blank. Five long seconds later, the list of Geraldo's accounts appeared, one by one. Each showed a zero balance.

"NO!" he roared at the screen. "Rory, you goddamned bitch! It's not yours to take!"

The dam burst. He grabbed the baseball bat and swung at the monitor with all his might. The bat connected with a solid *THUNK*. The screen exploded, showering his desk with shards and chunks. The plastic shell sailed across the room, smashing into the bookcase, collapsing a shelf. With a thunderous roar, legal texts, pictures, and trophies crashed to the floor in a heap of books and broken glass.

CHAPTER 56

Jason worked methodically to clean up the mess he'd made, forcing himself to focus on the task instead of his jumble of worries. As he reshelved the law books, he felt sheepish about destroying the flat screen. "Way to go," he mumbled to himself. "You killed the messenger." A new monitor would cost hundreds of dollars, which he couldn't afford. And he really shouldn't be surprised Rory took the money. She probably did it the minute she left his office.

After a half-hour of straightening and sweeping, only the monitor's plastic shell remained to be thrown away. He picked it up and found the Marlboro pack he always kept on the bookshelf. Slipping the pack in his shirt pocket, he smashed the shell with his foot until the pieces were small enough to cram into the wastebasket.

He fell into his desk chair and leaned back, stretching his arms over his head. "What the hell am I going to do?" he asked the ceiling. The pack in his pocket pressed against his chest. "I give up," he said to himself. "There's no point in fighting it any longer."

The crisp cellophane crinkled in his fingers. He ripped it off and opened the pack. The scent of fresh tobacco filled his nostrils. He found a book of matches from Posh in his desk drawer and lit a cigarette, taking a deep drag. Glorious smoke filled his lungs. Nicotine surged into his brain, tingling, and making him a bit lightheaded.

He held in the smoke as long as he could, savoring the taste. When he finally exhaled, he noticed his desk phone's dim red message light blinking. He never checked his landline anymore because no one called it these days. Flicking a long ash into his coffee cup, he decided to ignore the message. "I don't need any more surprises today," he growled at the annoying red light. He finished his cigarette and lit another. But what if it was a client?

Reluctantly, he picked up the receiver and entered his password for voicemail. The mechanical voice said, "You have three new messages. First message—1:30 p.m. today."

"Hi, Jason," Rory said. Despite himself, his heart tripped when he heard her voice. "This is the only number I could find for you, so I hope you get this. I took the money from the Grand Cayman account. You probably know that already. You'll say I stole it, but I didn't. It's mine. Don't even think about fighting me on this.

"I'm leaving tonight for my new life somewhere warm and peaceful. I promised myself I wasn't going to tell you where, but I guess I changed my mind. Well, sort of.

"I want you to know something. You really hurt me, Jason, like no one ever has before. When my father asked me to come up to Sea Cliff, I thought he was going to make peace with me, but he died so I'll never know if that's what he wanted. I certainly never made peace with him. I'll have to live with that pain the rest of my life, but I decided if I got his money that would be some closure. So I made up my mind to take the money and leave. You turned out to be the person I had to deal with, and I knew I could manipulate you. But a funny thing happened. I fell for you while I was playing my game. Really hard. I opened myself up to you. I told you things I've never told anyone, even Alex, when she was my world. I did everything but spread my legs, and I would've, and you still rejected me. It hurts even worse because I think we'd be so good together. I know you feel the magnetism between us. I can tell you do every time I touch you. Even when we're arguing or fighting, it's there—a force that connects us—something I've never felt with anyone before. But I think there's even more, something much deeper. It's like we were soul mates in another life, or the stars were aligned on the days we were born, or we're each other's destiny. Maybe we're halves of the same whole and make a complete person together, even though I don't believe in any of that stuff. I'd really like to find out, and I wish you'd come away with me to try a life together."

Jason sputtered, "Unbelievable! The last thing she said was, 'I'll destroy you,' and now she wants me to run away with her? And ... and 'we'd be so good together'? She nearly broke my jaw this morning!" He touched the tender spot that still ached from her punch. "There's no way. I hope I never see her again!" At the same time, however, he had to admit there was some kind of connection he couldn't explain, even though he didn't trust her for a minute.

Rory continued. "Of course it's not that easy, given everything that's happened. So here are my rules. I'm calling from a burner phone. It'll go dead at midnight, and you'll never be able to contact me again. If you want to go with me, call me back right now. I unblocked the number, so it's in your Caller ID. I'll text you instructions. Don't even think about trying to track me down because you think the money belongs to Geraldo's estate and I stole it. You're such a Boy Scout sometimes, but I guess I like that in you."

She paused before adding, "If you come after me, I will turn Alex and the FBI loose on you. She's the director of the LA field office, and she still cares enough to do one last thing for me. I promise, they'll ruin your life.

"I hope I hear from you, but if not, we'll both have to live with the 'what if's.' I know I'll always wonder, and I bet you will, too."

The message ended.

Jason held the receiver to his ear, dumbfounded. The mechanical voice said, "Second new message—1:34 p.m. today."

"One last thing," Rory said cheerily. "Remember you asked me to look through Geraldo's Next of Kin worksheets? The name Sonia Delgado was there. I heard through the family grapevine that Geraldo married her a few years ago in Phoenix, so doesn't that mean she should get half his estate?" She giggled. "Oh, well...."

The message ended. The voice said, "Third new message—1:35 p.m. today."

"This is Rory. I want you to know I did not kill my father."

The message ended. The voice said, "Goodbye."

Jason dropped the receiver into its cradle. Absently, he reached for a pad of sticky notes and wrote *Sonia Delgado-O'Brien—check Maricopa County, AZ vital records*. He stuck the note on the base of his desk lamp, lost in thought. The last message was totally bizarre. Why did she call back to say she didn't kill Geraldo? Did it mean she thought he thought she did? Did it mean she felt guilty because she did?

The list of local suspects caught his eye and he reached across his desk for it. He hadn't considered it since he learned where the injection site was. He hadn't included Rory before because he'd believed her when she said she didn't kill Geraldo. But now? She made her living by giving people Botox and collagen shots, so she had the skill to inject fragile skin like an eyelid. She was at the spec house the night Geraldo died, and she had plenty of motive. He wrote *Rory O'Brien* at the top of the page.

That decision led to another. He'd read that high-tech law enforcement agencies sometimes could trace burner phones. He retrieved her burner number from his desk phone's Caller ID memory, wrote it on another sticky note, and added it to his lamp base.

OK, who else could make such a tricky injection? He drew lines through the next three names: Jamie McDougal, Pedro Rodriguez, and El Carnicero. El Carnicero was evil, and had a $2 million motive, but he'd beat someone to death or slash their throat.

That left Mags Turlock, Tiffany Tedeski, and Danni Tedeski.

Jason inhaled a final lungful of smoke and dropped the butt in his coffee cup. He reached for another cigarette and lit it. Picking up the list, he thought Mags probably gave herself insulin shots twice a day, so she'd have lots of practice with a needle. But injecting the inside of an eyelid would be tricky. He pulled his upper lid and felt its thickness. There wasn't much flesh. It would be easy to punch through, or nick the eyeball. What if Geraldo jerked? That seemed unlikely because he would've been unconscious from smacking his head on the floor when he fell.

Was Mags that skillful? Maybe, maybe not. But she had motive and she was at One Bluffside the night Geraldo died. She had to stay on the list, even though she didn't know the exact site of the injection.

He stood and walked to the table under the front window to look for an ashtray. Finding one, he carried it back to his desk and sat, tapping away the ash. Tiffany was next on the list. He hated to think she could be the one, but she had tons of motive if Geraldo molested her and got her pregnant. She was at the spec house the night he died. Could she have injected his eyelid? She had needle tracks on her arm, so she had some skill with a syringe. As much as he wanted to cross Tiffany off the list, he decided he couldn't.

Finally, there was Danni. She used to be a nurse, so she would know how to inject fragile parts of the body, and the gossip mill said she used heroin. She had reasons galore to kill Geraldo, what with him beating her and screwing Tiffany. She was alone with him at One Bluffside after he passed out. And Mags said her fingerprints were on the hypodermic. "Yeah," he said, "she's definitely on the list."

His office door opened and slammed shut, interrupting his thoughts. The long bookcase blocked his view, so he couldn't see who came in. He reached for his baseball bat and propped it against his desk. The sounds of squishing shoes and jingling metal traveled the length of the bookcase. The squishing stopped. Deputy Hardesty's round face and beady eyes peered around the corner. He rapped his nightstick against a shelf. "Time to pay the piper."

Jason pushed back from his desk and stood, hoisting the bat to his shoulder. "What do you want?"

The deputy took a step forward. Using the end of his nightstick, he slid aside a folder on the corner of Jason's desk, uncovering a pile of papers. His mouth moved as he tried to read upside down. Jason swung the bat hard against the nightstick, knocking it to the floor. "You here to arrest me?"

"Huh? No."

"Am I a suspect?"

"Not officially, yet, but I bet you will be pretty quick."

"Do you have a search warrant?"

"No."

"Then get out of my office."

"Jeez, such hostility. You never heard of community policing?" Jason didn't respond. He reached for a cigarette, searched for his matches, and lit up in a cloud of smoke. "I'm just making my rounds," Hardesty continued, "introducing myself to all the people on my beat, you know, to give the community a good feeling about law enforcement. Thought

I'd start with you. Thought I'd drop by and pick up the information you promised me."

"What information?" Jason said, twisting the bat in his hands.

"Now, Brinkman, you know. What you promised me at the fire scene so's I wouldn't arrest you for arson and felony murder. Everything you know about the O'Brien babe." Without taking his eyes off Jason, he bent down to pick up his nightstick. He slapped it in his palm.

The list of local suspects lay face up in the middle of Jason's desk. He covered it with a legal pad before thumbing through a stack of papers on the far corner. Rory's client intake sheet was near the bottom, and he grabbed it. With bat in hand, he strode up to Hardesty, stopping inches from him. He looked down at the man's greasy, stubbly face. "You're blocking the copy machine. Move."

The deputy reached for the paper. "I'll take the original." Jason hefted the bat. Hardesty stepped aside, closer to the desk.

The machine clicked and whirred, and Jason returned a moment later. He handed Hardesty the copy. "That's everything I know about her."

Hardesty glanced at the sheet. "Driver's license number, cell phone— that's good." He folded the paper and shoved it in his pocket. "OK. That's it for now, but I'm gonna talk to Sepulveda about charges and a arrest warrant. You're not planning to go anywhere, are you?"

"Fuck you."

"Tsk, tsk. You oughta be making nice, 'stead of tryin' to piss me off." He turned toward the front door, stopped. "Hey," he said over his shoulder. "Did you see that little blue Neon out there? My grandma had one just like it."

Jason hefted his bat again. "I didn't notice."

"Really? It's in the spot where you usually park your Porsche."

"So?"

"Well, if you see the owner, tell him the tags expired two years ago. That's Vehicle Code sections 4000 and 4601.5, in case you ain't familiar. I left him little reminders under the windshield wiper."

Jason's desk phone rang. "We're done. Get out of my office." Keeping his eyes on Hardesty, he dropped into his chair and picked up the receiver.

An operator said, "Collect call from Mags Turlock. Will you accept charges?"

He knew a collect call meant she was using the jail's pay phone, so he said, "Yes," to the operator. To Hardesty, he repeated, "Get out of my office."

The fat little cop squished and jingled the length of the bookcase, *thwacking* each section with his nightstick. At the door, he yelled, "*Hasta la vista,* Brinkman. I'll be back." He slammed the door behind him.

CHAPTER 57

The din of televisions and loud male voices came through the receiver. Mags yelled over the noise, "I've gotta talk to you about my bail. I've gotta get out of here!"

"Where are you?"

"In the mess hall with twenty-five low-lifes. I'm losing my mind. You've gotta help me—"

"Look, you've probably got five minutes. You need to tell me where the hypodermic is right now, so I can start negotiating with the DA. That's how I'll get you out of jail."

"Uh-uh. No way. I thought about it while I was eating. That syringe is the only protection I've got. It's my safety net. I'm not telling you, or anyone, 'bout it 'til I figure out the best way to use it. Once I'm out on bail, I'll have all the time I need. I've decided on the assets I'm gonna use to secure the bond. I need you to get the documents and take them to the bondsman."

"But Mags, I can get you out of jail forever if the syringe checks out. This whole nightmare can disappear if you cooperate with the district attorney."

"Maybe, but I don't wanna play that card right now. Here's what I'm thinking: remember the drugs I hid in the closet at One Bluffside? I didn't tell anyone about them 'til the last minute, and then I told you, and you told the DA and got my bail reduced. I'm gonna leverage the hypodermic the same way. I'll choose my own time."

If he'd been sitting with Mags in the jail's interview room, he would've reached across the table, grabbed her by the shoulders, and shaken her until common sense took hold. As it was, he tamped down his frustration. Maybe if he tried a different angle.... "Suit yourself. But I have to say, if you won't tell me, your attorney, where the hypodermic is, I doubt you really have it."

"I've got it. It's in a safe place."

"They searched your house and car and didn't find it. I know the sheriff's team from other cases. They're very thorough."

"I'm not stupid enough to drive around with it. And I never said I hid it in my house."

"Your office?"

"You think I want the cops snooping through my business files? You're crazy."

"OK, so not your office."

Jason regrouped again. "Do you think you're protecting someone by withholding the syringe? We went through all that before. Remember? You decided it wasn't a good idea?"

"I told you, I'll choose my own time! And here's something else you need to remember. Chalmers and you aren't the only ones on my team. I've got the Lord watching over me, and He'll fix anything you two screw up, so I'm not worried. I'm gonna follow my own instincts."

"Sure, whatever. But be sensible. I'll go to the DA tomorrow if you tell me where it is. The cops will retrieve it, and if it checks out, you'll be off the hook. It's just plain stupid to stay in jail. You're jeopardizing yourself and your defense."

"What do you mean, 'if it checks out'?"

"If the cops find Danni's fingerprints on the syringe, or anyone else's, and none of yours. And if it has heroin residue."

Mags was silent.

"Are you there?"

"Shut up. I'm thinking."

A minute later, she said, "How about if you hint to the DA that you've got some, what do you lawyers call it, exculparty evidence, without saying what it is?"

"Look, I've got to deal with the DA's office from a position of strength. Right now, I don't believe you actually have the needle, and I don't feel strong. You've gotta give me something concrete so I don't make a fool of myself and blow your case."

She hesitated again. "I'll tell you this much. It's in the spec house."

"That doesn't help me. The cops searched One Bluffside and didn't find it."

"It's hidden there where no one but me can find it," Mags said, like she was lecturing a child. "I'm the only one who knows about the place where it's hidden."

In a flash, he understood what she wasn't saying. She didn't know that he knew about the crawl space and the stash box. The cops would've searched every inch inside the house, but they wouldn't have known to search under the house because the crawl space door was so well concealed. *She must've hidden it in Geraldo's stash box!*

Before he allowed himself to follow through on that thought, however, he had to settle one last detail. "If the hypodermic has Danni's prints on it, does it have yours also?"

"Damn you! You don't believe I'm innocent, do you? No, you won't find my prints on it. I'm not that stupid."

You may not be stupid, Jason thought, but you may not be innocent, either. He said, "Good enough for now, Mags. I'll go down to the DA's tomorrow morning and start negotiations."

He hung up the receiver. Reaching for his Marlboro pack, he shook out a cigarette. He lit up and leaned back in his chair, blowing smoke at the ceiling. Geraldo was the master of deception, it turned out. The crawl space door was virtually invisible when it was closed. The stash box was buried in the concrete pad under the elevator, so it was hidden when the elevator was down.

Those thoughts took him back to the afternoon he'd spent under One Bluffside with Admiral Bill. He tried to recall every detail as Bill opened the coffin/stash box. There were twelve bundles of marijuana inside arranged in two parallel rows of six each. They covered the bottom of the coffin. He hadn't seen the syringe, so Mags must've hidden it under one of the bundles.

He could go over there right now with a flashlight and latex gloves and check out the stash box more carefully. Move the bundles. Look under them. He pictured himself leaning over the coffin, breathing in the sweet, pungent odor of the weed, lifting up each package.

The vision brought to mind fragments of memories: his dream about GG discovering the buried safe under her burned-out house. Rory insisting Geraldo hid a lot of money before he died. El Carnicero demanding the missing $2 million. Rory describing the floor safe in the basement of her childhood home. Rory saying Geraldo was a creature of habit—that once he figured something out, he didn't like to change it.

These thoughts crystalized into two stunning conclusions: Geraldo duplicated his long-ago floor safe in the bottom of the stash box. It was hidden under the bales of dope. And that's where he hid the $2 million!

Jason stubbed out his cigarette and jumped up. "Gotta go to One Bluffside this minute. Gotta buy a flashlight and some gloves and go look." Grabbing his keys, wallet, and cigarettes, he dashed around the bookcase to the door. He had his hand on the knob when he realized the safe would have a combination. Frustration boiled over. "Goddammit!" he swore out loud. "I'm so close! Think! What do I know about Geraldo that I can use to figure out the combination?"

He slid down the door, sitting on his haunches, and listened to his pulse pound in his ears. "I just said it," he told himself a moment later. "He's a creature of habit. Rory said it and I know it." He stared into the distance without seeing. Maybe Rory was the key. That made sense. Geraldo would want her to be able to get at his money. Her words from yesterday echoed in his ears. "Geraldo told me when I was little, this is the secret code. Keep it safe forever. If you know it when you need it, you'll get the money."

He jumped to his feet and ran back to his desk. Searching his stacks of paper, he saw the list of local suspects was gone. *Damn Hardesty, but I can't worry about it now.* In another pile, he found the paper with the access code and jammed it in his pocket.

His hand was on the doorknob again when his cell phone buzzed with a text message. He glanced at the screen. It was from Erin. "Damn!" he swore, torn between finding the $2 million and needing a sign she really cared. He told himself he'd read her text later, but felt guilty. "Just a quick read," he promised himself, "then I'll go to One Bluffside." He opened her message:

Most wonderful news. Break in 15 min.
Please come so I can tell you in person. I ❤ yu.

The ❤ swelled his own heart and brought his first smile that day. *She does care!* The pounding in his ears stopped and his breathing slowed. Something really good must've happened, and she reached out to him all on her own. Maybe she was ready to make up. Maybe his life would finally start to turn around.

The spec house could wait a half-hour.

CHAPTER 58

A thick blanket of fog had descended over the village while Jason was in his office. Gusts of clammy ocean air stung his face and bare arms as he walked to his car. From his vantage point at the top of Charles Street, he watched the gray cloud settle over treetops, roofs, and buildings until all disappeared. Billows of dark mist blew in from the Pacific, arching across the sky, gathering and thickening, gradually obscuring the sun.

He shuddered in the ghostly half-light. Fear of fog was the hardest of his childhood traumas to control, and now the frightening memories took over. He was six years old, being dragged through the foggy night on Halloween by the big kids from his foster home. He bucked and twisted, struggling against the ropes that tied his hands and feet, straining to rip the blindfold from his eyes. Someone slipped a plastic bag over his head. The boys laughed as he choked and screamed for help. "You gonna die, you little puke," the oldest kid mocked, and they all pinched his arms and legs, like a hundred giant scorpions attacking him.

Still 20 feet from his car, Jason stopped, petrified and shivering. He gulped lungsful of damp air. "I can breathe," he said out loud. "I'm not choking." The images and sensations faded gradually, and many deep breaths later, he was able to force the memory back into its vault. He jogged to the Neon and scrambled inside to safety, yanking the door closed and locking it.

Driving down the hill in the heavy mist, Deputy Hardesty's Day-Glo green ticket envelopes stuck to the windshield. Jason turned on the wipers, flicking them into the street.

His first stop would be Posh to see Erin, then the hardware store for a flashlight and some latex gloves. After that, to the spec house. Finally. The plan had one major snag, however. He dreaded being anywhere near the coast when it was socked in like this. One Bluffside sat on a bluff above the Pacific and would be wrapped in a shroud that was even grayer, thicker, and wetter than the cloud he'd just watched engulf the village. "I've gotta do it now," he told himself, "before someone else finds the safe."

Jason trudged up Posh's back steps and pushed open the kitchen door. Pierre, the cook, looked up in surprise. "J-Man, what you doin' here at this hour?"

"My lady calls," Jason shrugged.

Pierre nodded in man-to-man understanding. "She's in the dining room. Busy night tonight. Lotsa A-list customers."

"I'll wait in the pantry 'til she's free." Pierre raised an eyebrow. "She said it was private."

Leaning against the long countertop in the pantry, Jason stared blankly at the jars and cans crammed into the cupboard in the corner. He drummed his fingers, wishing he could get going.

Erin burst through the door a few minutes later. Even in the harsh fluorescent light, he couldn't help thinking she was beautiful. She hesitated. Their eyes met, and for an instant, he imagined he saw uncertainty. She quickly looked away and turned to close the door. When she faced him again, she was her usual composed and confident self.

"I'm sorry I got tied up in the dining room. Mr. Green's not satisfied with anything tonight, and he's being very touchy-feely."

"Mr. Thirty Percent? Your best customer?"

She nodded, frowning. "A girl's gotta make a living, I guess."

"Yeah, you can't just slap him. Anyway, I'm glad I heard from you." He kept his relief out of his voice.

"Jason," she said solemnly, "I need to talk to you about something."

That didn't sound good. His gut began to clench, but then he remembered she'd just said, "I love you," in her text.

"That's what your message said. What's up?"

She leaned back against the edge of the counter, resting her elbows on the surface behind her. He slid next to her, staring at the opposite wall rather than the silky white fabric of her blouse as it tightened across her breasts. She said, "OK, I've got this all worked out in my head, so don't interrupt me. OK?"

"I won't."

"I've been thinking about the last couple days, and I decided I've been behaving like a ... well, like a not very nice person, so I want to apologize for fighting with you the other morning, and again today. I understand about you not wanting to leave Sea Cliff, and it's selfish of me to try to make you move to LA."

"You don't have to—" he began. She turned, resting her hip against the edge of the counter, and held a finger to his lips. Her eyes traveled to the bruise on his jaw and the red cut below his eye. "Oh my God! What happened to your face? Are you OK?" She touched the cut tenderly.

Another time, Jason would have told her everything that happened that afternoon—Rory attacking and punching him, his confrontation with El Carnicero, his car being repossessed, his house burning down, his fight with his father, his worries about losing his law license and earning a living, Courtney taking his son to New York. He told himself he'd tell her everything soon, when they were alone somewhere private and there was time to explain it all. But right now, he saw his chance to convince her that she had no reason to be jealous of Rory. "I'm embarrassed, but it was that Rory O'Brien. She thought I was lying about Geraldo's assets, and she punched me."

"But that looks like a cut. How did that happen? Now I'm worried about you." Erin cupped his face with both hands.

"She had a little ring on her hand. It's just a scratch, really."

"She's one crazy bitch. I shouldn't ever have doubted you. I'm so sorry."

"Yes, she is."

Erin stretched to kiss the bruise and cut. "That's the other thing. I have to apologize for not believing you when you said you didn't kiss that disgusting woman ... that Rory person. She really upset me, coming on to me, and ... and finding her there with you ...."

"I understand," he said, turning to face her, sliding closer. "You don't have to apologize." He put his arm around her shoulders and squeezed gently. "You said something wonderful happened—"

"Shhh!" she interrupted, pretending to be cross. "You promised to let me tell you my own way."

With a twinkle in her deep-blue eyes, Erin placed her hands on his hips and pushed him flat against the counter. "Let me in here," she whispered, playfully using her knee to scooch his legs apart. Sliding over his thigh, she stood between them. "That's better." She pressed the full length of her body against him and wriggled up on her toes. "Now I can feel you," she murmured. "Oh, yeah, that's nice."

He locked his arms around her back and pulled her tight, savoring the soft warmth of her breasts pressed against him and the heat radiating from her thighs. She leaned back just enough to speak to his face and whispered, "Something wonderful did happen, are you ready for it? Mr. Ivan Earle—he's the owner of the gallery in Big Sur where I consign a lot of my pictures…?"

"I remember him."

She nuzzled his neck. "He emailed me and said he sold three of my photographs to a gallery owner in Laguna Beach."

"That's wonderful, sweetheart! Which ones?"

"And, guess how much?"

The question distracted him from the sensations of her body. His mind cleared enough to think if he said too little, she'd be insulted. If he said too much, she'd be disappointed.

"Umm…."

"Ten thousand dollars! Can you believe it?" She held his face in her hands and bent his head down for a long, passionate kiss.

Any other time, Jason would have relished her soulful kiss and responded in kind. He would have been thrilled for her success. As it was, he struggled to say, "That's really fantastic."

She kissed his neck, murmuring, "I get to keep $6,000 after the commission, so I can pay Shorty's Garage for fixing my car, and …." She kissed him again. "Think of all we can do with $6,000!"

Like pay my bills for a couple of months. The thought popped into his head without warning, causing his body to tense.

Erin kissed his earlobe. "What's the matter?" she whispered. "Don't you like my kisses?"

"You know I do," Jason said, brushing his lips against her temple. He stroked her cheek, twirled a loose hair around his finger, straightened it, and tucked it behind her ear. As much as he wished otherwise, however, his mind returned to the spec house and his troubles. He pushed her back and rested his elbows on the countertop. "Tell me which photographs," he said, trying to focus on the moment.

She stiffened. "Well, OK, if you'd rather talk. No, I don't want to be that way. You're right, we should talk. My break's almost over and I have to be the perfect waitress again." She checked her reflection in the window over the sink and straightened her blouse. Unclasping her hair at the nape of her neck, she gathered it in one hand and secured it with the other.

Satisfied with her appearance, she said, "They were my Big Sur trip-tych that I loved so much, you know, three phases of the moon setting over the ocean, framed by the coastline and clouds and redwoods. You remember them? I worked so hard on them. I … I'm happy someone else thought they were that good, but I feel like I've lost a big part of myself."

"But you can make copies, can't you?"

"No, I can't. Mr. Earle had to promise Mr. Assan, the guy from Laguna, that they're the only ones, otherwise he wouldn't pay so much." Her eyes began to glaze. "I have to destroy the files and all the prints."

"Yeah, I guess you would," Jason said solemnly, taking her hands and pulling her to him. He kissed her teary eyes.

"They're beautiful pictures, Erin. They were my favorites. I got lost in them. But you'll take other photos that are even better. You have so much talent, it takes my breath away." She wiped her eyes carefully with her fingers, trying not to smear her mascara. "You're OK," he said, answering her question before she asked. She forced a smile.

"You know what Mr. Assan told Mr. Earle?" she said with a burst of enthusiasm a moment later. "He's going to come back next year, and if he likes my new photographs, he wants to take some on consignment to display in his galleries! He told Mr. Earle to tell me—wait, he put it in his email, it's here on my phone, I have to read it to you:

"'Tell Ms. Jones that her *milieu* informs her work brilliantly at present. However, I believe she has Weston- or Adams-like potential, and that to achieve it, she must subsume her artistic subconscious into her environment and ascend through ever higher planes of visualization, until it transcends the limitations of her physicality and merges with her spiritual vision. *That* is the vision which she must ultimately capture and express in her medium, and which, I am certain, will elevate her to the stature I am confident she can achieve."

He thought it sounded like a load of pretentious bullshit, but he said, "What does it mean?"

"It means I can stay here in Sea Cliff with you! We don't have to move to Los Angeles now. I've got it all figured out. I can take my photographs in Big Sur and wait tables, and we can live here, and we'll both work real hard and save our money. I'll get established with Mr. Assan. I Googled him, and he's got galleries in Newport and the other rich cities on the coast near LA. He'll be my entrée to the LA arts scene—you know, other galleries, and critics, and maybe even movie people. In fact, Mr. Earle told me Mr. Assan said my *milieu* is my *cachet* as I build a name. So we have to stay here for a while. Then, in a couple of years, we can move to LA, and I can support you if you need help while you're building your practice."

She beamed at him. Happiness danced in her eyes and she smiled from ear to ear. But he couldn't begin to match her enthusiasm. How could he tell her that he was broke and had no place to live? That he was about to lose his law license and would only drag her down?

For the first time, he saw his future if he stayed in the village—the *Sea Cliff Crier* running a front-page story about him being disbarred: "Local Track and Baseball Star Stripped of Law License" or "Brinkman Guilty of Fraud." Mandi Jo and the gossip queens digging up every bit of dirt and making up even more. Endless speculation on social media about his affair with the mystery woman he was seen kissing at Mostly's. His reputation would be ruined. Everyone would think he'd done something wrong or he was a sleaze. He'd never be able to make a living in Sea Cliff. His only option was to start over in LA.

He tried to hide the worry he knew showed on his face.

"Isn't that the most wonderful plan?" Erin asked, a slight edge creeping into her voice. "Isn't that what you wanted, to stay here and for us to be together?"

Jason searched for something to say that wouldn't bring her down, but that wouldn't be a lie. He rehearsed in his head how he'd begin: *Sweetheart, some things have happened today—*

The pantry door slammed open. Randy, the evening *maître d'*, shouted, "Erin, what the fuck are you doing? Table six wants their check right now. That's Mr. and Mrs. Green, in case you've forgotten." Glaring at Jason, he demanded, "Why are you in my pantry?" Without waiting for an answer, he barked at Erin, "Those are goddamned A-plus customers, girly. Three-hundred-dollar tab tonight. You don't piss them off. And you let him pat your ass or hold your hand if he wants." He stood in the doorway, holding it open for her.

"Alright, Randy, I'm on it. Don't have a stroke." Turning to Jason, she said, "I'll come over tonight." Again he caught a flash of uncertainty in her eyes, heard a hint of a question.

He started to say, "You can't, because I don't have a house anymore," but he checked himself. He dug deep for a smile and said, "Wonderful, sweetheart, but wait 'til I call you later."

Erin squeezed his hand before following Randy into the kitchen. The door swung closed behind her, leaving Jason alone in the pantry. "Well, OK then," he said to himself. "I guess it's finally time to go look for the treasure."

PART 6

END GAME

CHAPTER 59

In the darkest corner of Mostly's saloon, Danni and El Carnicero sat hunched over a table littered with empty shot glasses and beer schooners. An empty Cuervo Black bottle lay on its side in the center. Next to it, an ashtray overflowed with cigarette butts and burned-out matches.

Danni lit the filter end of a cigarette. "Shit!" she swore, jamming the blue flame into the ashtray. "Gimme 'nother."

"*No mas*," El Carnicero mumbled, shaking his head. He crumpled the empty pack.

"'S'OK. No worries." She stood. "I gotta pee, then we go ta the spec house. 'S dark an' foggy 'nough now. We get our tools an' tear it apart 'til we find the money." She stumbled down the hall, a stocky figure silhouetted by a dim bulb at the end of the corridor.

"*Dos millones de dólares!*" El Carnicero yelled at her back. "Two million *Yanqui* dollars!" He made a fist with his good hand and slammed the tabletop. The shot glasses jumped. Two crashed to the floor. "Barman!" he shouted. "*La cuenta!*" He patted his pockets and emptied them until he found his wad of bills.

Mostly walked cautiously to the table, carrying a tray and the check. El Carnicero waved at him. "*Ey estúpido! La cuenta!*"

Mostly slid the check in front of El Carnicero and began setting the glasses on his tray. Without looking at the total, El Carnicero shoved three hundred-dollar bills at him. "*Toma*," he grumbled. "Keep it."

"You want I should call you a cab?" Mostly asked, slipping the bills into his apron pocket. El Carnicero pulled himself to his feet unsteadily. He grabbed Mostly by his shirt collar with his good hand. "No taxi!" he growled, shaking his head. "*Motocicleta!*" He made *vroom, vroom* noises and twisted his right fist like it was on the throttle.

Danni staggered back to the two men. "Leave him 'lone, Guillermo. He my good frien." She draped her arm around Mostly's shoulders.

Mostly pried El Carnicero's fingers loose. "Let me get someone to drive you, Danni. You're both drunker'n pissants, and it's really foggy."

"Wha's a pissant?" Danni slurred. "I never know'd. People always say that."

"Danni," Mostly said. "Seriously. You need an Uber or a cab."

"No need, my frien'. We ride the Harley. We fly like the wind...."

"You sure?"

"Yeah, Mos'ly. You bin good frien'. Don' you worry none, 'cause I'll always 'member my friens. Guillermo an' me, we gonna get our tools now. We gonna be rich!"

* * *

The fog grew thicker and thicker on Del Mar Road as Jason got closer to the ocean. At Driftwood Lane, it was so dense he had to stick his head out the window as he crept toward Bluffside and the spec house. He turned right on Sunset, the street before Bluffside. Coasting to the middle of the block, he parked the Neon half on the sidewalk so it wouldn't get hit.

He cut the ignition and stubbed out his cigarette. Only two were left when he shook the pack for another. He decided to save them for when he was finished. Before leaving the warm interior, he switched on his new Sup-R-Brite LED Mini Flashlight and pointed it out the windshield. A white reflector on a mailbox 20 feet away glowed faintly in the beam. Satisfied, he slipped the flashlight into his pocket along with two latex gloves. His phone buzzed as he reached for the door handle.

Thankful for an excuse to stay out of the fog for a minute, he checked the screen. It was an email from Howie Simon with the subject *JASON READ THIS*. He debated reading it now or back at the office, but a few more moments of warmth won out. He opened the message:

Jason—This all happened this afternoon after I talked to you. I can't believe it. Gretchen vomited blood all over the conference table during our meeting and collapsed. Someone called 911, and the paramedics came and took her to USC Hospital. So the rumor about her having some kind of really bad cancer was true. But now, get this. The Executive Committee knew about her condition and had already agreed on a plan for when she became incapacitated. They met by Zoom late this afternoon and ratified the plan. Courtney is at the airport right now on her way to New York and her new position as senior managing partner. She had to be part of the planning for her to move so fast. Here's how this affects you. She and Gretchen filed their complaint with the State Bar, so Gretchen is after you even on her deathbed. Courtney got an Extraordinary Emergency Ex Parte Order for Custody from the Family Court, based on her urgent need to leave for NYC, your financial situation, and your refusal to cooperate in the divorce proceeding. She's taking Jason Jr. with her. She must've whupped a lot of court clerks with Whatley's big stick to get an order like that so fast. Technically it's only temporary custody, but this kind of order is hard to overturn once custody is awarded to a parent and the child is taken out of state. All of this information is from my trusted sources in the firm. I'm sorry, my friend. You sure can't catch a break.

—Howie

Jason stuck his phone into his pants pocket. He shook out one of the remaining cigarettes and lit it. "I guess that's it, then," he said to himself. "I've lost my son, at least 'til I have enough money to fight for him." He imagined a bicoastal custody battle that dragged on for years. Courtney would hire the best psychologists money could buy to prove that it was in Jason Jr.'s best interest for her to have sole custody. There'd be countless bare-knuckle court hearings, like those when his own parents divorced. Jason would struggle to keep up, but Courtney's money and prestige ultimately would prevail. Even if he did gain custody, he suspected Jason Jr. wouldn't want to leave the new home and life he'd become accustomed to.

Enveloped in darkness, Jason smoked his cigarette, fighting the tears for his son that would unleash all the tears he hadn't cried since he was a child. Those emotions gave way to fury at Courtney for this final betrayal and at himself for not being able to prevent it. When the cigarette burned down to the filter, he stubbed it out in the ashtray and made himself focus on the task at hand. He opened the car door and stepped onto the sidewalk.

The mist wrapped around him like a wet blanket, raising goose bumps on his bare arms. The heavy air caught at the back of his throat, choking him. Coughing and gasping, he struggled to take normal breaths, fighting the panic of the night years ago when the big foster kids pulled the plastic bag over his head and he thought he'd die. "Dammit!" he scolded himself. "Get a grip and do what you came here to do." He walked quickly to Driftwood and crossed it.

The spec house was nearly invisible in the mist. With a glance over his shoulder, he ducked under the crime scene tape, jogged across the back yard, and crouched at the rear corner of the house. Ironically, now he was grateful for the fog because it concealed him. The crawl space had to be his secret until he found the hypodermic and floor safe—or didn't.

The access door was near the center of the back wall, camouflaged by the shingle siding. He paced about fifteen steps along the wall until he judged he was near the middle. He squatted and duck-walked back and forth, pressing his palms against the shingles, searching for the pressure point to release the touch latch. Grunting from the exertion and shivering in the cold dampness, he worked his way farther from the center in each direction, pressing as many shingles as he could each time. After five minutes without success, he stood to catch his breath.

The mist grew colder, and he began to sweat despite the chill. He was about to give up and use the flashlight when his hand touched a shingle that was smooth, unlike the others. It had to be the one. It would stand out just enough in the daylight, if someone knew to look for it.

He pressed the shingle. Nothing happened. "Come on, come on," he mumbled, pressing it again, harder. The lock clicked this time and the door popped open an inch. He pulled it, and it swung away from the building on its articulated hinge. Slipping through the small opening, he closed the door behind him, stopping just before it latched.

The crawl space was pitch black and smelled of fresh dirt and raw lumber. The air was drier than outside, but just as cold. He waited for his eyes to adjust to the darkness. Now that he was concealed, he decided it was OK to use the flashlight to get his bearings. Sitting on his haunches, he switched on the light.

The blue-white beam flickered. He had to press the button several times before it shined brightly, illuminating the front foundation wall, about 40 feet from him. In the center of the space, about 20 feet away, was the cement pad that anchored the elevator assembly. In the center of the cement was Geraldo's stash box—the child-sized coffin buried up to its hinges.

His thighs and forearms ached by the time he crawled to the pad, and his nose was caked with fine particles of dirt. He propped the light against one of the elevator support girders. Looking at the two compression locks set in the casket's lid, he thought Mags's fate would be more clear in a couple of minutes.

He moved around the coffin to its hinge side, worked his hands into the latex gloves, and flipped the locks' loop handles upright. Unscrewing the locks, he strained to open the lid, but the suction of the hermetic seal was too great. He pulled the handles with all the strength of his back, shoulders, and arms. The top lifted a little, then a little more. Bearing down and grunting, the seal began to give way. With a cry of pain, he yanked one last time. The seal broke with a *thwucking* sound. The lid opened so fast, it caught him off guard. It hit the concrete with a metallic crash. He fell on his butt and rolled backward, nearly smacking his head.

Lying on the cold cement in the dim light, he worried someone might've heard the loud noise. "That's ridiculous," he muttered. "There's no one around to hear it." But as he dragged himself upright, heavy footsteps pounded across the floor above.

The hairs on the back of his neck stood. He held his breath, waiting for another noise, but heard nothing. After a few minutes, he decided he'd imagined the footsteps. He crawled around to the front of the casket and retrieved his flashlight. Wiping the metal tube on his pants, he stuck it in his mouth and checked his gloves to be sure they hadn't ripped.

The inside of the coffin was just as he remembered when Admiral Bill showed it to him a lifetime ago. The eleven remaining bread-loaf-sized bundles of marijuana were lined in two rows that ran the length of the box—five in the first row, closest to him, and six in the second row, closest to the hinge side.

Jason shined his beam into the casket. None of the bales looked like they'd been touched. The hypodermic had to be under one of them, so he had to be careful not to leave any clue they'd been moved. He picked up the bale in position number 2 in the first row, being sure not to drag it against the front wall of the box or the bundles around it. He looked under it. Nothing. Replacing it cautiously in its exact spot, he picked up bale number 3. Again, nothing. He put it back.

Working his way down the length of the row, he began to wonder whether he'd misinterpreted Mags. "No," he told himself. "This is the only logical place she could've hidden it."

It was finicky work, replacing each bundle so precisely it didn't appear to have been disturbed. Finally, he reached bale number 6 at the end of the first row. He lifted it carefully. Something filmy appeared to be wedged into the corner of the stash box. He shined his light on the object and leaned over it, so his head was level with the concrete. Still, it took him a moment to figure out what it was. "Son of a bitch!" he said triumphantly. "It's the syringe wrapped in a baggie. I'll go talk to the DA tomorrow, but this is a huge development, and Chalmers needs to know about it."

Sitting upright, he pulled out his phone and thumbed a text to Charles Chalmers:

Tip from reliable source. Syringe used to kill O'Brien hidden in crawl space under One Bluffside Drive, Sea Cliff, in stash box under elevator. Source says it exonerates Mags Turlock.

He pressed *Send* and replaced bundle number 6 exactly as it had been.

"One mystery solved," he said to himself. "Now, is the floor safe hidden under the other row?"

On the verge of a discovery that could change his life, questions he couldn't answer popped into his head. What if the safe was there and was full of diamonds or Krugerrands? What would he do? Keep it and be a crook like his father? Tell Rory because she's Geraldo's daughter? Turn it over to the court for the estate?

If I did keep it, it would solve my problems for a long time. But that would be wrong.

Tense with anticipation, he picked up bale number 7 and shined his light on the bottom of the coffin. Nothing. He put it back and picked up bale number 8. Again, nothing. "Come on, Geraldo, I know you too well. This is where it has to be." He used both hands to lift out bales 9 and 10. The floor was bare. "Dammit, Geraldo, come on!" His pulse raced. He picked up bales 11 and 12 at the same time.

The metal bottom gleamed in the blue-white beam, mocking him. "How can it not be here?" he raged. "It has to be! I had it all figured out. I was so sure!"

Admiral Bill once taught him a litany of sailors' obscenities. Jason repeated it over and over and added some of his own as he carefully replaced the two bales. He closed the lid and screwed the compression locks tight, flattening the handles against the lid, just as they had been.

He turned around and started crawling back to the access door. Halfway there, a heavy object clattered against the floor directly above his head. He stopped, held his breath, strained to hear. Focusing all his senses, he made out muffled voices, but no words. He heard what sounded like a grunt, followed by a thud—like a heavy soft object hitting the floor. Another thud followed, and the voices again. *Someone's on the first floor in the foyer.*

The flashlight quit without warning, leaving him in blackness. Crouched on his hands and knees in the cold space, he struggled to put the pieces together.

Who was up there? No one would cross the crime-scene tape except the cops, and they'd wait until daylight if they were going to search again. "No," he reasoned out loud, "it's gotta be someone who thinks Geraldo's money's hidden in the spec house, and they're looking for it. I've got to get up there. Right now!"

He began crawling rapidly through the dark. "Goddammit," he swore through clenched teeth, "the money's not theirs to find!"

CHAPTER 60

Danni and El Carnicero staggered around the foyer of the spec house, tearing out drywall, searching for Geraldo's missing drug money.

Despite being blind drunk and high on heroin and oxycontin, they fell into a routine. El Carnicero would smash a hole in the sheetrock with his short-handled sledgehammer. Danni would stick the claw head of her wrecking bar into the hole. El Carnicero would grip the jagged edge with his good hand. With a grunt, they'd jerk backward. The wallboard would make a ripping sound as it pulled away from the studs. They'd each grab a corner of the piece and heave it to the center of the foyer, where it would land with a thud, releasing a cloud of white plaster dust.

Next, they'd yank the sheets of insulation—usually white or yellow, sometimes gray or orange—from the stud bays. Finding nothing, they'd move on and repeat the process. The sounds of their labors became rhythmic. *Smash, grunt, jerk, rip, thud. Smash, jerk, rip, thud.* The travertine floor was covered with big and small chunks of drywall, dust, insulation, screws, and nails. Fine white powder clung to everything—the two of them, the debris, the staircase, the walls, and the elevator door.

"The money's here somewhere. Geraldo wouldn' of hid it at my house," Danni explained. She thought she might've said it before, but decided to repeat it to reassure Guillermo. And herself. "Tha's 'cause Geraldo knows Danni's one nosy bitch an' she gonna find it. He can't even hide his dope, 'cause I know all his li'l secret places an' I smoke it, or shoot it, or snort it, an' does he get pissed, 'cause there ain't none lef' fer him. I do it jus' ta piss him off, even if I don' wannit."

El Carnicero swung his mini-sledge against another section of wallboard, hitting a stud. The house shook from the force of the blow.

"Hey, dude," Danni laughed, "don' go knockin' the fuckin' house down 'til we get the money." He moved a few inches to the right and struck again, smashing through the surface. *CLAAANNG!* The hammer struck metal. The entire wall reverberated, rumbling like thunder.

"Guillermo! Ya dumb fuck, whaddja do now!" Danni bent her eye to the hole. "Shit. Can't see nothin' through my hair." She swept her silvery-white hair away from her eyes and flipped it over her shoulders. "Tha's better. Go turn on them lights," she said, pointing behind her at the panel of eight switches next to the front door. Guillermo flipped them all, and the foyer lit up brighter than day.

Danni said, "Gimme hand." They tore away the sheetrock. "Ya hit a copper water line, ya big dumb shit! Lookit that. See tha' big dent in th' metal? Lucky ya din't break it." They tossed the drywall to the center of the room and pulled the insulation out of the bay.

"*Nada!*" El Carnicero spat with disgust. He wiped the back of his hand across his dusty white forehead, exposing a streak of dark skin. Danni grabbed his elbow and tried to turn him to face her. He jerked his arm free. "Let go, woman."

"Ya lissen ta me. It's here. We just gotta find it." She motioned for him to smash more wallboard. "Geraldo tol' me one time 'bout a dealer buddy a' his," she continued while El Carnicero rammed his sledge into the next sections of sheetrock. "Th' guy goes an' stashes half-a-million bucks in th' stud bays a th' house he's buildin'. Five thousan' Franklins wrapped in plastic an' cover'd with drywall! Geraldo says th' guy's a genius an' it's th' smartes' thing he ever heard of. Thas' why I know it's here."

"*Lo dudo,*" El Carnicero growled. "That means nothing." He yanked on the drywall he'd just smashed. The entire 4x8 sheet crashed to the floor. He pulled the piece next to it, and it also crashed without breaking, exposing the stud bays from floor to ceiling.

A cloud of dust filled the air before settling on them. Danni coughed and covered her eyes until the air cleared. When she opened them, she gasped. "Ohmygod, I don' b'lieve it." She staggered over the pile of sheetrock and stared at the space between the studs. "It's all ... all ... pink!"

Eight square feet of pink insulation filled the stud bays, shining iridescently in the harsh light of the ceiling fixtures. Danni ran her palm up and down the fuzzy surface. "Oh, my sweet baby," she whispered. She pulled a sheet free and dug her hands deep into it. "Pink's her fav'rite color, Guillermo."

"*Que?*"

"Tiffany, ya dumb fuck. My baby girl." Danni clutched the puffy pink blanket to her chest and sank to her knees. "My darlin' li'l girl," she sobbed. "My darlin' dead li'l girl. She made me an' Tommy paint her room pink, back when we was married. We got her a Barbie in a pink box fer Christmas. She loves tha' doll. An' you know what?" Danni looked up at El Carnicero. Tears rolled down her cheeks, carving streaks of bare skin in the plaster dust. "She kep' that box ever since. Hid her treasures in it, even now."

El Carnicero waved his hand impatiently. All he said was, "*Agua.*" He pointed to the second floor and the kitchen.

"Goddamn you, Guillermo. You gonna lissen ta me. I got no earthly person ta talk to now Geraldo an' my baby are dead."

The big man hocked a wad of white phlegm into the pile of debris. He stomped through it, across the foyer to the elevator, and jabbed the button with his finger. The elevator creaked and groaned in its shaft, grinding to a stop without opening the door. "*Estúpido!*" He banged the button with his fist. The door screeched open halfway, exposing a 6-inch gap between the elevator's threshold and the foyer's floor.

"You go 'head an' get in it, shithead, an' git stuck 'tween floors, then you havta lissen ta me. HA! Tha's rich. A big dumb Mesican trapped in a cheapo el'vator made in Chink-land. Geraldo'd laugh his ass off."

El Carnicero swore in Spanish. He punched the door with his good hand. It squeaked closed, rattling in its track. He glared at Danni as he lumbered across the room to the staircase. "*Vaca fea,*" he growled over his shoulder as he climbed the stairs.

"*Chinga tu madre!*" she yelled at his back. "*Pinche chingon!*" Alone in the devastated room, Danni kneeled on the pile of drywall, clutching the pink insulation to her work shirt and jeans. "My baby," she moaned.

"You was so li'l, an' now yer gone. I know I ain't the best mother. Can't be helped really, 'cause I got all kinds a drugs an' shit in me, messin' up my head, makin' me forget shit, ya know. But I never forgot nothin' 'portant, like yer birthday, or pickin' ya up at school, did I? I did? Uh-uh. No way. Couldn' of. Ya tell me when."

Danni folded the insulation in half, cradling the rounded end in her arms. "You got such pretty hair," she said, stroking the curved pink surface. "Ya use ta love me brushin' it. I did try so hard, ya know. Ain't easy bein' a single mom on welfare, an' when Geraldo come along, he was s'posed ta take care of us. An' he did, but I let down my guard. I let him give ya a lollipop an' he stole yer cherry."

She squeezed the insulation with both hands, choking the life out of it. "Ya hurt me so bad, ya li'l bitch, ballin' him the way ya was. Ya think I din't know? Tha' I couldn' tell? Made me crazy. Coulda killed ya both, but I goes an' gets blind drunk 'stead, an' forgets 'bout you an' him, an' his li'l baby inside you."

Danni wept and wept, washing the plaster dust from her cheeks. "My precious li'l girl with her own bastard half-breed baby inside a her," she wailed. She cradled the pink blanket in her arms and sat cross-legged on the pile of sheetrock, gasping with sobs. Rocking back and forth, she moaned her dead daughter's name over and over. After a while, she collapsed on her side on top of the pile.

* * *

Like all the residents of Bluffside Drive, Mrs. Dottie Richardson was fascinated by the big gray house at the south end of the street because it had a connection to The Storm Drain Murder. So fascinated, in fact, she'd offered to babysit Harry and Meghan, her neighbors' English bulldogs, just so she'd have an excuse to walk past the house twice a day.

Unfortunately, Harry was proving to be very stubborn, and was downright obstinate this evening. He insisted on stopping to smell every bush, street lamp, garbage can, fire hydrant, and car tire on Bluffside— sometimes requiring return visits to reexamine them.

Mrs. Richardson shivered in the cold and damp, alternately coaxing and scolding Harry to resume walking so he could finish doing his business. Their goal, the corner of Bluffside and Driftwood, would take all evening at this pace, and she'd resigned herself to missing both her beloved *Jeopardy* and *The Insider*.

"Come along now, Harry, dear. Don't make me lie about what a good dog you've been when your masters get home." She yanked on Harry's leash, and they continued in fits and starts down Bluffside toward Driftwood. The dog snorted and rambled a few more steps before stopping. "Come on, will you?" Mrs. Richardson scolded. She pulled on the leash, but the dog sat and barked. "No treat! Just go to the bathroom so we can go home and get warm! You're being rude, you know that? You're just a...just a self-centered, spoiled, rude animal!"

Harry winced as if he'd been slapped. With a grunt, he shambled to his feet, taking the slack of the leash in his mouth and tugging on it.

They walked quickly now. "Young people are rude today, too," Dottie said as they finally neared Driftwood. "Like that young reporter, that Ally Booker, who promised me I'd be on television but never came to interview me." Hot blood rushed to Dottie's cheeks. She walked even faster, jerking the leash. "I'm the one who saw the body being dumped into the storm drain. Do you know that? No one else saw it, so why didn't she keep her promise and put me on TV? I had my hair done even though it wasn't my day! I told everyone in Mah Jongg that I was going to be on television! Now they all think I'm losing my marbles. Or even worse—that I'm a liar!"

Mrs. Richardson was so agitated by the time they reached the corner of Bluffside and Driftwood that what she saw didn't register at first. "That's not right," she muttered a moment later. She stared through the fog at One Bluffside. "See that, Harry? Those windows are always dark, but now the first floor's all lit up and the yellow tape's been torn down. It looks like the front door's open a crack. See the light along the edge? There's something wrong here. I'd better call the police, don't you think?"

Harry barked in agreement. Dottie fumbled in her coat pocket for her phone. With trembling fingers, she punched 9-1-1.

* * *

The heavy footsteps, thuds, and pounding hadn't made sense at first, but now Jason understood. Whoever was up there thought Geraldo hid the money in the house when he built it, and they were tearing it apart. Shaking his flashlight, he pushed the switch until it came on. He hurried through the dirt on all fours, ducking under water lines and heat ducts, and brushing cobwebs from his face every few steps.

It seemed to take an hour to reach the access door, and when he did, it was closed tight. *How the fuck did that happen?* He was sure he'd left it ajar. A deer could have bumped it, he supposed, or a raccoon, or the wind, but it didn't matter. He had to figure out how to open the touch latch from the inside.

He shined his flashlight on the lock mechanism, searching for a release button. There wasn't one. Claustrophobia wrapped its brawny arms around him and squeezed the air out of his chest. *NO! I'm not going to panic. I can get out of here. I just have to figure it out.*

He shoved the door, but it didn't move. Thinking the latch was designed to open when it was pushed from the outside, he tried pulling. The mechanism clicked, but didn't release. He remembered he had to push twice to get it to open, and really hard the second time. Planting his feet against the foundation, he grabbed the door's wooden structure with both hands and pulled with all his strength. It swung inward a fraction of an inch, creaking against its wooden frame. Just as he was about to give up, the mechanism clicked and the door opened. He blew out a sigh of relief and stooped through the opening.

Pressing himself against the back wall of the house, he worked his way around the side and then to the front. He crouched behind the bushes below the foyer's windows and popped his head up just long enough to peek inside quickly.

The bright lights in the foyer blinded him for a moment. When his eyes adjusted, he made out the elevator and the curved staircase on the far side of the room. The door to the garage was tucked behind and under the stairs. He ducked down again. Something was wrong with the wall on the right. He lifted his head up again. *What the hell?* The sheetrock was gone. It was all studs and insulation.

Jason crouched on his heels, thinking whoever was inside must believe the money was hidden in the walls. But they'd stopped working. His stomach twisted. That must mean they'd found it! He forced himself to be calm. Maybe not, he thought. Maybe they were taking a break or had moved on to another room. They could've given up. Maybe they left while he was crawling around to the front of the house.

It was so quiet in the foyer that he risked standing to get a better look. In the middle of the room was a pile of broken wallboard. There was something on the pile. It looked like a…. He pressed his forehead against the glass. *It is! It's a body!*

His heart leapt to his throat. He couldn't see the body's face because its back was to him, but he recognized the long silvery-white hair, baggy work shirt, carpenter's jeans, and heavy boots. *Geraldo?!?!* "It can't be!" he said to himself, struggling to explain what his eyes told him. "Geraldo's dead! I saw him hanging over the storm drain." He shivered, chilled to the bone by the apparition. "His corpse can't just materialize out of nowhere."

Jason's heart beat so fast he feared he'd pass out. His lungs refused to take in air. "It's not Geraldo, it's not Geraldo," he repeated out loud. "A dead body cannot reappear." Sinking back to his knees, he forced himself to inhale and exhale slowly to calm his jagged nerves. He knew that whoever was tearing up the house could still be inside, but he also knew there was only one thing to do: *I havta go in to see who's lying there, see if they need help.*

* * *

Deputy Hardesty jerked awake the instant the dispatcher's voice barked from his radio. He was disoriented, but only for a moment. He was parked at Vista Point because it was where kids came to make out on foggy nights, and he was going to bust one for indecent exposure.

Arresting men for indecent exposure was Duane's passion as a representative of The Law. And if he collared a flasher tonight, it would be a bonus point on his sergeant's exam.

He'd decided long ago that when he became sergeant, he'd assign his squad to scour the county to eliminate every kind of prevert, especially flashers. "Our mission is to cleanse this county of scum," he'd instruct his team at their pre-shift briefing. "Stop and question any adult male who's wearing a trench coat when it's not raining."

The dispatcher's call was especially annoying right now because Duane finally was on his righteous mission—one he'd been distracted from for too long. He debated ignoring the call because it merely requested unspecified assistance. On the other hand, he thought, taking it might lead to something worth more points than arresting a horny teenager.

He went back and forth while the radio squawked.

The possibility of arresting a real criminal who was committing a real crime finally won out. He decided to grab it before one of his competitors did and picked up his microphone.

CHAPTER 61

When Jason trusted his legs to carry him, he climbed the front steps and pushed open the door. He stepped in and leaned back against the door, pushing it until the latch clicked.

The bright lights forced him to shut his eyes so they could adjust. Thirty seconds later, he walked into the foyer and stopped a few feet from the body. Instinct told him to look for breathing, but he couldn't tell because of the bulky shirt. He circled the body so he could see the front. Its arms clutched a sheet of pink insulation, and another sheet lay in front of it. The face was obscured by the silvery hair. Crouching on his knees and fighting back waves of nausea, he brushed aside the hair. The skin was warm beneath his fingers. *A corpse is supposed to be cold.*

The face he saw was another shock. "Danni? What in the hell…?" He put his hand on her shoulder and felt her heat through the fabric. He shook her. "Danni, Danni, wake up. Do you need a doctor?"

She opened her eyes and stared at him blankly. He kneeled beside her on the pile of broken sheetrock, rubbing her shoulder. Her eyes became focused, and he saw signs of recognition.

"Brinkman?" she slurred. "Wha'…ya…doin' here?"

Looking for the money, Jason thought, same as you. Instead, he said, "Do you need help?"

"Hep? From you?" She pushed herself up on her elbow and seemed to consider the question. "Yeah, mebbe you can." She lay on her side, propped on her elbow. Her face was a mask of bloodshot eyes, caved-in nose, grainy skin, and sunken cheeks. She reeked of stale alcohol. Her lips twitched fitfully, baring yellow teeth.

Jason stared at her, trying to guess what was going on in her mind. She was beyond creepy, and he was uncomfortable being anywhere near her, but one thought kept him planted where he was: Did she know anything useful about Geraldo's money?

She appeared to drift in and out of consciousness for several minutes. He watched her, thinking she must believe the money was hidden behind the sheetrock. If it was cash, $2 million would be 20,000 hundred-dollar bills. That was hard to imagine, but not impossible. If it was something small, like CD receipts, or stored-value cards, or bags of diamonds, or even Krugerrands, it certainly could be hidden in the walls.

Finally struggling upright, Danni sat cross-legged, coughing and wiping strands of silvery hair from her face. She hacked loudly and spat a wad of phlegm on the floor. After taking a couple of breaths, she squeezed her nostrils, alternately blowing them onto a piece of wallboard. "Tha's better," she croaked, wiping her nose and mouth with her sleeve. "I hate breathin' tha' shit." She clambered to her knees and carefully arranged the sheet of insulation she'd been clutching on top of the one in front of her. "Got a Kleenex?" she asked, staring down at the fuzzy pink surface and running her hand back and forth over it.

"Uh-uh."

"Thought I had me one somewhere," she mumbled, picking up the edge of the insulation and searching under it. "Guess not." Her bloodshot eyes wandered to Jason's thighs and chest before reaching his face. She studied it as she stroked the pink surface. Her dazed expression faded and she seemed to reach a decision. "Yeah, Brinkman," she said in a voice that was unnaturally calm. Her eyes, drowsy just a moment ago, bore into him. She jutted out her jaw defiantly. "I do b'lieve ya can hep me."

"OK. Do you need a doctor? Are you alright?"

Danni gathered her legs under her. She rested her hands on the edge of the insulation.

"Is there anyone else here who could help?" he asked.

"Ain't no one here."

Jason knew he'd heard voices when he was in the crawl space, but figured she was so high, she could've been talking to herself. "You sure?"

"'Course I'm sure. You doubt me, go look fer yerself."

"Can I call someone for you?"

"Uh-uh. Got no one ta call. It's just Danni these days. Anyway, tha's not the kinda hep I need."

"What then?"

"Yer Geraldo's lawyer, the man tha' knows all his secrets."

"Hardly. I just kept him out of trouble."

Danni snorted. "Now, why don' I b'lieve that. Tell ya wha' I think. I think he must've tol' ya."

Jason barely knew Danni, other than by what the gossip mill said about her. Most important right now, the regulars at Mostly's said she punched out men she doesn't like, and Geraldo told him she'd attack him with a butcher knife when she was drunk. Jason pushed back a couple of feet and squatted on his toes, ready to move quickly if he had to. Looking over Danni's shoulder, he guessed he was at least 20 feet from the door. "What do you think Geraldo told me?"

"Where his money's at."

"Funny, that's what I want to ask you. I don't even know if it exists, but you obviously do."

Danni slid her hands under the edge of the insulation. "Oh, it's real. Uh-huh. Danni knows it's real."

Having had two violent drunks as parents, Jason recognized the menace in Danni's voice. He sensed he had seconds to decide whether to risk staying to pump her about the money or dash to the door. The sound of a toilet flushing upstairs made his decision for him. *There is someone else here. It must be El Crazy! Time to go!*

"Whatever you say," he said calmly. "You can have anything you find." He stood up in slow motion, hoping not to spook her.

The next few seconds were a blur. Danni reached under the insulation and grabbed a wrecking bar. She sprang to her feet, shaking the claw end in his face. "You an' yer LA clothes an' fancy car an' yer clever lawyer ways. You heped him scam it an' tol' him how ta hide it."

Jason had to back away, farther from the door. "Danni! Calm down! I don't know where he hid it."

"You jus' wan' it for yerself. He stole it from Guillermo, an' now you wanna steal it from him." She swung the wrecking bar at Jason's head. "It's Danni's!" she screamed.

Jason ducked, but felt the breeze of the blow. "For Chrissake! He didn't tell me."

"Yes he did. He tol' ya everything. You two was buddy-buddy." She crept forward, bent at the knees, shifting her weapon from one hand to the other. "He tol' ya he was fuckin' my baby girl. Ya had a good laugh 'cause ya wan'd it, too, some sweet young pussy. He tol' ya he knocked her up." She jabbed the claw at his stomach. "Ya think I din't know?"

Jason glanced over his shoulder and saw he was about to hit the wall behind him. He began circling backward, edging toward the front door. He stepped onto the pile of sheetrock. The broken pieces shifted beneath his feet, rocking his balance.

Danni stalked him, wrecking bar shoulder high, ready to swing. She stepped onto the pile. "Here's what'cha don' know, pretty boy." With a grunt, she swung at his chest. "I kill't Geraldo. I shot his brain fulla pure heroin."

Jason jumped back to avoid the claw, stumbling on the uneven surface. The sharp edge caught his shirt, ripping it to his navel.

Danni grinned at Jason's exposed flesh and the thin red line of blood below his ribs. "He kill't my baby by fuckin' her, made her so sad. Turned her 'gainst me so's I couldn't protect her no more."

By now Jason had circled around far enough that he had a clear shot at the door. He pivoted on his toe and bolted across the room, scrabbling for traction on the sheetrock.

"Now she dead," Danni screamed, chasing him over the pile. "Ain't no one left, so Danni gets the money!" She swung the wrecking bar at the back of his head. "Mama gets it, 'cause a how she earned it!"

The claw caught the back of Jason's neck, ripping away shirt fabric and flesh. He slipped on a chunk of sheetrock. His feet flew out from under him and he fell, crashing down flat, shoulders and hips thudding against the travertine. His forehead cracked against the tile with a sickening *thunk*.

* * *

Deputy Hardesty chewed his lip and drummed his fingers, waiting for dispatch to reply. The radio finally crackled. "Possible 459 in progress. In Sea Cliff, at ... One Bluffside Drive."

A "459" was one of those crimes Duane hadn't yet committed to memory. He removed his uniform cap and pulled his crib sheet from the headband. A "459" was a burglary, and "in progress" meant it was happening right now.

He paused to decide how to respond. Normally, he preferred to arrive at the crime scene after the burglary, carjacking, or robbery was completed. The smart thing was to wait until the perp was gone before the cavalry showed up with lights flashing and weapon drawn. After all, why should he risk his life to save some rich guy's flat-screen TV?

This situation seemed different, however. For one thing, this was Sea Cliff, where nothing violent ever happened, except for The Storm Drain Murder, and that was the first major crime in a decade. There certainly wouldn't be another for at least ten more years. The other thing—and the most important, really—was he'd earn bonus points on the sergeant's exam if he single-handedly captured a burglar while the crime was being committed.

Still, there was a fly in the ointment. He'd have to make the arrest by himself to get full credit, but he thought the Sheriff's Procedures Manual said he was supposed to have backup. He might lose points for not following procedures, but only get half-credit if he did. He wrestled with this dilemma for a moment before deciding a tiny lie was the solution. He'd tell dispatch he'd cruise by and check the situation. But he'd go in and make the arrest himself and explain later the situation called for urgent action.

He picked up his microphone and stated his call sign. "10-4, dispatch. I'll conduct a visual of the premises and advise." He beamed at his own cleverness. "The cavalry's on its way," he chuckled nervously.

CHAPTER 62

El Carnicero stomped down the stairs from the second floor. "*No hay papel higiénico,*" he grumbled. "Why you no tell me no toilet paper, woman?" He stopped when he saw Jason lying on the floor. "*Quien es? El abogado?*" He strode to the body and kicked its shoulder. "*Muerto?*" he asked Danni without looking at her.

Danni sat on the pile of sheetrock, hugging her knees and rocking back and forth. "I'm gonna burn in hell, Guillermo," she wailed. "I got three people's blood on my hands."

El Carnicero growled, "*Callate!* Shut up, stupid woman!" Bending down, he yanked on Jason's shoulder, flipping him onto his back. He felt for a pulse at his neck. "*Esta vivo.*" He slapped Jason's face. "*Abogado,*" he shouted. "*Despertar!* Wake up!" He slapped again, harder—one, two, three times—but got no response.

El Carnicero stalked to where Danni sat rocking on the debris pile. He slipped his switchblade from his pocket and snapped open the blade with a metallic click. Grabbing Danni's hair, he pulled her head back and pricked her neck with the knifepoint. "Woman, he tell you where is the money?"

"No," Danni whimpered, tears in her eyes.

"He know where is it?"

"Uh-uh, he thought I did. I don' think he does."

El Carnicero pushed the knifepoint into the flesh of Danni's neck, just enough to break the skin. A drop of blood pooled on the blade. "*You* want the money. You want take it all." He jerked her head back until she screamed.

"No, honest, Guillermo." Tears streamed down her cheeks, dripping onto the knife blade. "Ya gotta trust me. We's a team, 'member?"

"You betray me, I kill you." Guillermo twisted the knife tip slowly. When he withdrew it, a trickle of blood ran down Danni's neck. He slapped her hard across the jaw.

Crossing back to Jason's body, he kneeled on his chest. He felt for Jason's carotid artery and pressed the knife blade against it. "You are no use to me." Without applying pressure to the blade, he traced the curve from Jason's Adam's apple to the corner of his jaw. A faint streak of red followed its path.

"NO!" Danni screamed. "Don' sen' me ta hell, Guillermo. Please! He can die, but don' do it so's it's on my scorecard with God."

Still holding the knife to Jason's neck, El Carnicero looked in her direction. A sadistic grin twisted his lips. "*Como?*" he asked. "How does he die?"

"Lemme think. God hep me think." Danni's eyes flew wildly around the foyer. She pressed her fingers against her neck to slow the drops of blood.

The room was empty, except for the debris pile. The curved staircase and the elevator were the only architectural features. The door to the garage was tucked behind the staircase. "I know!" she cried. "Carry him up them stairs an' throw him down. Mebbe he hit his head an' die. Break some bones fer sure, an' might die from that. Be due ta chance if he did, an' not my fault."

El Carnicero slipped a foil packet from his pocket and selected two oxycontins. He looked at the stairs and counted them out loud while he chewed the pills. Kneeling beside Jason, he shoved his forearms under his shoulders and knees. He lifted the inert body an inch off the floor and shook his head. "*Pesa mucho y veinticino pasos,*" he complained. "Too much work. Cutting throat more easy." He held the knife to Jason's neck again.

"NO!" Danni screamed. "Please don' kill him like that. You do an' God'll strike me down right 'fore yer eyes."

"You test my patience, woman. *Como quieres matarto? Como? Rápidamente!*"

Danni stared at the knife pressed into Jason's neck. "Oh God, oh God. Come on, Danni, think a somethin'."

El Carnicero spat in Jason's face. "Too late," he snarled. "He die."

Jason's cell phone rang, shattering the silence. El Carnicero and Danni froze. "Thas' my Tiffany's ring tone," she said in a shocked voice. The phone rang four times. With each ring, Danni's eyes became more focused and the daze faded from her face. On the fourth ring, she announced, "It a mess'ge from t'other side. My baby's tryin' ta tell me somethin'. Why else'd it ring like that? She got somethin' 'portant ta tell me."

El Carnicero fished the phone out of Jason's pocket and read the Caller ID. "Erin? Who is this Erin? She know 'bout the money?"

"Nah, his ol' lady, I think. She wouldn' know nothin'."

Dropping the phone, El Carnicero shattered the screen with the butt of his knife. He pressed the blade against Jason's carotid. "He die now."

"Wait!" Danni cried. "Throw him in the el'vator. It din't never work. Throw him in there an' smash the button. We be long gone 'fore he dies, an' it won' be on my head."

"*Muy bien!*" El Carnicero grinned broadly, exposing dull metal teeth and missing molars. "He die slowly and suffer. *Buena* idea!" He dragged Jason's body to the elevator and jabbed the button to open the door. The door panel slid back halfway with a wrenching sound. Lifting Jason by one armpit, El Carnicero hoisted him over the elevator's threshold and tossed him inside. Jason's head hit the back wall, and he slid to the floor, toppling on his side.

El Carnicero pushed the button and held it until the door creaked closed. He retrieved his sledgehammer and shattered the button and its panel with one blow. "*Bueno,*" he said to the twisted faceplate and broken bits of plastic. He pressed his palm against the door and tried to slide it open. "*Bueno,*" he said again when it didn't budge.

Danni watched from the top of the sheetrock pile. "He can still open the door, ya know, an' get out."

"*Como?*"

"A button inside opens the door, *estúpido.*"

"*Pinche mierda!*" El Carnicero swore. Knocking the faceplate to the floor, he yanked the tangle of wires from the switch box. He clicked open his knife and severed the wires in one powerful stroke. "*No hay problema.*"

"Don' know 'bout that. Geraldo couldn't never get tha' el'vator ta work right. Swore it had gremlins."

El Carnicero lurched to where Danni sat. Pointing his switchblade at her face with his right hand, he jerked her to her feet with his left. He grabbed the front of her shirt and lifted her off the ground so they were eye-to-eye. He held the blade against her throat. "Geraldo make this problem. You fix so door no open." The tip of the blade pricked her skin, releasing bright-red drops of blood.

Danni flailed against his grip, but abruptly stopped struggling. "I ain't gonna meet my maker at your hands," she said under her breath. She locked eyes with him. "My Tiffany's sendin' me a message with her ring tone, and I unnerstand it now," she whispered. "She use ta tell me I shouldn' let men push me 'round so much, an' tha's what she's tellin' me now. I'm done bein' pushed 'round."

"*Que?* Louder, woman. *Habla mas alto.*"

"I'M DONE LETTIN' MEN PUSH ME 'ROUND."

"*Que? Me vuelves loco.* You make me crazy!"

"Here's how ya fix the problem." Danni spoke with confidence and authority now. "Put me down and I'll show ya." She used both hands to push the knife away from her neck. "Put me down now!"

The big man loosened his grip and dropped her on the pile of sheetrock. She staggered on the shifting pieces, but recovered her balance. "There's scrap wood in the garage," she said. "We get us some an' wedge it 'tween the jamb an' the el'vator door so's it can't slide open." She gestured toward the door beside the staircase. "That there door goes ta the garage. Le's go."

"*Veremos,*" El Carnicero grunted. "We will see." He walked in the direction Danni pointed. She followed him, stooping to pick up the wrecking bar and pressing it against her back. He opened the door to the garage and fumbled for the light switch inside.

"I got it," she said, flipping a switch on the foyer side of the wall. One bare bulb lit the three-stall garage. "See tha' pile a scrap wood?" she asked, pointing to the far end of the third stall. El Carnicero squinted into the dimness. "Well, go on. I gotta pee first 'fore I hep look fer th' right size piece."

El Carnicero stepped over the threshold and down to the concrete floor. The moment his balance shifted forward, Danni pushed his shoulders with all her might. His back foot caught the lip of the threshold and he stumbled forward, breaking his fall with his bandaged hand. "Ayyy-eee," he cried in pain.

Danni swung the wrecking bar like a baseball bat, smashing the side of his head. The blow was so hard she heard his skull crack. El Carnicero fell flat on his face. She shattered the back of his head on the downswing. Blood soaked his scalp and pooled on the garage floor.

Danni slammed the door closed and twisted the deadbolt. She giggled nervously. "Please, God, don' hol' tha' one 'gainst me, 'cause tha' sonofabitch surely had it comin'."

She walked back to the debris pile and picked up the sledgehammer. With a savage shriek, she crashed the head of the sledge into the next section of wallboard. It shattered. She rammed the wrecking bar's claw end into the hole and yanked. A four-foot-square piece crashed to the floor.

Pink insulation filled the stud bay. Danni gasped and jumped back. "My baby's spirit's ever'where in this house. 'S only right, after wha' Geraldo did ta you." She pulled out the pink sheet and hugged it to her chest. "You was right, baby girl," she whispered. "Men is easy. I never know'd it 'til right now."

CHAPTER 63

Deputy Hardesty stood under the portico at the front door of One Bluffside Drive. Heavy droplets of fog rolled off the roof over his head and plopped softly on the ground. The clammy air clung to his face and arms, sending shivers up and down his body. With a shaking hand, he drew his weapon from its holster. Its cold, dead weight gave him courage.

Duane had never been so nervous. His shirt was soaked through, but he knew it was from the dripping mist, not nerves. He twisted the doorknob. It was locked. What should he do? The entire first floor of the premises was lit up. He heard crashing and banging and a woman talking. *Maybe I should've requested backup.*

Staring at the front door, willing it to open, he noticed the shape of a chevron in the wood grain. It reminded him of his sergeant's stripes he'd yet to win. His bravado returned. Still, he wasn't sure how to proceed. Knock on the door? Smash a window and climb in? Was there something about knocking and entering in the Procedures Manual?

Duane stepped back three paces and rehearsed in his mind what he was going to do. He'd knock on the door, following procedure. Maybe the person inside would open it. If not, he'd break it down, again following procedure. He'd announce, "Deputy Sheriff! Don't move!" He practiced saying it, so he'd sound authoritative. Then he'd say, "You're under arrest for burglary, breaking and entering, and destruction of evidence." He repeated it several times to be sure he'd remember it.

Deputy Hardesty stood completely still and focused all his attention on the chevron wood grain. He charged the front door and fired his pistol at the knob. The report of the explosion echoed under the portico, deafening him temporarily. He burst through the door, weapon at arm's length, just like on TV. "Burglary!" he shouted. "Sergeant Duane! You're under breaking for arrest and entering! Don't move!"

He scanned the room. Ceiling fixtures filled the space with intense white light. A tall, stocky woman stood about fifteen feet in front of him. She had long, silvery-white hair and wore dirty work clothes and boots. Broken sheetrock lay in a pile behind her. Half the walls were bare studs. She stared at him in surprise. She looked stoned and smelled like a drunk. He thought he recognized other signs he'd seen before, too—dull eyes, twitching muscles, a sheen of sweat. She held a big crowbar in one hand and a short-handled sledgehammer in the other.

"Drop the gun!" He waved his weapon so she'd be sure to see it. "I've got a hammer."

She dropped the tools. They clanged on the tile floor.

"Hands on your knees! I mean, hands on your head and get on your knees."

The woman bent on one knee, then the other, and placed her hands on top of her head.

"OK, now don't move." Deputy Hardesty took a deep breath. *That wasn't so hard, was it?* Keeping his pistol trained on the woman's head, Duane walked around to her back. He fumbled with his handcuffs, holding his weapon between his knees while he untangled the cuffs from the clip on his utility belt. "OK, one hand behind your back." He clicked the cuff over her wrist. "Now the other one." Click. *There. I successfully secured the premises. Or did I?* "Anyone else here?"

"No, sir. No other livin' soul."

"Alright. That's good." He was starting to feel more confident, like the lawman he knew he was meant to be. "Alright. OK. What's your name, ma'am?" He sorted through his pockets for a scrap of paper and a pencil.

The woman blinked, like she was trying to recall her name. "Stoner," she said after a pause.

"First name?"

"Ima."

"Mrs.?"

"Yessiree. Mrs. Ima Stoner. Tha's me."

He wrote the names on his piece of paper. "Got some identification?"

"I knows who I am," the woman giggled. "So why do I need ID?"

"Do you have identification?" Duane repeated sternly.

"No, sir."

"No ID," he scribbled. "What're you doing here, ma'am? Why are you removing the wallboard in this room?"

"I…uh…I…lost my…uh…diamon' weddin' ring."

"OK, Mrs. Ima Stoner, right now I'm arresting you for burglary, breaking an' entering, malicious destruction of property, an' destruction of evidence. I'll think of more, but that's where we're at right now."

"God's gonna send me ta jail, 'stead a strikin' me down?" she mumbled. "Gonna let me off so easy, fer all my sins? Than' you, Lord."

"What? Speak up so I can understand you."

"Ain't nothin' fer ya ta hear. 'Tween me an' God."

With the woman and the premises secure, Duane looked around. It began to dawn on him this must be the house where Forensics found all the drugs.

"Ma'am, are there drugs hidden in this premises?"

"No, sir."

"You sure?"

"Yes, sir. I'd a' found 'em if they was." She giggled again.

"Were you looking for drugs?"

"No, sir. Like I tol' ya', I was lookin' fer my weddin' ring."

Deputy Hardesty barely listened. Like a bolt of lightning, it came to him this was the house where what's-his-name O'Brien was killed! This was his moment! He was going to crack The Storm Drain Murder case wide open all by himself, but he had to remember the deceased's first name. O'Brien…O'Brien…. Damn! It took him several moments to remember. "Do you know Gerald O'Brien?"

"No," the woman said slowly, "I don' know no one by tha' name."

The deputy tried to maintain his cool, knowing the answer to the next question could make his career. "Mrs. Stoner, do you know who killed Gerald O'Brien?"

"If I don' know him, how'd I know who kill't him?"

"Ma'am! Yes or no!"

"No need fer ya ta get all hissy. I already tol' ya, I don' know who kill't Gerald O'Brien."

Duane remembered the list of suspects he'd snatched from Brinkman's desk. He rummaged through his pockets, finding it crumpled with a used Kleenex. "Do you know anyone on this list?" He held out the paper so she could read it and watched her eyes move down the page. They stopped at one name before moving quickly to the bottom.

"No."

He turned the list so he could see it. She seemed to have paused at Tiffany Tedeski. That sent a jolt through him because he'd thought she was the killer all along, and sure as he was standing there, this woman was going to give him information that would prove he was right. "OK, Mrs. Stoner. In particular, do you know Tiffany Tedeski?"

"I don' know her no more, 'cause she dead!" she wailed.

Deputy Hardesty deflated like a spent Whoopee cushion. "What? She's not dead! She can't be! I can't arrest her if she's dead. How can she be dead?"

"She is."

"How?"

"She got hit by a car an' died."

"If you don't know her, how do you know that? Maybe you're wrong."

"The person that saw it tol' me."

"And she's dead? You're sure?"

"Yesss! An' I'm gonna burn in hell fer my sins, 'cause God don' forgive so easy." She burst into tears and shook with sobs, moaning, "My Tiffany, my sweet baby doll."

Duane tuned her out. Maybe it was just as well, he rationalized. It would've taken a lot of work to find that girl. He would've had to drive all the way down to Santa Luisa to question the ticket clerks at the Greyhound station and then drive all the way back to Sea Cliff. He would've had to learn how to do an Amber Alert, and he would've had to send out BOLOs all over the west. He would've had to follow up a hundred leads, and they'd probably all be dead ends. And even if he found her after all that bother, the sergeant's exam probably would be over.

He tore his note paper in bits and dropped them on the floor. "OK, Mrs. Stoner, I'm gonna take you down to the Rock Bay holding facility, where you'll be processed." He pulled her to her feet and pushed her toward the front door.

Outside, the dense fog muffled the normal sounds of night. Heavy drops of mist fell like rain, splashing on the walkway. Tiny wavelets lapped against the rocky cliffs just below Bluffside Drive. Somewhere offshore, restless sea lions barked on Seal Rock.

Deputy Hardesty escorted Danni to his patrol car and shoved her in the back. He imagined his sergeant's stripes fading into the mist. He'd made this arrest, but it wasn't going to be enough to win the prize. He climbed into the driver's seat and punched the steering wheel.

Suddenly, he was tired of the whole Storm Drain Murder thing, with its iffy suspects and murky facts. He hoped the DA would go ahead and charge the moose-woman Turlock and that would be the end of it. What Duane needed was a new crime to solve—one that was his from the start. Something sexy, to impress Commander Sepulveda. Like a big drug bust or a kiddy porn ring. Maybe he could find another dead body that'd be just his. A simple homicide with one suspect that lived in Sea Cliff. Something he could get his arms around and solve quickly, in time for the sergeant's exam. He flipped on his flashing lights and high beams, and headed up Driftwood toward Del Mar, deeper into the dense gray cloud.

That's what I need! He slapped the wheel in excitement. *Where can I find me a new dead body?*

CHAPTER 64

Victoria Viviano lay in her bed, clutching her favorite picture of her and Tiffany, the one with their arms around each other at the Junior Prom. "My dearest friend," she whispered, "where are you at? I tried to find you. I called the sheriff in Rock Bay and asked them to search for you, but they said they can't, 'cause it hasn't been seventy-two hours. I told them I'm so worried about you, but they don't care."

Pulling her phone from her pocket, Victoria scrolled through selfies of her and Tiffany—lying on the beach; shopping for prom dresses; hanging with some guys at homecoming—all happy times before T got so dark and dragged down by that creepy Geraldo.

The phone rang. The screen said *Unavailable*. Victoria decided to let it go to voicemail, but remembered Kyle said he'd call. She wasn't in the mood, but he was so gorgeous, and Kristen boobs was always flirting with him. She clicked on. "Hello?"

"Vic?"

"Oh my God! Tiffany?"

"It's me, sweetie. I miss you so much, but I can't talk long."

"Are you OK? Where are you at? I'm so worried, I could die."

"Listen, I'm fine. I'm staying with my stepdad Tommy and his wife, Heather, here in San Diego. They said I can stay as long as I want. I feel safe."

The relief Victoria felt in her heart slowly turned to anger. "Why didn't you text or call? Do you know what I've been going through? I was so frantic. I searched everywhere in that God's Helping Hands place and the Greyhound station—everywhere—but you disappeared. How could you ditch me like that?"

"Please don't be mad at me. It's just the way it had to be. I had to get away from everything so I could think and plan, even from you. Please don't hate me and try to understand."

"I could never hate you," Victoria said, trying not to sound hurt, "but you really devastated me. At least tell me you're coming home soon."

There was a long pause. Tiffany sighed. "Nooo, not for a long time. Listen. I've got a lot to tell you. Tommy said I could call, but only for a coupla minutes, so will you just listen?"

"I will, I promise, but why can't you come home? Please don't say that."

"I'm going to have the baby!" Tiffany blurted. "Me and Tommy and Heather, she's a nurse, well, we've decided I should have the baby and give it up for adoption. I think it's the right thing to do, he'll have a better life that way. Tommy said I can go to high school here after Christmas, and if I stay clean and get good grades, they'll help me go to college! I'm so excited, but sad about the baby 'cause, well, you know."

"Oh my God, Tiff. That's such a big decision. Are you sure...?"

"Tommy and Heather are the most wonderful people. They're gonna adopt me and make me their own daughter. He says it can be done without my mom knowing or trying to stop it. I don't know how but he says he knows people who can make it happen. Can you believe it? I'm gonna have a real home with a real mom and dad. I'm so happy. I'm already using his name."

"Can't you come back to Sea Cliff after the baby's born and finish high school with me?"

"That's what I said, but Tommy said no. I can't ever come back 'til I'm an adult. He says my mom could screw up the adoption if I do." She paused. "That means I can't see you for the longest time, but I had the greatest idea. Let's both go to UCLA! Let's just swear we'll do it right now, and if I can't call you, we'll meet by the Tommy Trojan statue on the first day of class! Isn't that a super idea? C'mon, let's swear. I swear!"

"I swear, too, but can't you come back here even for a day? If I could just see you...."

"You know how much I'll miss you, but Sea Cliff has such horrid memories for me."

"I know, sweetie. I can't imagine everything you went through with Geraldo, but the perv is dead. Did you know that? They found his body after you ran away. You'll never have to see him again."

The phone was silent so long Victoria thought her battery must've died. "Hello? Tiff? Are you still there?"

When Tiffany spoke, her voice was hollow and sounded far away. "Yeah. I know all that. That's the other thing I want to tell you, really why I called. I havta tell you 'cause it's killing me—I wake up at night ready to burst. But you havta swear you'll never tell anyone and it'll be our secret forever 'til we both die. You saw what happened when you told one person about me and Geraldo, so you can't tell anyone, ever! Promise!"

"I promise. You can tell me. You can tell me anything. You know you can."

"I killed Geraldo."

Victoria's stomach heaved. "*You* killed him? You don't even kill spiders. Oh, my dear, I can't imagine how horrible it is for you. Are you OK? Can you bear it?"

When Tiffany didn't answer, Victoria thought her friend must be scared about getting caught. To ease her mind, Victoria said, "Everyone thinks that amazon Mags Turlock did it. That's what that Ally Booker girl says. It's all over Facebook and Twitter and social media and TV."

Tiffany still didn't say anything. In the silence, Victoria was surprised to find a morbid curiosity growing inside her. She'd never even seen a dead person, except on TV. She wondered what it was like … what she did. "Umm, Tiff," she said hesitantly, "how did you do it? Will you tell me?"

"Oh God, Vic, he died! I felt him die. I saw his spirit fly away, like in a cartoon. I was at that party at One Bluffside, and he passed out and my mom cooked the pure heroin and filled the syringe and sat on his chest and held him down in case he woke up. Mags was there pacing circles, asking God if it was OK because he's such a perv. Mags made me wear plastic gloves and told me where to do it so the cops couldn't find it and I stuck the needle in his eyelid and pushed the plunger and I felt the life go out of him. It was like when we put your little Eddie Schnauzer down. Then my mom and Mags carried his body out to her van so she could dump it somewhere. I feel awful even though he deserved it and I know I'm gonna burn in hell for taking his life, and that's another reason for my baby to have a different family in case God strikes me down or the devil scoops me up."

Victoria pictured dead Geraldo hanging upside down from the crane. The image brought a wave of nausea and cold sweats. "Oh my God, Tiff," she mumbled, "to see him die and feel it ... ." Pity, horror, and love for her friend swirled inside her, but one thought emerged clearly: *I havta to tell her it's OK.* Victoria summoned every ounce of conviction and said, "He was so evil, he deserved to die for what he did to you. You did the right thing."

Tiffany raced on as if she hadn't heard, speaking without any expression. "I should've never told my mom I was pregnant and Geraldo was the father she called me a slut and a whore and slapped me she was so angry and when he passed out at the party she said it was a sign and it was his fault and he had to die and I had to do it to make it right and I did it, and then she went and got drunk and left me alone for a week and I had to run away." She began to sob. "I hadta run away, don't you understand? Please understand, V. Please help me, don't be angry with me, say you love me."

Victoria burst into tears. "I do love you, you are my dearest friend forever, my little sister, my other half. I wish I was there to hold you." She heard Tiffany sobbing and sniffling, and she cried even harder.

After a few minutes, Tiffany said, "Shit, I'm getting Tommy's phone all wet. I'll ruin it, and I've gotta go 'cause he said not to talk so long, but there's something else I havta tell you. I asked Tommy to send a anamomunus text to Ally Booker and the cops saying Mags didn't kill Geraldo. He said he did it so it couldn't be traced, but I don't know how. Maybe God will forgive me for letting Mags get in trouble. And the other thing, Tommy sent my mom a letter saying I was dead, so she wouldn't try to find me. Tommy says me an' you can never call or text 'cause my mom could find out and screw up the adoption, or maybe the cops could find me. You have to promise. I'm so sorry and sad, but we have to do it if I'm going to be safe."

"NO, TIFF! Say you'll call me. Say you'll send me pictures of you and the baby."

The strength returned to Tiffany's voice. "I love you like a big sister. Please take good care of yourself, sweetie, and study hard, and we'll meet by Tommy Trojan on the first day of class. I can't wait to see you and hug you, and then we'll have a good cry and tell each other everything, like always."

She clicked off.

Victoria dropped her phone in her lap and hunched over it. She grabbed a pillow and hugged it to her stomach, rocking back and forth and crying until she had no more tears.

CHAPTER 65

The first hint of consciousness flickered in Jason's brain. He lay perfectly still, aware of nothing but his throbbing head and pounding pulse. His blood roared in his ears, drowning out all other sound and making thought impossible. Time passed. Maybe minutes, maybe hours.

He imagined a woman was calling his name. Indistinct at first, the voice grew louder and louder. Like a spirit from beyond, Rory sighed, "Jaaaassson."

Did I really hear that? It took all his energy to form the question. Blackness rolled over him again, dragging him back into the abyss.

"Jason, wake up." Rory's words drifted through the void, nudging him back to awareness. "C'mon. You have to get out of here."

He bolted upright, blind in the total darkness. Sharp pain shot through his head. His face was crusty and smelled of saliva. The taste of dried blood filled his mouth, and the back of his neck was stiff and sore. He touched it and felt a jagged, bloody tear in his skin.

"Where am I?" He stretched his arms left and right and hit walls on both sides. He reached in front and found another. "I'm trapped in a cage!" Claustrophobia crushed his chest. He gasped for air, fighting for each breath. In a frenzy, he felt for the four walls that were his tomb. His heart raced faster and faster. *I'm going to die, right here. Wait. Do something! Try to stand up.* He pulled himself to his knees and slowly worked his way to his feet. Waves of dizziness washed over him, and he staggered against a panel beside him, hitting something with his elbow.

The tomb lurched upward.

"Holy Christ!" he screamed. "What is this?" He pounded on the walls. "HELP! HELP! Get me out!" The cage rose slowly, squeaking and groaning. Frantic to stop it, he pressed his palms everywhere on the panel, searching for the button or switch or whatever he'd pushed, but the tomb kept rising. "HELP! HELP!" He pounded the walls with his fists. Shaking and creaking, the cage ground to a stop. The sound of metal grating on metal was followed by a cool breeze blowing across his face. *Thank God!*

Momentary relief gave way to fear of what was next. He shuddered. Leaning against the wall behind him, he filled his lungs with the fresh air. His hands fell against his thighs. *What's this?* He felt a short metal tube in his pants pocket. *The flashlight! Of course!*

It all came back to him. The crawl space, the foyer, Danni trying to kill him with the wrecking bar, slipping, falling, the floor rushing toward his face. Now he understood. He was in the spec house elevator. Danni must have dumped him in it to die. He patted his pockets for his cell phone. *She took it so I can't call for help.*

Jason's head ached like he'd never experienced, and any movement caused pounding pain. He shined his flashlight in the direction of the cool air and saw the elevator door had opened all the way. That was the good news. The bad news was the cage had stopped between two floors. A structural steel beam blocked the opening about a foot above the elevator's threshold. The gap was too narrow to slip through. He lowered himself gently to his hands and knees and peered under the beam. The great room's ceiling was at eye level. The floor was ten feet below, dotted with furniture.

Looking up, he saw the rafters and insulation of the attic. The opening between the beam and the top of the elevator door was tall enough for him to climb through. That was his only option, but he hesitated. The attic was dark and drafty and cold. He decided to check what he could see before he climbed out.

His blue-white light shined all the way to the gable at the far end of the building, but he saw only roof framing, heat ducts, and insulation. A rush of air blew through the vents, soothing his throbbing temples. He imagined Rory's voice carried by the breeze. "Jaaasson, you neeeed to come up heeere."

He climbed onto the steel beam and hoisted himself into the attic. Turning in a circle, he shined his light on the two side walls and the opposite gable. Again, nothing unexpected. He slumped against a roof support and leaned his head back. Resting for a moment, he let waves of dizziness and nausea pass.

"Huh. Was that a light switch?" He pointed his flashlight at the elevator shaft's framing and saw a switch box tacked to a two-by-four. He stepped carefully on the joists to get to the switch and flipped it on. A light bulb high in the rafters cast a dim glow. It was just bright enough to reflect off something metallic next to the shaft. He knelt slowly, trying not to aggravate the ache in his head. Pulling away a half-sheet of insulation, he whistled. "I'll be damned."

Nestled in the joist bay was an expensive-looking leather briefcase with brass fittings. The initials "GOB" were embossed above the handle. "Geraldo, what have you been up to?" Jason whispered. He pressed the brass buttons to release the hasps and opened the lid.

Inside the briefcase were three matching oversized envelopes. Jason shined his light on them. They were heavy paper, perhaps vellum, and each was imprinted with the pastel logo of the Grand National Bank of the Cayman Islands. *Geraldo O'Brien* was typed on one and *Drake Quay Villa* on the second. *For your convenience* was typed on the third.

Jason's heart thumped against his ribs. "Oh my God! This is it!" The blood rushed to his head. The thudding ache was replaced by dizzy excitement, and for a moment, he feared he'd throw up.

He picked up the envelope addressed to Geraldo. The seal was broken and the flap tucked inside. He removed two typewritten sheets of heavy paper. Several credit-card-sized pieces of plastic fell to his feet.

Shining his light on the letter, he saw the date was a month ago. He read:

Kingston Easterday
President and General Counsel
Grand National Bank of the Cayman Islands

My dear friend Geraldo,

I am so pleased you have concluded your affairs in the United States and are prepared to retire to Grand Cayman Island. I look forward to renewing and continuing our decades-long friendship.

I have complied with your instructions, and this epistle confirms the arrangements I have made on your behalf.

All of your deposits in this institution have been consolidated and your accounts closed, save for some petty cash in one remaining account.

I have arranged a temporary, anonymous numbered account at ÜberBanc in Zurich, as you requested. The minimum deposit required for such an account is USD $1 million, and I have wired that amount to the bank. The account can be accessed only by means of the 10-digit alphanumeric code you possess. You will need to appear personally at the bank's headquarters in Zurich to enter a biometric identifier and the alphanumeric code in order to establish a permanent account and to deposit the remainder of your funds. Once this has been accomplished, you will be able to access your funds anywhere in the world.

Jason saw he was dripping sweat on the letter. He wiped his brow. "Unbelievable," he muttered. "A million dollars, a numbered Swiss account. The 'petty cash' must be the $780,000 Rory took."

He continued reading:

The balance of your funds has been converted to electronic debit cards, which I enclose herewith. I must emphasize these funds are as insecure as cash. I have complied with your instruction to forward them in this format, although it is contrary to accepted banking practice and my better judgment. I assuage my concern with the certain knowledge you have sound reasons for proceeding in this manner.

While the cards do not contain any logo or identifying information, they are compatible with the ÜberBanc system, and I strongly recommend you deposit them in that bank when you activate your account. For your convenience, I have written the value of each card on a Post-It and attached it thereto.

Jason whistled softly. He picked up the five plastic cards. Each was the size of a credit card and was a deep cobalt blue. None displayed any markings, except for a silver chip implanted on the front. Stuck to each was a Post-It that said "USD $1,000,000" in neat handwriting.

Forgetting the pain in his head, Jason jumped to his feet. "Holy Christ! Five million dollars! Six million altogether. This is too crazy!" And there was more to read. He leaned against the framing and turned to the second page:

Your final request concerns the villa at Drake Quay. Against my recom-mendation, the deed to this property remains in blank. I understand you wish to reserve your decision as to how title is held (and perhaps disposition of one or more of the debit cards) until you have attempted rapprochement with your daughter. Nonetheless, I urge you not to leave the document blank any longer than absolutely necessary. You will find the deed and the keys to the villa in a separate envelope.

I hope you will find these arrangements to be satisfactory, and I look forward to seeing you soon in George Town, my friend.

Your faithful and humble servant,

Kingston Easterday
President and General Counsel

"So Rory was right," Jason whispered. "Geraldo did want her to have some of his estate if they reconciled. Who'd have guessed? Who knew it would be so large?"

Bending down, he paused to massage his aching temples. He opened the second envelope. It contained the blank deed and an ornate key on an engraved brass fob. There were also several 4x6 color pictures of an imposing Mediterranean villa and the adjacent beach and grounds.

The third envelope bulged. He untucked the flap. Four bundles of new hundred-dollar bills fell out. He fanned one of the bundles. "Look at all this cash," he muttered. "There must be $10,000 here! Probably Geraldo's travel money."

He stuffed the bills back in the envelope and replaced it and the other envelopes in the briefcase. Closing the lid, he was about to snap the locks when he noticed the briefcase appeared thicker on the outside than it looked on the inside—perhaps six inches thick on the outside and three inches on the inside. He opened it again and removed the envelopes. The inside bottom piece fit neatly but sounded hollow when he tapped on it. *A false bottom!*

Jason tried to pry out the false bottom with his fingernail, but soon gave up in frustration. With his head splitting and stomach churning, he grabbed the briefcase, flipped it over, and shook it. The bottom piece fell on the insulation along with ten small, square leather boxes.

What the hell? He picked up the box closest to him. It was blood-red leather with perfect hand-stitching along the corners and edges. He pulled off the lid and gasped. On top was a Polaroid picture of young Rory. She was perhaps twelve, naked, except for a Little Mermaid wig. She thrust her budding breasts proudly at the camera and shoved her hips forward like a veteran pole dancer. But it was her gray eyes that caught Jason's attention. Hard beyond her years, they smoldered with hate. Her bitter voice shouted in his head. *"Now you have to believe me! I kept telling you, but you didn't."*

"Geraldo, you fucking pig," Jason swore. "Your own daughter! How could you even think it?" He thumbed through the nine other pictures in the box. All were of naked Rory at different ages in various costumes. A quick check of the remaining boxes confirmed he'd found the 100 missing Polaroids Rory accused him of hiding for Geraldo.

"Rory, I'm sorry I ever doubted you," he whispered. He replaced the boxes in the briefcase, inserted the false bottom, threw in the envelopes, and snapped the locks.

The contents of the briefcase raised unanswerable questions in his mind. Now that he'd actually found the money, what to do with it? What about the villa? What about Rory? What about the Polaroids?

The pounding pain had given way to a dull ache, and his head felt like it was stuffed with cotton. Thoughts got lost in the fuzz. "Slow down," he told himself. "You're not thinking clearly. No major decisions 'til you feel normal again. Anyway, you've gotta get out of this attic first."

But how to escape? The elevator wasn't an option. It might not go down. The door might close and he'd be stuck inside. It might free-fall into the crawl space.

He thought there might be an attic trap door with folding stairs. Shining his light from one end of the space to the other, nothing resembled folded stairs or even a bulge in the insulation.

That left one alternative. He lowered himself carefully into the elevator. On hands and knees, he peered through the gap under the steel beam, using his flashlight to examine the placement of the furniture in the great room. He silently thanked Mags for having the house staged.

Roughly in the middle of the room was a sectional sofa. Fixing on its location, he looked into the attic, trying to coordinate the sofa's location with the space above it. "It's probably under that vertical roof support," he decided.

He climbed out of the elevator. Waves of dizziness staggered him, and he knew he couldn't balance on the joists. He threw the briefcase in the direction of the post, crawled clumsily across the joists, threw the briefcase again, retrieved it, and crawled to the post. Reaching down, he pulled back the insulation. He stomped his heel against the drywall, once, twice, three times, until it shattered and fell to the floor below with a crash. Each blow resounded in his head, and he had to sit on a joist until the pounding eased.

It dawned on him that Danni might still be in the house. He cringed, hoping she didn't hear the noise. The hole in the drywall was about the size of his shoe. He pressed his ear to the opening and listened.

Jason sat on the joist for at least ten minutes, struggling to stay awake. The house was completely silent. He decided it was safe to get into the great room and leave through the back door. With a surge of adrenaline, he bashed his foot against the ceiling drywall repeatedly until he'd created an opening large enough to fit through. He dropped the briefcase through the hole. Grasping the joist, he lowered himself onto the sofa below.

CHAPTER 66

The fog was thick as gray cotton outside. Despite his throbbing head and churning stomach, Jason ran all the way to his car, chased by a swarm of Grey Widow spiders and giant scorpions. "Get away!" he cried hoarsely, kicking at them and swinging the briefcase to clear his path. "Leave me alone. Go away."

In the safety of the Neon, he collapsed in the driver's seat and threw the briefcase on the passenger's seat. The little car coughed to life after refusing to start several times. He slid the heater up to full blast and rummaged in the glove box for a package of GG's Handi-Wipes. The sheets on top were dried out, but he found a couple at the bottom that were moist enough to wipe the saliva and blood off his face. With the last ones, he wiped his arms, hands, and shoes. "The creatures can smell humans," he muttered. "No, dammit! They're just a nightmare from long ago."

He switched on the dome light and twisted the rearview mirror to see his face. In the dim glow, he saw a large black-and-blue bruise covering his forehead. Turning his head back and forth, his neck was stiff. He looked for damage to his nose and felt the bridge and cartilage gingerly. The movement and focusing his eyes caused waves of dizziness and dull throbbing. His nose didn't seem to be broken and didn't hurt at the moment. The back of his neck was raw with pain, like a bite had been taken out of it. He tried to examine the wound with his hands. The flesh was torn and caked with dried blood, and some fresh drops oozed and ran down his back.

As the car warmed up, he lit his last Marlboro. He pulled the smoke deep into his lungs and held it before exhaling. Grabbing a moment of clarity, he forced himself to think like a lawyer.

"First, what's the legal relationship between Geraldo's estate and the millions and the villa?" he asked himself out loud. Talking helped him stay focused. "Now that I know exactly what the assets are, does the estate have any claim to them? That's the fundamental issue." No, he corrected himself, the fundamental issue was only he knew about the assets. The money and villa were the proceeds of Geraldo's lifetime of criminal activity. The sheriff or the Feds would seize them in a heartbeat if they knew about them. "So," he concluded, "those assets don't exist, as far as the estate's concerned."

But it wasn't that simple. The Polaroid pictures of naked young Rory haunted him. He continued talking to himself. "She'd say she has a moral claim to it all because she endured so much at Geraldo's hands. But the Rory I know isn't at all sympathetic. And she never reconciled with her father. She took the $780,000 anyway, when she thought it was all the money, and ran away. So, since it's my decision, I'd say she has no claim."

He leaned back in the driver's seat and inhaled another long drag on his cigarette. "Well, Jason," he said to the ceiling, "it looks like this is your Barry Brinkman moment. He'd keep it all, no questions asked. Are you your father's son after all?"

Immediately a clamor of voices erupted in his head:

"Damn right I'd keep it," his father's voice said. *"You found it, you earned it, you keep it. No one else knows about it. Be smart for once, boy. It's enough money for a lifetime, plus a mansion in the Caribbean."*

GG said, *"It's your pot of gold, Jason dear, the one your father never had. I knew you'd find it. It's for you."*

"But Jason," Erin countered, *"it's tainted money and we don't need it. I can work at Posh and sell my photographs, and you can build your law practice, and we can make it together."*

Rory drowned them all out. *"You've seen what he did to me. I earned it. All of it. It's mine!"*

"And what about you, Jason?" he asked himself. "Your father's the most dishonest person you've ever known. You vowed when you were twelve you'd never be like him."

Jason shifted into first gear and pulled away from the curb. Suddenly, he was angry. "Goddammit!" he shouted. "I've lost my home and my car, and my law career's ruined. I'm broke. My father might as well be dead. My wife wants to crush me and I've lost custody of my son. I've got nothing left. Except Erin."

He imagined her blue eyes and tousled hair in the morning after a night together. "If I keep the villa and the millions," he asked his reflection in the windshield, "would she go with me to the Caymans? What if I moved to New York? I'd have enough money to fight Courtney for custody of Jason Jr. I could be a real father to him. It would probably take a half-million to win custody. Maybe three-quarters. I could set up Erin as a photographer, or she could go back to school. We could get a condo. That would be at least a million, plus living expenses. Would she be happy three thousand miles from her mother and everything she knows? Would she still love me if she knew I'd stolen the money?"

That was the crux of the matter, wasn't it? "Is it stealing if no one knows it's stolen? Am I the decent person I think I am? Does it matter that I've lost everything?"

With that, the thudding pain returned to his head and he felt fuzzy-brained again. "This is bad," he said. "I might have a concussion or a hematoma. I may have to go to the ER tomorrow."

Jason drove up Del Mar Road's hills and switchbacks toward Highway 1 and his office, where he'd sleep on the floor tonight. The fog was as impenetrable as the questions he faced.

"Tomorrow," he promised himself. "I'll think through it all again tomorrow when I'm fresh, and start making decisions. But if the options are turning it over to the cops, giving it to Rory, or keeping it, the choice is pretty obvious."

He glanced in the rearview mirror, and for just an instant, Rory's pale-gray eyes glared back at him.

CHAPTER 67

Five minutes to midnight. Rory walked swiftly through the fog up the Charles Street hill. No streetlamps lit her way. The only sounds were dripping eaves and her rapid breathing. She buttoned her collar and cinched her trench coat tighter as she walked.

Halfway up the hill, she made out faint squares of light from Jason's office at the top. She stopped when she reached the brick walkway that led to the deck and the open door.

She strode up the walk and into his office. Rounding the end of the bookcase, she saw Jason in his chair, slumped face-down on his desk. His forehead rested on his arms crossed in front of him. A gash in the back of his neck oozed blood.

With a quick glance at her watch, she went to him and felt his neck until she found his pulse. A Post-It note with her burner number was in his hand. She crumpled the note and slipped it in her pocket. Her foot grazed the leather briefcase on the floor next to his desk, where he said it would be.

She set the briefcase on his credenza and ran her fingertips over the gold monogrammed initials: *GOB*. Snapping open the locks, she lifted the top and examined the contents. Three cobalt-blue debit cards, two bundles of hundred-dollar bills, and the deed and key to the Cayman villa. Using a letter opener, she pried up the false bottom and counted the ten small leather boxes. "Thank you, Jason," she whispered. Tears ran down her cheeks as she opened several of the boxes. She closed them, replaced the bottom piece, and slammed the lid shut.

Checking her watch again, she picked up the desk phone's receiver and punched 9-1-1.

A sleepy operator answered. "Nine-one-one. What is your emergency?"

Rory spoke into the mouthpiece. "Unconscious male. Bleeding posterior neck wound, four or five inches long. Send medical help right away. 812 Charles Street, Sea Cliff."

"Ma'am, please remain at the location until the paramedics arrive," the operator said, urgency now in her voice. "Please open the front door."

Rory set the receiver on the desk. She kissed the back of Jason's head. "I'm sorry, Jason. I'd hoped it would work out differently for us. Maybe Destiny has another chapter in mind, but I've got a plane to catch right now. Help is on the way. Get healed and be well."

Tucking the briefcase under her arm, she walked quickly toward the door, but stopped halfway. "Dammit!" she swore. She hurried back to Jason's desk and set down the briefcase. "I really do have to go," she said, fumbling to unclasp her mantis pendant. She laid it beside him and kissed his head again. "Until then," she said, stroking his hair.

Briefcase in hand, she strode out the open door and jogged down the hill in the fog.

*****

Made in the USA
Las Vegas, NV
27 January 2024

84936715R00267